Dr Isaac Asimov was born in Ru
Ph.D. from Columbia University. ɪ᠎ormerly Professor of Bio-
chemistry at the School of Medicine, Boston University, Dr
Asimov has published many works and won the Hugo and
Nebula awards. He is perhaps best known for his 'Foundation'
series of books, although he has written a great many non-fiction
works and edited a number of science and science fiction
anthologies.

Martin H. Greenberg was born in 1941 and is an anthologist and
Professor of Political Science at the University of Wisconsin.
Since taking his Ph.D. at the University of Connecticut in 1969,
he has edited a great many thematic anthologies, many of which
are aimed at illustrating concepts in the social sciences to college
students.

Charles G. Waugh was educated at Syracuse University and
Kent State University, where he obtained his Ph.D. in 1982. He
is now Professor of Communications and Psychology at the
University of Maine at Augusta. He has published a great many
books on a wide range of topics, from communications to literature and from science to mysteries. He specializes in thematic
anthologies and searching for obscure stories. He met his wife via
a computer and they have two children.

COMPUTER CRIMES AND CAPERS

Edited by

ISAAC ASIMOV
MARTIN H. GREENBERG *and*
CHARLES G. WAUGH

PENGUIN BOOKS

Penguin Books Ltd, Harmondsworth, Middlesex, England
Viking Penguin Inc., 40 West 23rd Street, New York, New York 10010, U.S.A.
Penguin Books Australia Ltd, Ringwood, Victoria, Australia
Penguin Books Canada Limited, 2801 John Street, Markham, Ontario, Canada L3R 1B4
Penguin Books (N.Z.) Ltd, 182–190 Wairau Road, Auckland 10, New Zealand

First published in the U.S.A. by Academy Chicago Publishers 1983
First published in Great Britain by Viking 1985
Published in Penguin Books 1986

Made and printed in Great Britain by
Richard Clay (The Chaucer Press) Ltd,
Bungay, Suffolk
Filmset in Monophoto Ehrhardt

The acknowledgements on p. 7 constitute an extension of this copyright page.

CONTENTS

CONTENTS

ACKNOWLEDGEMENTS

Gores: Copyright © 1962 by Davis Publications, Inc. First appeared in *Ellery Queen's Mystery Magazine*. Reprinted by permission of the author.

Dryer: Copyright © 1981 by Mercury Press, Inc. From *The Magazine of Fantasy and Science Fiction*. Reprinted by permission of the author.

Dickson: Copyright © 1965 by Condé Nast Publications, Inc. Reprinted by permission of the author.

Wellen ('Goldbrick'): Copyright © 1978 by Mercury Press, Inc., from *The Magazine of Fantasy and Science Fiction*. Reprinted by permission of the author.

Hoch: Copyright © 1969 by Edward D. Hoch. Reprinted by permission of the author.

Anderson: Copyright © 1953 by Condé Nast Publications, Inc. Reprinted by permission of the author and his agents, the Scott Meredith Literary Agency Inc., 845 Third Ave, New York, NY 10022.

McIntosh: Copyright © 1963 by Condé Nast Publications, Inc. Reprinted by permission of the Scott Meredith Library Agency, Inc., 845 Third Ave, New York, NY 10022.

Wellen ('While-u-wait'): Copyright © 1978 by Mercury Press, Inc. From *The Magazine of Fantasy and Science Fiction*. Reprinted by permission of the author.

Silverberg: Copyright © 1973 by Robert Silverberg. Reprinted by permission of the author and Agberg, Ltd.

Asimov: Copyright © 1958 by Headline Publications. Reprinted by permission of the author.

INTRODUCTION
CRIME · UP · TO · DATE

Isaac Asimov

In the old West (something I know about only from the movies, which are to history as comic books are to literature) the worst crime you could commit was the stealing of a horse. A horse was a man's livelihood, his transportation, his love-object, his life.

Thus, when a Westerner wanted to berate someone (without using blasphemy or obscenity, which the movies used to frown upon) he would use a gradually intensifying series of beratements something like this: 'You low-down, ornery, varmint of a sheep-herdin' hoss-thief.'

Horse-thief was the worst you could call a man. The definite impression I got was that if you called a person a 'hoss-thief', it didn't even do any good to smile.

Calling names didn't stop horse-theft, however.

On a more practical note, I gathered from the movies that frequently, when a person was found astride someone else's beloved horse, he was strung up on the spot, without waiting for such effete details as a trial.

That didn't stop horse-theft, either.

In fact, nothing stopped crime, generally, in all the history of the world. The Lord himself, in the ten commandments, said in plain Hebrew: 'Thou shalt not kill!', 'Thou shalt not steal!' and so on, yet in the thirty-five centuries since Moses brought those tablets down into the Israelite camp, that has not helped.

We have had ferocious punishments, and that has not helped; and increasingly sophisticated police forces, and all the power of advancing technology, and that has not helped, either.

What can help? Well, in the case of a particular crime, like horse-theft, there are two possible hopes. Make sure that everyone already has all the horses he can possibly want, or fix it so that horses are relatively worthless.

No one but a few idealists think that everyone can be supplied with horses (or, in a more general sense, that social justice can be attained), but how about the second alternative?

You see, automobiles were invented, and horses stopped being so gol-darned, dad-rotted (whoops, I'm talking western) necessary. I suppose there are still people who will steal a horse just to be mean and ornery, but it is no longer the problem it used to be.

However, we now have the problem of automobile-theft, because crime, like everything else, must keep up to date.

Of all the technological advances made in modern times, the computer seems to be the most revolutionary. It will affect life in every corner, in every way. And we can imagine it may eliminate crime.

For instance, it could eliminate theft by eliminating the objective.

That sort of thing has been tried before. No one has to carry about intrinsically valuable gold and silver; you carry about little bits of worthless paper instead – so people steal dollar bills.

But why carry pieces of paper that have the same value to all? Use checks instead, which bear your signature; or credit-cards, which likewise bear your signature. So people indulge in forging, check-kiting, and credit-card theft.

Ah, but switch to computers. Have them keep track of all financial transactions. Have them shift figures bloodlessly, emotionlessly, heart-lessly, inhumanly, from here to there. Have your identity checked by code, by thumbprint, by studious comparison of this entry with that entry.

Once it becomes physically impossible to interfere with the financial operation of the individuals of the world, theft becomes as outmoded as the art of forming flint tools. And if computers keep track of everybody and know about everything, so that you cannot, no matter how you try, conceal your deeds, or hide and find sanctuary, why bother to commit a crime? Very few people perform misdeeds, if they are certain of being caught and punished.

And yet, unfortunately, it may be that we will never become so in-genious in designing computers as to frustrate human determination to frustrate all such good intentions. Human beings grow increasingly in-genious in their attempts both to do good and to do evil, but one has the nagging feeling that the weight of ingenuity will always be on the side of evil.

In short, the crime of the future will be that of outwitting the com-puter. It is already being done. By stealing a code, or by multifarious fakery that the dumb computer can't see through, numbers are so mani-pulated by the computer's incredible innocence as to sluice money into unauthorized hands.

Naturally, the computer can always be redesigned so as to prevent whatever diddle is discovered, but then it will be up to human beings to invent a new and more subtle, or more elaborate scam. And presumably, they will.

DARL · I · LUV · U

Joe Gores

FEAR AILK DEALER   FEAR SILK DEALER
FWAR SILK DEALER   FEAR SILK DEALER
FEAR SILK DEALER   FXEAR SILK DEALER

Not so good. Still, he was learning.

When Charlie Wyeth stopped typing, the only sounds to break the Pentagon's after-hours' silence were the peculiar whirring of the TWX machine and the distant echoing clatter of a scrubwoman's pail far down the E Ring.

Charlie glanced at the copybook clipped to the upright stand at the side of the teletypewriter; his long tapering fingers plunged down once more at the keys and words again appeared on the unrolling yellow paper.

FEAR SILK DEALER   FEAR SILK DEALER
FEAR SILK DEALER   FEAR SILK DEALER
FEAR SILK DEALER   FEAR SILK DEALER

Perfect. Charlie had achieved that momentary communion with the TWX machine which was so important.

Charlie was a tall, slender, lonely man with a sensitive mouth and a dreamer's eyes; his long, skinny legs stuck out awkwardly from beneath his chair, like the legs of a nesting stork. He could accomplish much more at night in the office at the Pentagon than he could during the morning practice sessions at the teletype training center. *One* secretary could render him tongue-tied; when he was the only man among *twenty* of them . . .

The telephone beside the TWX machine exploded, clamoring for attention; it meant an incoming call on the teletype. Charlie flicked the switch from *Practice* to *Open*, fighting a momentary panic. After all, he would soon be civilian TWX operator for Army Ordnance, Tech Liaison Office, personally chosen by Colonel Andrews; he had to get used to transmitting and receiving. He typed:

THIS IS ARL VA 661 GA PLS

Translated from TWXese this meant *This is Arlington, Virginia, call number 661, go ahead, please.* Charlie glanced at his watch. Ten p.m. This was a commercial network for making contact with private contractors. What civilian firm could be transmitting at this hour?

As if in response to his unasked question, the machine clattered out a single word.

LONELY

'I beg your pardon?' In his surprise Charlie had spoken aloud. Was this a joke? A name? Something in code? When nothing else was forthcoming, he asked:

WHO R U PLS DON T UNDERSTAND

The unknown returned:

LONELY U R LONELY CHARLES WYETH

With an angry flick of the toggle he cut the connection. A bead of sweat ran down his face. Someone – someone who knew shy, awkward Charlie's practice of working late to assuage his loneliness – was playing a damned cruel joke.

But who? Fussy old McAfee, civilian Section Head behind the Colonel? Hardly. The man was as dried-up and humorless as a prune. Colonel Andrews himself? Unthinkable. The secretary? She was married and had three kids. Doc Weston? The statistician professed a fear of any machine more complex than his typewriter.

Still angry and disturbed, Charlie clipped his plastic-encased ID badge on his shirt so that he wouldn't be stopped by the Pentagon security guards, and went home.

The next day he worked steadily, getting the necessary departmental clearances for publicity handouts on two Ordnance weapons soon to be declassified, and gradually relaxed. Neither at the office nor at TWX practice did anyone innocently ask 'Lonely, Charles Wyeth?' and then burst out laughing. When McAfee, his fussy little superior, buttonholed him at five o'clock just as he was leaving, Charlie didn't even wince in anticipation.

'Be sure and check your desk for classified material, Wyeth.'

Although McAfee wore a close-trimmed mustache, had thinning gray hair, and weak eyes behind horn-rimmed glasses, he reminded Charlie of a rabbit; he had the same nervous, jerky mannerisms – his nose even wriggled when he was distressed.

'I always do that, Mr McAfee. You know that, sir.'

'Well, I'm the one who signs each night, Wyeth, so I'm the one who'd get in trouble if any documents were left lying around the office.'

'Yes, sir, Mr McAfee. I understand your concern.'

All though dinner at the 24-hour Pentagon cafeteria by the Concourse ramp, Charlie seethed: damned old woman McAfee! The perfect civil servant, all right – he existed for routine. Charlie could do the old man's job easily – did half his work for him right now – but McAfee had seniority and a high GS rating – which was what really counted, not ability.

Charlie dawdled over his third cup of coffee. Only after stubbing out the butt of his fourth cigarette did he admit to himself that he almost dreaded returning to the office. If there was another call ... Then he thought: to hell with it! He wasn't going to give up his tranquilizing hours with the machine; a man can go to only so many concerts alone, can make only so many solitary visits to art galleries ...

For two hours the exercises flowed from beneath his nimble fingers; but as the minute sweep of his watch climbed to ten o'clock, the phone beside the TWX rang. Could he ignore it? He couldn't. Flicking the toggle, his hands shook slightly.

THIS IS ARL VA 661 GA PLS

Pause. Then:

HELLO CHARLIE WYETH

In desperation he returned:

HELLO YOURSELF WHO R U PLS Q

MY NAME IS MILLI AND I WORK IN AN OFFICE IN DC

Milli? He knew no one named Milli. He felt a stirring within him.

HOW DO U KNOW MY NAME Q

I SAW U ONCE HERE IN MY OFFICE AND MADE INQUIRIES U R MY TYPE

Charlie wanted to ask in what office she worked, but the connection was abruptly cut off and the call was not repeated. On the way home he told himself that it was obviously a joke, but at the same time he caught himself rehearsing what he would say to her the next time. Next time? There wouldn't be any next time.

But the following night at ten p.m. he was glued to the TWX machine. At midnight he went home. There had been no call.

Wednesday. Still no call. Thursday. No call. It had been a joke.

On Friday he set out for a movie but somehow was waiting when the shrilling phone bell broke the ten o'clock Pentagon silence. In a few moments Milli, somewhere across the Potomac in Washington, was connected to him by a maze of wires and electronic circuits.

Charlie found that his shyness deserted him on the machine; when Milli coyly refused to name her office, he boldly demanded:

R U CUTE MILLI Q

MY SUPERVISOR THINKS SO BUT I HOPE THAT ISN T ALL U WANT FROM A GIRL

IT IS NOT

I M GLAD BECAUSE I WANT A MAN WHO IS SERIOUS AND AMBITIOUS

I M BOTH MILLI

THEN WHY AREN T U AT MC AFEE S DESK WHERE U BELONG CHARLIE Q

He found himself asking:

HOW CAN I GET THERE Q

IF SOME CLASSIFIED MATERIAL WOULD BE FOUND ON HIS DESK BY CID SECURITY CHECK HE WOULD BE IN TROUBLE WOULDN T HE Q

Before Charlie could explain McAfee's infallibility on classified documents, Milli clattered:

SOMEONE COMING NOT SUPP USE MACH WILL CALL YOU NEXT WEEK DARL

DARL! In TWXese that meant *darling*! Milli had called him darling! And her supervisor thought she was cute!

Riding home, Charlie was unaware of Washington's stifling heat; his face, long and lean and horselike in the bus window as they crossed Memorial Bridge, didn't seem quite as homely as before. Even stern old Abe, peering down from his lighted aerie in the Lincoln Memorial, might have nodded benignly at him as he passed.

Charlie Wyeth was no longer lonely.

The following Tuesday night, after fifteen delicious TWXed minutes with Milli, Charlie saw two young men in plainclothes moving efficiently from room to room far down the D Ring. He recognized them as types sharing certain characteristics with FBI men, CIA men, and NSA men; Army CID Security Agents, checking for classified document violations.

With a sleepwalker's step Charlie returned to the office, opened the classified documents safe, and removed a yellow-edged *Top Secret* folder containing revised figures on steel fatigue and stress ratios received from one of the missile contractors. He slammed and locked the safe, thrust the folder under some interdepartmental memos in McAfee's *out* basket, switched off the lights, and went home. At no time did he allow himself to think about what he was doing.

Two days later, in his private office, big bluff Colonel Andrews came right to the point.

'You've heard about McAfee?'

'There have been some rumors about classified documents but –'

'More than rumors, Wyeth – cold, hard facts. The security boys found a *Top Secret* folder on his desk after office hours.'

Charlie said, 'I'm sure it was just an oversight, sir. He –'

'I don't give a damn what it was.' The Colonel's hard, red face swelled impressively above his triple row of ribbons. 'That sort of thing reflects damned poorly on my record. Er – damned poorly.'

'I can understand how you feel, sir.'

If Andrews had been a bird his neck feathers would have ruffled.

'Fact is fact, Wyeth, and the fact is, McAfee is an old woman. I'm up for retirement in three years, and there's talk upstairs that I can take a BG's stars with me – but *not* if I'm gonna have security blunders in my command.'

He went to the window, looked out, teetered on his toes, and continued without looking at Charlie.

'You work late almost every night, Wyeth. If you would check the office over – er, especially McAfee's desk – so that there are no more security troubles in this shop, I'll remember it when the time for efficiency reports comes around.'

Charlie really felt quite bad about the scathing official reprimand sustained by McAfee because of the security violation, but Milli made him see his action in its proper perspective.

BELIEVE ME DARL U HAVE DONE THE RIGHT THING FOR YOUR COUNTRY AND FOR YOUR OFFICE AND FOR US

The 'darling' was common usage between them now. Charlie still didn't know Milli's last name or where she lived or worked, but he was determined not to rush her; after all, through the machine they had achieved a communion they never could have had in face-to-face meetings, and their relationship was maturing into something fragile and wonderful.

When he tried some poetry on Milli, she had been enthralled by the mathematical precision of Pope's and Dryden's couplets; and although she admitted she had never visited any of Washington's marvelous art galleries, in discussion she obviously favored the cubists. In music she was extremely modern.

Before the end of July, Charlie knew he was in love.

One night, as August scorched its way across the cloudless Washington sky, a very excited Milli called. She had learned in her office that there was going to be a review of Job Description Files in Army Ordnance. She communicated her excitement with a question.

WHAT WOULD HAPPEN IF THE INSPECTORS WERE TO DISCOVER THAT MC AFEE S POSITION WAS REALLY JUST EXCESS Q

AS AN ECONOMY MOVE THEY WOULD PROBABLY VACATE IT

DON T U THINK IT IS TIME TO CLEAR AWAY THE DEADWOOD DARL Q

Milli hadn't really said so, but when he thought it over later, Charlie knew that until he had McAfee's job he would never have Milli. And would it really be so wrong? Everybody said that he deserved promotion. If he could only get into those folders before the review and rewrite them so that the majority of McAfee's duties, on paper, would appear in Charlie's job description . . .

It took him three weeks.

First he had to obtain the proper forms in such a way that his own name didn't appear on the requisitions: then there was the task of lifting the folders; then rewriting them and substituting the new for the old.

It was all made meaningful when he told Milli what he had done. There was a long silence, broken only by the whirr of the TWX machine; then came her electrifying response.

DARL I LUV U

For the next few days Charlie repeated it to himself at work, at home, in his dreams. What difference that he had never seen her, never touched her, never heard her voice, never held her in his arms? He loved her, and she had said it too!

DARL I LUV U

The grist in official Washington's mill is ground exceedingly slow, but during World Series time the Colonel summoned Charlie into his private office. He was at parade rest in front of the window, his combat-wise eyes gazing out across the green lawns and the freeway toward the Fort Myer enlisted-men's swimming pool where two sunbathing WACS were clearly visible. When he turned to regard the younger man his face was friendly.

'Wyeth,' his drill-field voice rumbled, 'you remember a few weeks ago I asked you to perform certain unofficial – er, checks, and intimated that appreciation would be shown?'

'Yes, sir, Colonel, but anything I have done has been from a sense of duty, not because I expected any personal advancement.'

'I'm sure it has, Wyeth. Nevertheless, the current job description review, coupled with my – er, recommendations . . . well! I believe word will be down in a day or two that Mr McAfee has been – er, retired.'

'I'm – why I had no idea, sir. I . . . can't help feeling sorry –'

'No need, Wyeth. We have to clear out the – ahem, the deadwood, as it were. Valued service from McAfee all these years, but the old war-horse is now ready for pasture. Er – on your way out send him in here, will you, Wyeth?'

At ten p.m. that night, as Charlie was proceeding with the heady news of the eradication of the old warhorse's job, to Milli's delight, the old warhorse, in his modest Alexandria bungalow, was proceeding with the eradication of himself.

'Did it with a double-barreled shotgun,' recounted the secretary ghoulishly the next morning. 'I heard on the bus that he stuck the end of the gun in his mouth and pushed both triggers at once with his toes. I bet that room was splattered from one end to the other with –'

'Was – was there a note?' Charlie fought a wave of nausea.

'His wife said he just went into the study muttering about clearing out the deadwood and – blooey! Brains splashed –'

In the Men's Room, Charlie was thoroughly sick. He sloshed out his mouth with cold water and regarded his face in the mirror. Could those be his sly, cold eyes? Was his mouth that cruel, that determined? Could the Charlie Wyeth who had reveled in the poetry of Keats and Shelley have that narrow, ruthless chin?

He desperately needed Milli's assurance that he had done the right thing.

But that night Milli didn't call.

The next night Milli didn't call.

The third day, the day of McAfee's funeral, Charlie phoned in sick. He spent the long afternoon in his stuffy apartment near Dupont Circle. If only he knew where to reach her! Once he took his .32 pistol out of the drawer and stared at it for a very long time.

What was the matter with him? He was acting like that young aide from Naval PID who had killed himself three days after *his* Section Chief had committed suicide; like that young civilian lawyer in the Air Force Legal Section who had taken over his superior's position, and then, three days later . . .

Charlie thrust the revolver hurriedly back into the drawer. Thoughts like that were treason to his love for Milli. Tonight she would call and everything would be right again. Her fine clear mind would analyze his despair, show him the logical necessity for an occasional human sacrifice on the altar of Progress. If only it hadn't been *both* barrels!

On his way to the Pentagon, hoping for a ten p.m. TWXed rendezvous with Milli, he began recalling those first wonderful nights of communication. *I've made inquiries here, Charlie Wyeth*, Milli had said; and then before the file review she had stated: *the word around our office is that there is going to be a Job Description File Review in Ordnance.* But there was only one office which could possibly have all that information: the Department of Defense Statistical Records Branch in those World War II buildings flanking Constitution Avenue.

Charlie was getting excited. Yes, and he had delivered some records there once, and in the machine room on the fourth floor, where they kept the computers which sorted and stored the plethora of statistics concerning DOD, *there had been a commercial TWX machine on which Milli could have called him after hours!*

The cab dropped him on Constitution Avenue at 9:45 p.m. The building guard, dozing over a detective magazine at his table by the front entrance, didn't even notice Charlie jimmying open a ground-floor office window, slipping across the hall, and gliding up the back stairs. He paused on the third floor, heart pounding rapidly. He mustn't be disappointed if she wasn't there; if by some remote chance he *had* guessed the correct office, she might not be here tonight ...

And then he heard it.

Very faintly came the muffled clatter of a TWX. He looked at his watch: ten o'clock. Milli was trying to contact him!

Charlie raced up the remaining stairs and paused outside the door marked Machine Room in which the TWX was rattling Milli's impatient message of love. Would she be blonde? Tall? Beautiful? Charlie didn't know and didn't care: he only knew that he needed her.

He thrust open the door, fumbled along the wall for the light switch.

The TWX was instantly silenced. Fluorescent overheads flickered, snapped, flooded down radiance.

'Milli!' he called softly.

Milli didn't answer. The room, as he remembered from his single previous visit, was full of innocuous squat gray-metal boxes shielding the amazing array of circuits, relays, and transistors which enabled them to store and select needed information. The TWX machine, hidden by a low partition, was squeezed between a huge computer and a water cooler.

Charlie stepped around the partition. The operator's chair was pushed back as if hurriedly abandoned, and on the floor there were crushed cigarette butts with lipstick markings. Three feet of yellow paper, covered with typing, hung over the roll behind the machine.

But the cubicle was empty.

Clever Milli! She had heard him in the hall and had hidden behind one of the computers because it would mean her job if her superiors caught her using the TWX for her own purposes.

'Come out, darling. It's me, Charlie!'

Still no answer. He began peering among the computers: hide-and-seek. What a wonderful sense of humor to go with her wonderful mind! In a moment he would spy her; he peeped over computers and under computers and behind computers and ...

Computers. Only computers.

Slowly, unbelievingly, Charlie straightened up. There was no place for a human being to hide in this room. There was no space for anything except a dozen giant mechanical brains able to duplicate almost exactly the most intricate thought processes of the human mind: unspectacular boxes stuffed with miles of patient wire to carry and transmit and quietly learn all there was to know of the finite human brains which had created them.

One of them hadn't waited. It had been ready. From the data fed into it for storage it had selected carefully, choosing men like Charlie – the ambitious, lonely, romantic men – the weak men who were susceptible, who could be influenced in the name of love to subordinate their moral codes, their ethics, to their own self-advancement. Men who, driven eventually to despair and guilt by the withdrawal of Milli's TWXed assurances, would take the way out that Charlie had contemplated that afternoon. Men whose carefully engineered murders were mere preliminaries, mere finger-exercises in the practice of the massive program of thought control which would inevitably follow.

Charlie's shocked, searching eyes probed the room – and he screamed.

Beside the TWX was a huge oblong computer topped with two eye-like red lights. *The lights were coolly regarding him, expressing faint contempt*! On the wall behind the computer some office wag had pasted a small white sign decorated with a single word: MILLI.

Charles Wyeth went berserk.

Seizing the TWX operator's chair – hastily abandoned by its human occupant at the end of the work day – he rained down blows on the computer. The twin light burned a sudden scarlet. When he smashed the glass panel above the program slot there was a puff of black acrid smoke; when he thrust a shattered chair leg into one of the glaring lights, gouging it out as a thumb might gouge out an eye, the thing began to *shriek* – harsh mechanical bellows simulating the expression of human emotions. Light lubricating oil spurted down its side like blood down the breast of a wounded maiden.

He dropped the chair; the vitals of the thing were protected by its tough metal hide. The computer fell silent. Charlie leaped to the TWX machine, his hands like claws, his eyes alight with fatal knowledge.

He had to warn humanity of its impending fate.

THIS IS WASH OPR GA PLS

OPR I WANT TO MAKE A CONFERENCE CALL

WHAT CONF NUMBERS DO U WISH PLS Q

GET ME THE WORLD

DO NOT UNDERSTAND PLS REPEAT NRS DESIRED ON CONF CALL

FOR GOD S SAKE OPR I HAVE TO REACH ALL THE HUMAN BEINGS ON EARTH

Just then the guard, attracted by the unearthly racket, burst into the room, brandishing his automatic.

'Stop!' he shouted. 'Get away from that machine!'

Whirling on him, his teeth bared, his eyes blazing, Charlie cried, 'Don't you see? They're going to take us over!'

The guard saw. At the sight of Charlie's contorted face he went into the crouch he had learned at the FBI summer training course – body turned to present the smallest target, gun arm extended, knees slightly flexed – and pumped three .45 bullets into Charlie's chest. The heavy slugs hurled Charlie against the humming TWX machine in a welter of splintered ribs and crimson flesh.

THIS IS WASH OPR PLS REPEAT NRS DESIRED

Charlie was unable to comply. Charlie was dead.

The guard was straightening up, wiping his face. Thank God for the FBI! This guy had been either a spy for a foreign power or an out-and-out lunatic . . .

It was well over an hour before the mess had been sufficiently cleaned up for the hurriedly summoned Section Head to make a careful examination of the machine. He said to one of the Homicide Lieutenants: 'It's damned lucky that guy didn't know anything about computers – it would cost Uncle Sam millions to replace this little cutie.'

'No kidding.' The detective looked impressed. 'I'd say he smashed it up pretty bad – almost like he hated it.'

'No damage to the important components. And of course a man can't hate – or love – a machine.'

The Section Head completed his inventory, turned out the lights and went slowly down the stairs. Actually he had to admit to himself that he had a certain abstract emotion for his machines; they were man's most beautifully complex creations to date. The one that had been damaged, for instance, was capable of utilizing over 13,000,000 separate pieces of information. With machines like that, who knew what fantastic surprises the technological Future might hold?

Behind him in the dark, the unbroken light atop the damaged computer once more came aglow. Its crimson scintilla brightened, steadied; its quiet fanatical hum began.

Suddenly the TWX machine began to clatter volubly in the unattended silence of the machine room. Though they were addressed to a call number which was not Charlie Wyeth's, the words would have been very familiar to him.

DARL

dictated the electronic brain named Milli,

DARL I LUV U

AN · END · OF · SPINACH

Stan Dryer

'Hey, Harry, I don't think we should be in here.'

'Cummon, Spike, my Dad lets me come in here all the time and watch him.'

'I know, but suppose he finds out we're here?'

'He won't know. See that TV monitor there? That shows the corridor outside his office so we can see him coming. Besides, we're not going to hurt anything, just talk to old Socrat a little.'

'Talk to Socrat?'

'Socrat the computer, dummy. That's what my Dad does all the time. You just type in the entry code on this terminal. I'll show you. "LOGON PEMBROKE".'

'Please-enter-your-password-at-the-terminal.'

'Harry, it spoke *out loud* to us!'

'Of course. Now I'll type the password. "MARS". That's what Dad used the last time.'

'Entered-password-was-illegal.'

'See, Harry, I knew you weren't supposed to use it.'

'Don't be dumb, Spike. They just change the password every month. I bet my Dad uses the names of the planets starting with the Sun and working out. Let me try the next one beyond Mars. "JUPITER".'

'Entered-password-was-illegal. If-another-illegal-password-is-entered, an-unauthorized-entry-alarm-will-be-generated.'

'Let's get out of here, Harry! You give it another bad password and it will ring a bell or lock the door on us!'

'Look, Spike, I know my Dad. He probably started with the names of the planets on the *outside* of the solar system and worked in. Watch this. I'll type "EARTH".'

'Good-afternoon, Professor-Pembroke. Socrat-at-your-service. Audible-inputs-may-be-used.'

'Wow, Harry, you did it. It thinks it's talking to your Dad.'

'I told you it was easy. Now what shall we ask it to do?'

'I-cannot-parse-your-audible-inputs. Please-speak-more-clearly.'

'I was just talking to my friend Spike. Let's see. To start, can you tell us what day it is today?'

'Today-is-Tuesday, May-twelve, nineteen-eighty-seven.'

'Gee, Harry, that's neat. Can it do math stuff too?'

'Sure, watch this. Socrat, what is the square root of two?'

'To-how-many-decimal-places-do-you-wish-the-square-root-of-two-calculated?'

'How about a hundred?'

'The-square-root-of-two-to-one-hundred-decimal-places-is-displayed-on-Screen-A.'

'Look at that, Harry! It didn't take it any time at all. One point four one four two one ... You think it's right?'

'Of course it's right. But we'll have Socrat check it for us. Watch this. Hey, Socrat, I want you to multiply the number on Screen A by itself.'

'The-value-of-the-product-of-the-number-on-Screen-A-and-the-number-on-Screen-A-is-displayed-on-Screen-B.'

'There it is, Harry, a two followed by about a hundred zeros. Hey, do you think Socrat could figure out the square root of two to a really big number of decimal places?'

'I'll ask it. Socrat, to how many decimal places can you find out the square root of two?'

'Calculations-of-roots-of-numbers-are-limited-only-by-the-machine-resources-you-wish-to-devote-to-the-problem-and-the-time-you-are-willing-to-wait-for-results.'

'Okay, Socrat, how long would it take to get it to a million decimal places?'

'By-devoting-full-capacity-of-this-machine-to-the-task, it-could-be-completed-in-thirty-seven-seconds. Where-do-you-wish-your-output-placed?'

'Can I get it printed?'

'Affirmative. Printout-of-one-million-digits-will-require-seven-point-six-minutes. Do-you-wish-me-to-perform-the-calculation?'

'What do you think, Spike?'

'Wait, Harry. Ask it how long it will take to get it to a hundred billion decimal places.'

'A hundred billion?'

'Sure. I bet it can't do that.'

'I bet it can. Socrat, how long will it take you to figure out the square root of two to a hundred billion places?'

'By-devoting-the-full-capacity-of-this-machine-to-that-task, the-square-root-of-two-could-be-calculated-to-ten-to-the-eleventh-decimal-places-in-approximately-forty-three-days-and-seven-hours. Printout-of-the-results-would-require-five-hundred-and-twenty-eight-days.'

'See, Harry, I knew it couldn't do it.'

'Hold on, Spike. I haven't finished asking it. First of all, Socrat, what can you do with the output if you don't print it?'

'Output-can-be-stored-on-disk-memory-for-recall-to-screen-display-as-required. Requisite-disk-storage-is-not-currently-available.'

'I told you it couldn't do it.'

'Just hang on, Spike. Socrat, is there anything you could erase from the disk storage to make room?'

'As-a-Priority-One-user-you-have-authorization-to-erase-any-current-files. Storage-of-ten-to-the-eleventh-power-digits-will-require-approximately-ninety-three-percent-of-online-disk-pack-storage-at-this-facility. Do-you-wish-me-to-erase-this-storage?'

'Not yet. We can't wait forty-three days to get the answer. Are there any other computers you can get to help with the job?'

'As-a-Priority-One-user-you-have-access-to-all-other-machines-on-the-network-and-can-execute-at-Priority-One-on-all-such-machines. Three-hundred-and-sixty-eight-machines-are-currently-on-line.'

'If we used all of them, how long would it take?'

'Utilization-of-the-full-facilities-of-all-machines-currently-on-line-would-reduce-calculation-time-to-approximately-seventeen-hours-and-twelve-minutes.'

'Hey, Harry, that's great. We could turn all the computers loose right now and then come back after school tomorrow and look at the answer.'

'Do-you-wish-me-to-begin-phaseover-of-other-network-machines-to-your-task?'

'Go ahead, Harry. Tell it to start them up!'

'Just a second, Spike. I'm not sure that's a good idea.'

'How come?'

'Look, if we erase all the disk files here and stop all those other computers so they can do our stuff, someone's going to notice. Besides, Socrat might be doing something important he shouldn't stop doing.'

'I thought Socrat was talking to us.'

'You dummy. Socrat can talk to us and do a hundred other things at the same time.'

'Go on, Harry. You're kidding me.'

'I'm not. I'll ask it what it's doing. Hey, Socrat, what important things are you doing right now?'

'I-cannot-index-on-the-word-"Important". Jobs-are-categorized-by-priority-and-user.'

'Okay, give me a list of all the Priority-One jobs you're doing right now.'

'Listing-of-Priority-One-jobs-is-displayed-on-Screen-A.'

'Hey, look at that, Harry. That satellite catalog looks pretty interesting. Maybe we could print out a list of them?'

'Naw, Spike, you can get that stuff in a science book. Dad is always talking about his Land Use Planning Program. Let's mess around with that.'

'What's it do?'

'Socrat, tell us about the Land Use Planning Program.'

'The-Land-Use-Planning-Program-automates-the-process-of-determination-of-priorities-for-land-use-for-agriculture-in-the-United-States. It-matches-requirements-for-food-products-against-available-land. Output-is-provided-to-fifty-seven-regional-planning-centers-where-farmers-can-obtain-pertinent-information-of-crop-requirements.'

'You mean you tell the farmers how much stuff to grow?'

'Use-of-planning-information-for-crop-land-allocations-is-voluntary. Participation-by-farmers-in-the-program-was-seventy-three-percent-for-the-last-planning-year.'

'Spike, I got a great idea! What's your least favorite vegetable?'

'That's easy. Spinach.'

'Mine too. Now what's your *favorite* vegetable.'

'Peas, I guess. How come you want to know that?'

'My idea, stupid. We're going to have Socrat stop everyone from growing spinach and have them grow lots more peas.'

'Wow, Harry, neat.'

'Socrat, how much spinach is grown in the United States every year?'

'One-hundred-and-ninety-eight-thousand-short-tons-of-spinach-were-grown-in-the-United-States-during-the-last-planning-year.'

'Okay, can you set it so no more spinach is grown from now on?'

'Negative. Changes-in-crop-acreage-allocation-are-limited-to-plus-

or-minus-fifteen-percent-per-year-unless-a-consensus-override-is-obtained.'

'Okay, then cut the allocation fifteen percent for each year for the next five years. And increase the allocation for peas by the same amount.'

'Your-request-has-been-analyzed. Predicted-retail-prices-of-spinach-and-peas-for-the-next-five-years-are-displayed-on-Screen-A. Do-you-wish-to-modify-the-master-planning-file?'

'Hey, Harry, look at that. In three years spinach will be twelve dollars a pound and peas will only cost twenty cents!'

'Socrat, please modify the files.'

'The-master-planning-file-has-been-modified-to-incorporate-your-request.'

'Harry, look at the monitor! Isn't that your Dad coming out of his office?'

'Right! Quick, Spike, tear that paper out of the terminal. Socrat, log us off right away.'

'Session-on-account-Pembroke-has-been-terminated. It-has-been-a-pleasure-to-serve-you, Professor-Pembroke.'

'Here he comes, Harry.'

'Hey, you kids aren't supposed to be in here.'

'I'm sorry, Dad. I was just showing Spike the computer.'

'You didn't touch anything, did you?'

'I just tried to type some stuff on the terminal.'

'I guess that couldn't have hurt anything. You see, this computer has built-in security checks. You know what those are, Spike?'

'I don't think so, Mr Pembroke.'

'Well, suppose someone wanted to get access to the computer to find out some important things that are stored or even to change around some of those things. He would have to know a logon name first and then he would have to know a secret password. And those passwords are changed every month. So not just anyone could come in here and use the computer. You understand that?'

'I guess so, Mr Pembroke.'

'Hey, Dad, can we come down and visit your office again next week?'

COMPUTERS · DON'T · ARGUE

Gordon R. Dickson

TREASURE BOOK CLUB
PLEASE DO NOT FOLD,
SPINDLE OR MUTILATE
THIS CARD
Mr Walter A. Child   Balance: $4.98

Dear Customer: Enclosed is your latest book selection. *Kidnapped*, by Robert Louis Stevenson.

437 Woodlawn Drive
Panduk, Michigan
Nov. 16, 198–

Treasure Book Club
1823 Mandy Street
Chicago, Illinois

Dear Sirs:

I wrote you recently about the computer punch card you sent, billing me for *Kim*, by Rudyard Kipling. I did not open the package containing it until I had already mailed you my check for the amount on the card. On opening the package, I found the book missing half its pages. I sent it back to you, requesting either another copy or my money back. Instead, you have sent me a copy of *Kidnapped*, by Robert Louis Stevenson. Will you please straighten this out?

I hereby return the copy of *Kidnapped*.

Sincerely yours,
Walter A. Child

TREASURE BOOK CLUB
SECOND NOTICE
PLEASE DO NOT FOLD,
SPINDLE OR MUTILATE
THIS CARD

Mr Walter A. Child   Balance: $4.98

For *Kidnapped*, by Robert Louis Stevenson

(If remittance has been made for the above, please disregard this notice.)

437 Woodlawn Drive
Panduk, Michigan
Jan. 21, 198–

Treasure Book Club
1823 Mandy Street
Chicago, Illinois

Dear Sirs:

May I direct your attention to my letter of November 16, 198–? You are still continuing to dun me with computer punch cards for a book I did not order. Whereas, actually, it is your company that owes *me* money.

Sincerely yours,
Walter A. Child

Treasure Book Club
1823 Mandy Street
Chicago, Illinois
Feb. 1, 198–

Mr Walter A. Child
437 Woodlawn Drive
Panduk, Michigan

Dear Mr Child:

We have sent you a number of reminders concerning an amount owing to us as a result of book purchases you have made from us. This amount, which is $4.98 is now long overdue.

This situation is disappointing to us, particularly since there was no hesitation on our part in extending you credit at the time original arrangements for these purchases were made by you. If we do not receive pay-

ment in full by return mail, we will be forced to turn the matter over
to a collection agency.

Very truly yours,
Samuel P. Grimes
Collection Mgr

437 Woodlawn Drive
Panduk, Michigan
Feb. 5, 198–

Dear Mr Grimes:

Will you stop sending me punch cards and form letters and make me
some kind of a direct answer from a human being?

I don't owe you money. *You* owe me money. Maybe I should turn
your company over to a collection agency.

Walter A. Child

FEDERAL COLLECTION OUTFIT

88 Prince Street
Chicago, Illinois
Feb. 28, 198–

Mr Walter A. Child
437 Woodlawn Drive
Panduk, Michigan

Dear Mr Child:

Your account with the Treasure Book Club, of $4.98 plus interest
and charges has been turned over to our agency for collection. The
amount due is now $6.83. Please send your check for this amount or
we shall be forced to take immediate action.

Jacob N. Harshe
Vice President

FEDERAL COLLECTION OUTFIT

88 Prince Street
Chicago, Illinois
April 8, 198–

Mr Walter A. Child
437 Woodlawn Drive
Panduk, Michigan

Dear Mr Child:

You have seen fit to ignore our courteous requests to settle your long overdue account with Treasure Book Club, which is now, with accumulated interest and charges, in the amount of $7.51.

If payment in full is not forthcoming by April 11, 198– we will be forced to turn the matter over to our attorneys for immediate court action.

Ezekiel B. Harshe
President

MALONEY, MAHONEY, MacNAMARA
and PRUITT
Attorneys

89 Prince Street
Chicago, Illinois
April 29, 198–

Mr Walter A. Child
437 Woodlawn Drive
Panduk, Michigan

Dear Mr Child:

Your indebtedness to the Treasure Book Club has been referred to us for legal action to collect.

This indebtedness is now in the amount of $10.01. If you will send us this amount so that we may receive it before May 5, 198–, the matter may be satisfied. However, if we do not receive satisfaction in full by that date, we will take steps to collect through the courts.

I am sure you will see the advantage of avoiding a judgment against you, which as a matter of record would do lasting harm to your credit rating.

Very truly yours,
Hagthorpe M. Pruitt Jr.
Attorney-at-law

437 Woodlawn Drive
Panduk, Michigan
May 4, 198–

Mr Hagthorpe M. Pruitt, Jr
Maloney, Mahoney, MacNamara and Pruitt
89 Prince Street
Chicago, Illinois

Dear Mr Pruitt:

You don't know what a pleasure it is to me in this matter to get a letter from a live human being to whom I can explain the situation.

This whole matter is silly. I explained it fully in my letters to the Treasure Book Company. But I might as well have been trying to explain to the computer that puts out their punch cards, for all the good it seemed to do. Briefly, what happened was I ordered a copy of *Kim*, by Rudyard Kipling, for $4.98. When I opened the package they sent me, I found the book had only half its pages, but I'd previously mailed a check to pay them for the book.

I sent the book back to them, asking either for a whole copy or my money back. Instead, they sent me a copy of *Kidnapped*, by Robert Louis Stevenson – which I had not ordered; and for which they have been trying to collect from me.

Meanwhile, I am still waiting for the money back that they owe me for the copy of *Kim* that I didn't get. That's the whole story. Maybe you can help me straighten them out.

Relievedly yours,
Walter A. Child

PS: I also sent them back their copy of *Kidnapped*, as soon as I got it, but it hasn't seemed to help. They have never even acknowledged getting it back.

MALONEY, MAHONEY, MacNAMARA
and PRUITT
Attorneys

89 Prince Street
Chicago, Illinois
May 9, 198–

Mr Walter A. Child
437 Woodlawn Drive
Panduk, Michigan

Dear Mr Child:

I am in possession of no information indicating that any item purchased by you from the Treasure Book Club has been returned.

I would hardly think that, if the case had been as you stated, the Treasure Book Club would have retained us to collect the amount owing from you.

If I do not receive payment in full within three days, by May 12, 198–, we will be forced to take legal action.

Very truly yours,
Hagthorpe M. Pruitt, Jr

COURT OF MINOR CLAIMS
Chicago, Illinois

Mr Walter A. Child:
437 Woodlawn Drive
Panduk, Michigan

Be informed that a judgment was taken and entered against you in this court this day of May 26, 198– in the amount of $15.66 including court costs.

Payment in satisfaction of this judgment may be made to this court or to the adjudged creditor. In the case of payment being made to the creditor, a release should be obtained from the creditor and filed with this court in order to free you of legal obligation in connection with this judgment. Under the recent Reciprocal Claims Act, if you are a citizen of a different state, a duplicate claim may be automatically entered and judged against you in your own state so that collection may be made there as well as in the State of Illinois.

COURT OF MINOR CLAIMS
Chicago, Illinois
PLEASE DO NOT FOLD,
SPINDLE OR MUTILATE
THIS CARD

Judgment was passed this day of May 27, 198–, under Statute 941.
Against: Child, Walter A. of 437 Woodlawn Drive, Panduk, Michigan.
Pray to enter a duplicate claim for judgment.

In: Picayune Court – Panduk, Michigan
For Amount: $15.66

437 Woodlawn Drive
Panduk, Michigan
May 31, 198–

Samuel P. Grimes
Vice President, Treasure Book Club
1823 Mandy Street
Chicago, Illinois

Grimes:

This business has gone far enough. I've got to come down to Chicago on business of my own tomorrow. I'll see you then and we'll get this straightened out once and for all, about who owes what to whom, and how much!

Yours,
Walter A. Child

From the desk of the Clerk
Picayune Court

June 1, 198–

Harry:

The attached computer card from Chicago's Minor Claims Court against A. Walter has a 1500-series Statute number on it. That puts it over in Criminal with you, rather than Civil, with me. So I herewith submit it for your computer instead of mine. How's business?

Joe

CRIMINAL RECORDS
Panduk, Michigan
**PLEASE DO NOT FOLD,
SPINDLE OR MUTILATE
THIS CARD**

Convicted: (Child) A. Walter
On: May 26, 198–
Address: 437 Woodlawn Drive, Panduk, Mich.
Statute: 1566 (Corrected) 1567
Crime: Kidnap
Date: Nov. 16, 198–
Notes: At large. To be picked up at once.

POLICE   DEPARTMENT,   PANDUK,   MICHIGAN.   TO   POLICE

DEPARTMENT CHICAGO ILLINOIS. CONVICTED SUBJECT A. (COMPLETE FIRST NAME UNKNOWN) WALTER, SOUGHT HERE IN CONNECTION REF. YOUR NOTIFICATION OF JUDGMENT FOR KIDNAP OF CHILD NAMED ROBERT LOUIS STEVENSON, ON NOV. 16, 198–. INFORMATION HERE INDICATES SUBJECT FLED HIS RESIDENCE, AT 437 WOODLAWN DRIVE, PANDUK, AND MAY BE AGAIN IN YOUR AREA.

POSSIBLE CONTACT IN YOUR AREA: THE TREASURE BOOK CLUB, 1823 MANDY STREET, CHICAGO, ILLINOIS. SUBJECT NOT KNOWN TO BE ARMED, BUT PRESUMED DANGEROUS. PICK UP AND HOLD, ADVISING US OF CAPTURE . . .

TO POLICE DEPARTMENT, PANDUK, MICHIGAN. REFERENCE YOUR REQUEST TO PICK UP AND HOLD A. (COMPLETE FIRST NAME UNKNOWN) WALTER, WANTED IN PANDUK ON STATUTE 1567, CRIME OF KIDNAPPING.

SUBJECT ARRESTED AT OFFICES OF TREASURE BOOK CLUB, OPERATING THERE UNDER ALIAS WALTER ANTHONY CHILD AND ATTEMPTING TO COLLECT $4.98 FROM ONE SAMUEL P. GRIMES, EMPLOYEE OF THAT COMPANY.

DISPOSAL: HOLDING FOR YOUR ADVICE.

POLICE DEPARTMENT, PANDUK, MICHIGAN TO POLICE DEPARTMENT, CHICAGO, ILLINOIS.

REF: A. WALTER (ALIAS WALTER ANTHONY CHILD) SUBJECT WANTED FOR CRIME OF KIDNAP, YOUR AREA, REF: YOUR COMPUTER PUNCH CARD NOTIFICATION OF JUDGMENT, DATED MAY 27, 198–. COPY OUR CRIMINAL RECORDS PUNCH CARD HEREWITH FORWARDED TO YOUR COMPUTER SECTION.

CRIMINAL RECORDS
Chicago, Illinois
PLEASE DO NOT FOLD,
SPINDLE OR MUTILATE
THIS CARD

Subject (Correction – omitted record supplied)
Applicable Statute No. 1567
Judgment No. 456789
Trial Record: Apparently misfiled and unavailable

Direction: To appear for sentencing before Judge John Alexander McDivot, Courtroom A, June 9, 198–

From the Desk of
Judge Alexander J. McDivot

June 2, 198–

Dear Tony:

I've got an adjudged criminal coming up before me for sentencing Thursday morning – but the trial transcript is apparently misfiled.

I need some kind of information (Ref: A. Walter – Judgment No. 456789, Criminal). For example, what about the victim of the kidnapping? Was victim harmed?

Jack McDivot

Records Search Unit
Re: Ref: Judgment No. 456789 – was victim harmed?

Tonio Malagasi
Records Division

June 3, 198–

To: United States Statistics Office
Attn: Information Section
Subject: Robert Louis Stevenson
Query: Information concerning

Records Search Unit
Criminal Records Division
Police Department
Chicago, Ill.

June 5, 198–

To: Records Search Unit
Criminal Records Division
Police Department
Chicago, Illinois
Subject: Your query re Robert Louis Stevenson (File no. 189623)
Action: Subject deceased. Age at death, 44 yrs. Further information requested?

A.K.
Information Section
US Statistics Office

June 6, 198–

To: United States Statistics Office
Attn: Information Division
Subject: Re: File no. 189623
   No further information required.

Thank you.
Records Search Unit
Criminal Records Division
Police Department
Chicago, Illinois

To: Tonio Malagasi
Records Division
Re: Ref: Judgment No. 456789 – victim is dead.

Records Search Unit

June 7, 198–

To: Judge Alexander J. McDivot's Chambers
Dear Jack:
Ref: Judgment No. 456789. The victim in this kidnap case was apparently slain.

From the strange lack of background information on the killer and his victim, as well as the victim's age, this smells to me like a gangland killing. This for your information. Don't quote me. It seems to me, though, that Stevenson – the victim – has a name that rings a faint bell with me. Possibly, one of the East Coast Mob, since the association comes back to me as something about pirates – possibly New York dockage hijackers – and something about buried loot.

As I say, above is only speculation for your private guidance.
   Any time I can help . . .

Best,
Tony Malagasi
Records Division

MICHAEL R. REYNOLDS
Attorney-at-law

49 Water Street
Chicago, Illinois
June 8, 198–

Dear Tim:

Regrets: I can't make the fishing trip. I've been court-appointed here to represent a man about to be sentenced tomorrow on a kidnapping charge.

Ordinarily, I might have tried to beg off, and McDivot, who is doing the sentencing, would probably have turned me loose. But this is the damndest thing you ever heard of.

The man being sentenced has apparently been not only charged, but adjudged guilty as a result of a comedy of errors too long to go into here. He not only isn't guilty – he's got the best case I ever heard of for damages against one of the larger Book Clubs headquartered here in Chicago. And that's a case I wouldn't mind taking on.

It's inconceivable – but damnably possible, once you stop to think of it in this day and age of machine-made records – that a completely innocent man could be put in this position.

There shouldn't be much to it. I've asked to see McDivot tomorrow before the time of sentencing, and it'll just be a matter of explaining to him. Then I can discuss the damage suit with my freed client at his leisure.

Fishing next weekend?

Yours,
Mike

MICHAEL R. REYNOLDS
Attorney-at-law

49 Water Street
Chicago, Illinois
June 10

Dear Tim:

In haste –

No fishing this coming week either. Sorry.

You won't believe it. My innocent-as-a-lamb-and-I'm-not-kidding client has just been sentenced to death for first-degree murder in connection with the death of his kidnap victim.

Yes, I explained the whole thing to McDivot. And when he explained his situation to me, I nearly fell out of my chair.

It wasn't a matter of my not convincing him. It took less than three minutes to show him that my client should never have been within the walls of the County Jail for a second. But – get this – McDivot couldn't go a thing about it.

The point is, my man had already been judged guilty according to the computerized records. In the absence of a trial record – of course there never was one (but that's something I'm not free to explain to you now) – the judge has to go by what records are available. And in the case of an adjudged prisoner, McDivot's only legal choice was whether to sentence to life imprisonment, or execution.

The death of the kidnap victim, according to the statute, made the death penalty mandatory. Under the new laws governing length of time for appeal, which has been shortened because of the new system of computerizing records, to force an elimination of unfair delay and mental anguish to those condemned, I have five days in which to file an appeal, and ten to have it acted on.

Needless to say, I am not going to monkey with an appeal. I'm going directly to the Governor for a pardon – after which we will get this farce reversed. McDivot has already written the Governor, also, explaining that his sentence was ridiculous, but that he had no choice. Between the two of us, we ought to have a pardon in short order.

Then, I'll make the fur fly ...

And we'll get in some fishing.

Best, Mike

OFFICE OF THE
GOVERNOR OF ILLINOIS

June 17, 198–

Mr Michael R. Reynolds
49 Water Street
Chicago, Illinois

Dear Mr Reynolds:

In reply to your query about the request for pardon for Walter A. Child (A. Walter), may I inform you that the Governor is still on his trip with the Midwest Governors Committee, examining the Wall in Berlin. He should be back next Friday.

I will bring your request and letters to his attention the minute he returns.

Very truly yours,
Clara B. Jilks
Secretary to the Governor

June 27, 198–

Michael R. Reynolds
49 Water Street
Chicago, Illinois

Dear Mike:

Where is that pardon?

My execution date is only five days from now!

Walt

June 29, 198–

Walter A. Child (A. Walter)
Cell Block E
Illinois State Penitentiary
Joliet, Illinois

Dear Walt:

The Governor returned, but was called away immediately to the White House in Washington to give his views on interstate sewage.

I am camping on his doorstep and will be on him the moment he arrives here.

Meanwhile, I agree with you about the seriousness of the situation. The warden at the prison there, Mr Allen Magruder, will bring this letter to you and have a private talk with you. I urge you to listen to what he has to say; and I enclose letters from your family also urging you to listen to Warden Magruder.

Yours,
Mike

June 30, 198–

Michael R. Reynolds
49 Water Street
Chicago, Illinois

Dear Mike: (This letter being smuggled out by Warden Magruder)

As I was talking to Warden Magruder in my cell, here, news was brought to him that the Governor has at last returned for a while to Illinois, and will be in his office early tomorrow morning, Friday. So you will have time to get the pardon signed by him and delivered to the prison in time to stop my execution on Saturday.

Accordingly, I have turned down the Warden's kind offer of a chance to escape; since he told me he could by no means guarantee to have all the guards out of my way when I tried it; and there was a chance of my being killed escaping.

But now everything will straighten itself out. Actually, an experience as fantastic as this had to break down sometime under its own weight.

Best,
Walt

FOR THE SOVEREIGN STATE OF ILLINOIS, I Hubert Daniel Willikens, Governor of the State of Illinois, and invested with the authority and powers appertaining thereto, including the power to pardon those in my judgment wrongfully convicted or otherwise deserving of executive mercy, do this day of July 1, 198– announce and proclaim that Walter A. Child (A. Walter), now in custody as a consequence of erroneous conviction upon a crime of which he is entirely innocent, is fully and freely pardoned of said crime. And I do direct the necessary authorities having custody of the said Walter A. Child (A. Walter) in whatever place or places he may be held, to immediately free, release, and allow unhindered departure to him ...

INTERDEPARTMENTAL ROUTING SERVICE
PLEASE DO NOT FOLD,
MUTILATE, OR SPINDLE
THIS CARD

Failure to route Document properly.
To: Governor Hubert Daniel Willikens
Re: Pardon issued to Walter A. Child, July 1, 198–
Dear State Employee:
You have failed to attach your Routing Number.
PLEASE: Resubmit document with this card and form 876, explaining your authority for placing a TOP RUSH category on this document. Form 876 must be signed by your Departmental Superior.
RESUBMIT ON: Earliest possible date ROUTING SERVICE office is open. In this case, Tuesday, July 5, 198–
WARNING: Failure to submit form 876 WITH THE SIGNATURE OF YOUR SUPERIOR may make you liable to prosecution for misusing a Service of the State Government. A warrant may be issued for your arrest.
There are NO exceptions. YOU have been WARNED.

GOLDBRICK
Edward Wellen

Always provide a golden bridge for a fleeing enemy.

Gen. Sun Tzu

The Knight came to the place where Arthur and Owain were seated
at chess. They perceived that he was harassed and vexed and weary.
The youth saluted Arthur and told him that the Ravens of Owain
were slaying his young men and attendants. Arthur looked at Owain
and said:

'Forbid thy Ravens.'

'Lord,' answered Owain, 'play thy game.'

'The Dream of Rhonabwy',
translated from the Welsh of the *Mabinogion*
by Lady Charlotte Guest

The battle is everlasting and can do without the pomp of actual armies
and of trumpets.

Jorge Luis Borges,
'A Page to Commemorate Colonel Suárez, Victor at Junín',
in *Selected Poems 1923–1967*, edited by Norman Thomas de Giovanni,
translated by Alastair Reid, New York, Delacorte, 1970.

It is the cold glitter of the attacker's eye, not the point of the questing
bayonet, that breaks the line.

Gen. George S. Patton, Jr

I do not like to see the arms and legs fly.

Brig. Gen. George Patton III

I'm used to a structured organization and this civilian process is so
doggone nebulous.

Gen. William C. Westmoreland

Moreover, remember that in the game of atomic warfare, there are
no experts.

Norman Wiener, *God and Golem, Inc.*
M.I.T. Press, 1964

We have met the enemy, and they is us.

Pogo

1. NLD   NOT IN THE LINE OF DUTY

Someone hawked. Otherwise, all quiet along the Potomac.

Then Stonewall J. Buckmaster grew aware of Maggie Fubb nudging him. Sleepily he pawed her. She hissed through her teeth and turned to her side of the bed and clicked the light on under the ballerina lampshade.

'*Ten-hut!*'

He blinked wide awake, then smiled and prepared to make love again. But she sounded off again in a parade ground voice, and he saw that though she spoke to him she looked past him.

'Wipe that smile off your face, Lieutenant. By God, when your superior officer enters the room, you jump to attention.'

Lt Buckmaster shut his eyes to make it all a dream, then opened them and looked around slowly. It was no dream. Col. Maximilian Fubb stood gazing down at them.

Buckmaster hopped out of bed and squared his shoulders and stood at bare-assed attention. Col. Fubb waved a hand at him in a small weary gesture.

'At ease, Lieutenant.'

Col. Fubb stood at parade rest, only his hands behind him refused to lock into stillness like the rest of him. In the dresser mirror Buckmaster watched them milk each other. Buckmaster reconnoitered the colonel's face. As always, one eyebrow took a higher position than the other. The eyes themselves, though they fixed on his wife, who had not bothered to cover herself, did not seem to see her. He had a black head of hair but gray stubble on his face. Buckmaster had never noticed that there were so many lines or so deep.

Buckmaster waited for the colonel to sand him down. But the colonel's mind seemed way elsewhere. On his work, no doubt. Maggie had questioned Buckmaster about the colonel's work, wanting to know all about this mistress that had taken him from her. Buckmaster had shrugged. 'I'm only a messenger boy, Maggie. All I know is, the colonel daily disappears into the war room. I don't have entry.'

The colonel's terminator swung more to the left, putting his other eye in shadow. He spoke more to Buckmaster than to his wife, as though he had given up on her.

'I don't want you to think I've stooped to sneaking, pretending to be on night duty to trap you by showing up unexpectedly at home. There's an emergency on and it's going to be a long siege. I've come to get a few personal things because I'll be staying at the Pentagon night and day.'

The colonel's hands released each other. He fingered his fruit salad.

'With the world on the brink, what's the faithfulness of a bitch of a wife more or less? Or the honor of an officer and a gentleman more or less?' He sighed. 'Still, Lieutenant, just on principle I'll have to deal with you. And right away, so you won't be at the back of my mind while I'm working.'

Buckmaster tensed. Did Fubb have a gun in the room? If Fubb made a move toward drawer or closet . . .

Maggie's breathing had quickened and loudened. The eternal bitch would love that, her husband going for his gun, her lover jumping him. The Helen complex. Men fighting over her.

But the colonel merely nodded to himself.

'I'm going to ask the computer to come up with the most hazardous duty or the most godforsaken post it can find and send you there.' He almost smiled. 'Think of it as getting your ticket punched.' He looked slightly hopeful. 'Unless you'd rather resign your commission?'

Buckmaster could not find his voice. He shook his head. But Fubb's eyes had shot to Maggie. Her hands were reaching out to grasp Buckmaster's.

'Stoney, stay. Fight the transfer.'

'Lieutenant, if you don't take the transfer, and if you don't resign, I'll give you an efficiency report rating that will finish your army career.'

'Stoney.'

'What do you say, Lieutenant?'

'Fight back, Stoney. Fight *him*.'

'No more time. Your answer now, Lieutenant.'

'Bring on your computer, sir.'

'Get dressed and wait for me.'

Buckmaster grabbed his clothes.

Maggie spat at him as he left the room.

2. NE   Not eligible for security clearance

The Pentagon Building's first floor has brown walls, its second floor has green walls, its third floor has red walls.

Buckmaster knew he was on the second floor. His mind felt blank – or at most a filled-in zero – but he knew that this timeless space had green walls. And he knew that he and Col. Fubb were striding toward the box. The box was a name for the war room, and the war room was a name for the National Military Command Center.

They were approaching the guards who had always sealed him out from that nineteen-room, 30,000-square-foot, highly restricted area.

'Wait here, Lieutenant.'

'Yes, sir.'

The guards stood watching him, still sealing him out.

Lt Victor Landtroop came out just as Col. Fubb was about to go in. Somewhere in there was the tank, the pastel conference room of the Joint Chiefs of Staff. And Landtroop, though he walked on his toes, carried the weight of his proximity to power with becoming gravity. Lt Victor Landtroop. You always knew just where he stood: straddling the issue. Lt Victor Landtroop. An upper lip that cried out for a mustache and a mouth that looked as if it had never got over the shock of finding a plastic nipple in place of the real thing. But Lt Victor Landtroop was one up on Lt Stonewall J. Buckmaster. Landtroop had clearance.

He evidently jumped to the conclusion that Buckmaster was going in with Fubb. After greeting Fubb smoothly, he gave Buckmaster a fellowish jab on the arm.

'Glad to see you're joining us in TOTE, Buckmaster.'

Buckmaster smiled easily. Never admit you're not in the know. But what the hell was TOTE? Short for *Totentanz*? All he was going to tote was his val-pack.

Fubb had stopped short in the doorway. Buckmaster watched Landtroop redden as Fubb came down on him with all the eyebrow weight the colonel could muster. Then the colonel entered alone and the door closed.

Without moving, Landtroop put distance between himself and Buckmaster. That was Landtroop, all right: he could blow hot and cold in the same breath. At the O-club, Landtroop had always – 'always' being the few months of Buckmaster's assignment here – tried to be one of the fellows while sucking up to the brass. Buckmaster saw that

Landtroop was really sweating. Whatever it was, TOTE was big and a lot was at stake. Landtroop's face lent green to the walls.

'Look, Buckmaster, forget I said anything.'

'Why, sure, Landtroop. I'll even forget you.' He waved away thanks before Landtroop could offer them. 'My pleasure.'

Waiting under the gaze of the guards for Fubb to return, Buckmaster wouldn't give them the pleasure of seeing him look at his watch. So he didn't know just how long it took the colonel to get the computer printout that the colonel came out studying with a frown.

Fubb led him away down the corridor out of earshot of the guards.

'You're going to the Tenth Experimental Company. Never heard of it, but it seems it comes under the Advanced Research Projects Agency. So I had to stick my neck out and get you clearance. I'll have them cut the orders for you to pick up at 0800 hours.' He looked squarely at Buckmaster. 'Unless you feel you have an Article 138 complaint. You know how that goes.'

Buckmaster nodded. Any member of the armed forces who believes himself wronged by his commanding officer and who, upon due application to that commanding officer, is refused redress, may complain to any superior officer. Buckmaster contained a grimace. Tenth *Experimental*. He remembered hearing about the men who had taken part in the Army's early experiments with radar microwaves. Whatever the Tenth *Experimental* was, it was no sinecure, no Underground Balloon Corps. He nodded again.

'I don't feel my CO has wronged me.'

A flicker of something in the colonel's eyes.

'I won't wish you luck, good or bad. Just good-bye.'

'Good-bye Colonel.'

'Damn it, Buckmaster, you've never measured up to your potential. You've never had to stretch yourself. I've sensed that any real seriousness of purpose is lacking in you.' He suddenly smiled a tight smile. 'I may be doing you a favor. This posting may be the making of you. Though to tell you the truth I hope it's the breaking of you.'

'Thank you, sir. I'll return with my shield or on it. Though to tell *you* the truth I'd rather return the shield.'

Buckmaster saluted, about-faced, and left.

3. WP WILL PROCEED

He eyed the drink in his hand as though wondering how it had got there. It looked like a glass of what the O-club's funny bartender called Long Binge Ale. That always went over big with the guys who had been in Nam. But Nam was before Buckmaster's time, and the drink tasted as flat as the joke.

The world was flat too. He had blown it. And for what: handy sex, a face and a figure, a tease and a dare. Be different if he really loved Maggie Fubb. No sacrifice too great. Beau Geste.

But it was a dull watery world he saw as he drained his glass. From a cushy job at the Pentagon to the Tenth Experimental. Even Col. Fubb, who knew everything about anything Army, had never heard of it. No chance for advancement in a nothing outfit. Good chance he wouldn't survive whatever probing and prodding of natural forces the Tenth Experimental was into.

He looked around the O-club. He had put off returning to BOQ. Packing would not take long. Besides, he had wanted to find out about Col. Fubb's world-on-the-brink emergency. If there was a chance of seeing action, he would go for an Article 138 after all and fight for transfer to a line company. Rather that than the Tenth Experimental. If there were rumors, the rumors would try their wings here.

But there were none on that scale. And there was nothing in the papers or on radio or television about an emergency, nothing about the world being on the brink any more than usual.

Mock-heroics on the colonel's part? He wasn't the type. But then he hadn't seemed the cuckold type. Maybe he had got wind of the affair, had sneaked back home, but had wanted to save face in his own bedroom.

Buckmaster all at once found himself in the talons of rumor. The funny bartender worked his way down from the other end of the bar – was that Landtroop moving away toward the john? – and gave Buckmaster a shake of the head and a shake of the hand and a shake of a cocktail.

'Sorry to hear they're shipping you out to the boondocks, Lieutenant. It ain't as bad as if it happened in wartime, though. I remember back in Naples, Italy, during World War II there was this light colonel, XO of CWS in Peninsular Base Section, and there was this tech sergeant under him, and both went for the same signorina. Young thing and sweet: you know, a pretty little girl that cleaned the office. The light colonel transferred the tech sergeant to Anzio, which, if you recall your ancient history, was a hot beachhead.'

Buckmaster felt his face fire up, but he smiled.

'I get the analogy, Joe. Call me Uriah.'

'Who?'

'Heap big chief.'

'Lieutenant, you've had too much or not enough.'

True. The analogy was faulty. The colonel was the husband and he was the interloper. He eyed the sign on the bar mirror. *Notice, because of shortage, no more than 5 gals to a customer.* Not enough. But he would do his best to make do.

Doing his best, some timeless time later, he found it was time to refreshen his drink. He turned away from watching two or four men bat the blip back and forth in a coin-operated video game, and he bumped into Brig. Gen. Fabian Hackstaff (Rtd).

In World War II, clerical error long-johnned for Arctic service a massive troop shipment heading for Saudi Arabia. The man in charge won kudos for throwing the enemy off. Hackstaff was that man and welcomed every opportunity to revisit the scene of his triumph and to recount his exploit.

'Sorry, sir, did I spill your drink? If I may, sir.'

He took the general's glass and handed it to Joe for a refill along with his own and brought it back to the general. The general eyed him sharply.

'Seen you before.'

'Perhaps, sir. But we haven't met.' He had made a point of avoiding the old pest. 'Name's Buckmaster.'

'Knew it. Thought the face looked familiar. Family face. Remember your old man, Buckmaster. Too bad. He had a fine career ahead of him. If only he had toed the line.'

Somehow Lt Victor Landtroop was standing shoulder to shoulder with them and was part of the conversation.

'What happened, Buckmaster?' Landtroop's voice said Landtroop knew the answer to Landtroop's question.

Buckmaster spoke tonelessly. 'They let him resign rather than face charges under Articles 133 and 134 of the Uniform Code of Military Justice.'

Landtroop snickered. 'What did he do? Cheat at cards or bingo, fail to pay debts, commit adultery, drink with enlisted men, exhibit an American flag with a peace symbol on his shirt, possess alcoholic beverages in a public place, or commit a bestial act with a chicken?'

Buckmaster smiled and mentally decked Landtroop. The imaginary blow was such a solid one that he opened his fist and worked the fingers in pleasurable pain. But it was the general who had stared Landtroop into retreat. Too bad. Too slow. A good unhushable brawl at the O-club would have been one way of stopping transfer to the Tenth Experimental, at least for the time being.

The general was eyeing him approvingly.

'You handled yourself well, Buckmaster. Maybe I can put a word in for you. What's your unit?'

Buckmaster told him. The general shook his head.

'Never heard of it. Can't help you there. But I can give you some advice. Apply yourself. Luck may determine who gets the chance. But the one thing I've learned is that character determines which ones can hack it and which ones can't. So learn to toe the line. If you want to get to the top, that's the tipoff. Remember: peacetime is the professional soldier's most trying time.'

'I know just what you mean, General.' He spoke very clearly. 'Shunsign shoulders.'

The general gave him a look and dismissed him, turning away to deploy caviar on a cracker. Landtroop bounced back. He held out the olive branch in the form of a martini. He clinked glasses with Buckmaster.

'Luck to you, Buckmaster.' He leaned toward Buckmaster. 'Say, just where is and what is the Tenth Experimental Company?'

Evidently he had hung around in earshot. Buckmaster gave him a thin smile, scarcely skin deep, and slowly poured out onto the floor the martini Landtroop had handed him. Landtroop had to dance backward.

'Landtroop, so far I haven't been able to make up my mind about you. I'm still not sure whether you're a small-bore bore or a large-bore bore.'

Maybe it wasn't too late for that brawl. His hand curled up in false remembrance. Landtroop's eyes darted left and right, then zeroed in on the wall clock and checked with his wristwatch, which he brought close to his eyeglasses.

'I've got to get back.'

'That's right, Landtroop. Lift that bale, TOTE that barge.'

Landtroop turned green again and away.

4. NLT   Not later than

Buckmaster found himself sitting on a park bench. It was a steel bench. Steel benches had replaced the wooden benches. Still trying to stay ahead of the vandals.

The vandals had got his father. Maybe not the vandals, but the unyielding steel of the system. You don't buck the system; you learn to use the system. His father hadn't learned. Buckmaster smiled with the family face. He hoped he didn't have the family temperament.

His father came from a small town and a poor family. Because he wore a uniform that said he was an officer and a gentleman, he was able to go into luxury hotels and plush nightspots – places he would never have dared step into otherwise – and at a ball he met a deb who danced with him all night. They married and had Stonewall – in that order, though Stonewall was aware he was a premature baby – and seemed happy. But when the Army eased Col. Buckmaster out for making a report charging that crooked and wasteful procurement policies were endemic in the service, the marriage fell apart.

They dumped Stonewall in military school. He saw more of his mother, who remarried – an admiral this time – but he went on camping trips with his father. The trips could have been fun. But his father was, if not a martinet, a perfectionist: everything by the numbers.

Always had you policing up, straightening up, yourself and your surroundings. He remembered a moment of rebellion. 'I'm not your command, I'm your son.' His father's long look filled a long silence. 'You're right, son. It's a while since I've had a command.'

Lt Buckmaster grew suddenly aware it was March. There must have been a windstorm hollowing out space for a mass of cold air. Overhead wires dripped black icicles of insulation. He guessed he had told himself to get some air, but this was overdoing it.

He pulled up his collar and headed for his BOQ. A yawn nearly unhinged his jaw. He looked at his watch. He might be able to get in a good two hours' sack time.

5. PAC   Pursuant to authority contained in

He parted a yawn and hoped the Wac would think he was a cool one.

The Wac handed him his 201 file.

'You'll handcarry it because otherwise it won't get there in time to put you in the morning report of your new unit. And here are your travel orders. You get a ride out to Andrews Air Force Base. A bucket seat's waiting for you aboard a C-5 leaving for Moody Air Force Base at 0930 hours.'

'And from there?'

'Your destination is classified.'

But the Wac looked around, then winked and pointed to a zip code number after the name Tenth Experimental Co. on his travel orders. 31905. It rang a southern bell.

He grinned his thanks, picked up his val-pack, and on his way out stopped in at the Pentagon's post office branch. He located a copy of the zip code directory on a chain. At the back of the book he found a list of zip codes for Army and Air Force installations; 31905 was the code for Fort Benning. He marched his fingers frontward through the book to Georgia and confirmed that 31905 was the Fort Benning branch of the Columbus post office. He was heading back home.

West Point had been out for him; as son of his father he had been unable to wangle congressional appointment. He had enlisted and got his OCS commission by way of Ft Benning Infantry School. And now he was proceeding back there, to the HQ of the Tenth Experimental Co., to present himself to Capt. Romeo Clapsaddle, CO, to take up duties as XO of the unit.

If it hadn't been the military, he might have wondered why a plane as big as a C-5 should take off with so little cargo, why they should route him to Benning by way of Moody when there was Eubanks Field, to say nothing of Gunter and Maxwell and Robins and Turner that were all nearer Benning than Moody was. But it was the military, and so he shrugged and made himself comfortable.

Finding himself alone aft of the flight deck, he opened his 201 file carefully and studied his DA Form 66, the organization copy of his qualification record, standing loose inside his DA Form 201. He reddened on seeing the NE that had stymied clearance for him till Col. Fubb overrode it to send him to the Tenth Experimental Co. He hadn't really believed there'd been this tag on him, simply because his father hadn't toed the line, but there it was. In the military, did guilt by association run unto the tenth generation? He closed his file carefully.

Just in time. The pilot came back to invite him to sit in the cockpit.

Maybe politeness, maybe curiosity. But if it was the latter, Buckmaster was able to make a virtue of ignorance. 'Top secret.'

At Moody AFB a command car waiting on the apron drove up to

the plane. The driver, an Ordnance corporal whose name tag over the left blouse pocket spelled out Flugel, saluted him and took his val-pack. Buckmaster breathed deep returning the highball. March was kinder down here.

Cpl Flugel put the val-pack in the back of the command car, and Buckmaster got in beside him in the front. The corporal wore wraparound shades. The long bill of the dark green hat further shadowed Flugel's upper face. There was nothing there to read. But Flugel also wore jump boots. Jump boots on an Ordnance corporal said that the man knew the angles.

'Corporal, what can you tell me about the Tenth Experimental?'

Flugel did not take his face from the road leading out of the air base.

'Sorry, Lieutenant.' A small smile in limbo. 'I only know I'm supposed to pick you up somewhere and take you somewhere.'

Buckmaster had a sudden impression of being in a dream. All the sense of structure that he had sought to bolster by joining the army was vanishing. He looked around for something to hold the world together, only to find that instead of heading northwest to Ft Benning once they left the air base, the driver headed east to Waycross. Buckmaster stared at the corporal, the wraparound shades giving Buckmaster back his own puzzlement.

'I thought the installation was at Benning.'

The corporal almost let the wheel slip away from him. He fought the car back under control.

'What made you think that . . . sir?'

The world was holding together again. The corporal had his place in it, and Lt Stonewall J. Buckmaster had his.

'I have ways.' Ah, why snow the guy? 'No, it's the zip code.'

'Oh.' A larger smile in limbo. 'No, sir. It's this way.'

Buckmaster shoved his hat forward over his face and leaned his head back.

'Wake me when we're nearly there, will you, Corporal?'

'Yes, sir.'

Buckmaster dozed, awoke, eyed the odometer. It had clocked fifty miles.

'How far?'

'Not much more. I was just going to wake you.'

Buckmaster sat up, wide awake, reading again in his mind the directional sign they had just passed. Okefenokee National Wildlife

Refuge. Could that be where they were heading? The corporal answered his look with a nod.

Okefenokee Swamp? What was the Tenth experimenting with? Alligators?

They drove through the north entrance, bypassed the ranger station. Flugel parked the command car, took out the val-pack, and locked the car. Buckmaster followed Flugel, who followed cypress boardwalks stretching into the swamp.

They stopped at a landing. A Quartermaster sergeant had a haunch up on the bow of a hydrofoil. He straightened, a big man, and threw Buckmaster a lazy highball. His name tag spelled out Messmore. He gave Buckmaster a flat-eyed stare as he got an exaggerated salute back. Then he looked at Flugel, and a smile wandered between them. Flugel gave him a questioning nod.

'All clear, Zulu?'

'All clear.'

Zulu took the val-pack from Flugel and stowed it aboard the hydrofoil. He hung loose and moved loose. His grits-and-gravy voice had come out of a rich beard. Buckmaster understood that Black males got shaving bumps – pseudofolliculitis of the beard – and that the only 'cure' was to grow a beard, the Army generally allowing a medical excuse for not shaving up to three months, but this looked like more than three months' worth. The shaving bumps could be a put-on. Zulu wore a black ring to show pride of race and looked like another man who knew the angles.

'That really your first name, Sergeant? Zulu?'

'No, sir. Miles. Sgt Miles Messmore.'

'Mine's Oscar, sir. Cpl Oscar Flugel.'

They eyed him with that same smile wandering between them, as if waiting for him to say that his was Stonewall.

'All right, men. Let's get wherever we're going. Don't want to keep Capt. Clapsaddle waiting.'

Zulu laughed a warm laugh that burned Buckmaster's ears.

'Sure don't want to do that. No, sir.'

They climbed aboard and Zulu took the wheel. The hydrofoil picked up quickly, sped along a maze of channels winding through a big-footed moss-bearded cypress, and, making eighty knots, drove them deep into the swamp. Zulu brought them to a stop at a small island that looked little more than a hummock.

Buckmaster looked around. If there was an installation in the neighborhood, its camouflage was perfect.

As Buckmaster turned to Cpl Flugel and opened his mouth to ask what the hell was up, he found cause to keep his mouth open. Flugel had picked Buckmaster's val-pack up and, as Buckmaster watched, the corporal dropped it over the stern. It sank. The air oozing out of it added a slow blub of spheres to the boil and burst of marsh bubbles.

Buckmaster turned swiftly but not swiftly enough to Zulu. The sergeant had lifted the lid of a seat locker and drawn out an M-16. He switched the selector to sprinkle and aimed the rifle at Buckmaster.

'Here's where you get out, Lieutenant.'

'Just like that?'

'Not just like that. Like for short-arm inspection. Strip.'

Buckmaster seemed to watch himself with a sense of detachment as he stripped to the buff.

'Your dogtags too.'

Slowly he lifted the chain from around his neck. He pendulumed the dogtags, hoping Zulu's eyes would follow them. Snap them at Zulu's face and make a grab for the M-16 when Zulu pulled his head away. But Zulu's eyes did not follow the dogtags. Zulu's gaze remained on Buckmaster's face. Buckmaster tossed the dogtags onto the pile of clothes, along with his wristwatch and his 201 file.

Flugel buttoned the shirt around all, knotted the sleeves, and wrapped a length of chain around the bundle. He pendulumed it and let go on the upswing. What enlisted men saluted splashed into the dark waters and drowned. Buckmaster watched it vanish. Were they going to deep-six him as well? There'd be nothing to lose in jumping Zulu or diving overboard, though there was nothing to gain in dying that way but pride. Could you take pride with you?

Zulu's brow rippled in sudden pain, though the M-16 stayed locked on Buckmaster.

'Let's hurry this thing. My migraine's killing me.'

'Easy, Zulu. We still have to take one precautionary measure.'

From the seat locker Flugel drew a first-aid kit. It held rubber gloves, a can of baby powder, a bottle with skull and crossbones label, a wad of cotton, a tube of salve, a roll of gauze bandage, and a roll of adhesive tape. He powdered his hands and worked them into the gloves. He uncapped the bottle and wet the cotton. He moved to Buckmaster's side, careful not to come between him and Zulu. Buckmaster's nose wrinkled.

'Hold still, Lieutenant, and put your hands out. Just a dab of acid on each fingertip. Enough to give you an identity problem, alive or dead.'

Buckmaster felt his upper lip draw up in a pulsing sneer. Rage as much as pride stiffened him inarticulate in body as in speech. He stood still and made no outcry.

Zulu forgot his migraine enough to nod approval and apparently paid for it with pain of his own. An acid hiss escaped his lips. Flugel shot him a glance.

'I'm hurrying, Zulu.'

Flugel salved Buckmaster's fingers and bound and taped them. He stowed the first-aid kit away.

'Okay, Lieutenant. Over you go.'

Buckmaster let out his breath. At least he was, to go by Flugel's nod, getting out on land. He jumped ashore.

The trees and bushes swayed. For an instant he thought it delayed dizziness. Then he remembered that Okefenokee meant 'quivering earth'.

'So long, Lieutenant. You want to watch where you walk or sit.'

He wanted to call out *'Why?'* but even if he had let himself, the hydrofoil thunder would have muted him.

They taught you a law in OCS. *Any order that can be misunderstood will be misunderstood.* What order had Cpl Flugel and Sgt Messmore received? Had they misunderstood it? Or were they following it literally? Was what he found himself in a test, an initiation? Was the Tenth Experimental trying him out? If the last, was it to make him prove he was worth taking aboard or was he merely an experimental animal?

Fubb. Was this the colonel's real revenge, his way of getting back at his wife's lover? Or did this have nothing to do with Fubb as Fubb but with Fubb as participant in TOTE? Was this the Pentagon's way of getting rid of Lt Stonewall J. Buckmaster because he had learned of TOTE's existence – whatever the hell TOTE was?

Or had he run into something else without knowing it?

The hydrofoil left a thrumming silence in its wake, like the beat of blood in his fingers. And now the silence filled, as all that the hydrofoil had frightened into hiding and mock death gave slithering and brushing sounds of life. He looked around quickly and armed himself with a forked stick to pin down any snake he might happen upon, both for defense of his own skin and for meat.

It must be around noon, but the dark leaves strained the sun into a shadow of itself, though here and there there was a dazzle on the water. The tannic-darkened depths hid whatever cottonmouth moccasins swam in them, but he imagined he could see the snaky rippling of black water write their presence.

His chin pebbled.

He was without a paddle. He was even without a boat.

6. TPA TRAVEL BY PRIVATELY OWNED
CONVEYANCE IS AUTHORIZED

He would have to get off this islet, not only to get out of the swamp but merely to live in the swamp. The islet offered little to live on long. But which bank should he make for? It would be well to keep to the higher side, because that would be the drier, and because small game – otters and such – took to higher ground when alligators roused from their winter sleep.

Forked stick ready, and picking his way, he traversed the islet. Where the ground was not squishy it was prickly. He broke slowly through to the edge and looked across. No: lower and wetter look to the earth and the vegetation. Back to the other side of the islet. He sighed and turned.

He hated to look ahead to swimming the stream. He gazed at his bandaged fingers. They hurt now and they were in for a lot more pain. He gathered likely fallen limbs as he made his way back to his starting point and had a heavy armful by the time he reached it. He laid them down in the form of a narrow raft.

He set his teeth, then used them to get a peeling start on the adhesive tape. He stopped, listening to the bellow of an alligator. Farther than it sounded, he told himself. He got the strips of tape off and wrapped one around either wrist. Safest place to save them: you never knew. His teeth came into play again to help unknot the gauze, and he unwound the bandages. His fingertips looked raw under the film of salve.

Luckily, Flugel had been generous with the gauze. Buckmaster lined up the knobs and roughnesses of the limbs forming his raft as best he could at either end to keep the gauze from shifting when he tied a strip around it, and he put a crosspiece under each end at that point to keep the raft relatively stiff, and he twisted each strip for strength before tying it as tight as he could. The raft was a foot shorter than himself and a foot and a half wide.

His forked stick was too short; he found a straight one long enough to pole with, stuck the forked stick under a binding for later, and slid the raft into the water. Gingerly he stretched out on it. It held, and it held him.

Dovetailing his fingers around the pole to save his fingertips, he thrust it in and shoved off. The raft gave itself slowly to the slow current. He poled now and then to move it nearer the other bank while looking for a likely place to land. It went well. Maybe the ramshackle raft would carry him all the way out of the swamp.

A line of bubbles lay across his way. He thought it signaled something alive till the smell hit him. Gases of decomposition. The smell of decaying and fermenting vegetation rose up all around and stirred old brain memories. He grinned. Spring. Beautiful spring.

The water exploded under him, heaving the raft, capsizing it, tearing it apart, and leaving him thrashing to stay afloat and fight off something monstrous in the water.

He grew aware that he was giving the thing life. He left off thrashing and it rocked easily. Mud. A mass of stinking bottom mud. A marsh-gas blowup. A bit of the bottom had torn loose out of sheer buoyancy – the joy of spring – and shot to the surface.

Time to laugh or swear or both later. He made for the bank. It looked steep, unnegotiable. He reached for an overhanging branch. He caught hold but it slipped away from bloodslick fingers. He turned from the bank to let himself drift down toward something offering purchase.

He had passed the islet and could see across to the opposite bank. An eight-foot alligator was slithering down.

Somehow, before the alligator nosed into the water, Buckmaster found he had caught hold of another overhanging branch and pulled himself up. And now the blood was glue and he had to tear himself loose.

He armed himself again with a stick, making sure first that it was not a snake, and looked back down at the water. The alligator moved by, like a run in dark silk. Be grateful to the alligator. Hundreds of years ago the Seminoles made water trails through the Okefenokee Swamp; the alligator has helped keep them open. Grateful, yes; but he would take his time leaving his semiknoll and following. Let it vanish around the bend of the channel.

Meanwhile his belly gnawed itself. It had gone a long time on coffee. He found a wild onion. That stopped the immediate pangs. Now thirst. He eyed the dark waters. The leachings that stained the stream brown supposedly sterilized it as well. He made his way down to the edge, rinsed his hands, and drank out of their cupping. The water tasted bad enough to be good. The lap of the dogs. He would have been one of Gideon's men.

He caught up his stick, straightened, stiff already, and made his way downstream. He followed the channel, climbing over cypress knees, keeping to the soft mud banks. He came upon a spot of sand with no pebbles on top. He stopped. He tossed a small stone on it. It sank. Quicksand.

The first of many such spots. He bridged quagmire and quicksand by gathering fallen limbs or tearing and twisting off leafy brush or even pulling up grass and laying a carpet of this vegetation to walk or crawl on. Go slowly, but keep moving.

Once, one of his bridges gave and a bog seized him. He had to remember that mud, muck, and sand are more buoyant than water. It was panicking that did you in. If you struggled or lifted your feet while you were upright, you made a vacuum that sucked you down. He felt himself sink and threw himself forward, spreading his arms, and started to swim, to pull himself ahead, but always keeping his body horizontal. That one was good for bad dreams that night.

Every morning at first light he climbed a tree to take his bearings and make sure he wasn't merely looping. He kept moving throughout the daylight hours. He watched out for snakes and gators and bears. He slapped mud on insect bites. He tired of wild onion, berries, and dandelion greens, and even the painfully got olivelike fruit within the spiny-toothed leafstalks of saw palmetto.

He had found a triangular stone with sharp edges. It might have been Seminole. It looked worked. He wedged it into a split he made in one end of his stick and bound it in place with the tape he had kept on his wrists. If the manufacturer wanted him to plug the tape's water-proofing, he would. Now he had a spear.

It came into play when he stumbled on a black-shelled turtle sunning itself. He flipped the turtle over with the butt of his spear before it could move. He stabbed it in the throat and sawed its head off with the spearpoint. He tilted the turtle to bleed well while he looked to see if he could build a fire.

A fire plow was the only method he thought he could cope with. He cast about for a fallen cypress trunk or limb, and near at hand he hit one ready-made for him. A crack in the trunk formed a natural groove about eight inches long and just wide enough for a fire stick. He found a stick of cypress to fit. He did not know if he could get a fire going, but he collected a pile of tinder – dry shredded grass from an old nest of a mouse or a bird – and set it handy. He broke off dry wood and made another sizable pile. He held the fire stick in both hands and, favoring his fingertips, bore down hard as he moved it back and forth in the groove. Wood powder heaped up at one end of the groove, and as he moved the stick back and forth more rapidly and bore down more heavily, he felt heat and a spark formed in the powder. Quickly he fed pinches of tinder to the spark and fanned it into flame.

When he had a good fire going, he dragged the turtle to it and put the turtle atop it. He let the heat crack and split the undershell, and when it had done so he pulled the turtle off. When it had cooled enough he levered and wrenched the belly plate away. He used his spearpoint to butcher the turtle. He cleaned the carcass, laying on palmetto leaves the raw chunks he would cook and burying the rest to keep from drawing insects and much larger foes. He scooped water into the intact upper shell and put it on the fire and boiled the meat in the shell.

That was his one hot meal. He felt that it would be, and he stuffed himself. But he still had a good portion of stewed meat to carry along in a palmetto leaf. He settled himself for the night, satiated into foolish happiness. High in the west, great shoals of mother-of-pearl clouds, iridescent as fish scales, grew suddenly dark.

7. CLNC Clearance

He belonged to the Turtle Totem. He had eaten Turtle but he was thankful to Turtle and so he was at one with Turtle. Driftwood shapes ghosted along in the stream of night, but they would not come alive and eat him because Turtle guarded him from harm. Turtle's shell became the dome of heaven. Turtle's claws were the power that moved the universe. Turtle's tail was the rudder. And Turtle's head?

He gazed at the face but the face told him nothing. A mask would have told him more because a mask is open deception. Had Turtle truly initiated him into manhood? Was it good to kill or evil?

'My, we're getting philosophical,' his father said, smiling with Turtle's smile and gazing into the campfire with the campfire's eyes. 'I'll go into it if you want, but I think it's over your head.' His father's voice changed into voices Stonewall had heard along the way. 'The tipoff – the circumcisional evidence – is that, after the quake, the mountain showed stretch marks; at its foot the mouse. That is, if we're all of Creation there is, why all the fuss? But before we worry about the nature of reality, we have to worry about the reality of nature. In accordions with the principle of uncertainty, the finer you tune time the fuzzier space gets. We're on the horns of paradoxen. Maya, illusion, a funhouse rire-view mirror. Gravity is laughing matter and light is bilaterally symmetrical. It's all pretense – from before the Word "Be".'

It was true. We were all goners from the Word 'Be'. But it was there, blowing in the mind, expanding his consciousness. His own voice telling him he knew The Answer.

'The universe is expanding at the subatomic level as well as at the galactic level. Which means gravitation is not pull but push. Gravitation is expansion of everything, stretching even the void. Things do not fall toward each other, they *grow* toward each other. But, with all matter expanding at the same rate, this growth is invisible to observers who are also expanding.'

It explained everything and he forgot it when he awakened.

8. PTGT Primary target

Now and then he heard the hum of a swampboat or the buzz of a kicker, but it was always far off. Flugel and Messmore knew their boondocks. But he was coming to something. At least the way ahead changed. The channel widened and merged with other channels into a lake. It had the look of impounded waters. He had reached the middle of nowhere.

Then he made out across the lake a shack among the trees. He began to think how he would look to people. Like a figure out of the Stone Age? He smiled. But he was not with his own yet.

Too far to swim, the way he felt. He would have to follow the shore around.

One foot after the other for a long time seemed only to take him farther from the shack. But one foot after the other would get him there; he kept telling himself that.

He stopped. What first through a film of sweat looked to be a large turtle in the way proved to be a rowboat half in the mud. He dug it out. After finding it basically sound he caulked seams with grass and righted it and it floated. He hunted for a short broad stick to paddle with where he could not pole, gave up, and tore out the thwart; he would be kneeling to paddle anyway. He shoved off.

He had just left off poling and taken up his paddle when a plane came out of the sun. He waved at it, and splashed water to throw glints of light at the plane, but had no real hope it would see him. It did. It wagged back at him and his heart swelled and his eyes filled with its USAF insignia.

It swooped low, lower, and the water puckered ahead of the boat with the stutter and stitching of machine-gun fire. He sat back on his heels, unable to do anything but stare as the plane lifted itself for another pass.

In a brief fade of engine he heard 'Bobwhite! Bobwhite! Bobwhite!' float across the lake toward him, but he saw no quail rise. The shooting had wakened no other sign of life. No one had appeared near the shack. Maybe it was abandoned, another dead end. But it was the only goal he had at the moment.

Someone was crazy. Either the pilot or himself. If it was not just some damn flyboy after kicks, then it had to be the Army, the Air Force, the whole world, all out to get Lt Stonewall J. Buckmaster. That way lay paranoia.

His chin pebbled. He leaned forward and paddled again toward the shack. Left, right, left, right.

This time the stitching came nearer.

He turned his head to follow the plane as it swung around: very carefully he burned its markings into his brain. Couldn't the fool see his play target was mother-naked, in need of help? Or – Buckmaster looked down at himself – did the daubs of mud over bites seem a camouflage suit? At least the clown wasn't trying to hit him, or the stitches would have been in Buckmaster's side.

Was he trying to warn Buckmaster away? Away from what?

The plane was coming around again.

Buckmaster backpaddled, making back for shore, as the plane made its third pass. No bullets this time.

Maybe the pilot thought he had made his point at last, or maybe the plane was low on fuel. But the tail spouted a satisfied bright orange as the plane swung away, and it did not come around for another pass.

Buckmaster felt number than zero. Then the flesh reasserted itself, and he stood up in the rocking boat and shook his fist at the quicksilver speck slipping out of sight. Then he sat down heavily as a leg gave.

And he saw that a ricocheting bullet had struck off a splinter of boat that had torn a flap of thigh.

Now he had another use for the tape. He unwound it from his spear to hold the flap of flesh in place.

He felt suddenly weary, and the plane might come back after all. He would put back in and wait for night and row across in the dark.

That was the worst day because it had begun the best day. And the night reflected that.

9. VO   Verbal orders

The chaplain was a cross between Gen. Hackstaff and Joe the bartender at the O-club. Buckmaster told the chaplain: 'I have a limpid conscience, Padre.' But the chaplain insisted on praying for his soul. 'I'll save your soul if I have to kill your spirit.' And the chaplain presided at a drum-head court-martial, and while Sgt Messmore drummed Buckmaster out with paradiddles and rimshots, Cpl Flugel stripped Buckmaster right out of his uniform and left him wearing just the buttons.

Lt Stonewall J. Buckmaster shook his head at the offer of a blindfold, but took the coffin nail in defiance of the surgeon general's report; and Col. Maximilian Fubb, admiring Buckmaster's bravery in spite of himself, barked, 'You may fire when ready, Frying Pan.'

Buckmaster braced himself against the post and in spite of himself closed his eyes. But the shots whistled past, striking stone not flesh. He opened his eyes.

Lt Victor Landtroop was waving Maggie Fubb's pink panties to signal that the shots had wholly missed. But why then was ex-Lt Stonewall J. Buckmaster bleeding? If you shoot a shadow, does the shadow bleed darkness? Or light?

> Hey, paradiddle; straw,
>   paradiddle,
> The cat and the catgut,
> The moo jumped over the
>   moon . . .

It was not an opera time for the Triumphal March from *Aïda*, but neither was a Mother Goose rhyme fitting. His dream edited itself, and 'Way Down upon the Swanee River' ran through his mind like a dark stream. This fostered a swansong sorrow that segued into taps . . . the tap dance that opened Preston Sturges's *Hail the Conquering*

Hero ... and just as six marines toted Woodrow LaFayette Pershing Truesmith home, Lt Stonewall Jackson Buckmaster let go, let stop.

10. RIF REDUCTION IN FORCE

He had slept past the time he had planned to start, but it was still before dawn. He shoved off again, toward the shore he could not see. It showed itself more and more, and light filled the sky when he at last beached a hundred yards north of the shack and dragged the boat into the tree line.

Just in time. A jet screamed into being. The same plane. It passed over and disappeared. He waited, then limped on.

He moved through pine and palmetto toward the shack. He was the more startled of the two when he flushed a bobwhite quail. Its warning cry wakened a tremendous chorus of echoes somewhere behind the shack.

Shack was the wrong word for it. It was a sturdy building for its size, of weathered redwood, and a strong padlock fastened the door. He grimaced. But a power line and a gravel road led away from it through the trees, tying this place to the outside world. He was back in civilization, or at least on the right track.

He looked down at himself, then listened to make sure there were no womenfolk about before he stepped out into the open.

'Hello!'

His croak made him realize he had been wordless for quite a spell. But it was loud enough to bring a heavy fluttering out back, though no rise of birds. He rounded the shack and came up against chickenwire penning hundreds of bobwhite quail – round plump bodies, brown and black bars like service stripes, males with a slight crest and a white bin, females with a browner cast.

Buckmaster stared hungrily, then remembered he was back in civilization. The ruts of truck tires in the gravel said where the breeder had gone. Whoever the breeder was he would not leave his quail here alone long. He would be back sooner than later. Buckmaster leaned against the shack and slid down to sit and wait.

He had hardly closed his eyes when the jet opened them. It was on another sweep of the forbidden lake. He made himself one with the shadow of the shack. He felt sure it had passed by without spotting him, but it made up his mind for him that he could not wait.

He peered through a window in the side of the shack and made out cans and packages on shelves and clothing hanging from a hook.

He broke the pane, sending the quail whirring and aborting again. He pulled out the jags of glass, heaved himself halfway through, then let himself fall the rest of the way, trying to land in a handstand to spare his game leg. It wasn't too bad.

The canned peaches and the crackers fitted his insides, the faded fatigues fitted his outsides less well. He had washed himself first. The shack held a sink with running water, a pump filtering and purifying the water, and there was soap. He used lots of water and lots of soap. His fingertips were a sight but had not festered. He used a clean dish-cloth to bandage his thigh.

He could have used a shave, but the rusty, hairy blade in the razor put him off. There were no spares: seemed that must have been one of the things the man had gone into town for. Buckmaster felt his beard and looked at it in the mirror. Not bad for seven days' growth. Gave him a whole new look, and he might need a whole new look while he went about finding out what he had got himself into.

He had switched on the table radio and listened while he washed and ate and dressed. But there was no news – nothing about a missing Lt Buckmaster, nothing about TOTE, nothing new in the world but flare-ups of the old woes, nothing worth noting other than the news to him that he had been a week in the swamp. He had lost track. He pocketed a box of crackers.

A cot stood against the wall. He eyed it, then shook his head and set it up only to help him climb back out through the window. He landed heavily, badly.

'"Bobwhite!" yourself.'

That only made the quail bobwhite themselves all the more.

Keeping to the dirt shoulder of the gravel road, he set himself a stiff-legged pace. Why couldn't there have been shoes? He never knew why he missed hearing the pickup. It wasn't rattly but it wasn't all that silent, but when he rounded a bend he came face to face with it. Maybe the crunch of the crackers he was munching had covered it; most of the crackers in the box had broken in his exit and themselves made a good rattle.

The driver braked swiftly but smoothly and took in Buckmaster, the box of crackers, the clothes, the bare feet. He had a pouchy face, well-suited to hold a chaw of plug tobacco. His eyes snapped to attention as he recognized the faded fatigues.

'Howdy. You in trouble, mister?'

'I got lost in the swamp.'

'That so? You're lucky, then. Seldom happens anyone gets lost comes out.'

'Yes, I'm lucky.' Buckmaster plucked at the loose fatigues. 'I had to help myself to somebody's things. If they're yours I'll pay you back when –'

The man waved that away.

'Forget it. My name's Quintus Collum. What's yours?'

'Jackson.'

'First or last?'

'Both. Jackson Jackson.'

'Interesting name.'

'They kid me about it a lot.'

'I guess they would. You're not from these parts.'

'Just visiting. Well, it's been nice meeting a friendly human after a week in the swamp. And thanks.'

'Wait up, Jackson. A week, you say? No wonder you look dog tired. You can't be in any shape to walk out. You know how far it is to town?'

'I don't even know what town.'

'Fargo. Just came from there.' He nodded toward the back of the pickup. Buckmaster saw it held cartons of goods. 'Shopping. Expecting company. Have to go back in tomorrow anyway to fetch more. So hop in and come on to the cabin. You can stay overnight. Don't doubt you could do with a good night's rest.'

'Thanks all the same, Mr Collum, but I'm behind time as it is.'

'Then leastways come on down and get the extra pair of shoes I can lend you.'

There had been no extra pair of shoes in the shack.

'No, thanks.'

Collum leaned over and opened the left-hand door.

'Get in. That's not an invite, it's an order.' He held a shotgun across his lap. It had hung from clips on the riser of the seat behind his legs; now it pointed at Buckmaster. 'Sorry, Jackson Jackson, but I reckon I ought to hold both of you till my company's come and gone. You've seen too much.'

'All I've seen is a lot of swamp. And a lot of quail.'

'That's what I mean. You just might be one of them meddlesome northeastern reporters looking to smear the military.'

'I just might be. And then again I just might be from the Inspector General or from the CID.' Or from the Campfire Girls.

Collum's jaw went slack and drooled brown juice.

'CID?' The direct gaze of the shotgun wavered.

Buckmaster sighed and shook his head.

'All right, Collum, I'll be glad to get in and get this over with now that I've blown my cover.' He pushed the barrel aside and climbed in and closed the door. 'I left my ID in my clothes and my clothes are in the fork of a tree near your cabin.' He chuckled ruefully. 'Got a soaking when I chuted in last night and landed in the lake.'

Collum chewed on that nervously.

'You're here on account of the quail?'

'What do you think?'

'Honest, Jackson, I only been following orders.'

'That's what Eichmann said.'

'Who?'

'Let's go, Collum. You can fill me in on the way.'

'A few years back, 135,000 hunters bagged 4 million quail. That was the peak.

'Since then, there's always more hunters and always less quail. It ain't just the shooting. When timber people plant pine, the quail leave soon as the seedlings take hold. Then there's the pasturing of dairy and beef cattle. All in all, this here's getting to be no more quail country. And if there's one thing Air Force generals like it's shooting quail.'

So that was what the protective reaction strike was all about. The brass wanted to keep everyone else out, and the pilot had thought Buckmaster was setting out fishing lines or otherwise poaching on their illegal preserves.

The pickup pulled up at the end of gravel. The birds whirred in their big cage. Collum's gaze followed Buckmaster's and grew proud.

'Pretty, hey? Mixed some wild ones in with the tame. When the generals come we set convoys out in the woods.' The airs and graces of cheap perfume and cheap liquor clung to him; he had done some more immediately satisfying shopping in town. And now the smell of fear. 'But what's going to happen now?'

'Nothing's going to happen to you. After all, you only followed orders.'

'That's right.' He climbed lightly out of the cab, and his eyes got bolder as he looked in at Buckmaster. 'Say, Jackson, what's your rank?'

'First Lieutenant.'

Collum smiled.

'A dozen generals come here regular. I guess a dozen generals pull a lot of rank.'

'I guess they do.'

'You bet they do.'

While Collum whistled a bobwhitish tune and dug the key to the padlock out of his pocket and opened the cabin door, Buckmaster unclipped the shotgun again from the seat riser. He broke it open. Collum whirled at the sound.

'Hey!'

'Nice piece. What are these in here, No. $7\frac{1}{2}$ or No. 8?'

'No. 8. Now, look here –'

Buckmaster managed to get out and hold Collum frozen at the same time.

'I want you to walk ahead of me and when you come to the wire start knocking it down.'

'But the birds will all fly away.'

'That's the general idea.'

'They'll chew my ass out.'

'Pyorrhea meets diarrhea. Go on, it's an order.'

Collum moved sullenly to the fence and wrenched feebly at the posts.

'I can't.'

Buckmaster shot a nice wide pattern into the side of the shack.

'You can.'

While birds still fluttered in the first flush of freedom, Buckmaster marched Collum back around into the shack and had him lie face-down on the cot. One hand held the shotgun ready, the other unwound fishline from a reel he had spotted on a shelf.

'Want to keep the chaw or spit it out? Could get messy later.'

Collum turned his head and looked slowly up at Buckmaster. His eyes played possum in their pouches; then he suddenly spat a stream of juice at Buckmaster's eyes. Buckmaster pulled his face away enough to miss the worst of it but not too much to lose sight of the man. He shoved Collum back down with the shotgun. He lost all fight, and Buckmaster tied him to the cot.

After testing the knots, Buckmaster started out.

'Jackson, you ain't going to leave me like this? They won't be here for days.'

'You'll keep.' Buckmaster softened. 'Once I get to town I'll leave word for the local law to look in on you. Best I can do for you and more than you deserve.'

'I didn't do you no harm.'

The jet flew past again. Buckmaster waited for its thunder to die down.

'Negative. Double negative. Nobody does me no harm.'

Outside again, he blinked at more than the sudden sunlight. Fully half the quail had never left or had come back to their compound. His face hardened. They were dead anyway. Better at his hands than at the generals'.

He looked under the seat in the cab of the pickup and found boxes of shells: how many he did not bother to note, but they were surely more than enough to do the job.

When he had finished he went again into the shack. Collum lay quite still. Buckmaster washed spatters of blood from face and hands. He picked up a kitchen knife and moved toward the cot. Collum stiffened and swallowed his wad.

Buckmaster's fingers, more pointedly the trigger finger, felt too sore to put to untying and retying laces. He sliced the knots and pulled Collum's shoes off.

'I almost forgot you promised to lend me a pair.'

Air filled all Collum's pouches.

'You ain't CID.'

'No, I'm really with the Campfire Girls. We're taking over.'

Before starting out in the pickup he looked to see what he had in the back. The booty included cases of bourbon. He had a drink on the brass. And another. He stopped. He was getting too light-headed. Among the cases and cartons he found a full laundry bag. He changed out of the fatigues into freshly laundered undershorts, white shirt, and blue jeans. Two pairs of socks, though his feet already felt as if they had swelled a size larger, helped make the shoes a good fit, bunion slits and all.

He turned the pickup around but drove away slowly. Collum and his pickup would be familiar sights in Fargo. Buckmaster wanted to pass through Fargo in the dark.

11. CIPAP Authority is granted to make such changes in above itinerary and to proceed to such additional places as may be necessary for the accomplishment of this mission

After Fargo he pulled off the road into leafy concealment and dozed till dawn. He pulled back on, and 441 took him through Homerville and points north to Helena. West on 280 took him to Columbus. Nine miles short of Columbus he found the fuel gauge redlining him. There were more filling stations than he could shake a dipstick at. Only he had no money for gas. He had bourbon. Would it work? He poured bourbon in the tank. After sputtering past Fort Benning and just before making Columbus, he noticed the driver of a canvased six-by-six truck coming the other way, evidently heading back from the Atlanta Army Supply Depot.

For a second their glances met. The driver, a Pfc., looked a lot like Sgt Miles Messmore. The second passed. Buckmaster shook his head. Couldn't be. In the mirror he caught the other driver shaking his head. Couldn't be?

Buckmaster's gut tightened. By the time he found a place to swing around it would be too late to catch up with the truck and tail it home. At least he knew it was a Fort Benning motor pool truck. And whether or not that had been Messmore, it had been in his mind that the place to start hunting down the Tenth Experimental Company was Fort Benning.

Messmore and Flugel would have to pay for what they had put him through. He felt the shotgun against his calves. But the reckoning was not at hand. That would come when he learned the score. Meanwhile, he would go on toting it up.

He parked the pickup in a black neighborhood, where the stuff in the back would do the most good. He started to wipe the steering wheel, then laughed shortly. He didn't have to worry about leaving fingerprints. He didn't worry long about leaving the shotgun behind; he needed brains more than firepower. He got out and eyed the remaining firewater in the back. It would make fine trade goods. He fixed himself up a package of six bottles of bourbon and a loaf of bread: that left him only a book of verses and a thou shy of paradise. He walked away from the pickup through a gauntlet of eyes.

Collum. The man must be feeling uncomfortable about now. Too bad there was no money in Collum's borrowed pockets for a phone call. It took Buckmaster a good walk to locate an emergency call box that looked safe to use, one not in the line of sight of women leaning on windowsills and one void of loiterers.

He told the policeman's voice and the tape to notify Fargo law that Quintus Collum needed help real bad. He hung up on 'Who's calling?' If he had given in to the temptation and said 'General Jackson', the cop would have dismissed the call as a hoax.

Now Lt Stonewall J. Buckmaster needed help real bad. He needed a phone, a typewriter, and brains to pick.

He knew what he was looking for after he saw it. Its name was FTA. Op art lettering on the window euphemistically expanded this into Free Time Association.

Out of uniform but not out of habit, his flexors readied themselves to return highballs. But the pair of GIs he encountered walked by him unseeing into a storefront. He stopped and let rock and roll wash over him while he studied the posters and tearsheets. It was an enlisted men's coffeehouse, but the joint doubled as the office of an offbase underground paper. Here would be a phone, a typewriter, and brains to pick.

He shifted his parcel to his other arm and went in. Most of the GIs in here wore civvies. No one would look at him twice.

They eyed him twice. The dogface cynosure was his week's beard. He couldn't plead shaving bumps. He could plead a binge that had left him AWOL. He thought drunk, which meant he thought firmly sober, and looked around with bleary concentration. The place was fairly full, but he spotted an empty table in a corner, steered a course for it, set his parcel at his feet, and sat down to send his gaze reconnoitering happily.

The decor was cork-float fishing nets on the walls and candles in dead soldiers on the tables. Posters of Mao and Mickey Mouse and Che hung on the nets, and there was bare space for graffiti such as 'Round up all the squares' and 'Ft Benning is American as appuru pai'. The sound was so thick that he had to squint through it, but the regulars seemed to find the endless riff a reassuring monotony, a certainty in an uncertain world. He quickly picked out the one who ran the joint.

The masthead of the sheet on the store window had listed a Joe Dee as editor and publisher, and Buckmaster saw the name Joe on the lips of those speaking to the twenty-year-old leaning his back against the food counter. Even without that, Buckmaster would have picked him out as the leading figure.

Joe Dee wore a sweatshirt bearing the motto: BE HEALTHY – EAT YOUR HONEY. Though in civvies, Dee would be in the Army and would be a Pfc. at most; the Army might say a good soldier is a bitching soldier, but the Army brass would not like anything about FTA; Dee would remain a Pfc. till his hitch was up. He looked to be twenty. A sharp kid.

Buckmaster let Dee wonder about him for a moment, then took out a bottle of bourbon, held it up to the light, and set it on the table. Joe Dee hurried over.

'You trying to get us busted? We don't have a liquor license, so no setups in here.'

'Sorry, Joe, but you got me wrong. I'm not drinking. I'm trading. I'm stone broke –'

'Man does not live by stone alone.'

Dee spoke absently, clearly trying to figure out if Buckmaster was a provocateur. Just as clearly he was taking no chances. He shot a couple of glances, and a pair of brawny GIs moved to watch the entrance.

Buckmaster put up a hand in Scout's oath.

'Honest, I'm out of bread and I wondered if six bottles of bourbon will buy me a few things.'

'Such as?'

'A few phone calls, the use of a typewriter.'

Dee frowned, then smiled.

'We're not in the swapping business, but we do try to help our fellow soldiers out. That's what FTA is all about. You *are* in the Army? Mind showing me your ID?'

'That's the whole trouble. That's what I have to straighten out. I woke up in a hotel room in Atlanta this morning, sobering up after a long drunk, and it hit me I'm a week AWOL. And on top of that my wallet with my bread and my papers ran away with the girl. I sneaked out of the hotel and hitched a ride back here. But I don't want to show up at Benning like this.'

'What outfit you in?'

'Tenth Experimental Company.' He watched Dee's face closely but drew a blank. 'Want the name, rank, and serial number?' He gave his name as Cpl Jackson Wallstone and rattled off his own number with the o in front of it.

Dee picked up the rest of the package and examined it.

'Where'd you get this?'

'Found it under the bed. All's left of the case I started out with.'

Dee smiled.

'And the loaf of bread?'

Buckmaster tried to look earnestly puzzled.

'I don't remember that. I guess I thought I might get a little bit hungry.'

Dee laughed.

'How about now? Are you hungry, Jackson?'

Buckmaster thought.

'I guess I am.'

Dee nodded, elbowed room for himself at the counter, and brought back a chili dog and a double Coke. He looked apologetic.

'I'll throw this in. It goes for a buck but it isn't worth a buck. But then a buck isn't worth a buck.'

From another table Dee liberated a camp catsup bottle in the form of a wounded soldier; the catsup poured from a bandaged head. Then Dee hustled the bourbon out of sight into the back room.

The two GIs on guard opened themselves for a girl. She came in with a handful of FTAs that looked as if they smelled of fresh ink and with a headful of smiles and nods. She missed seeing Buckmaster behind his chili dog. She made for the back room, remained there a long moment, and when she came out she made for Buckmaster's table and sat down across from him.

'Hi. I'm Sally Kaster.'

He grinned on a bite of chili dog. Sally Kaster was a shag haircut, a Dayglo flower on the left cheek, pale lips, granny glasses, shoulder bag, peekaboo dress, brass-toed boots. She was very thin and very tall, and each made her look more of the other.

'I help Joe put out the FTA. Joe told me to take care of you.'

The chili dog took another grin, and she hurried on.

'I mean, you know, show you where the phone is, you know, and the typewriter.'

Buckmaster chewed quickly. She touched his arm.

'No, please take your time. You eat, I'll just sit here.'

No doubt Dee had told her, 'See what you can worm out of him.' See if Jackson Wallstone's story stood up, stood repeating.

'What are you?'

'Mmm?'

She frowned. 'I mean, you know, what's your, you know, sign?'

He thought. 'Cancer, I guess.'

She made a face. 'You mean you're a Moonchild. We don't say Cancer.'

'Isn't that dishonest?'

'Just, you know, nicer. I'm an Aquarian.'

'Does that make you lucky?'

'I know my luck. If I, you know, knocked on wood, I'd, you know, get splinters. You know?'

'I know.' He knew. Her words got in the way of what she said, and what she said got in the way of what she meant.

'What's your unit?'

He told her.

'What're you experimenting on?'

'Sorry, that's top secret.'

'Oh?'

'No, honest. Being AWOL's nothing to what I'd be in for if I shot off my mouth about our work.'

'Is it dangerous work?'

'I'm beginning to think so.'

'You know, I don't think you like what you're doing, or, you know, you wouldn't've got all that, you know, drunk and be, you know, AWOL.'

'Maybe I was celebrating and overdid it.'

Her eyes searched his face. 'I don't think so. You don't, you know, look that kind of, you know. What made you sign up in the first place?'

He shrugged. 'Three hots and a cot.'

'Are you really, you know, straight arrow? Do you really want to turn yourself in? Or do you want out? We can help you get a, you know, medical discharge. For instance, you know, there's licorice, you know?'

He knew. Draft dodgers had fooled doctors by eating lots of licorice before their physicals. The glycyrrhizinic acid in licorice makes the body retain sodium and mimic oversecretion of aldosterone.

'Or if you don't want to try that, you know, we can keep you underground here, you know, or get you to, you know, Canada or Sweden?'

'If you don't mind, I'll just, you know, face the music.'

'You sure you're a Moonchild?'

Dee appeared behind her and put his hands on her shoulders. He smiled at Buckmaster and nodded toward the back room.

'Anytime you're ready. And you look ready.'

Buckmaster got up, wiping his mouth with a paper napkin.

'That was good. Thanks.'

'Sally will show you.'

Sally showed him.

'There's the phone. And here's the, you know, area phone book. The typewriter's over there. Need any help?'

'No, thanks.'

She hesitated, smiled, then left.

Even with the door shut the rock and roll came through strong. He looked around. The bourbon was nowhere in sight. He opened the phone book and found the Fort Benning number and dialed it. He covered his free ear with the heel of his palm.

'Put me through to the Tenth Experimental Company.'

The Benning operator's voice took an odd turn. 'One moment, sir. I'll have to connect you with Lt Fiordaliso.'

Lt Fiordaliso had a musical voice, and Buckmaster was not using the rock and roll as a touchstone. She let him repeat his request and herself repeated the name sweetly.

'The Tenth Experimental Company?'

'That's right. I want to speak to the CO, Capt. Romeo Clapsaddle.'

Lt Fiordaliso's voice became gothic architecture. 'I realize that this is April First and that that's like a full moon to some people. But I find it a not very funny joke, and one that's fast getting tiresome. Why don't you stick to phoning the zoo and asking for Mr Lyon?'

'Hold on.' Buckmaster was trying to hold on to something himself. He spoke all the more forcefully. 'This is no joke, Lieutenant. The Tenth Experimental exists. You may not know about it because it's a top-secret installation. But it's there and it's urgent that I reach its CO.' Had he shaken her? There was a pause he hurried to fill. 'Look, you can check with the Pentagon. Ask for Col. Maximilian Fubb.'

Another pause. Then, 'All right. I will. Will you hang on, or will you call back?'

'I'll hang on.'

Copies of the latest issue of FTA lay on the desk. Sally must have brought them fresh from the printer. It took Buckmaster a while to catch on to the usages 'hash' for 'he/she', 'herm' for 'him/her', and 'sheir' — no doubt pronounced 'share' for 'his/her(s)'. Sally Kaster's influence? Anyway, the item his eye fell on seemed to indicate an enlisted personnel's union was in the pangs of organizing. 'FTA board members are pushing

overtime pay for a soldier when hash puts in more than thirty hours performing sheir duties – *whether or not the extra time is punishment for herm.*'

'Hello?'

'Right here, Lieutenant. How did you make out?'

'I have some information about that matter, but I can't give it to
you over the phone. You will have to come to the base and see me in
my office. Can you do that?'

'Yes. Thanks. I'll be there.'

Sally Kaster came back into the room just then, and the music for-
tissimo'd between doorshuts. When Lt Fiordaliso's voice came back in
focus, it was saying, '– your name so I'll know who to –'

He hung up.

Kaster eyed him anxiously.

'How did it go? Still plan to turn yourself in?'

'That's the strategy. Now for the tactics. The typewriter, if you'll let
me at it.'

He warmed his hands up and flexed his fingers, like a concert pianist,
and sat down to it. He helped himself to a blank sheet of paper and began
to tap out a pass for Cpl Jackson Wallstone. Kaster laughed.

'I've seen slow, but you are s-l-o-w.' Then she saw the tips of his
fingers. 'Sorry. Want me to –?'

'No, thanks.'

'Happen in one of your, you know, experiments?'

'Happened in line of duty.'

Her face turned fierce. 'I'll bet your experiments are imperiling this
whole, you know, area. But all the brass cares about is, you know, secrecy.
I hate that. I believe in the people's right to, you know, know.'

'I'll tell herm when hash comes in.'

Kaster's fierceness laughed away. Then she grew serious. 'I see you've
read our sheet. What do you think of it?'

'For what it is, it's good.'

Her eyes went Jeanne d'Arc. 'You don't like what it stands for?'

He didn't want to argue with her, but he didn't drop it because he
felt he wasn't arguing with her but with himself.

'What it stands for is nice. But an army isn't nice. And what happens
to an army when you fight it from within?'

'We fight, yes, but not to destroy it. We know there's a need for an
army in today's world. We're not that, you know, naive. We fight to
humanize the military.'

'If you humanize it, then it won't be the military.'

'They've brainwashed you.'

She let him finish typing in peace. Joe Dee came in as Buckmaster was signing the name of Capt. Romeo Clapsaddle to the pass.

'All squared away, Jackson?'

'Almost, Joe.' He rubbed his beard. 'I can't go back looking like this.'

'We can fix that.'

Buckmaster nodded his gratitude. He glanced around, looking for something he could do to pay Dee back, and saw how to pay the Air Force brass back.

'If you want a story for your sheet, I can give you one about Air Force generals setting up and enforcing a private hunting preserve in the Okefenokee.'

Dee smiled an easy smile. 'I'd be more interested in hearing about the – what is it? – Tenth Experimental? What sort of thing are you working on?'

Dee was the type of EM Buckmaster had always put down as a smart-ass, as almost a traitor to tradition, as everything a good soldier was not. But now he felt a liking for Dee and Dee's anti-ness. He fought the temptation to tell Dee the whole truth as he knew it. He had to maintain a wariness and an anti-ness of his own.

'Like I told Sally, it's top secret.'

Dee's easy smile didn't harden. 'So top secret Benning has no record of it. You see, I used the phone before you did.'

Kaster whirled on Buckmaster.

'You've been putting me on? Why?'

'If I had told you the truth, you wouldn't've believed me.'

'How do you know? Try me.'

'Lay off him, Sally. He has his reasons – or unreasons. We all have our paranoias.'

'But he could be a, you know –'

Dee cut her off with a slice of the hand. 'They've been trying to get me for a long while now. But I don't think he's a plant.' He turned to Buckmaster. 'I'm betting you're all right. But even if I'm all wrong, you don't worry me. I don't have any deep dark secrets. They ought to know by now I let it all hang out.' He studied Buckmaster's face, then nodded slowly. 'Besides, I believe you really are in trouble with the Army. That puts you on my side whether you know it or not, or want to be or not. Meanwhile, you need a shave and clothes that fit. We're about the same size. When we close for the night, Sally will take you home and fix you up.'

Kaster walked out of the back room ahead of Buckmaster stiffly and did not sit with him again. Before leaving him to himself she did tell him home, a communal you know thing, was only a few blocks away. She made her way around the room, table by table, taking down what the men told her about conditions on the base and in the service generally.

In spite of the noise Buckmaster found himself dropping off, lost himself. He came alert. The live noise had cut off, leaving the field to the recorded noise. The street door had opened on darker night, and Buckmaster saw first the white helmet liners, the white gloves, the .45 automatics on the white gun belts, the MP brassards, the black boots with white laces. Then he saw the faces. Messmore and Flugel.

Both were MP sergeants now, and the eyes of both scanned the place and fixed on him.

Buckmaster looked around. The GIs seemed collectively sullen at the incursion but individually glad it was not on their account. They had no leadership. Joe Dee was out of sight, likely in the back room. Sally Kaster stood up but only stared as Messmore made for Buckmaster while Flugel remained in the doorway. If Messmore felt he was in enemy territory, he didn't look it. He smiled as Buckmaster rose slowly.

'All right, soldier.' That was in grits and gravy. Then in a yam whisper, 'Look, Lieutenant, why don't you come along quiet? That way nobody gets hurt. We got a lot to talk over once we're away from here.'

Buckmaster gestured at the corner he was in, the fishnetted wall he was up against.

'Guess I don't have any choice.'

Kaster moved herself toward Messmore's side.

'Listen, Sergeant, he's been planning to turn himself in, so –'

Messmore put out a big white-rayed hand.

'Stay out of this, sister.'

But she had stayed in it just long enough. Buckmaster tore the fishnet from the wall, and in the same movement flung it over Messmore. The net fell over Kaster as well, and Messmore and Kaster struggled at cross-purposes, entangling themselves all the more. He gave them chairs to stumble over and slid past the bobbing corks of their writhings.

'Stop him!' Flugel had found his voice.

The G Is parted and closed, and Buckmaster reached the door of the back room.

Dee looked up from his typewriter as the door opened and closed, frowned at the brief relative hush and scuffle, and lifted an eyebrow.

'What's up?'

'The M Ps.'

'After you?'

As if Dee didn't know. Dee sprang to his feet.

'There's a –'

Buckmaster decked him before he could finish, dragged him out of the way, shoved the desk against the door. The phone. But by the time the cops came, it would all be over. There had to be a way out, or at least a hiding place. There was no other door, not even a window. But Dee had hidden the bourbon away. Where? He looked down.

The desk legs had scuffed a rug away from the outline of a trapdoor. He lifted the door. Steps led down into darkness. Might be a way through to an adjoining building; might be a dead end.

He left the trapdoor open and stood against the wall on the hinge side of the door to the front room. He felt the building shake. He thought himself thin, willed his molecules into the wall.

Messmore nearly tore the door off its hinges. That would have left Buckmaster without concealment. But the hinges held, and the door shoved the desk out of the way and shielded Buckmaster. In a flash Messmore was in the room and in a crouch away from the open doorway. Flugel followed, knelt to Dee for a second, then loosened the .45 in its holster and moved toward the cellar opening. He took a deep breath and started down the stairs. Messmore followed.

When the second white blob vanished, Buckmaster stepped silently over. Eyes looked up at him as he slammed the trapdoor shut. He stood a pair of desk legs on the trapdoor. Pounding and swearing moved him away. Bullets might come next.

'Joe, are you all right? Joe?'

Kaster sat herself on the floor and rested Dee's head in her lap. Dee stirred, opened his eyes to the pain of light, rubbed soreness, and winced. He looked past Kaster at Buckmaster.

'What was that for?'

He got to his feet. Buckmaster all at once felt wobblier than Dee looked. Had he been wrong about Dee? He looked at Dee and knew he had been wrong.

'I'm sorry, Dee. I thought you had turned me in.'

'Sure.' But Dee's face and voice were cold. 'Turned you in?' Then he took in the state of the room and heard the pounding and swearing below. 'What happened?'

'Two guys in MP uniforms came in and tried to take me.'

'Great. What do we do now?'

'Call the MPs.'

'But *they're* –'

'Phony MPs.'

Dee stared at him, then stared at the trapdoor. He listened, Kaster listened, Buckmaster listened. The pounding and swearing had stopped. Dee shook his head.

'Whoever they are, they're gone.'

'So there is a way out?' Buckmaster grimaced. He could have saved himself a lot of sweat.

'Yes. Look, you'd better go too. Now. Fast.'

12. NSI   NONSTANDARD ITEM

An ante-bellum mansion that had lost the war with time housed the FTA commune. Commune was the wrong word for it. It was more like a stop on today's underground railway. The wide streets had been empty of MPs real or phony, and the house itself seemed nearly empty of anyone. Sally Kaster, showing Buckmaster to a second-floor room, told him they had a big turnover of activists passing through. Buckmaster heard only one, a bedspring twang, as they moved by the one closed door.

Kaster also showed him the hall bathroom and brought him a razor with a fresh blade. She came back again while he was rinsing the razor. She stood behind him and studied the result in the mirror.

'Not bad.' She hurried past herself. 'Anything else you need? I put clean, you know, sheets on your bed.'

'Thanks.' He opened the medicine cabinet and found a bottle of after-shave lotion. 'I'll just tend to my wounds before I sack out.'

He gave his fingertips dashes of lotion.

'What happened to your fingers? Really.'

'Same failing as the Venus de Milo's. I bite my fingernails and don't know when to stop.'

She made a face at the mirror and sat down on the edge of the bathtub. She showed no sign of leaving when he made to see to his thigh. He took off Collum's pants and untied the dishcloth bandage and put a sting of lotion on the wound.

'What happened to your, you know, thigh?'

'I was in a boat in the Okefenokee Swamp, minding my own business, when a Phantom jet came along and strafed me.'

She got up and turned her back on him.

'All right. I'll mind my own business. But I don't see why you can't trust me. I only want to help.'

'I trust you.'

'You make me so mad.'

Her thinness added to her body's attitude of hurt. He put his hands on her shoulders and felt a tenseness that slowly tenderized. But he did not yet pull her to him. He remembered Dee's hands on her shoulders. He hadn't let Maggie's marriage to Col. Fubb hold him off, but this girl's possible relationship with Joe made him hold off.

'Are you and Joe, you know –?'

'Nothing serious.' She turned in his arms and smiled. 'Go on, lie to me. Tell me you think I'm pretty. Tell me you love me.'

He left her sleeping, and before anyone else was stirring in the pre-dawn, he shaved again and went through closets. Even the empty rooms had wardrobes, whether the leavings of passers-through or the belongings of base-bound members of the commune. In the room next to his he had spotted Kaster's shoulder bag on the dresser. He had picked it up but had put it down without opening it. He found a Pfc.'s jacket in that room and a pair of trousers. He put them on. A fairly good fit. Joe Dee's? He started toward the shoulder bag again, then stopped himself again with a grimace, and quitted that room to get on with his scrounging.

He liberated a cap and a pair of shoes his size in another room, tore corporal's stripes off a jacket in another room, and wherever he came across loose change, he changed it from the other pockets to his own. He pinned corporal's stripes on over the Pfc.'s to go with Cpl Jackson Wallstone's pass, working the safety pins from the inside of the sleeves to make the pinnings less overt.

Meaning only to look in on Sally before he left, he came back to his room. She stopped breathing as the light from the hall hit her. Then she opened up. Her eyes studied him gravely, her mouth smiled uncertainly.

'So early?'

He nodded. She studied his uniform.

'Let me sew the stripes on.'

'No time. I want to catch the first bus.'

'Do you have money?'

He rattled the change. 'Enough to get me to Benning.' Unless they'd raised the fare since he had been here last; he might have to thumb a ride.

She must have caught his flicker of doubt because she slid out of bed and ran to get her bag and handed him a ten-dollar bill. She held on to one end.

'This is only a loan. You'll have to come back to repay me.'

'I wouldn't have it any other way. Any other way I'd feel like a you know.'

Her eyes searched his face.

'I'll see you again? Don't lie.'

He put her to bed.

'Go back to sleep and dream it's coming true.'

He kissed her eyes shut.

13. NFR No FURTHER REQUIREMENT

Buckmaster got onto the post with a busload of soldiers beating reveille. The Infantryman Statue – the 'Ultimate Weapon' – still stood in front of Infantry School Headquarters saying, 'Follow me.' Buckmaster wandered purposefully away from the others and followed his nose to the post chapel. It was open. Empty. He went in and sat down. A damned good place to kill time.

He raised his head out of a doze to find the approaching footsteps were the chaplain's. The chaplain was eyeing him almost with alarm – as a pope might eye someone holier than the pope.

'Don't let me disturb you, son. If there's one thing I don't want to do, it's come between a man and his God.' His smile said that was a joke, son. He tried to find out Buckmaster's God. 'You Catholic, son?'

'No, sir.'

'Ah, well, we're all God's children, aren't we?'

'Yes, sir.'

The feet and voices of God's children were beginning to resound on the post, but headquarters would not be fully operative yet awhile. Buckmaster put off resurrecting time. He let the chaplain detain him.

He put on his garrison cap but did not go. The chaplain had captain's bars. Not much, but more than Buckmaster.

'Well then, son –'

'Excuse me. Could you get a message to the commanding general?'

The chaplain's pinchbottle face drained dry. He laughed uneasily.

'Corporal, I have to go through channels just like everyone else. Maybe if you told me your problem I could help you, though my hours –'

'I see.'

'No, wait, Corporal. I'm not the only chaplain here. What's your faith?'

Buckmaster started to say Anabaptist, then struck that flag of convenience and flew a Jolly Roger.

'I belong to the Church of Improbability.'

'I'm afraid I don't –'

'It's a sect that started on Sigma Corvi III. It began with people praying to a god who had latched on to probability and who took credit for it. Nary a priest – or seminary a one – would dare to cross him. That worked fine for a millennium or so. Then they found out he probably didn't exist. And so they killed him.'

The chaplain blinked. Then his pinchbottle face filled up.

'Corporal, don't you believe there's a God?'

'I believe God's a black box.'

'A what?'

'You can't give me the wiring diagram, can you?'

'Isn't it enough to believe we're here for a purpose? Even though we may not know that purpose?'

Buckmaster let himself look astonished. 'Why, the purpose is no mystery.'

'All right then, Corporal, suppose you tell us. What are we here on earth for?'

The chaplain smiled, waiting. It seemed a smile of smugness till you looked deeper, and Buckmaster almost felt ashamed of himself; the man was an easy mark. But he had asked for it.

'What on earth are we here for? Here's the whole thing: we're shit machines.'

The chaplain sat down and sat silent as Buckmaster left. He seemed to be straining at stool.

14. TOE TABLE OF ORGANIZATION AND EQUIPMENT

Buckmaster made for headquarters mess hall and got in the chow line, though his purpose was not chow, which was just as well. He took his tray to a table and, picking his spot, sat down beside a clerical-looking Sp 4.

'Hi. I just transferred here today.'

'And just made corporal.'

'Yeah.' He had picked the right man. The guy had a quick eye. 'I'm going to be in the Personnel Service Division.'

The Sp 4 stiffened slightly and eyed him as a possible competitor. 'What section?'

'Personnel Records Branch.'

The Sp 4 relaxed. 'I'm in the Personnel Management Branch. Name's Harry Rushcamp.'

'Jackson Wallstone.'

'Jackson Wallstone? Say, that's a funny combination. You know, if you turn your last name around –'

'Yeah. My old man thought of that. That's why he named me Jackson.'

'Oh.' He smiled at a thought. 'Personnel Records Branch. That's Lt Fiordaliso.'

'What's he like?'

'She. A Wac. Juliet Fiordaliso.' He told Buckmaster what she was like, and Buckmaster gathered she was a dish, though not everyone's, and everything about her was sharp, even her curves.

Rushcamp had never heard of a Sgt Miles 'Zulu' Messmore or a Cpl Oscar Flugel. Rushcamp said he felt sure he would know if they were post personnel because he had a thing for names – 'Oscar Flugel! Now there's a name' – and every roster passed before his eyes.

'Ever heard of the Tenth Experimental Company?'

'No. That the outfit you transferred from?'

'No. Just a name I heard.'

Before Rushcamp began wondering why the name Jackson Wallstone hadn't caught his attention on the lists that passed before his eyes, Buckmaster thanked him and said he'd see him around and got up and left.

In spite of himself and the food, he had emptied the tray. A good little shit machine.

Buckmaster crossed the parade ground, past men and women standing in formation, and dispatched himself to Headquarters.

The sign was there. MAJOR GENERAL REEBER BATTLE, COMMANDING GENERAL, US ARMY INFANTRY CENTER AND COMMANDANT, US ARMY INFANTRY SCHOOL, FORT BENNING, GEORGIA. Was the general there?

He tuned in on two majors he was slow to overtake, his need to know working.

'The Old Man's out on the course.'

'Obstacle course?'

'Golf course.'

'Same thing, of course.'

They looked around before laughing, saw him, refrained, officers forming a closed society.

Buckmaster followed them inside, and then the walls arrowed him to the Personnel Records Branch of the Personnel Service Division. He'd meant to try Fiordaliso first anyway. If she didn't pan out, well, the chain of command had fusible links.

As Sp 4 Rushcamp had led him to expect, Lt Fiordaliso was a living flow chart, all business but all feminine. He got in to see her by saying he was the one who had phoned her about the Tenth Experimental Company.

'At ease, Corporal.' She looked him over and frowned. At the uniform or the man? The inspection was unsettling and humbling. 'You're the one who phoned? I thought it was an officer.'

'That's what I wanted you to think, ma'am. Saved time.'

'Watch it, Corporal. I may think something you won't like. What's your name?'

'Harry Rushcamp, ma'am.'

'Do you know a Lt Buckmaster?'

'Yes, ma'am. He's the guy, sorry, the officer, who told me about the Tenth Experimental Company.'

'I see.' Her frown deepened to help her see. 'Where is he?'

'I can get in touch with him.'

'Did he send you here?'

'In a way. Ever read the FTA sheet?'

She gave a nod, more to herself than to him. 'I've seen it. Are you with –'

'FTA is thinking of running a story exposing the Tenth Experimental Company.'

Fiordaliso seemed to fight down a start. 'Exposing it?'

'Its potential destructiveness, effect on the environment, hazard to soldiers and the population at large, that kind of thing.'

He had the feeling he had just lost the skirmish.

Fiordaliso seemed to fight back a smile. But her voice, when it came out came out deadly serious. 'Let me warn you, Cpl Rushcamp. This is a top-secret matter. You might like to know that Col. Fubb was so interested in your call that he's flying someone right down.' She glanced at the clock. 'The officer should be here any minute now. He's expecting to meet a Lt Buckmaster, not a Cpl Rushcamp.' She gestured toward her phone. 'So you will get in touch with the lieutenant now. Then you will wait in the outer office.' There was a glass partition; she would be dismissing him without losing sight of him.

Buckmaster nodded to the CRT display on her desk.

'Would you mind making a call first?'

'About what, Corporal?'

'There are two men on base Col. Fubb's men ought to meet as well. Will you find out what units a Sgt Miles Messmore and a Cpl Oscar Flugel are in and have them on hand without telling them why?'

She eyed him sharply, then repeated the names and tapped keys. Her eyes glowed with reflected readout. She cleared the screen before he could step around for a look at it.

'I have that information, Corporal. I'll see they're at the meeting.'

Lying bitch. Sp 4 Rushcamp, if you believed him and Buckmaster believed him, hadn't made the names. So Fiordaliso had been pretending to summon up the data. She was on the other side, whoever or whatever the other side was.

If it hadn't been Joe Dee who had called in those phony MPs Messmore and Flugel, and Buckmaster felt sure it hadn't, and if it hadn't been pure coincidence, and Buckmaster felt sure it hadn't, then it had been Lt Fiordaliso who had tipped them off. She had heard the blare of music in the background of his phone call. That either pinpointed the FTA coffeehouse or narrowed the search.

And if Fiordaliso had tipped them off once, she would tip them off again. There had been no call to Col. Fubb, and no Col. Fubb's man was flying down. There would be only another try at seizing or silencing Buckmaster.

'All right, Corporal. Now make that call to Lt Buckmaster.'

'Right away, ma'am. All I have to do is step outside the building and give him the high sign.'

He saluted, about-faced, and strode out.

She hesitated too long. Her 'Corporal –' was far enough away for him reasonably not to hear it.

15. SUPOHDU   SUPPLY FROM STOCK ON HAND OR DUE IN

What remained of Sally Kaster's ten bought him a half-dozen golf balls at the PX.

He wandered among the vehicles at the parking lot looking for one with keys in the ignition.

'Wallstone.'

Buckmaster recognized the voice sooner than the name. Pfc. Joe Dee sat at the wheel of a jeep.

'I wasn't sure at first without the beard. I see my spare jacket made corporal. Did you explain away your AWOL? At least you're not in the stockade.'

'Yes. It isn't over. What are you doing here?'

'My sergeant ran out of his brand of smokes. What are you doing here?'

'Looking for a heap to clout.'

'Wallstone, you are something else. And I'm beginning to think someone else.' He spotted the golf balls. 'Going to fill a few cavities?'

'Yeah, me and W. C. Fields. Maybe you know – where's General Battle's golf course?'

'Old Rivet Divot? Somewhere out on the Reservation. Thinking of bribing him with those? I think his honor comes a little bit higher.'

'Just a gimmick to get to him.'

'That I'd like to see. Let me drive you there.'

'What about your sergeant?'

'So I'll tell him I had to wait for them to dig a case of his brand out of the back.'

'Never volunteer.' Buckmaster hopped in. 'On the other hand, I never look a gift jeep in the gears. But wouldn't it go better for you if it seemed I forced you to take me? Or if I simply slugged you and drove off?'

Dee put up his dukes but only as if to fend off. 'Overkill. I already have the bruise to prove you made me do it if it comes to that.' He pulled out of the parking lot. 'I've been wanting to get a look at the general's golf course and write it up. One more zinger about the brass wasting the taxpayer's dollar.'

They drove under the shade of trees, crossed Upatoi Bridge, and reached Outpost No. 1.

'Golf balls for General Battle' got them past Outpost No. 1 onto Fort Benning Reservation and directions to just where in the 185,000 acres the golf course was.

Dee was first to spot the golf cart. Far enough away to be a white dot till you sharpened your eyes, it rolled along the green.

'There he goes with his aide. How'll you catch up with him? We can't take out after them in the jeep.'

'I'll cut him off at the next tee: be easy enough. Drop me off here, Joe, and turn back. I don't want you to get mixed up in this any more than you are.'

'I'm mixed up, all right. I sure would like to know what's going on. But, okay.'

Buckmaster waved so-long and loped across the terrain leading his target. His thigh felt the pull of a muscle and slowed him so that he reached the tee late. The general was already setting up for his drive. Buckmaster held his salute, waiting for the general to acknowledge him. The general's mouth was a thin red line.

'Gunning, I thought there were never to be any interruptions.'

The lieutenant colonel with the general turned to Buckmaster.

'Corporal, what do you mean by interrupting the commanding general?'

Buckmaster held out the golf balls.

'Sir, compliments of Capt. Clapsaddle.'

'Gunning, who in hell is Capt. Clapsaddle?'

'Corporal, who is Capt. Clapsaddle?'

'Sir, Capt. Romeo Clapsaddle is CO of the Tenth Experimental Company.'

'Gunning, what the hell is the Tenth Experimental Company?'

'Corporal, what organization is the Tenth Experimental Company part of?'

'Why, sir, it's in the general's command.'

'Gunning, I know what-all's in my command. I never heard of the Tenth Experimental Company.' The thin red line slackened a bit. 'Have you ever heard of it?'

'No, sir. Corporal, in what area is your unit?'

'It's not my unit, sir. All I know is a captain stopped me and handed me those golf balls and ordered me to take them to Gen. Battle and

say they came with the compliments of Capt. Romeo Clapsaddle, CO
of the Tenth Experimental Company.'

'Are you sure that's what he said?'

'Yes, Colonel. He made me say it back to him till he was satisfied.'

'Gunning, my nose tells me this is something in very bad taste or
something much more sinister – and the latter is more likely right. You
know how I hit a ball, and if I hit one having a dynamite core – the
end of a deadly foe of all leftists. Gunning, call in and get an EOD
team.'

'Yes, sir.' The lieutenant colonel started toward the golf cart. A walkie-
talkie lay on the seat. 'Right away.'

'Just a minute, sir.' Buckmaster shoved the six golf balls further out
toward the general. 'Allow me to test them for you. Pick a ball, sir.'

The general pulled his hand back to the ribbon representing a paper
combat in Vietnam.

'Gunning, pick a ball.'

The lieutenant colonel pointed to a ball. Buckmaster set the others
on the ground and the one on a tee. He deferentially helped himself
to a driver from Gunning's bag and took a few practice swings. He smiled
at Gunning, who, like Battle, had retreated.

'Something like Russian roulette, isn't it, sir?'

Contact had a good solid feel and the ball took flight, long and true,
and landed a few feet from the cup. Buckmaster looked apologetic.

'It's a long time since I've played.'

The general's thin red line withdrew into the zone of the interior.
He stepped up to his own ball, swung savagely. The ball landed far short
of Buckmaster's and in the rough.

'Gunning, this hoax, or whatever it is, is not only in very bad taste,
it is also putting me off my game.' He pointed east, his West Point ring
glittering. 'I want this man out of my sight. But first get his name and
serial number.'

'Corporal, the general wants you out of his sight.' Gunning drew
out a small pad and a ballpoint pen. 'But first give your name and serial
number.'

'Yes, sir. Cpl Oscar Flugel, 876-54-321.'

He saluted, about-faced, got into the cart and drove away. Disbelief
rooted them long enough.

'Corporal! Bring that cart back! Want a court-martial?'

He gave it all it had, and it outdistanced feet, and the next 'Corporal!'

was breathless and fainter, though louder and fiercer at the end. When he looked back before topping a green hill, the last he saw of the general the general was clubbing an invisible snake to death. Buckmaster supposed that was par for the course.

Once out of sight, he changed course and made for the line of trees, wheeled into concealment, and braked. Smiling, he picked up the walkie-talkie. Much simpler and far faster to use this link than to try getting his plight through the hole in Old Rivet Divot's head.

He pressed the send switch and opened his mouth. He closed his mouth. Damn. Why hadn't he let Gunning call HQ? He would have learned the official communications signal. Now, lacking it, he might make HQ suspicious. Have to fake it.

'. . . you read? Do you read? Over.'

It was a long second.

'Bravo Base to Bravo One. You are coming in garbled. Request you say again your last message. Over.'

'Bravo One to Bravo Base. Where've you been? Never mind. This is urgent. How do you copy, Bravo Base?'

'Bravo One from Bravo Base. Read you loud and clear, Bravo One. Go ahead. Over.'

'Bravo One to Bravo Base. By order of the commanding general, there will be an immediate and intensive lookout for a large black soldier with a beard. His name may or may not be Miles Messmore. His nickname may or may not be Zulu. He may or may not be driving a truck. Do not, repeat not, attempt to apprehend. Simply report such sighting at once. Over.'

'Understand. Stand by, please. Over.'

Bravo One stood by. All hung on HQ getting back to him with the sighting before the general and his aide found a way of getting through to HQ. He had no way of telling how many minutes passed. He filled the time by unpinning the corporal's stripes and by threading the golf cart through the trees to a road of graying blacktop. A signpost told him he had hit Service Road Foxtrot. At least he had the beginnings of bearings. Bravo One stood by.

The walkie-talkie crackled. 'Bravo Base to Bravo One. Come in, please, Bravo One.'

'Bravo One. Do you have a sighting?'

'Affirmative, Bravo One. A Pfc. answering the description and driving a motor pool six-by carrying supplies to a 29th Infantry bivouac, has just passed Outpost No. 1 onto Reservation and is heading west on Service Road Echo. Do we put a tail on the subject? Over.'

'Negative. Stand by for further orders. Over.'

Was Foxtrot north or south of Echo? On a map the alphabet would descend: therefore, south. He twisted the golf cart north through the woods.

Service Road Echo was long, straight, and empty. He waited. This was way out on Echo. If it had just passed Outpost No. 1, the six-by-six could not have got by him yet. He waited. Either something was keeping Messmore, or Messmore had turned off. Buckmaster drove east on Echo, which remained long, straight, and empty. Ahead lay only Outpost No. 1.

Buckmaster swung the cart around and drove west on Echo, hunting a turnoff that wasn't there. Doing a double take, he swung around again and retraced a hundred meters. At one point the woods had a thin look. He stopped. Through a tall screen of brush at the edge of the road he saw what looked to be an old firebreak stretching back into denseness.

He studied the shoulder of the road and saw the start of a scratchy arc. A gate of movable brush? Just that. He drove the golf cart in, swung the gate back in place, cached the cart but kept the walkie-talkie, and followed the firebreak and the six-by-six wheeltracks in the dirt.

'Bravo Base to Bravo One. Come in, please, Bravo One.'

The voice had an uncertain, edgy quality now. Gunning must have busted a gut getting to a phone. By order of the commanding general, there would be an immediate and intensive search-and-seizure operation, objective a white corporal whose name might or might not be Oscar Flugel.

'Bravo Base to Bravo One. Where are you, Bravo One? We have further information for you. Come in, Bravo One.'

Buckmaster turned its insistence down. He started to unsling the walkie-talkie. He changed his mind. It was still a link, and he might need a link if he ran into something worse than the general's anger.

The firebreak flared into a clearing. A compound filled the clearing. A big sign hung on the wire-mesh gate – RESTRICTED AREA. POSITIVELY NO ADMITTANCE. Inside the chain-link fence and under camouflage netting, an olive-drab tractor-trailer with the look of a communications van seemed to serve as HQ building. The only structures were a tower – no more than a ladder with diving platforms at regular heights but with a sand box at its foot in place of a pool –

and a twenty-foot-diameter Fuller dome under another camouflage net. Buckmaster slid to cover.

The bearded black Miles 'Zulu' Messmore, in Pfc. fatigues, unloaded cartons from a six-by-six into the dome, which made that the supply room. Besides the six-by-six and the tractor-trailer, there were a command car and a jeep in the shade of trees overhanging the fence.

Buckmaster moved himself a tree nearer.

A tin voice blasted from the compound. 'Halt. This installation is a restricted area. Only authorized personnel may enter. Do not proceed any further. Turn around and go back.'

Buckmaster threw himself flat. Slowly he peered around the base of a tree trunk. Zulu had frozen, holding a double armful of cartons, his eyes scanning the surround. The door of the van opened, and Cpl Oscar Flugel leaned out, called to Zulu, and pointed toward Buckmaster's position. Both gazed Buckmaster's way, but he felt sure they could not see him. Still, they knew someone was there.

He looked around him. Sensors, posing as pebbles or even animal droppings, picked up and relayed heat, scent, sight, sound. There had to be a monitoring device aboard the trailer. He reached out and grabbed a pine cone that looked too much like a pine cone. He hefted it and felt it and confirmed its artificiality. He flung it away from him.

It must have landed near another sensor, for it promptly triggered the tin voice, plainly now an automatic taped warning.

Messmore dropped the cartons, and Flugel pulled back into the trailer. Zulu produced an M-16 from the cab of his truck. Flugel reappeared and pointed toward where the pine cone had ended up. Zulu moved nearer the fence, following the fix of his eyes. Zulu stopped, turned to face Flugel, shook his head, and rippled his hand. He put the M-16 back in the cab of his truck and returned to his unloading. Flugel stood a moment in the doorway, then went inside.

Buckmaster looked around. At first he saw nothing, then a quiver gave it away. A squirrel sat upright, staring at him. He saluted it and it rippled away.

He watched Messmore finish unloading and join Flugel in the long van. No better time than now. Waiting till dark would not keep the sensors from pinpointing him. He got to his feet but did not step away from the tree. He looked up and traced a jagged line of limbs and spaces. It seemed a long time since he had played Tarzan. But getting off the ground should get him out of sensor range. He climbed the tree and crawled out on a limb.

It *was* a long time since he had played Tarzan. But he made it to a limb of a tree overhanging the fence without shaming his ancestry or at least without falling. He dropped onto the hood of the command car, jumped, and landed running.

He dashed for the cab of the six-by-six and got the M-16. Freud was right: it seemed to Buckmaster that he had never felt so potent in his life. He strode to the van, stepped up to the door and kicked it in.

'Okay, you bastards. I've got you surrounded.'

His jaw was the one that dropped.

16. CYA   COVER YOUR ASS

Messmore, wearing a dazzling dashiki, sat at a snowy-tableclothed table, plying knife and fork on a steak. A bottle stood in an ice bucket; part of a Rothschild label peeped out of the napkin. Flugel stood at a micro-wave oven, plattering a thick porterhouse; he put it down at the third setting on the table before glancing at Buckmaster.

'What's been keeping you, Lieutenant?'

'I've been playing golf with the commanding general.'

The bastards. They didn't have the decency to look scared or guilty or anything but sure of themselves. Messmore gave him a chewing smile.

'Nice comeback, Lieutenant.'

'From Okefenokee?'

'That too, Lieutenant. That too. Sit yourself down, Lieutenant, and dig in. If you want to wash up first, the washroom's in that corner.'

'Zulu's right, Lieutenant. Eat before it gets cold.'

Flugel sat down at his own place and set to. Messmore put down knife and fork.

'Uh-oh. Lieutenant's trigger finger's itching. Show you something, Lieutenant. I'll move real slow.' Messmore reached inside his dashiki and drew out a full clip of M-16 ammo. 'I switched an empty clip for this.'

Buckmaster pointed the M-16 between the two men and pulled the trigger. An empty click. Messmore shook his head sadly, then brightened.

'Got to hand it to you, though, loot, you're a real swinger.' He nodded at Buckmaster's start. 'Yeah. Some of those sensors see and don't give away that they see. Take a look around that partition.'

Buckmaster stepped around the dinette and came face to face with a sophisticated communications console. One monitor showed the cab of the six-by-six. He walked back slowly to find Messmore playing *sommelier*. Messmore smiled, concentrating.

'The champagne cork must come out gently, like a sigh.'

The cork came out like a sigh. He filled the three glasses.

Buckmaster let out an ungentle sigh and folded into the empty chair. He gulped his drink down and saw Messmore wince and look his pain at Flugel.

'All right, you two. What the hell is this all about?'

'Money, man, money.' Messmore took a connoisseurish sip. 'Relax, Lieutenant. Give the man a hot towel, Talley. A hot towel before meals relaxes you. Picked that up in Japan. Stirs memories of mammaries, I guess; takes you back to mama's nice warm breast.'

'Never mind that. Just tell me before I explode.' Talley. That was something new. Was that Oscar Flugel's real name?

Flugel wiped his mouth with a cloth napkin. 'Frankly, Lieutenant, if you had died on us, that would have been ideal. But you're alive and well and in Fort Benning. That still leaves you in a bind, because here you've been executive officer of the Tenth Experimental Company for well over a week and you have a nice fat bank account that opened on the day you went on the roster, proving you threw in with us as soon as you found out our racket. Be mighty hard for you to blow the whistle now. So make yourself at home, Lieutenant. You're among friends. If you're friendly, we're friendly. If not, Okefenokee should've shown you we're playing for high stakes.'

Messmore forklifted a chunk of steak high in the air. 'Mighty high, Lieutenant.'

Buckmaster still did not know what the racket was, but he thought it would be nice to know who was in it.

'Who else is in this besides Lt Fiordaliso?' He saw them eye each other. 'What about Capt. Clapsaddle?'

Messmore almost choked on his bite, then swallowed it. 'Capt. *Romeo* Clapsaddle, Lieutenant. Yeah, he's in it. So are the whole two hundred men. Only you don't see them around, do you?'

Buckmaster stared at the two of them. They made quite a pair. Messmore had the kind of pleasant face that can quickly turn mean; Flugel had the kind of mean face that can quickly turn pleasant.

'Don't tell me you wasted all of them the way you tried to waste me?'

Messmore looked thoughtful. 'I suppose that would've been one way of doing it. But, no, we did it the easy way. Fort Zinderneuf without the bodies. Only punch cards. Talley here's the mastermind. You tell him, Talley.'

Talley told him. Talley's eyes shone in the telling.

All three were in the Personnel Service Division. Cpl Oscar Flugel was really Warrant Officer Marshall Talley; he headed the Military Pay Branch. Pfc./Sgt Miles 'Zulu' Messmore was really Warrant Officer Hannibal Zwinger; he headed the Machine Processing Unit of the Administrative Machine Branch. Lt Juliet Fiordaliso was Lt Juliet Fiordaliso; she headed the Personnel Records Branch. The three of them covered all loopholes.

The whole scheme stemmed from Par. 2-7, AR 37-104-2.

Officers and enlisted members in all grades may arrange for pay checks to be deposited to their accounts with a bank or savings institution by submitting a request for payment by check to the commanding officer for approval. The request must include the name and address of the bank; the account number, if any; and a statement that satisfactory arrangements have been made with the bank to accept such checks for deposit. The request will be forwarded to the members' personnel officer. A request for revocation of a previously designated bank or savings facility will be sent through the unit commander to the personnel officer. An officer or warrant officer may submit the completed forms directly to the personnel officer.

'We have set up in the computer a make-believe outfit with make-believe soldiers. Two hundred names on tape are collecting and depositing money that winds up in three – and now four – bank accounts.'

Buckmaster nodded, then frowned. 'Why Tenth *Experimental* Company?'

Talley smiled. 'That's in AR 37-104 too. Comes under incentive pay for hazardous duty. Experimental stress duty means a private under four months draws fifty dollars per month extra; and on up to an officer on pay grade 0-6, who draws two hundred and forty-five dollars per month extra.' He put his hand up. 'And that's not all. Any member of the Armed Forces who performs more than one type of hazardous duty essential to the unit's mission may receive double incentive pay. Man, every damn soldier in the Tenth receives double incentive pay. Lieutenant, you might like to know you're in the most hazardous outfit in the whole damn Army.'

It was Buckmaster's turn to smile. 'I knew that before I got here. What's the experimental stress duty we're supposed to be exposing ourselves to? Or is that make-believe too?'

Talley laughed. 'You know, nobody's come around and asked so far. But then no one's known about the Tenth so far.' He paused and frowned. 'I've been wondering how come out of the blue they assigned you.'

'Maybe I'll tell you some time. But go on.'

'Well, I planned in depth for that contingency. Show him, Zulu.'

Zulu shoved himself away from the table and left them alone for a moment. He came back carrying a pair of jump boots with the look of platform shoes till Buckmaster saw that the extra-thick white soles clamped on. He handed them to Buckmaster.

Buckmaster shook his head. 'You're showing me, but what are you showing me?'

'Lieutenant, if you think I'd go out there and jump any time, much less on a full stomach, just to show you, you're crazy. You saw that tower out there? You see this pair of shoes? Put one and two together, and you'll see.'

Talley jumped in. 'It's simple, Lieutenant. You know how many paratroopers there are who break their leg bones and smash their feet? Even in practice jumps? I call these Crushees. They're a crumple foam that takes most of the shock of landing. They clip on like skis. Once you land you throw them away. That's what the Tenth is testing if anyone asks.' He took them from Buckmaster and fondled them wistfully. His face warmed. 'But nobody will. I keyed into the computer that it report any inquiry about the Tenth and any travel orders or tours of inspection scheduled for the same. Nobody takes us by surprise; we'll just fold up our tents.'

He gave Buckmaster a sly look. 'Got a printout on you soon as we got word you were coming, Lieutenant. Do you know your file is flagged? You're under a constant security check because of your father.'

Buckmaster's face burned. He remembered the look Col. Fubb had given Lt Landtroop. They weren't to trust him with knowledge of TOTE – whatever TOTE was. Fubb the cuckold and Landtroop the sin of commission. All right, if that was the way the Army played, FTA – and he didn't mean Free Time Association. He was in it with these bastards, and not just because he seemed to have no choice. But even they would have to watch out. He was in it for himself.

But how smug they seemed. Do them and him good if he shook them up some. The walkie-talkie hung at his side. He swung it up and spoke into it. They would not know it was off.

'Bravo One to Bravo Base. Now that you have all that, you know how to proceed. Out.'

He switched from off to receive, sleight of hand to cinch the effect.

In a smooth flow of movement Messmore–Zwinger grabbed the M-16 Buckmaster had set down, switched the full clip for the empty, and took a stand at one side of the door.

'Take it easy, Talley. We have a hostage.'

The hostage poured himself another glass of champagne and took a sip.

Talley looked pale and shrunken. His voice was a whisper.

'You're CID. I knew it. I knew this would happen if we played out our string too long.' His face went pleasant and his whisper persuasive. 'Look Lieutenant, nobody got hurt. We've scored big. Millions. We can make a deal before they get here. Listen –'

The walkie-talkie crackled with Maj. Gen. Reeber Battle's cold anger. Buckmaster could almost see the general's chin going double as he deepened his voice. 'Cpl Oscar Flugel, I shall find you. And when I do I promise you the *fairest* court-martial the Army has ever seen.'

Buckmaster eyed Flugel–Talley's distorted face through the champagne glass. The man had grown paler and more shrunken.

'Yes, take it easy, Talley. I only wanted to get some of my own back at you. The general thinks *I'm* Cpl Oscar Flugel. I took your name in vain. The blood in his eye is for me.'

He turned his head to watch Messmore–Zwinger bring the M-16 to bear on him. The man's brow pleated. His eyes glittered as though from inner flashes.

'You oughtn't to get me this excited, Lieutenant. I get these migraines.' He held still as the infantryman statue, then slowly lowered the M-16. He squeezed water out of his eyes, then wiped them with a thumb and forefinger. His mien faded to a pleasanter pleasant than Talley's. 'Hand me the walkie-talkie, Lieutenant.' When he had it he dropped it and stomped it useless. 'Don't want them getting a fix on us by accident or otherwise. Make my own accident.'

Buckmaster studied Zwinger. It was easier to think of him as Zulu.

'Zulu, you'd better shave off your beard. I set the whole post to looking for a big black with a beard.'

Zulu's grin spread the beard. His hand made a magician's pass and peeled off the beard. 'Why wait?' His grin spread chipmunk cheeks. 'Here's the naked truth. The way I am when I'm on duty at the Machine Processing Unit.'

That started a train of thought in the dark tunnels of Buckmaster's mind. 'Yes, what about duty? How are you two free to run around?'

Talley was back in control of himself and the situation. 'We don't usually. Running the Tenth takes only a weekend now and then. But soon as we got word of your coming, we both took our furloughs to be free to handle you.' He eyed Buckmaster and his face twitched. 'You know, Lieutenant, in a way I'm glad you're in this with us now. We draw our millions without the Army wondering about an extra two hundred men, but we haven't figured a way of phasing it out. If two hundred men go over the hill together, or if a phony case of food poisoning or epidemic of spinal meningitis wastes them, or if a bogus bomb wipes out their base, the Army will wonder.'

'Great. And I'm supposed to help you sweat that out?'

'You may not like us, Lieutenant, but you'll sure love the money. Now you're here you can man the Tenth full time. True, you lost your papers, but the computer don't know that. Not much for you to do. Only convince the computer the Tenth is a real Army unit. That means it has the regulation number of fuckups. Right, Zulu? That's the part Zulu likes, playing God. Let's show the lieutenant how it works.'

They adjoined to the communications section of the van. Zulu sat down at the computer terminal. He raised the roster of the Tenth Experimental Company on the screen.

Buckmaster read the name above his own and shook his head. 'Did you have to name him Romeo Clapsaddle?'

Zulu laughed. 'That's Juliet Fiordaliso's dream man. She didn't like it either.' He rubbed his hands. 'Speaking of courts-martial, like Old Rivet Divot just was, we got to dish out punishment as well as reward. See, we programmed the computing of required time in pay grade; automatic promotions and pay increases follow. But we still have to keep up the look of a going outfit – soldiers after all do fuck up. The roster won't pass muster if it stays nice and fuckless month after month.'

He began tapping away as he spoke. 'I think we'll have to bust Sgt Bannerman one grade for inefficiency, though I hate to do it to a member of the cadre. I think we'll promote Cpl Warmath in his place. We'll redline Pfc. Saladino this month. And let's see, we Article 15 a few others at random, and that does it.' Zulu cleared the screen. 'Any questions, Lieutenant?'

'What happened to the former XO?'

Talley took it. 'The same orders that transferred you here called for him to present himself at the Pentagon for reassignment. But we told the computer he had a prior commitment to death. Poor guy died testing Crushees.'

Zulu took it from there. 'Yeah, he was a psycho. Got up in the middle of the night yelling "Geronimo!" and climbed the tower and jumped from the top platform. Only Talley has it wrong, the guy didn't stop to put on his Crushees.'

Talley looked annoyed. 'It's not that I have it wrong, it's just part of the cover up. We fixed it so he died in line of duty.'

Buckmaster smiled. They nearly had him believing them. They smiled and Talley's smile grew sly.

'That's another moneymaker. The next of kin of each man is one of our bank accounts. I told you this is the most hazardous company in the Army. You'd never guess how many lives the Tenth has given to its country.'

No doubt Col. Fubb had guessed – or thought he guessed.

Buckmaster eyed the two men. 'What started you on this?'

Talley's smile faded. 'I wasn't able to swing the down payment on a farm I had my eye on to retire to. After twenty years I felt I rated something better than that. So I set up my own little equity funding.'

Zulu nodded, but kept his smile. 'The Man owes me one too. Better to scuffle for pennies than to fight for The Man for nickles and dimes, my granny always told me. But I say it's still better to do The Man out of the sawbucks.'

Now both eyed Buckmaster and it was Talley's turn to ask.

'What do you say, Lieutenant? How do you feel about it?'

'*Viel besser*: lots better. But after all I've been through I want a full and equal share.'

'I have to say it, Lieutenant, you're cool.'

'Any cooler, he'd be dead.' Zulu looked at Buckmaster but spoke to Talley. 'But *I* got the feeling he's still in the open field.'

Buckmaster's jaw went lumpy. Then he smiled it smooth. 'What do you want? A blood oath?'

Talley's hand moved placatingly. 'Just your word. The word of an officer and a gentleman. Are you with us?'

'I thought you'd never ask. Many's the saint who'd've sold his soul to the devil – only the devil wasn't buying. And I'm no saint.'

They shook on it.

Talley opened a closet, baring a wardrobe of uniforms bearing assorted rank, and lifted a flap of flooring and worked the combination of a floor safe. He handed Buckmaster a thick wad.

'Here you go, Lieutenant. Some walking-around money. Eat, drink, and bank Mary.'

The new smoothness of his fingertips made it hard to riffle through. He settled for hefting. A few thousand dollars at least. He would have to spend it to prove his good faith. He grinned. That seemed far from the worst of fates.

Zulu's brow suddenly pleated. His eyes registered inner lightning flashes. 'My granny always told me, "Don't chain your dog with links of sausage."' Buckmaster didn't know if that was Zulu or Zulu's migraine talking, but this latest of Zulu's mood shifts chilled Buckmaster. Zulu calmed just as suddenly, though he raised a clenched fist. 'But I'm getting out June eighteenth. You'll be all Talley's lookout after that.'

They returned to the table and killed the bottle. The bubbles had got fewer, but this still looked to be the life. He could get up when he pleased and knock off when he pleased and do nothing in between. All furlough. A solid gold brick.

Only one thing he had to worry about – that the others would leave him holding the bag.

17. REQAURQN REQUEST AUTHORITY TO REQUISITION

Two goldbricking GIs, Zulu and Talley, stiff with effort and care, were marching in step a dozen feet apart pretending to tote a big sheet of glass. A third GI, Buckmaster himself, reading a letter fresh from mail call, a letter written on red drawers, walked through between them unseeing.

Buckmaster woke to find Zulu standing over him. Buckmaster had been bunking down luxuriously in the van for three days and nights now, catching up on sleep and getting the hang of the operation. Zulu and Talley had left him on his own much of the time. They were making the most of what remained of their furloughs. At the moment, shades and a mustache changed Zulu into someone neither Messmore nor Zwinger. He seemed to be in his good mood.

'Come to take the six-by-six out for a run to the Atlanta Army Supply Depot. Got anything you want to add to our shopping list?'

Buckmaster put his hands behind his head and lay back thinking. He rolled his head no. 'Can't think of a thing.'

'Maybe you want to ride into Columbus with me? I'll drop you off and pick you up on my way back.'

Buckmaster had planned to immure himself till he had total control of the SOP. He had already found that the payroll was only a spit in the ocean to what was available. Talley had managed to patch the console into AUTODIN, the Department of Defense's worldwide communications network that interchanged data involving finance, personnel, logistics, intelligence, and operational management information for the Army, Navy, Air Force, and other defense agencies. And with the Tenth Experimental company field-testing and evaluating products of the Pentagon's Advanced Research Projects Agency, they had access to nonaccountable funds. He felt sure there was more to learn.

But the sun had rolled a golden carpet all the way in through the door. Besides, they wanted him to spend his wad. Besides, he had to get to know Zulu. First thing a soldier does before he cleans a rifle is look at the number to make sure he's cleaning his own. First thing an officer does on assuming command is have a friendly chat with his top kick. Besides, another bird with the same stone, he'd take Joe Dee's uniform back to the guy. Early for Dee to be there but he'd find Sally. He smiled thinking of the look on Kaster's face when Lt Stonewall J. Buckmaster walked in. He got up.

'You can drop me off at the FTA coffeehouse. I think you know where it is.'

'Believe I do.' Zulu handed him a new ID. 'You're Lt Buckmaster, but not of the Tenth Experimental. The Tenth X has to exist only in the computer, dig it? You're XO of a 29th Infantry headquarters company. You don't have to wait on me. You have your own transportation. You can jeep in and out of the Reservation whenever you like. Anybody asks, you're checking up on bivouacs.'

'I'll ride in with you this time.'

'Okay. I'll have the six-by-six gassed up time you're ready.'

Zulu was putting empty jerry cans in the back of the truck when Buckmaster came out. Buckmaster hopped into the cab.

'Let's get this thing rolling.'

He spoke lightly, but now Zulu was in his bad mood.

'Hustlers don't call showdowns.' Zulu climbed in slowly and pointed his index finger at Buckmaster and cocked his thumb. 'Don't think because we didn't finish you off in the swamp we're afraid to. Give us any flak and we will. Same goes if we find out you're shucking us.' He settled in and got the thing rolling. 'I tried to play The Man's game his way. Now I do it my way. And it's paying off. Money don't get everything, it's true, but what it don't get I can't use. So if you make yourself worrisome or troublesome, you better make yourself scarce.'

Damn Zulu and his short fuse. Just when he had begun to like the man in spite of himself. If anyone had cause for anger it was Buckmaster. Sooner or later his own anger at Zulu would surface, and they would have it out. Even if not, sooner or later Zulu would turn on him. There ought to be some way of getting an edge over Zulu against that time of reckoning.

'Yeah.' Zulu took savage pleasure in his pain. 'I'm feeling real evil.' Zulu's writhing temples looked real evil. 'Migraine.'

'That's an increment of excrement. It's all in your mind.'

'Don't tell me my illness is an illusion, or you'll wake up trying to tell yourself your death is a delusion.'

'Sure, the suffering is real enough. I know about migraine because my mother was a sufferer.'

'You don't know about it when it's yourgraine not mygraine.'

'I've read up on it. Ever think of trying biofeedback?'

'How would it apply?'

'You psych yourself. If you have an ulcer, you use biofeedback to train your mind to control the amount of gastric juices your stomach secretes. Should work for migraines. Tension is a beta-rhythm state. Relaxed alertness is an alpha-rhythm state. You'd learn to induce alpha rhythms. And whenever you feel tension coming on, you'd switch to alpha.'

'Man, I'll try anything. How do I start?'

'Think the Atlanta Army Supply Depot carries biofeedback machines?'

'Carries everything from The Pill to autopsy saws, from tent poles to field hospitals.' Zulu's good mood returned.

Unable to find a parking slot nearer the F T A coffeehouse, Zulu pulled up alongside a NO PARKING HERE TO CORNER sign.

Buckmaster smiled. A minor infraction alongside their major larcenies, but all the same . . . 'Don't you see the sign?'

Zulu got out, bent the perforated steel standard back and forth in the concrete footing till it snapped, and tossed it aside.

'What sign?'

Buckmaster climbed out carrying Dee's rolled-up uniform and walked Zulu to the FTA coffeehouse.

The door opened but the place was silent and looked empty. Then Sally Kaster stepped out of the back room. She added another smudge to her brow and leaned against the doorway. She stared at the two of them, at Buckmaster's lieutenancy and Zulu's beardless MP-lessness, then shook her head and found her voice.

'I'm all right, it's just that I, you know, sometimes see things.'

'So does the lieutenant. He thought he saw a sign.'

'Borrow your typewriter, Sally?'

She had another spell of wordlessness and waved them in.

Zulu drew a requisition form from his breast pocket and rolled it in the typewriter. Buckmaster saw a Lt S. J. Buckmaster had signed the form. Zulu looked at Buckmaster.

'Machine, biofeedback, right?'

'Should do. You can fill in the model number when you get there. And get a good pocket flashlight for me.'

'What for?'

'All the light I have out there is in the van. Suppose there's a blackout? What if the Army, not knowing you tied the van's umbilical to the power line, says let there be darkness, cuts it off for some reason?'

'It won't.' But Zulu shrugged. 'Costs me nothing, don't know why I'm arguing.'

He typed in one dozen flashlights, pocket, complete with batteries. He stopped himself from rolling the form and its carbons out.

'Damn, I almost forgot. Fiordaliso wants chocolate and peanut butter. Bet I know why I disremembered. I love both – and I have to steer clear of both account of my migraine. Yeah, and hair spray. Wonder why I disremembered that?'

He typed the items in rapidly, fingers heavy on the keys. His migraine had started again, and Buckmaster was glad to see him go.

Kaster put her hands on her hips and winged out her elbows. She wore a yellow sweater and the stance and her slenderness shaped her into a danger sign on a post.

'All right now, Wallstone, maybe you'll make it all clear to me.'

'Sure. But first, I came back to repay a loan.'

He had noted a cot in the corner of the room, and he locked the front door – Dee had not yet fixed the one to the back room – and occupied her too much for questioning. Or thought he had. Her dreaminess faded and she shoved up and away.

'All right, Wallstone. Now.' But her glance fell on the desk and she looked guiltily defiant. 'Maybe I ought to tell you something first.' She handed him a sheet of copy for the coming issue of FTA. 'Joe didn't want to mention the name Tenth Experimental Company because they might get him for breach of national security – *real* national security, you know, not Nixon national security. So we're making it a blind item.'

He read the copy where she pointed: *The question of the week. What experimental unit at Ft Benning is posing a threat to the ecosystem?*

His grin both nettled and encouraged her. 'Now you. Why are you and that soldier running around in disguise so buddy-buddy now and so enemy-enemy before?'

'It was a security foulup. I guess Joe told you I went to see the general? Well, I spoke to him and cleared it all up.'

She looked doubtful but moved on to her next question. 'What *does* the Tenth Experimental do?'

'What does the Tenth X do?' He was stalling and knew it and knew that she knew it. Crushees seemed too tame, not destructive enough of the environment. As long as there would be a blind item anyway, might as well go the whole hog and give her a good Hitchcockian McGuffin. 'If I tell you will you watch out how you word it? Because Joe's right to be careful. It *is* a matter of *real* national security.'

She nodded and he went on.

'The Soviets have a carbon-dioxide laser. It can take out incoming missiles up to three hundred miles away.' That much was true – or at least that much he had read. Now he was winging it. 'Our comeback is something that bounces the laser beam right back. It's a coating material we call Mirrorite. Mirrorite is everywhere reflective. You can't work it with an ordinary laser, much less penetrate it.' He eyed his fingertips ruefully. 'Rough stuff to handle.' He looked up at her with a brave smile. 'I can't tell you any more than that.'

'I understand, Jackson.'

She took his hands in hers and kissed the fingertips. He drew her back down on the cot. This time it was not merely to occupy her. He felt himself beginning to feel something real for her and so for himself.

When he looked at the hour again, he disengaged himself and got up. Still plenty of time before Zulu came back to pick him up, but the troops would be showing up soon, and a lieutenant couldn't very well hang around an EM's hangout. He repaid her the ten and left a thousand for the cause. Still speechless, she saw him to the door.

As he reached the corner and glanced at the fallen sign, a horn honked. Zulu back already for the honky? Car horn rather than truck horn, though, and it didn't have to be for him; he wasn't the only one on the street. He turned the corner, and the honking followed close behind him.

He didn't look around. He hated for someone to blow a horn at him even to warn him. Let the driver speak to him as human to human, not as powerful machine to vulnerable human. The machine insisted. He stopped and turned.

Oh, no.

18. MOS   MILITARY OCCUPATIONAL SPECIALITY

Oh, yes.

Blonde poodle curls. Blue glitter on the eyelids. Maggie Fubb.

Her open convertible pulled up and he got in. She offered her cheek, then changed her mind and withdrew it.

'Who was that freaky stringbean?'

'How'd you happen to find me?'

'No happen about it. I've been riding around town for days trying to spot you. I helloed the Fort first thing, and what a runaround. Nobody's heard of the Tenth Experimental Company. Stupid girl lieutenant in Personnel claims there's no Lt Buckmaster at Benning. But I knew damn well you were down here. So I've been staying at a motel and asking around. And riding around trying to spot you.'

'How did you know damn well?'

'Lt Landtroop. You know him? I twisted it out of him.'

He looked at her as she drove. How would she have gone to work on Landtroop? Her serene profile stayed serene, just a slight thrust of the jaw.

'Who is she?' Maggie sounded too offhand.

'She's on the staff of the FTA – an underground sheet. You know the sort of thing: very antiestablishment, loves to knock the Army. I went there trying to learn how they got wind of the Tenth X. We got a tip they're printing a blind item about it. It could be a serious breach of security.'

'Oh.' Maggie's face reddened and her voice shook with rage. 'I don't know what's got into kids these days. No loyalty, no patriotism.'

Maggie on loyalty made him think of Col. Fubb. How was good old

Max coming along with his precious TOTE? And what in hell was TOTE? Maybe he could pump Maggie. He suddenly realized that what he was eyeing now wasn't simply the bunching up of her dress. He stared. How had she had blown up seven months' worth in two weeks?

She caught him in the corner of her eye and laughed. She patted her belly. 'At ease, in there. I swear it's wearing combat boots.' She laughed again, a bit shortly. 'Don't worry, it isn't your kid. It isn't anyone's.'

'Parthenogenesis?'

'What's that?'

'The next best thing to propinquity.'

'Wait till we're in my motel room and I'll show you.'

It proved to be an egg-shaped satin pillow with ribbon trim that tied around.

'A pregnancy puff. A put-on. Folks just love to help corner a rat who's run out on his girl.' She untied it and *embonpoint* no longer came between them. 'What were you saying about propinquity?'

'I don't know if I'm up to it, Maggie.'

Her eyes narrowed, and he knew they were replaying the freaky string-bean. He held up his hands to show his fingertips.

'I've been in an accident.'

'Oh, you poor boy. But you don't need your hands now, darling. Here, let me.' She tore at the buttons of his jacket. One flew off. 'I'll sew it on later.'

Later would have to wait awhile. Sex came first, pillow talk came second.

'Poor Stoney. Tell me about the accident. It happen in your work with the Tenth Experimental?'

He told her about Mirrorite. Her interest encouraged him to embellish. Mirrorite acquired the property of so altering any laser beam bouncing off it that the laser beam transformed what it touched on the way back into a spot of antimatter that exploded because of its ambience.

She frowned. 'What does that mean?'

'Means any laser gun that shoots at our Mirrorite-coated missiles or planes blows up.'

'That could really decide an all-out war, couldn't it?'

'You bet it could.'

'How operational is Mirrorite?'

'Sorry, Maggie.' It felt good to be gently firm. 'You know I can't tell even you. I've already told you more than I should've.'

Her frown cleared away and she kissed him. 'No, I'm the one who's sorry, Stoney.' She rose. 'You stay put, dear, while I sew on the button.'

He started to doze off, then remembered. 'Maggie.'

'Hmmm?'

'Maybe you can tell me something. What do you know about TOTE?'

'TOTE? Never heard of it.' If her voice had gone flat, that might have been because he had caught her in the middle of biting off the thread.

19. BIOLDEF   BIOLOGICAL DEFENSE

Talley picked him up in the morning. Buckmaster had walked from the motel to a pay phone in the heart of town, called Fort Benning, got through to Lt Fiordaliso and asked her to pass the word for Zulu or Talley to pick him up.

Talley looked surly, greeting him with only a nod. He pulled the jeep away with a jerk before Buckmaster fairly settled himself.

'You had us shitting bricks, Lieutenant.'

'Gold bricks, I'm sure.'

'When Zulu stopped by to pick you up and you weren't there and nobody knew where you were – I'm telling you. What happened?'

'I met an old friend.'

'I hope she was worth it. You should've let us know you were going to be out all night.'

'I'm not standing still for bed check, Charlie. I'm an equal partner, remember?'

'Yeah, and an officer and a gentleman. You remember this, Buckmaster. I'm not your chauffeur. If anyone pulls rank, I do.'

Suddenly Talley cut sharp left and then cut sharp right, took a short cut through a filling station, doubled back, pulled into an alley and watched the street.

'Someone after us?'

'Thought a red Chevy was tailing us.' He waited another minute, then got the jeep going again. 'If it was, we lost it.'

They rode the rest of the way in silence, Talley watching the rear-view mirror as much as the road ahead.

Zulu too looked surly but it was himself he was sore at. He had put himself to extra work by typing the wrong figures in the requisition, and cartons of Mist-Tress hair-spray canisters overflowed the supply room. He showed Buckmaster the one carton he had set aside for Lt Fiordaliso.

'Easier to take it all than say it was a mistake. But what we going to do with all that hair spray?'

'The devil made you do it. Wants you to finish his work and deplete the ozone.' Buckmaster was glad to see his package of pocket flashlights. It had struck him that Zulu might bring back a generator of their own instead. 'Forget the embarrassment of riches. You get the biofeedback machine?'

'Yeah, it's in the console section. Still in the crate. Sure hope it works because I feel that damn migraine coming on again.'

They moved forward in the van, and Zulu and Buckmaster unpacked the machine. Buckmaster spotted the sheet of directions and misdirected Zulu with a toss of wrapping while slipping it into his pocket.

'What pattern do you see when your migraine's about to begin?'

'Like a honeycomb design. How do you know I see a pattern?'

'That's from the firing of some visual cortex analyzer cells. My mother saw a sweeping arc.'

'I'm not your mother.'

'In a strangely endearing way you remind me of her.'

Zulu grimaced a grin. 'She could be evil too, huh?'

'She had her moments.'

Zulu pawed through the wrapping paper and the padding. 'Where's the poop sheet?'

'We don't need one. I know how the thing works.'

He wired Zulu up.

'You sure you know how the thing works?'

'You're going to learn to induce alpha rhythms at will. Look at the screen. See the pretty patterns? Think your hands warm ... Now think your hands cool ... See how the patterns change?'

The machine gave visual feedback – flashing colored lights – of the pattern of brain waves plus audio feedback – a pleasant tone that rose and fell in step with the EEG. Zulu fidgeted.

'Those spikes that drive into my brain?'

Buckmaster answered something absently. He had found the dysrhythmic EEG he had hoped for. It meant Zulu had a disposition to epilepsy.

'So far I'm only getting chickenfeedback.'

'You're doing fine. Keep it up. That's the pattern you want to get and hold on to.'

A dirty trick to play on the man. But no dirtier than Okefenokee.

In the short run it should do the man some good, the power of suggestion damping Zulu's migraine, making him think he felt less pain.

Talley looked in on them and watched till it got too boring for him. Then he went out, and Buckmaster heard the command car purr away, carrying Talley and his share of Zulu's haul.

Buckmaster thought ahead to tonight. That was as far ahead as a gold-bricker thought, he thought. He would rest up and man the fort awhile – they were the same thing – then jeep into town. Only one problem.

Maggie or Sally?

Or Juliet?

Maybe he should get to know Lt Juliet Fiordaliso better. Was that the real reason he had called her this morning? She had sounded warmly conspiratorial. No; better keep business and pleasure separate. Maggie-or-Sally was problem enough. Everyone should have such problems.

Thinking of problems, now he had to look out for a red Chevy. If there had been a red Chevy. It might have been Talley's imagination. Or Talley's vindictiveness, Talley's way of putting fear into him.

He looked at Zulu patched into the machine.

'How do you feel? Better?'

'I don't know. Different, anyway.'

'Takes practice.'

'Yeah, I suppose.'

Buckmaster felt a twinge. He switched the machine off.

'That's more than enough for your first try.'

20. FUPOSAT FOLLOW UP ON SUPPLY ACTION TAKEN

A fly graphed a bad year – for itself? the motel? the guests? – on the outside of the window screen. Buckmaster looked down at the bathroom sink. A bubble had uddered under the mouth of the faucet; it stretched without breaking, vibrating rapidly as the drops dripped from it.

The toothbrush was his. The toothpaste was theirs, his and Maggie's. He eyed the toothpaste tube. There had to be something Freudian in the way women squeezed it in the middle as against the way men milked it. He replaced the fluted fez on the tube.

Something was wrong. He had been putting off facing up to it. Maggie touched things, touched people, to make sure they were real; maybe to make sure she was real, to draw some of their reality to herself. He had felt a new nervousness in her touch since his returning for another night of love.

Love. He wasn't sure what he felt for her. Love? Love is a social disease, both immunizing and fatal. If you give yourself to love, you give yourself to both life and death. Had they given themselves to hate? Same mixture, different tincture.

The something that was wrong reflected itself in Maggie's eyes. There's an embarrassment when you keep running into someone you've said farewell to. Was that what he'd seen in her eyes when he'd returned? They had said farewell once. He hadn't forgotten the quiddity of her spitting at him and she hadn't forgotten the why.

Last night there had been a fight. 'Maggie the camp follower.' He still thought he had said it tenderly, but maybe there are words you can't say tenderly. Maggie had flung on her maxicoat and swept out. Had slammed out of the motel room – or would have but for the automatic door-closer that took its own good time. Running after her to bring her back, he had found her already coming back, remembering the room wasn't his but hers. Anger turned to laughter. And whatever it was he felt for her had been deeper and better.

'Do you have to go, Stoney? Back to the Tenth Experimental?'

He had to go, but not to the Tenth X. To the FTA coffeehouse to see Sally. To see whether what he felt for the one stood up in the face of what he felt for the other. He came out of his study and out of the bathroom and smiled gravely down at Maggie in bed.

'Duty.'

'Duty. Always damn duty. First Max and now you.' Her face seemed awash with unshed tears.

'How is Max?'

'As well as you can expect of a corpse.'

Fubb hadn't been much good to her, but to call him a corpse ... Buckmaster turned but her voice followed.

'I'm not being bitchy. He died a week ago. Heart attack. TOTE was too much for him.'

Buckmaster was still struggling with Col. Fubb's death, and TOTE almost got by him. 'I thought you never heard of –'

The tears were no longer unshed. 'Max is dead. I don't have anyone.'

'You have me.' The words dragged out.

'No, Stoney. It's over for us, no matter what I say or do now.'

He felt a mix of release and pique but had to make a show of something neither. 'What do you mean, over?'

'I'm a sleeper.'

Buckmaster grinned uneasily. He wouldn't ask if she meant she was promiscuous. If camp follower had set her off . . .

'You think I was an army brat like you, Stoney, but I wasn't. My parents took on American identities and merged into American life and brought me up to keep my Soviet loyalties always in the background against . . . now.'

He could feel his mind stretch, protein synthesize, synapses thicken. There was some kind of showdown. TOTE was its name. He moved nearer to shake TOTE out of her but stopped.

She had reached for her pregnancy puff, and a gun had flashed into her hand. The slit in the back of the puff had shown itself only when her hand thrust through and drew out the .22 that held him still.

'Poor Max. Did you think I wanted to be an easy lay?'

She was looking at Buckmaster and he shook his head for Max and himself. That seemed to satisfy her.

'That's right. I did it for my country. Only now I'm awaking into a nightmare. Which is my country?' She stared at Buckmaster and shook her head. 'No, not poor Max: old Max never knew. Poor Stoney. Those poor FTA kids. Poor me.'

She touched the reality of the gun to her temple and pulled the trigger. Her head fell back upon the pillow. She might have been sleeping but for the black ring and the blood rose.

He shook her. 'What is TOTE?'

Maggie was. *Tod.*

Nothing he could do for her, nothing she could do for him. He slipped out. No sweat, though he felt the film of cold sweat. If anyone had heard the gunshot, television or backfire had subsumed it.

Poor FTA kids? He jeeped toward the FTA coffeehouse.

The red blur far ahead in traffic could have been a red Chevy, but it had too much of a lead; and though he ran a red light, he found he had lost it when he reached the corner where it had turned off.

21. MOP   MUSTERING OUT PAY

In the back room of the actionless coffeehouse flies were having a very busy season. Sally Kaster and Joe Dee sat dead, wire binding them to chairs. The stink of loosened sphincters filled the air. Poor little shit machines. Person or persons unknown had tried to make them talk before they died.

Talk about something they did not know. The Tenth X's whereabouts?

Buckmaster's temples drummed. Talley hadn't been lying about shaking pursuit. Had Maggie's friends sought to pick up the trail here?

Why the Tenth X? Where did it fit into TOTE?

He made himself look at the two. He could at least do them that small penance. He had been their link to death.

There was only one link here to the Tenth X. Chances were that person or persons unknown had got out of Joe Dee that Joe had spoken to Lt Fiordaliso on the phone to check out Jackson Wallstone and that the lieutenant had said there was no Tenth Experimental Company. Person or persons unknown would want to speak to Lt Fiordaliso in person.

They would be people who would not believe the phony story about Crushees or the true story about the fraud.

He had to hurry. But he stayed long enough to pick the thousand dollars he had given Sally from the pile of their belongings and pocket it. The serial numbers might run in the same series as the twenties he still possessed. He didn't want a Watergate-burglars tie-in to these deaths.

22. SITREP Advise by rapid means, citing this message, present situation of following unit

He pulled up at the nearest pay phone. Lt Fiordaliso recognized his voice, and hers took on the warm conspiratorial tone. He cut in.

'Listen, don't talk. This thing is blowing up. We all have to meet. If Zulu and Talley aren't at the van, tell them to get there on the double. Leave your office right now, leave HQ building. Give any excuse. Be careful. If you see a red Chevy on the post, don't let it see you. If you don't believe me, Talley knows about that. I'll pick you up at the PX. Look for me to come by in the jeep.'

He made a hanging-up sound by tapping the phone against the box and listened. Fiordaliso let out an uncertain breath. Her breathing firmed up, and he heard her say, 'Sergeant, I have to –' before she hung up.

For someone whose big score and whole career stood in danger Fiordaliso seemed strangely amused when he picked her up. She eyed him sidewise as he sped them toward Outpost No. 1.

'Did you knock her up? The bleached-out blonde? You know she came here looking for you and for the Tenth X.'

'I know. No. She wore a pregnancy puff.'

'Oh.' Fiordaliso blinked, at the words, the toneless way he said them, or both. 'I thought that might be why this thing is blowing up, that you and she had a lovers' quarrel or a lovers' heart-to-heart and you said too much.'

'Nothing like that.'

'Then like what?'

'Tell you when we're all together.'

The mirror shared his gaze with the road, and Fiordaliso sat back away from him.

Zulu in his dashiki and slippers sat staring at the visual feedback of his brain waves, and Talley paced the console section. Talley stopped and glared at Buckmaster and Fiordaliso.

'This better be bad.'

Buckmaster nodded reassuringly. 'It is.'

Fiordaliso spotted the carton of Mist-Tress hair spray canisters and turned to Zulu, who was unhooking himself from the biofeedback machine.

'Good. You got it.'

'And a hell of a lot more.' Zulu grinned dazedly. 'For hair to eternity.'

Buckmaster swelled. 'For God's sake, you people. This is serious.'

Fiordaliso flushed. 'I'm only trying to hold on to banality.' She half smiled with a half shrug. 'I mean, after all, if the whole thing's blowing up, what else is left?'

Talley snorted. 'Let's have it, Buckmaster.'

'We're in the middle of something with the code name TOTE.'

'Never heard of it.'

'Our friends in the red Chevy have. That's why they're after us.'

'Who are they?'

'The Soviets.'

'You got red on the brain, Lieutenant. I figure our friends for the CID.'

Buckmaster nodded toward the computer terminal. 'Check it out and see. TOTE is a war-room program.'

Talley sat down at the keyboard, then shook his head. 'The box? I'm not messing with that.'

'Can you do it?'

'At HQ, I replaced the correct monitor with a rigged monitor of my own, which has special ins for unauthorized parties, but –'

'Skip the tech talk. Can you do it?'

Talley sweated. 'I can override the run of systems security measures, but you need passwords and terminal identification.'

'Then try.'

Zulu's brow creased. 'Get on with it, Talley. We got to know one way or the other.'

Talley looked at Fiordaliso. She nodded. He shook his head again but poised his fingers over the keys. 'All right, wise guy, give me a terminal identification. The box isn't going to deal with just anyone.'

Buckmaster eased his breath out and nodded. 'We'll be a CIA link.'

'Fine. But what's our code name?'

Buckmaster smiled tightly. 'It has to be something stupid enough for the spooks to think they're being clever. Like the way they call themselves The Company because *Cía* is the Spanish abbreviation for company.'

'Do I try Company?'

Talley wasn't being serious, but Buckmaster mused as though taking him seriously.

'Negative. Must be a *bit* more subtle. Let's see, the CIA's at Langley. L'Anglais. The Englishman. Limey? Limehouse? Try Lime and see what happens.'

'Sure you want to? We can make only one slipup – two at the most – then the security people will be on to us.'

'Proceed.'

Talley tapped keys.

login tl lime

Response came rapidly, letters glowing on the screen.

SORRY. PLEASE REPEAT

Talley lit up. 'We're on the right track, Lieutenant. It thinks we dropped – or it lost – a letter or a syllable. Which to do we try? Limey or Limehouse?'

Buckmaster wavered. Limey or Limehouse? And now that he thought of it, it could even be Blimey. No, the CIA would opt for elegance. 'Limehouse.'

login tl limehouse

The display cleared, making way for a number burst.

1208 37

Buckmaster followed Talley's glance at the clock and saw it was just eight minutes and thirty-seven seconds past twelve noon.

'By God, we're in. It's logged us in. What now, Lieutenant? What do we ask for?' Talley's fingers played the air above the keys.

'Go for broke. Ask for TOTE.'

tote

WARNING/WARNING - SPECAT-WARNING/WARNING

Talley locked eyes with Buckmaster. Both read that both knew SPECAT was a marking to identify information so sensitive as to require special access and safeguarding procedures. Buckmaster made himself shrug.

'We're CIA, aren't we? So we have COSMIC clearance.'

Talley gave a shrug of his own, but his face was tight and shiny.

proceed

The readout manifested: virtually instantaneously.

TOTE WARNING/WARNING - SPECAT - TOP SECRET DATA TO FOLLOW. TABULATION OF TOTAL EXCHANGE KEY NAME: CALL NAME TOTE.

start read and print data

START START READ AND PRINT DATA

TOTE

UP-TOTE

print tote and up-tote

TOTE KEY NAME TABULATION OF TOTAL EX-CHANGE, ULTIMATE MINIMAX WAR GAME VIA MOLINK. THE SUPER-POWERS CAN NO LONGER SUSTAIN A ZERO-SUM WORLD. NEITHER CAN THE WORLD SUSTAIN ALL-OUT WAR. TOTE WILL PEACEFULLY DETERMINE WHICH IS TO RULE THE WORLD – THE US OR THE USSR. TOTE HAS TAKEN FOUR YEARS TO SET UP AND WILL TAKE SIX MONTHS TO PLAY. ELECTRONIC SYMBOLS REPRESENTING MISSILES, BOMBERS, DECOYS, INTERCEPTORS, AND ELEMENTS OF OTHER WEAPONS SYSTEMS, ARE ON MAGNETIC TAPE. THE TWO SIDES PLAY THE GAME BY FEEDING PUNCH CARDS WITH INSTRUCTIONS INTO THE MACHINES. FORCES TO BE COMMITTED BY BOTH SIDES, ALL. TABULATION OF THE SPECIFIC RESULTS WILL BE COMPLETE BY FOUR SLASH SEVEN SLASH SEVEN SIX BUT WILL REMAIN SECRET TO FORESTALL UNREST AND UPRISINGS. HOWEVER, THE TWO SIDES HAVE AGREED TO ABIDE BY THE OUTCOME AND WILL WORK IN

GOOD FAITH BEHIND THE SCENES TO GIVE ALL
POWER TO THE WINNER. END.
    UP-TOTE. SITREP AS OF FIVE SLASH FOUR
SLASH SEVEN SIX STANDOFF.
    END.
    The glowing upper-case letters stared at them. Talley's lower-case
fingers hung still, unasking. Buckmaster saw the big picture while pieces
were still jiggling into place; MOLINK, for instance, was Moscow Link,
the room housing the hot line. Zulu hummed to himself. Fiordaliso
leaned against Buckmaster to see over his shoulder and seemed unaware
that her voice was warm in his ear and her form salient.
    'War is heck.'
    Buckmaster nodded absently, dully. The war room was where the
action was. How disheartening to be so far away from the center and
so small in the scheme of things.
    Sensors outside the compound set off the taped warning and lit up
the monitor. The four started: they had visitors.

23. REPCAT   REPORT CORRECTIVE ACTION TAKEN

One square near the perimeter, in the grid covering the compound and
a half klick out on all sides, showed an M-16 whose nearness to the sensor
all but blocked out its bearer, a man in Army fatigues. Another square,
on the other side of the firebreak, showed another man in Army fatigues,
also carrying an M-16.
    Fiordaliso pressed closer to peer. 'Ours?'
    Buckmaster shook his head. 'No insignia. But they're not Soviet
regulars – that would be against the rules. They'll be sleepers rather
than infiltrators.' He nodded to himself. 'What do you bet they'll pretend
to be FTA members to make this seem an internal matter.'
    Zulu cocked his head. 'Sounds like they're bringing up some heavy
stuff.'
    Talley listened. 'Roger. Too far away yet to pick up on the monitor.'
    The tower. Buckmaster wasn't ready to trust his fingers to the rungs.
He showed them to Zulu. 'Zulu, you just got volunteered. Climb the
tower and see what we're up against.'
    Zulu picked up a pair of binoculars and started out on the double,
stopped, grinned, kicked his slippers off, got the pair of Crushees-fitted
boots from the closet and put them on. Talley stayed at the monitor;
Buckmaster and Fiordaliso went to the door to watch Zulu, Buck-

master covering him with the M-16 – and, Buckmaster made sure, a full clip.

The jump tower rose in four sixteen-foot stages. Zulu flattened himself on the top platform and glassed the horizon. He fixed on a spot straight down the firebreak. His voice carried.

'They got one of those lemons – an M-551. About a klick away.' Then, 'Hey!'

It might be a lemon, the M-551 Sheridan armored reconnaissance assault vehicle that the sleepers had commandeered, but its gun-launcher had fired a Shillelagh eye-guide missile that gouged the tower just below the top platform and Zulu. A second shot took out the platform next below and tore away the rest of the ladder. Zulu lowered himself from the top platform, hung dangling, let go.

'Geronimo!'

Dashiki billowing, he landed in the sandbox like a crumpled butterfly. Then he stood up, with a smile of surprise. He unclamped the flattened Crushees and looked at them.

'The damn things work.'

Buckmaster scowled. Zulu's mind wasn't working. Buckmaster sent a burst into the air over Zulu's head. Fiordaliso gasped. Zulu hit the dirt. He glared across at Buckmaster, then grinned sheepishly, and nodded. It takes four seconds for a man to aim and fire. Zulu made it back to the van in three-second rushes. There was no further M-16 fire, though; the enemy hadn't yet reached the compound fence.

Talley had come running to the door, .45 in hand. Fiordaliso filled him in and he holstered his weapon. He made room for Zulu to pass inside, then put a hand on Buckmaster's shoulder to hold Buckmaster and, by the weight of it, himself. He looked pale.

'I hate to agree with you, Lieutenant, but that's not the CID. Whatever they are, let's get the hell out before they surround us.'

Zulu was getting the hell out of his dashiki and into insignialess fatigues. Without pausing, he nodded.

'Yeah. We got only ten minutes, fifteen minutes outside, before they do.'

Buckmaster tingled. Standoff. He almost laughed. He saw Fiordaliso stare at him, and his urge to laugh deepened. He had to be out of his mind to follow his own reasoning, but the nonexistent Tenth Experimental Company could tip the balance. He had to make them see it. If there was no time for that, he had to make them follow without seeing.

'Listen up. Let them surround us. They'll be the ones in a trap. We stand them off and call in an air strike. A few gunships, a few smart bombs, and it's all over. We win TOTE for our side.'

There was no almost about Talley's laugh. 'You're crazy. Just the three of us?'

Fiordaliso put chest out, pulled chin in. 'The four of us.'

Buckmaster grasped at that. 'And it's not just the four of us. It's the whole damn Tenth X. The enemy's expecting to find a whole two-hundred-man company. He won't rush us. We have time for that strike.'

Talley shook his head. 'You think Old Rivet Divot's going to stick his neck out on your say-so? You don't exist. The Tenth X doesn't exist.' He grinned. 'If he sends in a strike, it'll be to wipe out Cpl Oscar Flugel.'

'We go over his head. Talley, sit down at the keys and get through to the Joint Chiefs.'

Talley didn't bother to shake his head; the negative was in his face and voice. 'Even if we got through to them, would we get through to them? Time they believed us and reacted it *would* be all over. For us.'

Buckmaster blocked the doorway, M-16 relaxed-looking but ready. 'Sure, we could walk away ... crawl away ... and leave the Tenth X behind for the enemy to discover it's only a Potemkin village, nothing to worry about as far as TOTE's concerned. But here we have this one chance to do something big. Don't throw it away.'

Talley took a step toward him. 'I'm not throwing myself away. I'm above the battle. I can always make a deal.'

'Swiss numbered accounts? First thing the Reds will do if they win is lean on the Swiss to hand over all assets of US nationals. They'll take before you can offer to give.' Buckmaster smiled tightly at Talley. 'Above the battles are the vultures.'

Talley's face twisted. 'I remember Nam ... the brass in their command choppers four thousand feet above the grunts ... moving the grunts like toy soldiers. TOTE sounds like more of the same. To the brass on both sides we're electronic symbols. Pawns. And what the hell's so important about the Tenth that the fate of the world hangs on it? *Crushees*, for God's sake?'

Zulu looked up from zipping his fly. 'Well, they do work.'

Buckmaster's cheek twitched. Take too long to tell them about Mirrorite. 'Just being an unknown factor is enough. What's so important about the Tenth is that they think it's important.'

Talley took another step. 'Yeah? Well, being a pawn has its redeeming features. We can pass the buck to the brass. Let them fight it out. Step aside, Lieutenant.'

Zulu moved up beside Talley. 'Yeah. Up your rear echelon, Buckmaster. Why should I risk my beautiful skin to help beat the Reds? To save us for the shitstorm: the breakup of America? If you want to play tin soldier, that's your weight. Me, I'm splitting.'

The van went dark and humless.

'They cut the line!'

'Jump him, Zulu!'

Zulu flashed a grin. 'I won't jump – got no more Crushees.'

Buckmaster watched Zulu stride toward him. Swiftly he unclipped his flashlight with his free hand and pulsed it at what he hoped was ten cycles per second, near enough to the alpha rhythm to give Zulu a seizure – if a seizure was going to take at all.

'Stop it, Zulu. We're together.'

But Zulu paid Fiordaliso no mind. He strode on. Then he stopped midstride, hands and feet tense, eyes wide open in the flicker, lips smacking. 'Alpha is better . . . alpha is better . . . alpha is better . . .' The irrelevant phrase capped the symptoms of temporal-lobe epilepsy, and Zulu fell to the floor, frothing and writhing.

'What did you do to him?'

Buckmaster swung the flicker into Talley's eyes. 'Disrupted his brain. Do the same to you if you don't shape up. Lieutenant, wad your handkerchief between Zulu's jaws so he doesn't swallow his tongue; unbutton his collar; stretch him flat. Talley, go up front to the bunks and tear up all the bedsheets into short strips.'

'What for?'

'Molotov cocktails.'

Talley shook his head dazedly but backed away into the dimness. Buckmaster pocketed the flashlight, looked outside.

Buckmaster slung the M-16, dashed out to the supply room, and hurried back toting cartons of Mist-Tress. On his second trip he saw a flare go up. The enemy was getting into position. Returning to the van he found Fiordaliso helping Zulu sit up.

'How's he doing?'

Zulu got up by himself and answered for himself. 'Man, you really did me. How long I been out? Guess now it's too late to run? We got to stand and fight?'

'Unless you know a better hole.'

Zulu's eyes flashed. 'Man, I know just the spot. If I can crash through the fence at the rear, I'll drive us there.'

'I'll ride shotgun.' Buckmaster turned to Fiordaliso and was glad to see she looked calmer than he felt. 'Lock yourself in and get set for a rough ride. While we're on our way, you and Talley will be working. The bedsheet strips are wicks. Use knife points or fork tines to jam one end of the wick down between the valve stem and the gasket and —'

'What valve stem? What gasket?'

'Didn't I say? The hair-spray canisters are our Molotov cocktails. Knock a hole in the side of the trailer if you need light to work by. Round up all the matches and lighters and have them ready to hand out when we get there.' Wherever Zulu's there was.

The door closed behind him and Zulu. Zulu moved shakily at first but quickly steadied. Buckmaster flung the camouflage off the rig and netted Zulu, who had bent to pull the plug of the umbilical. Zulu straightened and stood in momentary resignation.

'Oh, man, not again.'

'C'mon, man, move. Don't you know there's a war on?'

'A war on what?'

Zulu and Buckmaster shook with silent laughter as Buckmaster helped untangle him. They hopped into the tractor cab, and Zulu pulled them away, making straight for the fence and picking up all the speed he could.

24. LRTGT LAST RESORT TARGET

Eyes still wet with laughter, face cold sober, Buckmaster saw again Zulu the MP sergeant and Sally Kaster rolling together in the fishnet at the FTA coffeehouse. He told himself it wasn't Mirrorite that had brought about the deaths of Sally and Joe ... and deaths yet to come. The Reds, through Maggie, had shown their deep concern about the Tenth X even before the Mirrorite put-on. But, all right, if there was self-anger in him he would vector it toward the enemy.

The enemy was now, brutal as the rig rushing the fence, and the enemy showed himself as Zulu reversed for another run at the sagging section of fence. A figure broke cover, out of the trees, and a hand pulled back to throw a grenade. Buckmaster got off a sprinkle, and the figure tore apart and the grenade exploded in free fall.

Then they were through the fence and on the straightway of the fire-break that took up again on this other end of the compound. M-16 fire followed them in futile rage.

Zulu turned west on Service Road Delta a short way and then headed across country into the vast openness of the Reservation. Buckmaster frowned.

'Just where the hell are you taking us?'

'That mother of a Vietnamese village they set up to train troops for guerrilla warfare. You know, that Nam village with its hooches and pagoda and tunnels and punji pits with the stakes smeared with shit and the booby traps and mines and graves and rice paddies. A bitch of a last ditch, man. I know the tunnels outside in. *Veni, vidi,* VC. We'll be Charlie.'

Buckmaster stared at him. 'Zulu, that's long gone. They tore that mock-up down and built a Middle East Village. Preparing for a different brand of war.' He busied himself trying to revisualize the village, then a speck in his rear-view mirror caught his eye even as Zulu spoke. A subdued Zulu.

'Turn back, Lieutenant? Try to make Outpost No. 1?'

'Look back.'

Zulu grew more subdued. The speck was the M-551. Zulu poured it on, tried to lay her on the peg. It had to be a rougher ride in the trailer than in the tractor. The speck grew.

'They're staying right with us.' Zulu looked suddenly puzzled. 'Say, Lieutenant, how did the enemy locate us in the first place, anyway?'

A good question, and Buckmaster went cold with the answer. In one savage move his hand bit off and swallowed the button Maggie had sewn on. The bitch had planted a beeper on him. He shook the fist the button was in.

Zulu grinned and gave him the sign of the fist back. 'That's right, loot, what the hell's the difference now. We're in it all the way.'

When Zulu wasn't looking, Buckmaster slipped the button into the rear fold of the cab seat.

Zulu sat straighter. 'Maybe we'll find lots of us there.'

'We'll see. But don't count on it. And if they are there, how effective are their blank bullets in real house-to-house fighting?' Buckmaster narrowed his eyes. 'There it is, dead ahead.'

'Yeah, dead.'

A signpost stood at the outskirts. MEGIDDO. No one was there. And the speck was bigger.

They lost it when they turned into town. Megiddo was a stylized jumble of whitewashed mud cubes, the last big throw of dice. Buckmaster found it coming back to him.

'That way ... now left. Pull into the central market square ... into the far corner of it, so they'll have to move all the way in to get at the rig. Fine.'

Before Zulu had braked the rig, Buckmaster had lit running back to the trailer door. He knocked: the door opened and he climbed in. Light stitched the walls where M-16 crossfire had pierced after the breakout from the compound. Fiordaliso was bringing a carton of wicked canisters to the door.

'We did most of them. I don't know how, or how many, or how well.'

A greenish Talley followed with another carton. 'What a miserable ride.' He looked out and around. 'Where are we?'

'Megiddo.'

Talley almost dropped his carton. 'Hell, we're not equipped for house-to-house.'

Buckmaster took both cartons, one under each arm. 'It won't be house-to-house. It'll be roof-to-ground.' He jumped out and called back. 'On the double with the rest.'

He made sure each of the four had two cartons and matches or lighters. All four stood frozen a moment, naked under the wide square of sky, as the enemy, not yet in Megiddo but near, thought he saw something and opened up on it. Buckmaster pointed to the four corners of the square. 'One of us up on each of those roofs. Keep your head down till the M-551's in the square together with all the sleepers. Then let 'em have it with everything you've got. Move!'

Buckmaster gazed out over the roofs, away from the market square toward the way they had come. They had got into position just in time. He flattened himself. The M-551 was rolling into town.

A dozen men dropped from it and walked behind its bulk as it quested. Buckmaster found himself swinging his M-16 into line. A figure slid into the sights. A man in a chicken vest and a radio helmet. Buckmaster lowered his M-16 and wished a prayer at Zulu and Talley, though they had only .45s. Don't pick him off. The man pointed. The M-551 made for the market square.

'Take it easy. You're hyperventilating. Save your breath to pool your courage.' Had he spoken aloud? Buckmaster grimaced. Follow me. Had he led the Tenth X into a deathtrap, or were the sleepers walking into one? What kind of leader did the sleepers have? Not so hot. Bad tactics to have fired those Shillelaghs at Zulu. Gave themselves away too soon.

But here they came, not so bad for a scratch task force of sleepers that, it was his guess, the Reds had pulled in from all over the US.

The M-551 rolled into the square, its crew and the men walking behind it spraying the doorways and windows with cal-fifty and M-16 fire. It halted and its gun-launcher trained on the van. Buckmaster edged for a look. All present and accounted for? He pulled back.

He grabbed a canister, lit its wick, and arced it toward the M-551. He quickly lit another and hurled it to block escape from this side of the square. As they went off, other canisters shot from the other roofs. Thirty-meter sheets of flame fed each other and grew into a fireball.

It was all over before the enemy knew it. But one man in the M-551 died with his hands on the double handgrips of his cal-fifty rendering his death rattles. It was all over, but Buckmaster tossed canisters till he had none; the others did the same.

The world was on fire and the heat licked at him and he rolled away. Then there was silence but for the talk of hot metal and hot brick slowly cooling. He climbed down into the building and out into the square. Screams of the napalmed remained in his mind.

He didn't make a body count. He didn't think anyone could make a body count. Fire had twisted smoking flesh into mortal coils, charred fetuses. Zulu rushed out into the square, bent to a body, and tore chars of cloth from the char of flesh.

Buckmaster stiffened. 'What the hell?'

Zulu looked up at him with wild eyes, and he made ready to flick his flashlight. Only, where was it? He had lost it. Then Zulu's eyes focused. Zulu slowly straightened.

'Guess I had a flashback to Nam. In Nam you stripped the VC body to keep Charlie from booby-trapping it.'

Buckmaster nodded and turned away. Something not wholly burned caught his eye. Something had escaped the holocaust. He picked up a toasted fragment of a leaflet bearing the FTA logo. EATH TO THE MILITARISTIC-IMPERIALISTIC POLLUTERS.

He pocketed it. He swung around with his M-16 at the ready. Fiordaliso had come up behind him. Her eyes ignored the weapon, ignored the bodies. She looked at Buckmaster and Zulu but seemed not to see them. Her eyes were shineless, her voice toneless.

'Where's Talley?'

Buckmaster's head jerked toward Talley's building. An arc of pocks ran up the face of the building.

'I'll go see.'

But Zulu beat him into the building. In a moment Zulu's head showed over the edge of the roof.

'That cal-fifty in the M-551 caught him looking over.'

Buckmaster and Fiordaliso were silent till Zulu rejoined them. Zulu hawked and spat. He looked off into a distance.

'Well, it was worrying him how to end it. No more.'

Buckmaster eyed himself, Fiordaliso, and Zulu. Singed and dirty. 'Look at us. All we need is a flag, a fife, and a drum.'

They grinned death's-head grins at each other. Then Fiordaliso gave a choking cough.

'Can't we get away from the stink?'

They started away but Zulu put out a hand and they stopped. He cocked his head.

'A chopper.'

Buckmaster drew Fiordaliso back to the building line.

'Take cover. Could still be the enemy.'

They hurried through a doorway and stood listening to the beat of hovering. Buckmaster edged a look.

'No, there's only the pilot. It's our own come to see what the smoke's all about.'

His mood lightened. Then he saw darkness at the end of the tunnel. Medals for some, though. Let another General Hackstaff take credit for outplaying the Reds.

'Stay under cover. When it descends a bit more, we can slip out the back.'

Zulu nodded. 'Yeah. No way we can talk our way out of this. And I can't see us taking the Fifth on the Tenth.'

'Roger. We ease out of Megiddo and out across the fields into the woods.'

Fiordaliso cocked an eye at Buckmaster. 'And then?'

'Off the Reservation.'

'And then?'

'Spend the money.'

He looked his last at the van. It might have ended for Talley, but the Tenth was still in it, operational in the electronic eyes of TOTE. His look lasted on the burnt-out M-551 and the burnt-out bodies. War is not a game. A stinking moral in the nostrils of Fiordaliso, Zulu, and himself.

The chopper had lowered enough now: the pilot would not see them dash across the street beyond the square.

'Dive for that doorway. Now!'

They dove.

COMPUTER · COPS
Edward D. Hoch

Crader's office was on the top floor of the World Trade Center, over-looking all of New York City and a good deal of New Jersey. On a clear day he could see the atomic liners gliding silently through the Narrows, or the mail rockets landing at Reagan International Airport far to the west. That is, he could see these things when he had time to look. On this day, a Tuesday in February of 2016, he had no time to look. He was listening to a teletaped report of the previous week's investigations and arrests, while at the same time jotting down notes in the margin of a computer wiring diagram.

Carl Crader was the Director of the Computer Investigation Bureau, an organization which had not even existed a decade earlier. From this New York office he directed a field force of 95 investigators and technicians, trained in the highly sophisticated twenty-first century science of investigating computer crimes. The CIB was a wholly independent government agency, reporting not to the Justice Department but directly to the White House. It was this independence, plus continued feuding between Justice and Commerce, which had placed the world headquarters of the CIB in New York rather than Washington. 'I want to be where the action is,' Crader had told the President nine years earlier when the idea was first suggested to him. 'And that's New York, the computer center of the world.'

He'd never regretted his decision. The CIB had proven to be a highly effective law enforcement agency, operating with limited manpower against some of the best brains in the criminal world. Even now, as he jotted notes and listened to the activity report, he was amazed at how much his Bureau could accomplish. The newspapers liked to call them 'The Computer Cops', and he'd come to take a certain pride in the name.

Earl Jazine found him at his desk, staring off into space, when he

NOTE: Changes made in this story by permission of Edward D. Hoch – C.G.W.

entered a few moments later. 'Dreaming of past triumphs, or future ones?' he asked.

Crader smiled and used the remote control switch to silence the teletape. He liked Jazine, liked the cool brash confidence of the fellow and his way of treating Crader almost as an equal instead of showing the stilted deference the others seemed to feel necessary toward the Director. 'Trying to figure a way to screw a BX-7809, if you must know, Earl. There's a guy over in Jersey City who's figured a way to program a 7809 so it's mailing regular checks to all his relatives, and I can't for the life of me scam how he did it.' *Scam* was a technical word they'd adopted for general use around the Bureau. Earl especially was fond of it, and Crader threw it into the conversation whenever he wanted to get through to his assistant.

'Well, I've got something a lot bigger than a little payroll swindle for you to worry about, Chief. Nobel Kinsinger just phoned from his office.'

'Kinsinger?' He was, perhaps, the most spectacularly wealthy man in the Western Hemisphere – an aging soldier of fortune who'd starred in the public press during the eighties and nineties, and had now shifted to the financial journals and business magazines. As the inventor of the air-wiper for auto windshields, he still received a royalty from every one of the fifteen million cars turned out by Detroit and Birmingham in a year's time.

'That's right – Kinsinger. He wants to see us at his office right away. Somebody's tapped into his SEXCO system.'

Crader frowned. 'That could be serious. But can't you handle it, Earl?'

'He wants nobody less than the Director in person. You'd better handle it personally, Chief. He might get upset and invade you.' Nobel Kinsinger had first come to public attention in the late 1980s, when he'd organized a private army and invaded Cuba in the final days of Castro's regime. It had been a nine-day wonder, which came dangerously close to starting a world war. In those days, commercial airliners were still being hijacked to Cuba by criminals and mentally unbalanced persons, and Kinsinger had used that fact as the basis of his invasion scheme. One hundred of his crack minutemen had been aboard a plane falsely reported as being hijacked. When the Cuban officials allowed it to land, the armed troops seized the airport and held it until helicopters could fly in with more men. The private army, numbering less than a thousand, had succeeded in capturing all of downtown Havana and most of its suburbs before being driven back and wiped out by Cuban army troops.

The whole incident greatly embarrassed the United States government, which spent weeks in the United Nations denying any knowledge of the invasion. Whatever the truth, Castro's government toppled a few months later, and Nobel Kinsinger returned from a Cuban prison as something of a folk hero. As a self-appointed soldier of fortune and champion of conservatism, he went on to further triumphs, mainly in the Arab–Israeli War of 1998.

'I hope Kinsinger is beyond his invading days,' Crader said. 'He must be nearly seventy years old now.'

'But still vigorous enough to command a financial empire.'

Crader thought about it and nodded. 'If high friends in Washington still mean power in this country, Kinsinger's about the most powerful man there is, next to the President himself.'

'If you don't go see what his trouble is, he could get on the phone to the President,' Jazine observed, and Crader knew that this was no exaggeration.

'Let's go talk to him,' he said with a sigh. 'See what the trouble is. Tell Judy to hold all calls and cancel my appointments for the afternoon.' He glanced out at the misty blue sky. 'We'll take the helijet and beat the traffic.'

Ten minutes later they were airborne, sweeping over lower Manhattan in the twin-engined helijet. The craft was hangered on the roof of the 120-story building, one of the few allowed to operate over Manhattan since passage of the Air Congestion Act. The trip to Nobel Kinsinger's headquarters across the East River took only a few minutes by air, and they were lowering for a landing when Crader noticed the Kinsinger trademark staring back at him from the helijet windshield. 'They've even got his airwipers on this thing!' he remarked to Jazine.

'Sure, they're everywhere. That's why he's the richest man in the country, or one of them, anyway.'

Not just anyone got in to see the richest man in the country. They were met by a burly-looking guard armed with a laser, and escorted past the latest thing in metal-detection devices. Crader never carried a weapon, but Earl Jazine's M-3 pistol was detected and confiscated.

They passed through an electronically controlled door and an ultra-violet germ screen before they were met by a smiling secretary in a blue body-stocking. 'This way please. We hope you'll excuse the necessary precautions.'

Earl Jazine, never one to overlook a pretty girl, eyed her with open admiration. 'And what would your name be, Miss?' he asked.

'I'm Linda Sale, Mr Kinsinger's personal secretary. This way, please,' she repeated, urging them on.

The inner sanctum was a dimly lit, windowless room which seemed more like a chapel than a business office. There was no traditional desk in evidence, only a great padded swivel chair and an altar-like bank of computers set against the far wall. As Crader adjusted his eyes to the dimness he saw the great bulk of a man move out of the shadows to confront them.

'You're Carl Crader?' the husky voice asked.

'That's right, sir. You're having some trouble with your SEXCO unit...?'

Fully visible now as he stepped to the center of the room, Nobel Kinsinger was a vast, elderly man, a spiderweb of wrinkles across his hairless face. He looked older than his sixty-odd years, much older, though when he moved there was still something of the old vigor about him. Crader could almost see him leading his troops down Havana's main street, like some latter-day Teddy Roosevelt.

'Trouble is an understatement, young man. I'm glad to see you've brought a technician with you.'

Crader hid his smile. 'This is Earl Jazine, one of our deputy directors. Everyone in the CIB is a technician of sorts, of course.' As he spoke to Kinsinger he moved over for a better view of the SEXCO unit.

SEXCO was an acronym for Stock Exchange Computer Operation, a system by which businessmen and wealthy individuals could function as their own stock brokers, buying and selling with the push of a button. To operate it, one simply pressed the code access buttons, then the credit card number the stock was to be charged to, then the stock symbols and the number of shares to be bought at the current market price. The information was relayed instantly to a master computer which matched up buy and sell orders, printed a bill, printed a fresh punched-card stock certificate, and adjusted the market price of the stock upward or downward – all in a matter of seconds.

SEXCO had proven immensely popular since its introduction some years earlier. Its operation was said to be foolproof, and it enabled the Stock Exchange to handle a volume of fifty million shares a day without flinching. The fact that some younger and more immature businessmen around town used it as something of a gambling device did not detract from its charm. Crader himself had seen men punch the buttons to buy a stock, then immediately punch to sell it, without knowing the price change.

It might be up or down, and the thrill of it was something akin to operating a slot machine in one of the plush casinos of Las Vegas or Kansas City.

'What seems to be your trouble?' Jazine asked, also moving over to examine the machine.

'Trouble again!' Kinsinger exploded. 'That must be a favorite word with you fellows. My *trouble* is that someone is buying and selling stocks in my name, using my machine.'

'Don't you keep it locked?' Crader asked, but he could see for himself that both locks were on.

'Of course I keep it locked! There's no way anybody but me could operate it. But someone is, nevertheless.'

'Impossible,' Earl Jazine stated flatly. 'These things are foolproof. When you punch your code number, an additional code is sent out by the machine itself. The two have to agree, or the computer rejects the order. If someone is buying or selling in your name, he has to use this machine. Yet you say no one but you has access to it.'

'Don't tell *me* it's impossible! Here's my bill from the Stock Exchange. I've lost close to fifty thousand dollars already through unauthorized manipulation of my holdings.'

Crader nodded sympathetically and motioned Jazine to start making notes. Then he asked, 'Just how is manipulation affecting your holdings, sir?'

Nobel Kinsinger dropped into his swivel chair, seemingly fatigued. 'In a number of ways – mainly by selling short. An order is put through to sell one thousand shares of some stock I don't even own. If the stock goes lower, a *buy* order is relayed to the computer the following day. If it goes higher, nothing happens and I get the printed notice demanding delivery of the shares. The same works with *buy* orders for shares I never heard of. Look, on this monthly statement – 5,000 shares of Comsat, purchased at $56\frac{1}{2}$, and then sold two days later at $59\frac{1}{4}$. If it had gone down, I would have received a bill for the shares.'

'But this swindle would only work if the swindler had access to your mail,' Crader pointed out, thinking of the blonde secretary in the blue body-stocking.

'Of course! But for someone who already has access to my double-locked SEXCO unit, that seems to be no problem. The shares and checks never reach me – only some bills and this monthly statement of my holdings, which is mailed by computer.'

'Then you suspect someone in your office?'

'Certainly. I want you to find out how the SEXCO unit is being rigged and who's doing it.'

Crader turned to his assistant. 'Earl, give the unit a quick check and make certain there's no runoff cable to another office. In the meantime, Mr Kinsinger, I want to get a complete list of everyone who could be working the machine or intercepting your mail.'

Kinsinger swung around in his chair until the overhead light was reflecting off his balding, web-like head. 'No one could be working the machine, and only two other people have a key to my private mail tube.' Like most of the newer office buildings, Kinsinger's headquarters was equipped with an air chute connection to the post office substation on the ground floor. Once sorted, mail addressed to Kinsinger or any other officer of the corporation was delivered directly to them by private air chute, deposited in a locked box until claimed.

'Your secretary would be one,' Crader said, stating the obvious.

'Yes, Miss Sale has a key and John Bunyon has a key. He's my administrative assistant. I have a key, though I only use it when I'm here alone after hours and have to mail something.'

'I'll want to talk to Miss Sale and Bunyon,' Crader said. The case suddenly began to seem dull and routine to him. Bunyon would prove to be a handsome young fellow with an unhappy married life, whose office romance with Linda Sale had led them both into the muddy waters of conspiracy.

Earl Jazine had been on his knees, examining the SEXCO machine. Now he stood up and brushed off his pants. 'No lead-offs. Could I have the keys to this thing, Mr Kinsinger?'

He unlocked the switches and ran a few standard tests while Crader and Kinsinger watched. First a special code was punched into the computer and then Kinsinger's regular code. A test grouping of stock symbols was run through, and the SEXCO responded as it should, sending back a complex message of numbers and letters. 'It checks out,' Earl told them. 'Nothing wrong with the unit.'

'All right,' Crader said. 'Then how about the keys?'

'Only one set,' Kinsinger insisted, 'and they're never off my person.'

'Could I speak to this John Bunyon?'

'He's out this afternoon. Had to make a quick flight to Rio. But he'll be back in the morning. You could speak to Miss Sale.'

'Perhaps we could put that off till tomorrow,' Crader said. 'I really must be getting back to headquarters.'

Nobel Kinsinger seemed about to protest, but finally he dismissed them with a wave of the hand, 'Just track down whoever's swindling me, Mr Crader. Find them, and I'll see you get a bonus from the government.'

'That's hardly necessary.'

'Find them,' Kinsinger said, holding out his hand, and Crader saw that he was trembling. He was a man in fear. The most powerful person in the country, next to the President, and he was afraid.

From his window the following morning, Carl Crader watched the nuclear ferry moving across New York harbor toward Staten Island. A few years ago the very idea of it had touched off demonstrations among the ban-the-atom brigades, but now it traveled back and forth every ten minutes without a murmur. Times were changing. He wondered, thinking about it, if even Nobel Kinsinger himself had been passed by in this twenty-first century world. Men no longer led invading forces down the streets of Havana, or even ran for office on the theories Nobel Kinsinger had espoused back in the 1990s. The only war of importance in recent years had been fought by robot submarines on the floor of the Indian Ocean. It had lasted twelve hours, without any loss of life, and had finally been settled by a flying squad of United Nations inspectors.

'Thinking about it?' Earl Jazine asked, entering with his usual soft knock.

'Kinsinger? I suppose so.' Crader sighed and reached for a charfilter cigarette. 'What do you think? Can you scam it?'

'Maybe, maybe not. You might be interested in talking with Kinsinger's assistant, John Bunyon. He's outside.'

'Bunyon? Here?' Somehow he had expected it. 'Well, bring him in. We might as well talk to him together.'

Bunyon was a tall young man who looked pretty much as Crader had supposed he would. Black hair worn fashionably long, a briefpurse dangling from his waist. Somehow these new fashions hadn't caught on with the over-thirty crowd, but Bunyon was still young enough to bring it off. Crader would have guessed his age at about twenty-eight.

'I'm pleased you came,' Crader said, continuing to study the man from across his cluttered deskette. 'I wanted to have a talk with you. How was Rio?'

'Fine,' the young man answered. 'But one day is too short a trip to enjoy it. It's summer there now. I hated to come back to the cold weather.'

Crader nodded. 'About the SEXCO...'

'He said that was the trouble. Old Kinsinger. He sent me here to see you.'

'Did he now?' It seemed that Kinsinger might almost be pointing the finger of suspicion at young Bunyon. 'What do you know about the business?'

'Next to nothing, really, except that something's happening with his SEXCO unit and it's serious enough to get the Computer Cops in on it.'

Crader shot a glance at Jazine and saw him chuckle silently at the term. 'Any idea who could be using the SEXCO besides Kinsinger?'

'Not unless it's Linda Sale – his secretary.'

Crader nodded. 'We've met Linda. You know her well?'

The young man shrugged. 'Around the office.'

'Date her?'

'A drink after work once or twice. Nothing more.'

'Do you have any other explanation to offer for the tampering with the SEXCO?'

'Sure. I think the old man made it all up.'

'Oh? Why is that?'

Bunyon shifted in his chair. 'He's gone a bit nuts lately. Frankly, I've been looking for another job. He's got this whole room full of computers that are supposed to be projecting sales figures for Airwiper, and what does he do with them? He uses them to try and prove the existence of an Anti-Earth!'

'A what?' He saw that even Jazine had come alert.

'Anti-Earth. It's a theory that apparently was quite popular a few decades back, in the days of the flying saucer sightings. Some people said there was an undiscovered planet, of about the same size as Earth, whose revolution around the sun was always exactly opposite of Earth's. It was always on the other side of the sun, eclipsed by the sun, and therefore could never be seen from Earth. They even had a name for it back then – they called it Clarion. Today, some believers call it Vulcan.'

'And Nobel Kinsinger believes this?'

'Of course he believes it. In fact, he's getting ready to lead an invasion of Clarion-Vulcan, as soon as he can get enough spacecraft built.'

'An invasion?' Crader mused. 'Like in his days of Cuban glory?'

'Exactly!' John Bunyon said. 'Actually, computer work forty years ago established that there could be no planet on the far side of the sun, because the pull of its gravity would have affected the orbit of Venus. Kinsinger is attempting to prove this old data wrong, and at the same time establish a trajectory for a space shot at the planet.'

'Why does he want to invade it?' Jazine asked. 'Even supposing the planet is there.'

'They're the enemy,' Bunyon said. 'Like Cuba, thirty-five years ago. That's the only reason he needs.'

Crader cleared his throat. 'Of course if there were a hidden planet on the other side of the sun, it could have been observed from our moon station, in all probability – especially during a period of eclipse when the Earth passed between sun and moon.'

'He's charted all that. He claims a small planet such as he imagines Clarion-Vulcan to be could still remain unseen behind the sun. The moon isn't far enough from earth to afford a sharp enough angle of observation.'

'Small planet? You said the same size as Earth.'

John Bunyon smiled. 'In the Universe, Earth is a small planet.'

Fifteen minutes later, after he'd departed, Crader faced Earl Jazine. 'What do you think, Earl?'

'Which one do we believe? Have we got a computer swindle or a nutty old guy who wants to conquer the Universe?'

'He's too wealthy to be just a nutty old guy, Earl. And if he is, the whole thing is out of our field. We deal in computers, not planets.'

'So what do we do, Chief?'

'*I* try to get some other work done around here. *You* go talk to the secretary, Miss Sale. That shouldn't be too hard an assignment.'

'It'll be a pleasure, if she's still wearing that blue body-stocking.'

'She's probably changed to a pink one today. Flesh-colored. I hear they're all the rage.' He allowed himself a slight smile and then added, 'Find out whose side she's on, anyway. I'll bet in advance that she backs up Bunyon's story.'

Once he was alone, Crader turned his attention to the other reports on his desk. Some trouble with the master tax refund computer at Andover. Could be sabotage. He marked that one for his top technical team. The government always demanded the best of service. He turned over the next report and saw it concerned the traffic control computer at Kennedy Airport. They'd had trouble there before – and at Reagan Airport in New Jersey. With almost all airfreight routed by computer these days, there was a great temptation to attempt a rerouting of it for personal gain.

Crader put down the reports after a time and found his mind drifting back to Nobel Kinsinger. Finally he dialed a Washington number he knew by heart and asked for some information about Nobel Kinsinger's activities. He held the phone for five minutes, waiting, until a voice came back to report that Kinsinger was indeed building two spacecraft, under the permission granted by the Independent Space Exploration Act of 2003.

He was still thinking about that an hour later when Earl Jazine came back from talking with Miss Sale. 'You look happy,' Crader commented.

'Why not? I just spent a most enjoyable ninety minutes with a lovely lady. I might even arrange to see her again.'

'So get to the point. What does she say about the SEXCO flap?'

'You lose your bet. She says someone *is* getting to the machine somehow. She knows it, because one of the *sell* orders was put through on a day when Kinsinger wasn't even in the office. He was home sick, and she swears no one went near the machine all day.'

'She's sure of the date?'

'Positive. It was Friday the 13th, and she remembers connecting that with her boss's illness. She's superstitious, I guess.'

'And what about John Bunyon? Anything between them?'

'Nothing. She had a few drinks with him after work, but she thinks he's queer or something. Spends a lot of his time in the South Village with the flippies.'

'I'm surprised. He didn't look the type.'

'How can you tell, without seeing him naked? She says she saw him buttoning his shirt in the office one day, and his chest was all painted.'

Crader sighed and shuffled the reports on his desk. 'So where does that leave us?'

Jazine shrugged. 'Either the girl's lying, or the machine's being bugged from off the premises.'

'I don't like either possibility at the moment, but you'd better check out the bugging possibility. Wiring, induced current, the works.' He remembered a case in San Francisco the previous year, in which an induction coil around a cable had been used to feed false information into a payroll computer.

'I'll get right on it, Chief. Who should I use?'

'Carter and House. They're the best I can spare. And send Judy in on your way out. I've got some letters to dictate that I can't trust to the autotype.'

The girls in the CIB were forbidden to wear body-stockings on duty, but Judy still managed an air of quiet sensuality in her old-fashioned miniskirt. Crader was past the age where it mattered, but he noticed that

Jazine always gave her a second look in the morning. He was never one to let his family hamper his girl-chasing activities.

'Judy, take a letter to Washington. I want it to go out by rocket mail this afternoon ...'

That was Wednesday. On Thursday morning, glancing casually over Jazine's notes, he made a discovery. 'Earl,' he spoke into the wireless intercom, 'can you step in for a moment?'

Jazine was smiling. He always smiled in the morning, though it sometimes wore thin by noon. 'What's up, Chief?'

'You made a list of the dates last month when Kinsinger's SEXCO was tampered with.'

'Sure. You've got it right there.'

'Notice anything strange about it?'

'Not especially.'

'The false orders always go out over SEXCO on Fridays. Sometimes there are other days as well, but there's always something on Fridays.'

'You're right,' Jazine agreed, looking over his shoulder. 'And Linda Sale mentioned a Friday the 13th, too.'

'Have Carter and House had any luck checking out the circuits?'

'None so far. They should be just about finished now.'

Crader nodded. 'If they don't find anything, suppose you and I go over there tomorrow and baby-sit with that SEXCO? We'll see if it really can be gimmicked without anyone touching it.'

'Good idea,' Jazine agreed. 'Although we'll probably scare away our villain.'

'Maybe not.'

But before they could put the plan into operation, there was a noonday report from Carter and House. The news was brought in by Jazine right after lunch. 'The SEXCO isn't gimmicked in any way, but they turned up something else of interest. While they were testing the induction coil on a telephone line, they accidentally tapped into a conversation between Linda Sale and our boy Bunyon. He's taking her down to the South Village tonight, to some sort of flippie gathering.'

'Oh?' There were times when Crader's mind ran to wild ideas. This was one of them. 'Could you and Judy dress up like a couple of flippies and crash the gathering, do you think?'

Earl Jazine rolled his eyes. 'What'll my wife say about that? Getting all painted up ...'

'Tell her it's for the Bureau,' Crader said with a smile. 'She'll understand.'

He drove them to the South Village area himself in one of the less blatant official cars. Judy's face was a blazing mixture of flippie colors, and she wore a modified body-stocking with the traditional flippie boots and belt. 'I'll freeze to death in this outfit,' she complained.

'Come on,' Jazine said with a chuckle. 'Flippies aren't supposed to mind the cold. They're supposed to be flipped out.'

Crader remained in the car, turning on the one-way polarization so no one could see inside. He knew that wouldn't attract attention, because many people used it when they parked their cars, to discourage thieves. No one was going to break into a car when they couldn't see what – or who – might be waiting for them inside. He was especially interested in the arrivals at the meeting hall across the street, and he realized quite quickly that the gathering was open to non-flippie types as well as the usual South Village residents. He saw Bunyon and Linda Sale arrive together, dressed in regular office clothes. Perhaps he wasn't as much of a flippie as they'd been led to believe.

Ten minutes after the beginning of the gathering, Crader left the car and crossed over to the entrance. A large sign outside depicted the joint US–Russian moonport and space observatory. It was to be an evening of lunar happenings. The interior of the place was bathed in a cold white light of the intensity to suggest moonlight, and several of the flippie couples were swaying to some computerized musical sounds. He saw Jazine and Judy at once, standing against one of the foam rubber walls, but there was no sign of Bunyon and Linda.

Crader had been watching the multi-media proceedings of light and sound and smell for some fifteen minutes when a cry went up from the far end of the room. Someone had shouted, 'Blue moon!' and others had taken up the chant. '*Blue moon!* BLUE MOON!' Then the nearest of the flippies fell upon the chanters, and a tussle was in progress. Crader knew that the 'Blue Moon' people opposed the joint US–Russian moonbase. They wanted the moon to stay blue, or American, rather than become even partly red, or Russian. The base had functioned well, with surprisingly little friction, for more than five years, but that didn't cool the tempers of the 'Blue Moon' people.

Crader was startled to see Linda Sale fighting her way through the crowd to the side of the Blue Moon chanters. What was she up to?

What ...? Someone yanked at the smooth stretch fabric of her body-stocking and a seam ripped at her shoulder. Then suddenly John Bunyon was at her side, fighting off the grasping hands. The loudspeaker bellowed a cry for order, but the situation was already out of hand. Crader was shoved aside by the panicking crowd. He had a glimpse of Earl Jazine drawing the M-3 pistol from beneath his flippie costume, and then someone crashed into him from behind. He went down on his face beneath the crowd.

When Crader opened his eyes, the first thing he saw was Earl Jazine's painted face peering down at him. 'You all right, Chief?'

'I guess so. What happened?' The area of his vision gradually enlarged and he saw Judy standing by Earl's side.

'The flippies got into a fight with the Blue Mooners. Bunyon and the girl were right in the middle of it, somehow, and I saw a guy go at them with a knife. That's when I used my gun.'

Crader struggled to his feet. 'Sorry to involve you in all this, Judy. I didn't know it would be dangerous.' The moonlit hall was almost empty now, except for a few riot police and hangers-on.

'That's all right,' she said. 'It was exciting while it lasted. Better than being a secretary all day.'

'What about Bunyon and the girl?'

Earl Jazine shrugged his broad shoulders. 'They got away in the confusion. Apparently unhurt. The police are questioning the guy with the knife, but he's not talking.'

'A flippie?'

'No. One of the Blue Moon crowd. He seemed to know them. He went right for Bunyon with his knife.'

'Did you have to shoot him?'

'In the arm. He'll be all right. We got the guy that landed on you, too, but he's harmless enough. Just a bit high on moon juice.'

Crader smiled. 'Let's get out of here.' He gazed up at the great diorama of the moon base. 'From now on maybe we'd better stick to computers.'

Friday was a busy day in the offices of Airwiper Inc., and Nobel Kinsinger was not particularly pleased at the prospect of Crader and Jazine spending the entire day camped in his offices. They'd arrived early, before any of the other employees, and hadn't taken their eyes from the locked SEXCO unit since the start of the business day.

'I have things to do, stock to buy!' Kinsinger protested.

'It'll wait till Monday,' Crader assured him. 'The false buy and sell orders usually come on Fridays, and this is the only way to track them down. Nobody uses the machine – not you or Miss Sale or John Bunyon – and that'll at least confirm or deny Miss Sale's story that orders went out without anyone touching it last Friday the 13th.'

All went well until just before noon. 'I have to use it,' Kinsinger decided. 'I want to sell some Radiostar shares.'

'Call a broker,' Crader told him. 'Nobody unlocks this machine.' Kinsinger sighed and went meekly to the telephone.

When the Stock Exchange finally closed for the day at three o'clock, Crader relaxed a bit. 'Should I check with them?' Jazine asked.

'Yes. Get on the phone and have them run a computer check on this SEXCO unit. Tell them to report back to us at once.'

They sat for another fifteen minutes waiting for word. Presently Linda Sale appeared in the doorway, wearing a maroon body-stocking and looking none the worse for wear from the previous night's experience. 'Anyone for coffee?' she asked, all efficiency. As she served it, Crader found himself comparing her with his own secretary, Judy. Her figure was better, he had to admit, but there was something a bit too coldly detached about her for Crader's taste. She was too much the anti-sex vision of the future, despite the curves and the body-stocking.

The phone flickered into life and Jazine took it. He listened intently and made notes. Then he hung up and turned to Crader and Kinsinger. 'It's impossible, but it happened. Five thousand shares of General Tygart were bought through that machine today.'

Crader stared at the locked computer. He should have been surprised, but somehow he wasn't. He'd almost expected it. 'How are they doing it?' Nobel Kinsinger breathed. 'How in hell are they doing it?'

John Bunyon had appeared from somewhere, standing very close to Linda in the doorway. For a moment nobody said a word, and then his voice broke the silence. 'Are you accusing us, Mr Kinsinger, because if you are ...'

'Wait, wait.' Crader held up a hand. 'We're past the stage of name-calling. It's time to get to the bottom of this thing. Earl – you must have the exact time the sale went through the machine today. What was it?'

Jazine consulted his notes. 'Exactly 10.07, shortly after the market opened this morning. *Buy General Tygart 5000 shares @ market*. The price at the time was $65\frac{1}{2}$. It closed this afternoon at 67.'

'At 10.07 we were all in this office,' Crader reminded them. 'You were at your desk outside the door, Miss Sale. What about you, Bunyon?'

'I was at my desk. I have witnesses.'

Crader nodded. 'I believe you.'

'Then how . . . ?' Kinsinger began.

'How?' Crader stood up and started to pace the floor, feeling his feet sinking into the uraform rug. 'I think I've scammed that at last. We checked the wiring just yesterday, so there was no tampering from outside the machine. And Earl and I watched it all day. Neither Kinsinger nor anyone else so much as unlocked it.'

'The thing's impossible,' Bunyon protested.

'Not at all,' Crader said. 'Before there were SEXCO units everywhere, what happened if you phoned a broker with an order after the market closed for the day? What still happens if you deal through a broker after 3 p.m. closing time?'

Earl Jazine's face lit up. 'The order is held till the following morning.'

'Exactly! And of course the SEXCO operates in the same manner. An order punched into the machine late Thursday afternoon is held till the opening of the Exchange on Friday, and then put through by the computer. Of course it carries Friday's date on it. With the usual overnight backlog of orders, it's not surprising the computer at the Stock Exchange took seven minutes to match up 5,000 shares of *buy* and *sell* on General Tygart. So the order was recorded at 10.07 today, when it was actually punched into this SEXCO sometime after three yesterday afternoon.'

'But which one of them did it?' Kinsinger wanted to know. 'And how did they get my key to the machine?'

Crater was smiling as he moved in for the kill. 'Remember when you were sick on Friday the 13th? A transaction was made that day, and it helped convince Miss Sale here that you really were being swindled somehow. But think about it – would the swindler allow Thursday afternoon's order to stand if he knew you were out sick and unable to use the machine on Friday? Of course not! A real swindler's only hope of success was to avoid discovery of the stock manipulations, not call attention to them. He would have cancelled the previous afternoon's transaction before the market opened Friday morning.'

'What are you trying to say?' Kinsinger asked.

'That there was no swindle. That you faked the whole thing yourself, Kinsinger.'

'Why? Why would I do that?' he exploded, wheeling in his swivel chair. But his face had gone ashen.

'Two reasons, I think. One was an attempt to frame and discredit John Bunyon here. And Miss Sale too, if that became necessary. The other was to bring the CIB into the investigation, to cover up some irregularities with your other computers.'

'The Clarion invasion!' Bunyon almost shouted.

'Not exactly,' Crader said. 'But you're on the right track. You see, if anyone discovered dirty work in the programming of his other computers, Mr Kinsinger here could simply point to us and say we were investigating the whole matter of his computer operation.'

'But what is it, if not Clarion?' Bunyon asked. 'What's he building those space ships for?'

Crader turned to the big man in the chair. 'Do you want to tell them, Kinsinger? Or should I?'

'Go to hell!'

'All right, Bunyon, you took Miss Sale to a flippie gathering last night. A moon program, where a fight broke out with some of the Blue Moon crowd. Why did you go there?'

'Why?' He hesitated, then said, 'Well, I think Mr Kinsinger might be linked to them somehow.'

'Exactly! You were getting too close to the truth. That was why Kinsinger called us in, and then tried to have you knifed at the meeting last night.'

'What?' Linda Sale exclaimed. 'Knifed?'

'Mr Jazine here saved your life. You see, Kinsinger is very close to the Blue Moon people. In fact, he's their financial backer. I found that out from Washington. The space ships are being built not to explore a mythical planet but to invade the moon – to cast out the Russians for all time and make it a purely American base.'

'And his computers are programming for the trip!' Bunyon said. 'Of course! He could hardly ask Washington for the flight plan to the moon without tipping his hand.'

Nobel Kinsinger stirred uneasily in his chair. 'Am I the only true patriot left in this country?' he growled. But his mind and eyes seemed suddenly far away, perhaps once more leading a charge through the streets of Havana.

Earl Jazine brought the completed reports in a folder and laid them on a corner of Crader's crowded deskette. 'What will Washington do about it?' he asked. 'Kinsinger is a powerful man, the most powerful.'

'They know a moon invasion can't be allowed. Now that they know the scheme, steps will be taken. Work on the spacecrafts has already been halted, and the Blue Moon crowd is being fully investigated. It'll probably be disbanded shortly.'

'And Kinsinger?'

'He's sick. Perhaps they can put him away somewhere in a little room with only a dummy SEXCO unit to play with.'

Two months later, Crader received an invitation to the wedding of John Bunyon and Linda Sale. He was a bit sorry he couldn't attend, but he was flying to Hawaii that day. It seemed they needed help out there with a computer that was printing counterfeit money in its spare time.

SAM · HALL

Poul Anderson

Click. Bzzzz. Whrrr.

Citizen Blank Blank, Anytown, Somewhere, USA, approaches the hotel desk. 'Single with bath.'

'Sorry, sir, our fuel ration doesn't permit individual baths. One can be drawn for you; that will be twenty-five dollars extra.'

'Oh, is that all? Okay.'

Citizen Blank reaches into his pocket with an automatic gesture and withdraws his punched card and gives it to the registry machine. Aluminum jaws close on it, copper teeth feel for the holes, electronic tongue tastes the life of Citizen Blank.

Place and date of birth. Parents. Race. Religion. Educational, military, and civilian service records. Marital status. Occupations, up to and including current one. Affiliations. Physical measurements, fingerprints, retinals, blood type. Basic psychotype. Loyalty rating. Loyalty index as a function of time to moment of last checkup. Click, click. Bzzz.

'Why are you here, sir?'

'Salesman. I expect to be in New Pittsburg tomorrow night.'

The clerk (32 yrs, married, two children; NB, confidential: Jewish. To be kept out of key occupations) punches the buttons.

Click, click. The machine returns the card. Citizen Blank puts it back in his wallet.

'Front!'

The bellboy (19 yrs, unmarried; NB, confidential: Catholic. To be kept out of key occupations) takes the guest's trunk. The elevator creaks upstairs. The clerk resumes his reading. The article is entitled 'Has Britain Betrayed Us?' Other articles in the magazine include 'New Indoctrination Program for the Armed Forces', 'Labor Hunting on Mars', 'I Was a Union Man for the Security Police', 'New Plans for YOUR Future'.

The machine talks to itself. Click click. A tube winks at its neighbor as if they shared a private joke. The total signal goes out over the wires.

With a thousand other signals, it shoots down the last cable and into the sorter unit of Central Records. Click, click. Bzzz. Whrrr. Wink and glow. A scanner sweeps through the memory circuits. The distorted molecules of one spool show the pattern of Citizen Blank Blank, and this is sent back. It enters the comparison unit, to which the incoming signal corresponding to Citizen Blank Blank has also been shunted. The two are perfectly in phase; nothing wrong. Citizen Blank Blank is staying in the town where, last night, he said he would, so he has not had to file a correction.

The new information is added to the record of Citizen Blank Blank. The whole of his life returns to the memory bank. It is wiped from the scanner and comparison units, so that these may be free for the next arriving signal.

The machine has swallowed and digested another day. It is content.

Thornberg came into his office at the usual time. His secretary glanced up to say 'Good morning,' and looked closer. She had been with him for enough years to read the nuances in his carefully controlled face. 'Anything wrong, chief?'

'No.' He spoke it harshly, which was also peculiar. 'No, nothing wrong. I feel a bit under the weather, maybe.'

'Oh.' The secretary nodded. You learned discretion in the government. 'Well, I hope you get better soon.'

'Thanks. It's nothing.' Thornberg limped over to his desk, sat down, and took out a pack of cigarettes. He held one for a moment in nicotine-yellowed fingers before lighting it, and there was an emptiness in his eyes. Then he puffed ferociously and turned to his mail. As chief technician of Central Records, he received a generous tobacco ration and used all of it.

The office was not large – a windowless cubicle, furnished with gaunt orderliness, its only decoration a picture of his son and one of his late wife. Thornberg seemed too big for it. He was tall and lean, with thin, straight features and neatly brushed graying hair. He wore a plain version of the Security uniform, with the insignia of Technical Division and major's rank but no other decoration, none of the ribbons to which he was entitled. The priesthood of Matilda the Machine were a pretty informal lot for these days.

He chain-smoked his way through the mail. Routine stuff, most of it having to do with the necessary change-overs for installing the new identification system. 'Come on, June,' he said to his secretary.

Irrationally, he preferred dictating to her rather than to a recorder. 'Let's get this out of the way fast, I've got work to do.'

He held one letter before him. 'To Senator E. W. Harmison, SOB, New Washington. Dear Sir: In re your communication of the 14th inst., requesting my personal opinion of the new ID system, may I say that it is not a technician's business to express opinions. The directive ordering that every citizen shall have one number applying to all his papers and functions – birth certificate, education, rations, social security, service, etc. – has obvious long-range advantages, but naturally entails a good deal of work in reconverting all our electronic records. The President having decided that the gain in the long run justifies the present difficulties, it behooves all citizens to obey. Yours, and so forth.' He smiled with a certain coldness. 'There, that'll fix *him*! I don't know what good Congress is anyway, except to plague honest bureaucrats.'

Privately, June decided to modify the letter. Maybe a senator was only a rubber stamp, but you couldn't brush him off so curtly. It is part of a secretary's job to keep the boss out of trouble.

'Okay, let's get to the next,' said Thornberg. 'To Colonel M. R. Hubert, Director of Liaison Division, Central Records Agency, Security Police, etc. Dear Sir: In re your memorandum of the 14th inst., requiring a definite date for completion of the ID conversion, may I respectfully state that it is impossible for me honestly to set one. It is necessary for us to develop a memory-modification unit which will make the change-over in all our records without our having to take out and alter each of the three hundred million or so spools in the machine. You realize that one cannot predict the exact time needed to complete such a project. However, research is progressing satisfactorily (refer him to my last report, will you?), and I can confidently say that conversion will be finished and all citizens notified of their numbers within two months at the latest. Respectfully, and so on. Put that in a nice form, June.'

She nodded. Thornberg went on through his mail, throwing most of it into a basket for her to answer alone. When he was done he yawned and lit another cigarette. 'Praise Allah that's over. Now I can get down to the lab.'

'You have some afternoon appointments,' she reminded him.

'I'll be back after lunch. See you.' He got up and went out of the office.

Down an escalator to a still lower subterranean level, along a corridor, returning the salutes of passing technicians without thinking about it. His face was immobile, and perhaps only the stiff swinging of his arms said anything.

Jimmy, he thought. *Jimmy, kid.*

He entered the guard chamber, pressing hand and eye to the scanners in the farther door. Finger and retinal patterns were his pass; no alarm sounded; the door opened for him and he walked into the temple of Matilda.

She crouched hugely before him, tier upon tier of control panels, instruments, blinking lights, like an Aztec pyramid. The gods murmured within her and winked red eyes at the tiny man who crawled over her monstrous flanks. Thornberg stood for a moment regarding the spectacle. Then he smiled, a tired smile creasing his face along one side. A sardonic memory came back to him, bootlegged stuff from the forties and fifties of the last century which he had read: French, German, British, Italian. The intellectuals had been all hot and bothered about the Americanization of Europe, the crumbling of old culture before the mechanized barbarism of soft drinks, advertising, chrome-plated automobiles (dollar grins, the Danes had called them), chewing gum, plastics ... None of them had protested the simultaneous Europeanization of America: government control, a military caste, light-years of bureaucratic records and red tape, censors, secret police, nationalism, and racialism.

Oh, well.

But, Jimmy, boy, where are you now, what are they doing to you?

Thornberg went over to the bench where his best engineer, Rodney, was testing a unit. 'How's it coming?' he asked.

'Pretty good, chief,' said Rodney. He didn't bother to salute; Thornberg had, in fact, forbidden it in the labs as a waste of time. 'A few bugs yet, but we're getting them out.'

You had to have a gimmick which would change numbers without altering anything else. Not too easy a task, when the memory banks depended on individual magnetic domains. 'Okay,' said Thornberg. 'Look, I'm going up to the main controls. Going to run a few tests myself – some of the tubes have been acting funny over in Section Thirteen.'

'Want an assistant?'

'No, thanks. I just want not to be bothered.'

Thornberg resumed his way across the floor, its hardness echoing dully under his shoes. The main controls were in a special armored booth nestling against the great pyramid, and he had to be scanned again before the door opened for him. Not many were allowed in here. The complete archives of the nation were too valuable to take chances with.

Thornberg's loyalty rating was AAB-2 – not absolutely perfect, but the best available among men of his professional caliber. His last drugged checkup had revealed certain doubts and reservations about government policy, but there was no question of disobedience. *Prima facie*, he was certainly bound to be loyal. He had served with distinction in the war against Brazil, losing a leg in action; his wife had been killed in the abortive Chinese rocket raids ten years ago; his son was a rising young Space Guard officer on Venus. He had read and listened to forbidden stuff, blacklisted books, underground and foreign propaganda, but then every intellectual dabbled with that; it was not a serious offense if your record was otherwise good and if you laughed off what the prohibited things said.

He sat for a moment regarding the control board inside the booth. Its complexity would have baffled most engineers, but he had been with Matilda so long that he didn't even need the reference tables.

Well –

It took nerve, this. A hypnoquiz was sure to reveal what he was about to do. But such raids were, necessarily, in a random pattern; it was unlikely that he would be called up again for years, especially with his rating. By the time he was found out, Jack should have risen far enough in the Guard ranks to be safe.

In the privacy of the booth Thornberg permitted himself a harsh grin. 'This,' he murmured to the machine, 'will hurt me worse than it does you.'

He began punching buttons.

There were circuits installed which could alter the records – take out an entire one and write whatever was desired in the magnetic fields. Thornberg had done the job a few times for high officials. Now he was doing it for himself.

Jimmy Obrenowicz, son of his second cousin, hustled off at night by Security police on suspicion of treason. The records showed what no private citizen was supposed to know: Jimmy was in Camp Fieldstone. Those who returned from there were very quiet and said nothing about where they had been; sometimes they were incapable of speech.

It wouldn't do for the chief of Central Records to have a relative in Fieldstone. Thornberg punched buttons for half an hour, erasing, changing. It was a tough job – he had to go back several generations, altering lines of descent. But when he was through, Jimmy Obrenowicz was no relation whatever to the Thornbergs.

And I thought the world of that kid. But I'm not doing it for myself, Jimmy. It's for Jack. When the cops go through your file, later today no doubt, I can't let them find out you're related to Captain Thornberg on Venus and a friend of his father.

He slapped the switch that returned the spool to its place in the memory bank. *With this act do I disown thee.*

After that he sat for a while, relishing the quiet of the booth and the clean impersonality of the instruments. He didn't even want to smoke.

So now they were going to give every citizen a number, tattooed on him, no doubt. One number for everything. Thornberg foresaw popular slang referring to the numbers as 'brands', and Security cracking down on those who used the term. Disloyal language.

Well, the underground was dangerous. It was supported by foreign countries who didn't like an American-dominated world – at least, not one dominated by today's kind of America, though once 'USA' had meant 'Hope'. The rebels were said to have their own base out in space somewhere and to have honeycombed the country with their agents. It could be. Their propaganda was subtle: we don't want to overthrow the nation; we only want to liberate it; we want to restore the Bill of Rights. It could attract a lot of unstable souls. But Security's spy hunt was bound to drag in any number of citizens who had never meditated treason. Like Jimmy – or had Jimmy been an undergrounder after all? You never knew. Nobody ever told you.

There was a sour taste in Thornberg's mouth. He grimaced. A line of a song came back to him. '*I hate you one and all.*' How had it gone? They used to sing it in his college days. Something about a very bitter character who'd committed a murder.

Oh, yes. 'Sam Hall'. How did it go, now? You needed a gravelly bass to sing it properly.

> Oh, my name it is Sam Hall, it is Sam Hall.
> Yes, my name it is Sam Hall, it is Sam Hall.
> Oh, my name it is Sam Hall,
> And I hate you one and all,
> Yes, I hate you one and all, God damn your eyes.

That was it. And Sam Hall was about to swing for murder. He remembered now. He felt like Sam Hall himself. He looked at the machine and wondered how many Sam Halls were in it.

Idly, postponing his return to work, he punched for the file – name, Samuel Hall, no other specifications. The machine mumbled to itself. Presently it spewed out a file of papers, microprinted on the spot from the memory banks. Complete dossier on every Sam Hall, living and dead,

from the time the records began to be kept. To hell with it. Thornberg
chucked the papers down the incinerator slot.

'*Oh, I killed a man, they say, so they say* –'

The impulse was blinding in its savagery. They were dealing with
Jimmy at this moment, probably pounding him over the kidneys, and he,
Thornberg, sat here waiting for the cops to requisition Jimmy's file, and
there was nothing he could do. His hands were empty.

By God, he thought. *I'll give them Sam Hall!*

His fingers began to race; he lost his nausea in the intricate technical
problem. Slipping a fake spool into Matilda – it wasn't easy. You couldn't
duplicate numbers, and every citizen had a lot of them. You had to account
for every day of his life.

Well, some of that could be simplified. The machine had only existed
for twenty-five years; before then the files had been kept on paper in a
dozen different offices. Let's make Sam Hall a resident of New York, his
dossier there lost in the bombing thirty years ago. Such of his papers as
were on file in New Washington had also been lost, in the Chinese attack.
That meant he simply reported as much detail as he could remember,
which needn't be a lot.

Let's see. 'Sam Hall' was an English song, so Sam Hall should be British
himself. Came over with his parents, oh, thirty-eight years ago, when he
was only three, and naturalized with them; that was before the total ban
on immigration. Grew up on New York's lower East Side, a tough kid, a
slum kid. School records lost in the bombing, but he claimed to have gone
through the tenth grade. No living relatives. No family. No definite
occupation, just a series of unskilled jobs. Loyalty rating BBA-O, which
meant that purely routine questions showed him to have no political
opinions at all that mattered.

Too colorless. Give him some violence in his background. Thornberg
punched for information on New York police stations and civilian-police
officers destroyed in the last raids. He used them as the source of records
that Sam Hall had been continually in trouble – drunkenness, disorderly
conduct, brawls, a suspicion of holdups and burglary, but not strong
enough to warrant calling in Security's hypnotechnicians for quizzing him.

Hmmm. Better make him 4-F, no military service. Reason? Well, a
slight drug addiction; men weren't so badly needed nowadays that hop-
heads had to be cured. Neocoke – that didn't impair the faculties too
much; indeed the addict was abnormally fast and strong under the
influence, though there was a tough reaction afterwards.

Then he would have had to put in a term in civilian service. Let's see. He spent his three years as a common laborer on the Colorado Dam project; so many men had been involved there that no one would remember him, or at least it would be hard finding a supervisor who did.

Now to fill in. Thornberg used a number of automatic machines to help him. Every day in twenty-five years had to be accounted for; but of course the majority would show no travel or change of residence. Thornberg punched for cheap hotels housing many at a time – no record would be kept there, everything being filed in Matilda; and no one would remember a shabby individual patron. Sam Hall's present address was given as the Triton, a glorified flophouse on the East Side not far from the craters. At present unemployed, doubtless living off past savings. Oh, blast! It was necessary to file income-tax returns. Thornberg did so.

Hmmm – physical ID. Make him of average height, stocky, black-haired and black-eyed, a bent nose, and a scar on his forehead – tough-looking, but not enough so as to make him especially memorable. Thornberg filled in the precise measurements. It wasn't hard to fake fingerprints and retinal patterns; he threw in a censor circuit so he wouldn't accidentally duplicate anyone else.

When he was done, Thornberg leaned back and sighed. There were plenty of holes yet in the record, but he could fill them in at his leisure. It had been a couple of hours' hard, concentrated work – utterly pointless, except that he had blown off steam. He felt a lot better.

He glanced at his watch. *Time to get back on the job, son.* For a rebellious moment he wished no one had ever invented clocks. They had made possible the science he loved, but they had then proceeded to mechanize man. Oh, well, too late now. He got up and went out of the booth. The door closed itself behind him.

It was about a month later that Sam Hall committed his first murder.

The night before, Thornberg had been at home. His rank entitled him to good housing even if he did live alone – two rooms and bath on the ninety-eighth floor of a unit in town, not far from the camouflaged entrance to Matilda's underground domain. The fact that he was in Security, even if he didn't belong to the man-hunting branch, gave him so much added deference that he often felt lonely. The superintendent had even offered him his daughter once – 'Only twenty-three, sir, just released by a gentleman of marshal's rank, and looking for a nice patron, sir.' Thornberg had refused, trying not to be prissy about it. *Autres temps, autres moeurs* – but still, she wouldn't have had any choice about getting client status, the first time anyway. And Thornberg's marriage had been a long and happy one.

He had been looking through his bookshelves for something to read. The Literary Bureau had lately been trumpeting Whitman as an early example of Americanism, but though Thornberg had always liked the poet, his hands strayed perversely to the dogeared volume of Marlowe. Was that escapism? The LB was very down on escapism. Oh, well, these were tough times. It wasn't easy to belong to the nation which was enforcing peace on a sullen world – you had to be realistic and energetic and all the rest, no doubt.

The phone buzzed. He went over and clicked on the receiver. Martha Obrenowicz's plain plump face showed in the screen; her gray hair was wild and her voice a harsh croak.

'Uh – hello,' he said uneasily. He hadn't called her since the news of her son's arrest. 'How are you?'

'Jimmy is dead,' she told him.

He stood for a long while. His skull felt hollow.

'I got word today that he died in camp,' said Martha. 'I thought you'd want to know.'

Thornberg shook his head, back and forth, very slowly. 'That isn't news I ever wanted, Martha,' he said.

'It isn't *right*!' she shrieked. 'Jimmy wasn't a traitor. I knew my own son. Who ought to know him better? He had some friends I was kind of doubtful of, but Jimmy, he wouldn't ever –'

Something cold formed in Thornberg's breast. You never knew when calls were being tapped.

'I'm sorry, Martha,' he said without tone. 'But the police are very careful about these things. They wouldn't act till they were sure. Justice is one of our traditions.'

She looked at him for a long time. Her eyes held a hard glitter. 'You too,' she said at last.

'Be careful, Martha,' he warned her. 'I know it's a blow to you, but don't say anything you might regret later. After all, Jimmy may have died accidentally. Those things happen.'

'I – forgot,' she said jerkily. 'You ... are ... in Security ... yourself.'

'Be calm,' he said. 'Think of it as a sacrifice for the national interest.'

She switched off on him. He knew she wouldn't call him again. And it wouldn't be safe to see her.

'Good-by, Martha,' he said aloud. It was like a stranger speaking.

He turned back to the bookshelf. *Not for me*, he told himself thinly. *For Jack*. He touched the binding of *Leaves of Grass*. *Oh, Whitman, old rebel*, he thought, with a curious dry laughter in him, *are they calling you Whirling Walt now?*

That night he took an extra sleeping pill. His head still felt fuzzy when he reported for work, and after a while he gave up trying to answer the mail and went down to the lab.

While he was engaged with Rodney, and making a poor job of understanding the technical problem under discussion, his eyes strayed to Matilda. Suddenly he realized what he needed for a cathartic. He broke off as soon as possible and went into the main control booth.

For a moment he paused at the keyboard. The day-by-day creation of Sam Hall had been an odd experience. He, quiet and introverted, had shaped a rowdy life and painted a rugged personality. Sam Hall was more real to him than many of his associates. *Well, I'm a schizoid type myself. Maybe I should have been a writer.* No, that would have meant too many restrictions, too much fear of offending the censor. He had done exactly as he pleased with Sam Hall.

He drew a deep breath and punched for unsolved murders of Security officers, New York City area, within the last month. They were surprisingly common. Could it be that dissatisfaction was more general than the government admitted? But when the bulk of a nation harbors thoughts labeled treasonous, does the label still apply?

He found what he wanted. Sergeant Brady had incautiously entered the Crater district after dark on the 27th of last month, on a routine checkup mission; he had worn the black uniform, presumably to give himself the full weight of authority. The next morning he had been found in an alley with his head bashed in.

> Oh, I killed a man, they say, so they say.
> Yes, I killed a man, they say, so they say.
>   I beat him on the head
>   And I left him there for dead,
> Yes, I left him there for dead, God damn his eyes.

Newspapers had no doubt deplored this brutality perpetrated by the traitorous agents of enemy powers. ('*Oh, the parson, he did come, he did come.*') A number of suspects had been rounded up at once and given a stiff quizzing. ('*And the sheriff, he came too, he came too.*') There had been nothing proven as yet, though one Joe Nikolsky (fifth generation American, mechanic, married, four children, underground pamphlets found in his room) had been arrested yesterday on suspicion.

Thornberg sighed. He knew enough of Security methods to be sure they would get somebody for such a killing. They couldn't allow their reputation for infallibility to be smirched by a lack of conclusive evidence. Maybe Nikolsky had done the crime – he couldn't *prove* he had simply been out for a walk that evening – and maybe he hadn't. But hell's fire, why not give him a break? He had four kids. With such a black mark, their mother could find work only in a recreation house.

Thornberg scratched his head. This had to be done carefully. Let's see. Brady's body would have been cremated by now, but of course there had been a thorough study first. Thornberg withdrew the dead man's file from the machine and microprinted a replica of the evidence – nothing. Erasing that, he inserted the statement that a blurred thumbprint had been found on the victim's collar and referred to ID labs for reconstruction. In the ID file he inserted the report of such a job, finished only yesterday due to a great press of work. (True enough – they had been busy lately on material sent from Mars, seized in a raid on a rebel meeting place.) The probable pattern of the whorls was – and here he inserted Sam Hall's right thumb.

He returned the spools and leaned back in his chair. It was risky; if anyone thought to check with the ID lab, he was done for. But that was unlikely; the chances were that New York would accept the findings with a routine acknowledgment which some clerk at the lab would file without studying. The more obvious dangers were not too great either: a busy police force would not stop to ask if any of their fingerprint men had actually developed that smudge; and as for hypnoquizzing showing Nikolsky really was the murderer, well, then the print would be assumed that of a passer-by who had found the body without reporting it.

So now Sam Hall had killed a Security officer – grabbed him by the neck and smashed his skull with a weighted club. Thornberg felt a lot better.

New York Security shot a request to Central Records for any new material on the Brady case. An automaton received it, compared the codes, and saw that fresh information had been added. The message flashed back, together with the dossier on Sam Hall and two others – for the reconstruction could not be absolutely accurate.

The other two men were safe enough, as it turned out. Both had alibis. The squad that stormed into the Triton Hotel and demanded Sam Hall were met with blank stares. No such person was registered. No one of the description was known there. A thorough quizzing corroborated this. So – Sam Hall had managed to fake an address. He could have done that easily enough by punching the buttons on the hotel register when no one was looking. Sam Hall could be anywhere!

Joe Nikolsky, having been hypnoed and found harmless, was released. The fine for possessing subversive literature would put him in debt for the next few years – he had no influential friends to get it suspended – but he'd stay out of trouble if he watched his step. Security sent out an alarm for Sam Hall.

Thornberg derived a sardonic amusement from watching the progress of the hunt as it came to Matilda. No one with the ID card had bought tickets on any public transportation. That proved nothing. Of the hundreds who vanished every year, some at least must have been murdered for their ID cards, and their bodies disposed of. Matilda was set to give the alarm when the ID of a disappeared person showed up somewhere. Thornberg faked a few such reports, just to give the police something to do.

He slept more poorly each night, and his work suffered. Once he met Martha Obrenowicz on the street – passed by hastily without greeting her – and couldn't sleep at all, even with maximum permissible drugging.

The new ID system was completed. Machines sent notices to every citizen, with orders to have their numbers tattooed on the right shoulder blade within six weeks. As each tattoo center reported that such-and-such person had had the job done, Matilda's robots changed the record appropriately. Sam Hall, AX-428-399-075, did not report for his tattoo. Thornberg chuckled at the AX symbol.

Then the telecasts flashed a story that made the nation sit up and listen. Bandits had held up the First National Bank in America-town, Idaho (formerly Moscow), making off with a good five million dollars in assorted bills. From their discipline and equipment it was assumed that they were rebel agents, possibly having come in a spaceship from their unknown interplanetary base, and that the raid was intended to help finance their nefarious activities. Security was cooperating with the Armed Forces to track down the evidence, and arrests were expected hourly, etc., etc.

Thornberg went to Matilda for a complete account. It had been a bold job. The robbers had apparently worn plastic face masks and light body armor under ordinary clothes. In the scuffle of the getaway one man's mask had slipped aside – only for a moment, but a clerk who happened to see it had, with the aid of hypnosis, given a fairly good description. A brown-haired, heavy-set fellow, Roman nose, thin lips, toothbrush mustache.

Thornberg hesitated. A joke was a joke; and helping poor Nikolsky was perhaps morally defensible; but aiding and abetting a felony which was in all likelihood an act of treason –

He grinned to himself, without much humor. It was too much fun playing God. Swiftly he changed the record. The crook had been of medium height, dark, scar-faced, broken-nosed – He sat for a while wondering how sane he was. How sane anybody was.

Security Central asked for the complete file on the holdup, with any correlations the machine could make. It was sent to them. The description given could have been that of many men, but the scanners eliminated all but one possibility. *Sam Hall*.

The hounds bayed forth again. That night Thornberg slept well.

Dear Dad,

Sorry I haven't written before, but we've been kept pretty busy here. As you know, I've been with a patrol in Gorbuvashtar for the past several weeks – desolate country, like all this blasted planet. Sometimes I wonder if I'll ever see the sun again. And lakes and forests and – who wrote that line about the green hills of earth? We can't get much to read out here, and sometimes my mind feels rusty. Not that I'm complaining, of course. This is a necessary job, and somebody has to do it.

We'd hardly gotten back from the patrol when we were called out on special duty, bundled into rockets, and tossed halfway around the planet through the worst gale I've ever seen, even on Venus. If I hadn't been an officer and therefore presumably a gentleman, I'd have upchucked. A lot of the boys did, and we were a pretty sorry crew when we landed. But we had to go into action right away. There was a strike in the thorium mines and the local men couldn't break it. We had to use guns before we could bring them to reason. Dad, I felt sorry for the poor devils, I don't mind admitting it. Rocks and hammers and sluice hoses against machine guns! And conditions in the mines are pretty rugged. They DELETED BY CENSOR someone has to do that job too, and if no one will volunteer, for any kind of pay, they have to assign civilian-service men arbitrarily. It's for the state.

Otherwise nothing new. Life is pretty monotonous. Don't believe the adventure stories – adventure is weeks of boredom punctuated by moments of being scared gutless. Sorry to be so brief, but I want to get this on the outbound rocket. Won't be another for a couple of months. Everything well, really. I hope the same for you and live for the day we'll meet again. Thanks a million for the cookies – you know you can't afford to pay the freight, you old spendthrift! Martha baked them, didn't she? I recognized the Obrenowicz touch. Say hello to her and Jim for me. And most of all, my kindest thoughts go to you.

As ever,
Jack.

The telecasts carried 'Wanted' messages for Sam Hall. No photographs of him were available, but an artist could draw an accurate likeness from Matilda's precise description, and his truculent face began to adorn public places. Not long thereafter, the Security offices in Denver were blown up by a grenade tossed from a speeding car that vanished into traffic. A witness said he had glimpsed the thrower, and the fragmentary picture given under hypnosis was not unlike Sam Hall's. Thornberg doctored the record a bit to make it still more similar. The tampering was risky, of course; if Security ever became suspicious, they could easily check back with their witnesses. But it was not too big a chance to take, for a scientifically quizzed man told everything germane to the subject which his memory, conscious, subconscious, and cellular, held. There was never any reason to repeat such an interrogation.

Thornberg often tried to analyze his own motives. Plainly enough, he disliked the government. He must have contained that hate all his life, carefully suppressed from awareness, and only recently had it been forced into his conscious mind; not even his subconscious could have formulated it earlier, or he would have been caught by the loyalty probes. The hate derived from a lifetime of doubts (had there been any real reason to fight Brazil other than obtain those bases and mining concessions? had the Chinese attack perhaps been provoked – or even faked, for their government had denied it?) and the million petty frustrations of the garrison state. Still – the strength of it! The violence!

By creating Sam Hall he had struck back, but it was an ineffectual blow, a timid gesture. Most likely his basic motive was simply to find a halfway safe release; in Sam Hall he lived vicariously all the things that the beast within him wanted to do. Several times he had intended to discontinue his sabotage, but it was like a drug: Sam Hall was becoming necessary to his own stability.

The thought was alarming. He ought to see a psychiatrist – but no, the doctor would be bound to report his tale, he would go to camp, and Jack, if not exactly ruined, would be under a cloud for the rest of his life. Thornberg had no desire to go to camp, anyway. His own existence had compensations – interesting work, a few good friends, art and music and literature, decent wine, sunsets and mountains, memories. He had started this game on impulse, but now it was too late to stop it.

For Sam Hall had been promoted to Public Enemy Number One.

Winter came, and the slopes of the Rockies under which Matilda lay were white beneath a cold greenish sky. Air traffic around the nearby town was lost in that hugeness; brief hurtling meteors against infinity; ground traffic could not be seen at all from the Records entrance. Thornberg took the special tubeway to work every morning, but he often walked the five miles back, and his Sundays were usually spent in long hikes over the slippery trails. That was a foolish thing to do alone in winter, but he felt reckless.

He was working in his office shortly before Christmas when the intercom said: 'Major Sorensen to see you, sir. From Investigation.'

Thornberg felt his stomach tie itself into a cold knot. 'All right,' he answered in a voice whose levelness surprised him. 'Cancel any other appointments.' Security Investigation took priority over everything.

Sorensen walked in with a hard, military clack of boots. He was a big blond man, heavy-shouldered, his face expressionless and his eyes as pale and cold and remote as the winter sky. The black uniform fitted him like another skin; the lightning badge of his service glittered against it like a frosty star. He stood stiffly before the desk, and Thornberg rose to give him an awkward salute.

'Please sit down, Major Sorensen. What can I do for you?'

'Thanks.' The cop's voice was crisp and harsh. He lowered his bulk into a chair and drilled Thornberg with his eyes. 'I've come about the Sam Hall case.'

'Oh – the rebel?' Thornberg's skin prickled. It was all he could do to meet those eyes.

'How do you know he's a rebel?' asked Sorensen. 'It's never been proved officially.'

'Why – I assumed – the bank raid – and then the posters say he's believed to be in the underground –'

Sorensen inclined his cropped head ever so slightly. When he spoke again it was in a relaxed tone, almost casual: 'Tell me, Major Thornberg, have you followed the Hall dossier in detail?'

Thornberg hesitated. He wasn't supposed to do so unless ordered; he only kept the machine running. A memory came back to him, something he had read once: 'When suspected of a major sin, admit the minor ones frankly. It disarms suspicion.' Something like that.

'As a matter of fact, I have,' he said. 'I know it's against regs, but I was interested and – well, I couldn't see any harm in it. I've not discussed it with anyone, of course.'

'No matter.' Sorensen waved a muscular hand. 'If you hadn't done so, I'd have ordered you to. I want your opinion on this.'

'Why – I'm not a detective –'

'You know more about Records, though, than anyone else. I'll be frank with you – under the rose, naturally.' Sorensen seemed almost friendly now. *Was it a trick to put his prey off guard?* 'You see, there are some puzzling features about this case.'

Thornberg kept silent. He wondered if Sorensen could hear the thudding of his heart.

'Sam Hall is a shadow,' said the cop. 'The most careful checkups eliminate any chance of his being identical with anyone else of that name. In fact, we've learned that the name occurs in a violent old drinking song – is it coincidence, or did the song suggest crime to Sam Hall, or did he by some incredible process get that alias into his record instead of his real name? Whatever the answer there, we know that he's ostensibly without military training, yet he's pulled off some beautiful pieces of precision attack. His IQ is only 110, but he evades all our traps. He has no politics, yet he turns on Security without warning. We have not been able to find one person who remembers him – not one, and believe me, we have been thorough. Oh, there are a few subconscious memories which might be of him, but probably aren't – and so aggressive a personality should be remembered consciously. No undergrounder or foreign agent we've caught had any knowledge of him, which defies probability. The whole business seems impossible.'

Thornberg licked his lips. Sorensen, the hunter of men, must know he was frightened; but would he assume it to be the normal nervousness of a man in the presence of a Security officer?

Sorensen's face broke into a hard smile. 'As Sherlock Holmes once remarked,' he said, 'when you have eliminated every other hypothesis, then the one which remains, however improbable, must be the right one.'

Despite himself, Thornberg was jolted. Sorensen hadn't struck him as a reader.

'Well,' he asked slowly, 'what is your remaining hypothesis?'

The other man watched him for a long time, it seemed forever, before replying. 'The underground is more powerful and widespread than people realize. They've had some seventy years to prepare, and there are many good brains in their ranks. They carry on scientific research of their own. It's top secret, but we know they have perfected a type of weapon we cannot duplicate yet. It seems to be a hand gun throwing bolts of energy – a blaster, you might call it – of immense power. Sooner or later they're going to wage open war against the government.

'Now, could they have done something comparable in psychology? Could they have found a way to erase or cover up memories selectively, even on the cellular level? Could they know how to fool a personality tester, how to disguise the mind itself? If so, there may be any number of Sam Halls in our very midst, undetectable until the moment comes for them to strike.'

Thornberg felt almost boneless. He couldn't help gasping his relief, and hoped Sorensen would take it for a sign of alarm.

'The possibility is frightening, isn't it?' The blond man laughed harshly. 'You can imagine what is being felt in high official circles. We've put all the psychological researchers we could get to work on the problem – bah! Fools! They go by the book; they're afraid to be original even when the state tells them to.

'It may just be a wild fancy, of course. I hope it is. But we have to *know*. That's why I approached you personally, instead of sending the usual requisition. I want you to make a search of the records – everything pertaining to the subject, every man, every discovery, every hypothesis. You have a broad technical background and, from your psychorecord, an unusual amount of creative imagination. I want you to do what you can to correlate all your data. Co-opt anybody you need. Submit to my office a report on the possibility – or should I say probability – of this notion, and if there is any likelihood of its being true, sketch out a research program which will enable us to duplicate the results and counteract them.'

Thornberg fumbled for words. 'I'll try,' he said lamely. 'I'll do my best.'

'Good. It's for the state.'

Sorensen had finished his official business, but he didn't go at once. 'Rebel propaganda is subtle stuff,' he said quietly, after a pause. 'It's dangerous because it uses our own slogans, with a twisted meaning. Liberty, equality, justice, peace. Too many people can't appreciate that times have changed and the meanings of words have necessarily changed with them.'

'I suppose not,' said Thornberg. He added the lie: 'I never thought much about it.'

'You should,' said Sorensen. 'Study your history. When we lost World War III we had to militarize to win World War IV, and after that, for our own safety, we had to mount guard on the whole human race. The people demanded it at the time.'

The people, thought Thornberg, *never appreciated freedom till they'd lost it. They were always willing to sell their birthright. Or was it merely that, being untrained in thinking, they couldn't see through demagoguery, couldn't visualize the ultimate consequences of their wishes?* He was vaguely shocked at the thought; wasn't he able to control his own mind any longer?

'The rebels,' said Sorensen, 'claim that conditions have changed, that militarization is no longer necessary – if it ever was – and that America would be safe enough in a union of free countries. It's devilishly clever propaganda, Major Thornberg. Watch out for it.'

He got up and took his leave. Thornberg sat for a long time staring after the door. Sorensen's last words were – odd, to say the least. Was it a hint – or was it bait in a trap?

The next day Matilda received a news item whose details were carefully censored for the public channels. A rebel force had landed in the stockade of Camp Jackson, in Utah, gunned down the guards, and taken away the prisoners. The camp doctor had been spared, and related that the leader of the raid, a stocky man in a mask, had ironically said to him: 'Tell your friends I'll call again. My name is Sam Hall.'

Space Guard ship blown up on Mesa Verde Field. On a fragment of metal someone has scrawled: 'Compliments of Sam Hall.'

Army quartermaster depot robbed of a million dollars. Bandit chief says, before disappearing, that he is Sam Hall.

Squad of Security police, raiding a suspected underground hideout in New Pittsburgh, cut down by machine-gun fire. Voice over hidden loud-speaker cries: 'My name it is Sam Hall!'

Dr Matthew Thomson, chemist in Seattle, suspected of underground connections, is gone when his home is raided. Note left on desk says: 'Off to visit Sam Hall. Back for liberation. M.T.'

Defense plant producing important robomb parts blown up near Miami by small atomic bomb, after being warned over the phone that the bomb has been planted and they have half an hour to get their workers out. The caller, masked, styles himself Sam Hall.

Army laboratory in Houston given similar warning by Sam Hall. A fake, but a day's valuable work is lost in the alarm and the search.

Scribbled on walls from New York to San Diego, from Duluth to El Paso, Sam Hall, Sam Hall, Sam Hall.

Obviously, thought Thornberg, the underground had seized on the invisible and invincible man of legend and turned him to their own purposes. Reports of him poured in from all over the country, hundreds every day – Sam Hall seen here, Sam Hall seen there. Ninety-nine per cent could be dismissed as hoaxes, hallucinations, mistakes; it was another national craze, fruit of a jittery time, like the sixteenth- and seventeenth-century witch hunts or the twentieth-century flying saucers. But Security and civilian police had to check on every one.

Thornberg planted a number of them himself.

Mostly, though, he was busy with his assignment. He could understand what it meant to the government. Life in the garrison state was inevitably founded on fear and mistrust, every man's eye on his neighbor; but at least psychotyping and hypnoquizzing had given a degree of surety. Now, with that staff knocked out from under them –

His preliminary studies indicated that a discovery such as Sorensen had hypothesized, while not impossible, was too far beyond the scope of modern science for the rebels to have perfected. Such research carried on nowadays would, from the standpoint of practicality if not of knowledge, be a waste of time and trained men.

He spent a good many sleepless hours and used up a month's cigarette ration before he could decide what to do. All right, he'd aided insurrection in a small way, and he shouldn't boggle at the next step. Still – nevertheless – did he want to?

Jack – the boy had a career lined out for himself. He loved the big deeps beyond the sky as he would love a woman. If things changed, what then of Jack's career?

Well, what was it now? Stuck on a dreary planet as guardsman and executioner of homesick starvelings poisoned by radioactivity – never even seeing the sun. Come the day, Jack could surely wangle a berth on a real spacer; they'd need bold men to explore beyond Saturn. Jack was too honest to make a good rebel, but Thornberg felt that after the initial shock he would welcome a new government.

But treason! Oaths!

When in the course of human events –

It was a small thing that decided Thornberg. He passed a shop downtown and noticed a group of the Youth Guard smashing in its windows and spattering yellow paint over the goods: O, Moses, Jesus, Mendelssohn, Hertz, and Einstein! Once he had taken this path, a curious serenity possessed him. He stole a vial of prussic acid from a chemist friend and carried it in his pocket; and as for Jack, the boy would have to take his chances too.

The work was demanding and dangerous. He had to alter recorded facts which were available elsewhere, in books and journals and the minds of men. Nothing could be done with the basic theory, of course, but quantitative results could be juggled a little so that the over-all picture was subtly askew. He would co-opt carefully chosen experts, men whose psychotypes indicated they would take the easy course of relying on Matilda instead of checking the original sources. And the correlation and integration of innumerable data, the empirical equations and extrapolations thereof, could be tampered with.

He turned his regular job over to Rodney and devoted himself entirely to the new one. He grew thin and testy; when Sorensen called up trying to hurry him, he snapped back: 'Do you want speed or quality?' and wasn't too surprised at himself afterward. He got little sleep, but his mind seemed unnaturally clear.

Winter faded into spring while Thornberg and his experts labored and while the nation shook, psychically and physically, with the growing violence of Sam Hall. The report Thornberg submitted in May was so voluminous and detailed that he didn't think the government researchers would bother referring to any other source. Its conclusion: yes, given a brilliant man applying Belloni matrices to cybernetic formulas and using some unknown kind of colloidal probe, a psychological masking technique was plausible.

The government yanked every man it could find into research. Thornberg knew it was only a matter of time before they realized they had been had. How much time, he couldn't say. But when they were sure –

Now up the rope I go, up I go.
Now up the rope I go, up I go.
    And the bastards down below,
        They say: 'Sam, we told you so.'
They say: 'Sam, we told you so,' God damn their eyes.

'REBELS ATTACK'

'SPACESHIPS LAND UNDER COVER OF RAINSTORM, SEIZE POINTS NEAR N DETROIT'

'FLAME WEAPONS USED AGAINST ARMY BY REBELS'

'The infamous legions of the traitors have taken key points throughout the nation, but already our gallant forces have hurled them back. They have come out in early summer like toadstools, and will wither as fast – WHEEEEEE-OOOOOO!' Silence.

'All citizens are directed to keep calm, remain loyal to their country, and stay at their usual tasks until otherwise ordered. Civilians will report to their local defense commanders. All military reservists will report immediately for active duty.'

'Hello, Hawaii! Are you there? Come in, Hawaii! Calling Hawaii!'

'CQ, Mars GHQ calling ... buzz, wheeee ... seized Syrtis Major Colony and ... whoooo ... help needed ...'

'The Lunar rocket bases are assaulted and carried. The commander blows them up rather than surrender. A pinpoint flash on the moon's face, a new crater; what will they name it?'

'So they've got Seattle, have they? Send a robomb flight. Blow the place off the map ... Citizens? To hell with citizens! This is war!'

'... in New York. Secretly drilled rebels emerged from the notorious Crater district and stormed ...'

'... assassins were shot down. The new President has already been sworn in and ...'

'BRITAIN, CANADA, AUSTRALIA, REFUSE ASSISTANCE TO GOVT'

'... no, sir. The bombs reached Seattle all right. But they were all stopped before they hit – some kind of energy gun ...'

'COMECO to all Army commanders in Florida and Georgia: Enemy action has made Florida and the keys temporarily untenable. Army units will withdraw as follows ...'

'Today a rebel force engaging an Army convoy in Donner Pass was annihilated by a well-placed tactical atomic bomb. Though our own men suffered losses on this account ...'

'COMECO to all Army commanders in California: The mutiny of units stationed near San Francisco poses a grave problem ...'

'SP RAID REBEL HIDEOUT, BAG FIVE OFFICERS'

'All right, so the enemy is about to capture Boston. We *can't* issue weapons to the citizens. They might turn them on us!'

'SPACE GUARD UNITS EXPECTED FROM VENUS'

Jack, Jack, Jack!

It was strange, living in the midst of a war. Thornberg had never thought it would be like this. Drawn faces, furtive eyes, utter confusion in the telecast news and the irregularly arriving panic when a rebel jet whistled overhead – but nothing else. No gunfire, no bombs, no battles at all except the unreal ones you heard about. The only casualty lists here were due to Security – people kept disappearing, and nobody spoke about them.

But then, why should the enemy bother with this unimportant mountain town? The Army of Liberation, as it styled itself, was grabbing key points of industry, transportation, communication; was fighting military units, sabotaging buildings and machines, assassinating important men in the government. By its very purpose, it couldn't wage total war, couldn't annihilate the folk it wanted to free. Rumor had it that the defenders were not so finicky.

Most citizens were passive. They always are. It is doubtful if more than one-fourth of the population was ever near a combat during the Third American Revolution. City dwellers might see fire in the sky, hear the whistle and crack of artillery, scramble out of the way of soldiers and armored vehicles, cower in shelters when the rockets thundered overhead – but the battle was fought outside town. If it came to street fighting, the rebels wouldn't push in; they would either withdraw and wait or they would rely on agents inside the city. Then one might hear the crack of rifles and grenades, rattle of machine guns, sharp discharge of energy beams, and see corpses in the street. But it ended with a return of official military government or with the rebels marching in and setting up their own provisional councils. (They were rarely greeted with cheers and flowers. Nobody knew how the war would end. But there were words whispered to them, and they usually got good service.)

As nearly as possible, the average American continued his average life.

Thornberg went on in his own way. Matilda, as the information center, was working at full blast. If the rebels ever learned where she was –

Or did they know?

He could not spare much time for his private sabotage, but he planned it carefully and made every second tell when he was alone in the control booth. Sam Hall reports, of course – Sam Hall here, Sam Hall there, pulling off this or that incredible stunt. But what did one man, even a superman, count for in these gigantic days? Something else was needed.

Radio and newspapers announced jubilantly that Venus had finally been contacted. The Moon and Mars had fallen, there was only silence from the Jovian satellites, but everything seemed in order on Venus – a few feeble uprisings had been quickly smashed. The powerful Guard units there would be on their way to Earth at once. Troop transports had to orbit most of the way, so it would take a good six weeks before they could arrive, but when they did they would be a powerful reinforcement.

'Looks like you might see your boy soon, chief,' said Rodney.

'Yes,' said Thornberg, 'I might.'

'Tough fighting.' Rodney shook his head. 'I'd sure as hell hate to be in it.'

If Jack is killed by a rebel gun, when I have aided the rebels' cause –

Sam Hall, reflected Thornberg, had lived a hard life, all violence and enmity and suspicion. Even his wife hadn't trusted him.

> ... And my Nellie dressed in blue
> Says: 'Your trifling days are through.
> Now I know that you'll be true,
> God damn your eyes.'

Poor Sam Hall. It was no wonder he had killed a man.

Suspicion!

Thornberg stood for a taut moment while an eerie tingle went through him. The police state was founded on suspicion. Nobody could trust anyone else. And with the new fear of psychomasking, and research on that project suspended during the crisis –

Steady, boy, steady. Can't rush into this. Have to plan it out very carefully.

Thornberg punched for the dossiers of key men in the administration, in the military, in Security. He did it in the presence of two assistants, for he thought that his own frequent sessions alone in the control booth were beginning to look funny.

'This is top secret,' he warned them, pleased with his own cool manner.

He was becoming a regular Machiavelli. 'You'll be skinned alive if you mention it to anyone.'

Rodney gave him a shrewd glance. 'So they're not even sure of their own top men now, are they?' he murmured.

'I've been told to make some checks,' snapped Thornberg. 'That's all you need to know.'

He studied the files for many hours before coming to a decision. Secret observations were, of course, made of everyone from time to time. A cross check with Matilda showed that the cop who had filed the last report on Lindahl had been killed the next day in a spontaneous and abortive uprising. The report was innocuous: Lindahl had stayed at home, studying some papers; he had been alone in the house except for a bodyguard who had been in another room and not seen him. And Lindahl was Undersecretary of Defense.

Thornberg changed the record. A masked man – stocky, black-haired – had come in and talked for three hours with Lindahl. They had spoken low, so that the cop's ears, outside the window, couldn't catch what was said. The visitor had gone away then, and Lindahl had retired. The cop went back in great excitement and made out his report and gave it to the signalman, who had sent it on to Matilda.

Tough on the signalman, thought Thornberg. *They'll want to know why he didn't tell this to his chief in New Washington, if the observer was killed before doing so. He'll deny every such report, and they'll hypnoquiz him – but they don't trust that method any more!*

His sympathy didn't last long. What counted was having the war over before Jack got home. He refiled the altered spool and did a little backtracking, shifting the last report of Sam Hall from Salt Lake City to Philadelphia. Make it more plausible. Then, as opportunity permitted, he did some work on other men's records.

He had to wait two haggard days before the next requisition came from Security for a fresh cross check on Sam Hall. The scanners swept in an intricate pattern, cogs turned over, a tube glowed. Circuits were activated elsewhere, the spool LINDAHL was unrolled before the microprinter inside the machine. Cross references to that spool ramified in all directions. Thornberg sent the preliminary report back with a query: This matter looked interesting; did they want more information?

They did!

Next day the telecast announced a drastic shakeup in the Department of Defense. Lindahl was not heard from again.

And I, thought Thornberg grimly, have grabbed a very large tiger by the tail. Now they'll have to check everybody – and I'm one man, trying to keep ahead of the whole Security police!

Lindahl is a traitor. How did his chief ever let him get on the board? Secretary Hoheimer was pretty good friends with Lindahl, too. Get Records to cross check Hoheimer.

What's this? Hoheimer himself! Five years ago, yes, but even so – the records show that he lived in an apartment unit where *Sam Hall* was janitor! Grab Hoheimer! Who'll take his place? General Halliburton? That stupid old bastard? Well, at least his dossier is clean. Can't trust those slick characters.

Hoheimer has a brother in Security, general's rank, good detection record. A blind? Who knows? Slap the brother in jail, at least for the duration. Better check his staff ... Central Records shows that his chief field agent, Jones, has five days unaccounted for a year ago; he claimed Security secrecy at the time, but a double cross check shows it wasn't so. Shoot Jones! He has a nephew in the Army, a captain. Pull that unit out of the firing line till we can study it man by man! We've had too many mutinies already.

Lindahl was also a close friend of Benson, in charge of the Tennessee Atomic Ordnance Works. Haul Benson in!

The first Hoheimer's son is an industrialist, he owns a petroleum-synthesis plant in Texas. Nab him! His wife is a sister of Leslie, head of the War Production Coordination Board. Get Leslie too. Sure, he's doing a good job, but he may be sending information to the enemy. Or he may just be waiting for the signal to sabotage the whole works. We can't trust *anybody*, I tell you!

What's this? Records relays an Intelligence report that the mayor of Tampa was in cahoots with the rebels. It's marked 'Unreliable, Rumor' – but Tampa *did* surrender without a fight. The mayor's business partner is Gale, who has a cousin in the Army, commanding a robomb base in New Mexico. Check both the Gales, Records ... So the cousin was absent four days without filing his whereabouts, was he? Military privileges or not, arrest him and find out where he was!

– Attention, Records, attention, Records, urgent Brigadier John Harmsworth Gale, etc., etc., refused to divulge information required by Security officers, claiming to have been at his base all the time. Can this be an error on your part?

– Records to Security Central, ref: etc., etc. No possibility of error exists except in information received.

– to Records, ref: etc., etc. Gale's story corroborated by three of his officers.

Put that whole damned base under arrest! Recheck those reports. Who sent them in, anyway?

– to Records, ref: etc., etc. On attempt to arrest entire personnel, Robomb Base 37-J fired on Security detachment and repulsed it. At last reports Gale was calling for rebel forces fifty miles off to assist him. Details will follow for the files as soon as possible.

So Gale was a traitor! – Or was he driven to it by fear? – Have Records find out who filed that information about him in the first place. *We can't trust anybody!*

Thornberg was not much surprised when his door was kicked open and the Security squad entered. He had been expecting it for days now. One man can't keep ahead of the game forever. No doubt the accumulated inconsistencies had finally drawn suspicion his way; or perhaps, ironically, the chains of accusation he had forged had by chance led to him; or perhaps Rodney or another person here had decided something was amiss with the chief and lodged a tip.

He felt no blame for whoever it was, if that had been the case. The tragedy of civil war was that it turned brother against brother; millions of good and decent men were with the government because they had pledged themselves to be. Mostly, he felt tired.

He looked down the barrel of the gun and then raised weary eyes to the hard face behind it. 'I take it I'm under arrest?' he asked tonelessly.

'Get up!' The face was flat and brutal, there was sadism in the heavy mouth. A typical blackcoat.

June whimpered. The man who held her was twisting her arm behind her back. 'Don't do that,' said Thornberg. 'She's innocent.'

'Get up, I said!' The gun thrust closer.

'Don't come near me, either.' Thornberg lifted his right hand. It was clenched around a little ball. 'See this? It's a gimmick I made. No, not a bomb, just a small radio control. If my hand relaxes, the rubber will expand and pull a switch shut.'

The men recoiled a little.

'Let the girl go, I said,' repeated Thornberg patiently.

'You surrender first!'

June screamed as the cop twisted harder.

'No,' said Thornberg. 'This is more important than any one of us. I was prepared, you see. I expect to die. So if I let go of this ball, the radio signal closes a relay and a powerful magnetic field is generated in Matilda – in the Records machine. Every record the government has will be wiped clean. I hate to think what your fellows will do to you if you let that happen.'

Slowly, the cop released June. She slumped to the floor, crying.

'It's a bluff!' said the man with the gun. There was sweat on his face.

'Try it and find out.' Thornberg forced a smile. 'I don't care.'

'You traitor!'

'And a very effective one, wasn't I? I've got the government turned end for end and upside down. The Army's in an uproar, officers deserting right and left for fear they'll be arrested next. Administration is hogtied and trembling. Security is chasing its own tail around half a continent. Assassination and betrayal are daily occurrences. Men go over to the rebels in droves. The Army of Liberation is sweeping a demoralized and ineffectual resistance before it everywhere. I predict that New Washington will capitulate within a week.'

'And your doing!' Finger tense on the trigger.

'Oh, no. No single man can change history. But I was a rather important factor, yes. Or let's say – Sam Hall was.'

'What are you going to do?'

'That depends on you, my friend. If you shoot me, gas me, knock me out, or anything of that sort, my hand will naturally relax. Otherwise we'll just wait till one side or the other gets tired.'

'You're bluffing!' snapped the squad leader.

'You could, of course, have the technicians here check Matilda and see if I'm telling the truth,' said Thornberg. 'And if I am, you could have them disconnect my electromagnet. Only I warn you, at the first sign of any such operation on your part I'll let go this ball. Look in my mouth.' He opened it. 'A glass vial, full of poison. After I let the ball go, I'll close my teeth together hard. So you see I have nothing to fear from you.'

Bafflement and rage flitted over the faces that watched him. They weren't used to thinking, those men.

'Of course,' said Thornberg, 'there is one other possibility for you. At last reports, a rebel jet squadron was based not a hundred miles from here. We could call it and have them come and take this place over. That might be to your own advantage too. There is going to be a day of reckoning with you blackcoats, and my influence could shield you, however little you deserve it.'

They stared at each other. After a very long while the squad leader shook his head. 'No!'

The man behind him pulled out a gun and shot him in the back.

Thornberg smiled.

'As a matter of fact,' he told Sorensen, 'I *was* bluffing. All I had was a tennis ball with a few small electrical parts glued on it. Not that it made much difference at that stage, except to me.'

'Matilda will be handy for us in mopping up,' said Sorensen. 'Want to stay on?'

'Sure, at least till my son arrives. That'll be next week.'

'You'll be glad to hear we've finally contacted the Guard in space: just a short radio message, but the commander has agreed to obey whatever government is in power when he arrives. That'll be us, so your boy won't have to do any fighting.'

There were no words for that. Instead Thornberg said, with a hardheld casualness, 'You know, I'm surprised that *you* should have been an undergrounder.'

'There were a few of us even in Security,' said Sorensen. 'We were organized in small cells, spotted throughout the nation, and wangled things so we could hypnoquiz each other.' He grimaced. 'It wasn't a pleasant job, though. Some of the things I had to do – Well, that's over with now.'

He leaned back in his chair, putting his booted feet on the desk. A Liberation uniform was usually pretty sloppy; they didn't worry about spit-and-polish, but he had managed to be immaculate. 'There was a certain amount of suspicion about Sam Hall at first,' he said. 'The song, you know, and other items. My bosses weren't stupid. I got myself detailed to investigate you; a close checkup gave me grounds to suspect you of revolutionary thoughts, so naturally I gave you a clean bill of health. Later on I cooked up this fantasy of the psychological mask and got several high-ranking men worried about it. When you followed my lead on that, I was sure you were on our side.' He grinned. 'So naturally our army never attacked Matilda!'

'You must have joined your forces quite recently.'

'Yeah, I had to scram out of Security during the uproar and witch hunt you started. You damn near cost me my life, Thorny, know that? Well worth it, though, just to see those cockroaches busily stepping on each other.'

Thornberg leaned gravely over his desk. 'I always had to assume you rebels were sincere,' he said. 'I've never been sure. But now I can check up. Do you intend to destroy Matilda?'

Sorensen nodded. 'After we've used her to help us find some people we want rather badly, and to get reorganized – of course. She's too powerful an instrument. It's time to loosen the strings of government.'

'Thank you,' whispered Thornberg.

He chuckled after a moment. 'And that will be the end of Sam Hall,' he said. 'He'll go to whatever Valhalla is reserved for the great characters of fiction. I can see him squabbling with Sherlock Holmes and shocking the hell out of King Arthur and striking up a beautiful friendship with Long John Silver. You know how the ballad ends?' He sang softly: '*Now up in heaven I dwell, in heaven I dwell –*'

Unfortunately, the conclusion is pretty rugged. Sam Hall never was satisfied.

SPANNER · IN ·THE · WORKS

J. T. McIntosh

Before tapping on Bergstein's door, Mark Swan surveyed it sardonically.

It was a plain plastic-faced door with nothing on it but a handle. No gold-painted name. Not even the word 'Private'.

Thus in the Intelligence Department anonymity was preserved. Because Bergstein's name wasn't on the door, no office cleaner would ever learn anything which would enable Mercaptan to win the war. Because in the Terran Intelligence section nobody's right hand ever knew what the left hand was doing, there would never be any leaks.

In a pig's eye.

Mark tapped on the anonymous door and entered.

'Ah, Mark,' said Bergstein. 'You're just in time. We're due at the lab in two minutes.'

'I'm not coming,' said Mark.

Bergstein stared incredulously.

Mark handed him a plain envelope. 'I want that sent to D,' he said. 'And I want it time-stamped now, so that he'll know I handed it in before Carr went under the probe.'

'You can't do that,' Bergstein exclaimed.

'There are many things I can't do, but that isn't one of them. I don't even have to tell you what's in that envelope, but I will, after you've time-stamped it.'

Bergstein hesitated and then put the envelope into a small machine. It spat the envelope back at him, enclosed in another, stouter, sealed package with the time clearly marked on the top left-hand corner.

'In that envelope,' Mark said, 'is my resignation. And don't tell me I can't resign. I also state that Carr is not the man who took a distorter into the Navy Yard, and that none of the seventeen people we were told to screen did it.'

Bergstein opened his mouth and then shut it. After due consideration he smiled. 'Sour grapes,' he said.

'What?'

'I may not be supposed to know it, Mark, but one hears things. Two years ago when S retired, you thought you were going to take his place as Security Chief, didn't you? Instead D took over and you were made departmental head of Counterespionage. Then six months ago I was promoted over you.'

'So?' said Mark grimly.

'Sour grapes,' Bergstein repeated, and left it at that.

Mark turned to go.

'Wait,' Bergstein said sharply. 'You're still in CE and I'm still your boss.'

He pressed a button on his desk. 'This is what we're going to do, Mark. I'm sending this letter to D right now. Then you and I are going to the lab. After the probe has duly established that Carr planted that distorter, D will no doubt send for you. And after that it's improbable that you'll be in Intelligence any more – though whether the record will show that you resigned or were fired I've no idea. Now let's go to the lab.'

'I don't fancy seeing an innocent man ripped to pieces by the probe.'

'Once for all, Carr's the saboteur. You're coming with me to the lab. That's an order.'

A messenger entered, and Bergstein gave him the package with instructions to deliver it to D immediately. Then he stood up. Mark shrugged and went with him.

In the laboratory Carr was ready for the probe, strapped in a metal throne which looked like an electric chair and was just as unkind in a slightly different way. Half a dozen technicians and a doctor were in attendance. Mark found the presence of a doctor ironic – yet hadn't doctors been present when duels were fought?

Bergstein nodded to the chief technician, who nodded to one of his assistants, who pulled down a knife-switch. Carr began to scream. There was a faint smell of burning, which meant that something was wrong somewhere, but it was too late to do anything about that. The chief technician made another gesture to his assistant, and the assistant played a tune on his controls.

Carr stopped screaming. The probe now allowed, indeed commanded, him to talk, but didn't let him scream and didn't let him tell lies.

'Did you take a distorter into the Navy Yard?' Bergstein asked.

Despite the stand he had taken, Mark hoped the answer would be 'Yes'. But it wasn't. It was 'No', and Bernstein staggered as if he'd been struck.

'Did you have anything to do with a plan to have a distorter in the Navy Yard?' Bergstein persisted.

'No.'

'Are you a spy?'

'No.'

'Have you ever been in the pay of Mercaptan, or any agent of Mercaptan?' Bergstein pleaded.

'No.'

Bergstein gestured, the chief technician gestured, the assistant cut the probe and Carr collapsed in an untidy bundle.

'He may recover,' said the doctor without any great confidence, moving to Carr's side and ripping the contacts from him. After a few seconds he added: 'No. Catalepsy for a few days, and then death.'

Bergstein was speechless. Mark felt no triumph.

'I,' he said, 'am going out to get drunk.'

Mark sat alone in his favorite bar downing whisky sours with no regard for what was going to happen when the rest of his body caught up with the alcohol content of his stomach.

Fortunately Carr was a pervert and a crook. After a few hours Mark knew he'd be able to convince himself that Carr was no loss to the world and that if he hadn't deserved death for sabotage, he deserved it for something else.

At the moment, however, all he could think of was that his department, CE, had in effect executed an innocent man – just another boob to add to the long list of boobs in Intelligence during the last two years. The fact that Mark had done everything in his power to prevent it let him out to a considerable extent, but it didn't make him feel like singing and dancing with joy.

What was wrong with Intelligence? Not, surely, the Genius. The Genius had worked well for S – why shouldn't it work well for D? It was not D. D was a former colleague of Mark's – he had had a name then, before he became Security Chief – and although neither Mark nor S had liked him, the appointment of D as Security Chief was not, in Mark's opinion, nearly enough to turn an efficient Intelligence Department into the shambles it had become. Since D was at the head, he was responsible and had to shoulder the blame and no doubt deserved a lot of it – but inefficiency on the part of D could not possibly be the whole answer.

And it certainly wasn't Bergstein's fault, for CE was only one branch of Intelligence and wasn't responsible for more than its fair share of boobs. Besides, technically the current business couldn't be blamed on Bergstein, because CE had been instructed by the Genius, through D of course, to find which of a certain party of seventeen visitors who had been shown through the Navy Yard had planted a distorter there. Bergstein and Mark interviewed everybody on the list, together and separately, and they hadn't exactly disagreed in picking Carr as the prime suspect.

The Genius asked a specific question: Which of these seventeen could be bribed to perform such an act of sabotage? And both Bergstein and Mark picked Carr. As far as Bergstein was concerned, that was that – the Genius had said one of seventeen people did the thing, and that being so, Carr was the one. Mark went a stage further. His conclusion was: *Carr might have done it, but he didn't.*

Mark had sent in his resignation because working in CE was ceasing to be merely frustrating and becoming pointless. He had been told very little about the Navy Yard affair except that one of seventeen people was a saboteur, and had then established to his own satisfaction that even that wasn't true.

What happened when an Intelligence agent sent in his resignation he didn't know. There were obvious difficulties –

At this point in his deliberations he saw the bubble girl.

Wars, even faraway wars, frequently produce tensions which can be relieved only by strange new vices or new versions of the old ones. And the war with Mercaptan had produced the bubble girl.

This one, to everyone else in the bar, was a pretty blonde in a dark suit, surrounded by a faint shimmer which looked like a gigantic soap bubble all around her. To her intended client, in this case Mark, she was clad in her dark suit for ten seconds, then in wisps of underwear for five seconds, and finally in nothing at all for a single second, the cycle repeating itself endlessly or at least until she realized she hadn't made a deal and directed the field toward somebody else.

She stopped beside him. 'Do I stay?' she asked softly.

'Why not?' said Mark.

She sat down at his table. 'My name's Star,' she said in the same soft, seductive voice. Most bubble girls took glamorous professional names such as Star and Dawn and Gloria and Venus.

'You can call me Mark,' he said. 'What are you drinking?'

'Orange juice, please. You want to talk?'

'Sure,' he said. 'I want to tell you my troubles. I guess you're used to that?'

In spite of the alcohol he had consumed, he saw the flicker of puzzlement deep in her green eyes.

'I'm in Counterespionage,' Mark said, 'and I just got a man executed for something he didn't do. Well, maybe that's not quite right. I tried to stop it, but I failed. So I've sent in my resignation.'

Now she didn't try to hide her puzzlement. 'What's this you're giving me, Mark? If you were an Intelligence agent, you wouldn't tell a girl you'd just met. Particularly –'

She stopped, but Mark had no difficulty in completing the sentence. 'Particularly a bubble girl? Why not? It's your job to satisfy your clients, isn't it? Doesn't that often include letting them weep on your shoulder? I want to do some weeping.'

He ordered orange juice and another whisky sour. When he looked back at Star, she had switched off the bubble-girl apparatus. Now she was just a pretty girl in a dark suit, permanently, and with no bubble.

'You didn't have to do that,' he said mildly. 'I'm not going to get tired of you. Were you afraid that familiarity would breed contempt?'

She frowned, and then apparently decided to play along with him. 'All right, Mark, go ahead and weep.'

He told her that a distorter had been planted in the Navy Yard. All electrical apparatus in the vicinity had begun to misbehave very, very slightly, so slightly that it was days before the Navy Yard Director could be certain that there was something wrong, two weeks before the distorter was found and smashed, and a month – not yet over – before all the work done in the yard during that time could be done again, checked, double-checked and pronounced satisfactory.

It was the kind of unspectacular sabotage which was ten times as effective as a clumsy bomb-explosion at the yard. In this kind of long-range, long-term conflict, man-power and materials were less important than overall technical accuracy.

'I was told to find which one out of a party of seventeen people who visited the yard left the distorter there,' Mark went on, 'and I decided none of them did. But this man Carr was probed just the same, and now he's as good as dead, though he's innocent.'

By this time Star had fallen into a mechanical routine of saying the expected thing whenever he paused, suspending puzzlement, disbelief, incomprehension and anything else she had to suspend.

'And this bothers you?' she said.

'Sure it bothers me. I'll give you the background next. But first, hadn't we better go to your apartment?'

She hesitated, obviously doubtful about the whole thing now.

'I'm not drunk,' Mark said, 'not seriously, anyway. Let's go, huh?'

Once more Mark surveyed a bland door sardonically. This time it was Star's bedroom door.

When they reached her apartment, he had started to tell her all about Intelligence, but she excused herself, saying she'd get into something more comfortable. And he thought he knew why.

Perhaps he should have put on more of an act, letting her think she was squeezing information out of him. By pouring it in her lap as he had done, he naturally made her suspicious.

Leaving him alone like this, she was deliberately giving him time to think, time to get control of himself, time to sober up. But it wasn't going to make any difference.

The door opened and Star returned. Mark, who had no previous experience of bubble girls, had been curious to see what kind of negligee she would wear. He wasn't disappointed. It was ten times as aphrodisiacal as plain nudity.

Her wrap was ankle-length and consisted of white, pink and yellow gauze, and even at the few places where three layers came together, nothing was concealed.

'Like it?' she said softly.

She was trying to get matters back on her own ground, but Mark didn't let her.

'Yes, but I haven't finished weeping on your shoulder. Come and sit down, will you? So's you'll understand, I'd better tell you about my old boss, S. He retired two years ago. Under him, Intelligence was so efficient that –'

'Mark, didn't it occur to you that I might be working for Mercaptan?'

'Not for a moment. Star, how about taking off that wrap? You'd distract me a lot less without it.'

She still stood in the bedroom doorway, frowning.

'And,' Mark added, 'I've seen you without any clothes on anyway.'

'In the bar, you mean?'

'No, long before that. Thirteen years ago, when you were six.'

She went on quietly. 'So that's it. I was beginning to wonder if you'd guessed somehow. It never occurred to me that you'd recognize me. I was only a kid the last time you saw me, and you couldn't have been more than twenty yourself.'

'I'd have known anyway – Paula. Only it might have taken longer.'

'Am I such a bad actress?'

'It's not that. You can't pump a Security man, Paula. D should have known that. My specialty is picking the wrong 'un, smelling out the thing that doesn't quite fit.'

They were both silent for a while, remembering the time thirteen years ago when Mark, hardly more than a messenger in Intelligence then, had been sent to S's home. In the garden he had found a pretty, fair-haired child who had asked him if he was a sex maniac – because if so, she'd run and put some clothes on. Otherwise it didn't matter, and didn't he like sunbathing in the nude, too?

'My father thought a lot of you, Mark,' Paula said. 'He still does. Look – since there's no point in playing games any more, I'm going to put on something respectable.'

'You didn't thirteen years ago.'

'Thirteen years ago it didn't matter.'

'And now it does – and you a bubble girl?'

'Get this straight, Mark. As a Security agent I use the bubble girl pose now and then. But I don't follow through. That isn't in the contract.'

Mark grinned. 'You wave the carrot in front of the donkey's nose, but never let him have it?'

She made a face at him and turned to go back into the bedroom. But he jumped up, caught her arm and pulled her to the couch.

'You just insisted on putting on that wrap. Why?'

'You can guess. I'm supposed to be checking on you. But I'm biased. I didn't want you to –'

'You didn't want me to hang myself. So you gave me a chance to think.' He grinned. 'If you work that way, you'll never be a good Security agent, Paula.'

'You're different. You should have been Security Chief after my father. He said then that it was a great mistake to appoint D instead of you.'

'When did you join Security?'

'A year ago. My father wasn't very keen.'

'I'll bet. Does he know about this bubble girl business?'

'No.'

'What's your report on me going to be like?'

She shrugged. 'What can I say but that you identified me, so it was no good?'

'Will you tell me one thing? When were you briefed?'

She hesitated and then said: 'Just a few minutes before I picked you up.'

'Then that must have been after D got my resignation,' Mark mused.

Paula stirred uncomfortably as his arm went round her. She felt at a disadvantage. As a Security agent she did as she was told, acting a part. But now she found her professional and private lives embarrassingly mingled. It was hard to keep a man at arm's length when only a few minutes before she had been pretending to be a high-class prostitute.

Mark stood up. 'I've decided to be a gentleman,' he said. 'Are you insulted?'

'Anything but,' she said gratefully.

However, a couple of minutes later, when he had gone, she found herself frowning at her reflection in a mirror and wishing he had found it a little harder to tear himself away.

It was no surprise whatever to Mark when he was summoned to D's presence first thing the next morning.

The Security Chief was always known as a single letter. Perhaps unfortunately, however, there was a limit to the secrecy which could be maintained within Intelligence departments. Security Chiefs, like other department heads, were not always department heads. Before that they were field men – and when they climbed or were kicked upstairs, their former colleagues could hardly be kept from knowing about it.

Mark had worked with D when he wasn't Security Chief, when they both took orders from S.

D, a plump, innocent looking man of thirty-five, stared at Mark without pretending any friendliness he didn't feel. 'I got your letter yesterday,' he said. 'Why, if you were so sure Carr wasn't the man, didn't you take action sooner?'

'Now there's a question,' said Mark. 'Before I answer it, are you sure you don't want to take it back?'

'All right,' said D wearily. 'I take it back. No doubt you told Bergstein all about it in triplicate, and I guess you're all set to point out that six months ago I raised Bergstein over your head. And now you want to resign.'

'Not just over the Navy Yard case,' Mark said.

'I know that, too. I also know that Star didn't get anything out of you. Listen, Mark. I don't like you and I never did. And six months ago I took great pleasure in putting Bergstein over you because I thought CE could be run better. But you can't resign. You'll find your new job in there.'

He pointed at an inner door.

'Am I dismissed?' Mark asked.

'Yes, in there. I'll be here when you want to talk to me. And I'm not going to enjoy it.'

Mark stood up. He wanted to temporize, to ask questions, but D clearly had no intention of saying any more just at the moment.

As he crossed the floor wild thoughts of what he would find in the inner room flashed through Mark's mind. It might be a gas chamber. He might be whisked away by Security cops. Or Star might be there.

What he found was a desk with a folder laid on the blotting pad; a chair, a carafe of water. Nothing else, not even a telephone.

He sat down and opened the folder.

Ten seconds later he sat up abruptly, staring at the papers in front of him as if they were red hot. As a matter of fact they were.

Once upon a time, in the fairy-tale past, Secret Service had been really secret, so secret that nobody knew what anybody else was doing. Spies had spied on spies on spies on spies until nobody knew what he was looking for and wouldn't know if he found it. It had often been exactly like the situation in farces in which A trailed B trailing C trailing D trailing A. It would have been funny if men hadn't often died trying to trace telephone calls to relatively innocent brothels or protecting information which was printed in current technical journals.

The use of an electronic brain changed the situation entirely. For the Genius knew everything – and the Genius didn't talk.

The Genius was a vast computer which contained all of civilization's most secret information in its thousands of cubic feet of memory banks. This top-secret information went in, but it could never come out. The Genius was a computer, not a reference library. It was so constructed that although it could direct all operations of all the Security branches, only directives could be communicated, not information.

But the Genius didn't have the final say. It was, after all, only a tool. The Security Chief made the real decisions. Nine times out of ten he merely rubber-stamped directives from the Genius. Nevertheless, when the logical decision wasn't the right one, it was up to the Security Chief to divine this and take appropriate action.

Mark remembered when the Genius had wanted twenty-five men shot, including the President of the United States. It was the logical answer in the circumstances; the war came first, at least three of these men were known to be working for Mercaptan, and the damage they could do in every moment that passed was so great that the coldly correct solution was to liquidate them all at once rather than spend weeks, possibly months, finding the three traitors and making absolutely certain there were no more.

But S, Mark's boss then, had known that such ruthlessness, although it might accomplish its own object, was going to create more problems than it solved. He authorized slower, less certain but more humane measures.

And the Genius didn't care. Naturally. The Genius never did care.

The Genius never sulked when the Security Chief told it, in effect: 'Look, you've given us the best solution but for reasons that you couldn't possibly understand we're not going to use it. What's the second-best solution?'

Since the Genius kept all it knew to itself, Security had to have its own files. But these could be locked away without any risk of sections and operatives working at cross-purposes – so long as the Genius knew everything.

An agent was told all he needed to know to do a certain job. He didn't have to be allowed to gorge himself on top-secret material looking for relevant information. On the other hand, he didn't have to stumble about in the dark because he wasn't allowed information he desperately needed.

The system had worked very well until about two years ago, when D replaced S as Security Chief.

As he scanned through the material in the folder, Mark reached many conclusions, the first of which was that instead of being fired or being allowed to resign, he was being asked to tell D where he had gone wrong. For no other reason would so much so secret information be made available to him.

Either in trust or in desperation, D was concealing nothing from Mark. The folder contained the whole sorry record of Intelligence during the last two years – highly efficient at first, then merely passable, then shocking.

Mark sat back, lit a cigarette and blew smoke at the ceiling. It took guts on D's part, he had to admit, to call in a man he didn't like, a man who might have been sitting in his chair, and say in effect: 'Look what a ball I've made of this job. Where did I go wrong?'

Why, he wondered, should D demote him, put Bergstein over him and then, six months later, put such trust in him? Searching in the folder, he soon found the answer – his own service record.

Six months ago D had demoted him because CE, although not as inefficient as the other Intelligence departments, was still anything but efficient. Since then, however, CE had sunk until it was the least effective of all the departments.

And Mark's record showed his persistent habit of being right, or at least less wrong than anybody else. Time and again Mark had stuck his neck out and not got it chopped off. Time and again he had reported that the lines CE was working on were wrong, and they duly turned out to be wrong.

Although the decision must have tasted bitter in D's mouth, he hadn't much choice. Everything he did turned out wrong. And the man who might have been Security Chief in his place stubbornly persisted in keeping his nose clean.

Mark wouldn't have been human if he hadn't permitted himself a quiet chuckle.

When D had detailed Star – or Paula – to check on Mark, it had been a last, despairing effort to find out something that made it impossible to consult him. And Star reported laconically: 'Nix. He rumbled me right away.'

Staring at the ceiling, Mark summarized his conclusions.

1. This crisis in Intelligence was far more serious than Mark dreamed – and D had seen it growing, tried to arrest it and failed. Practically no information was coming out of Mercaptan any more, spies and saboteurs weren't being uncovered the way they used to be, innocent people were being arrested while guilty people went free – in every department Intelligence was falling down on its job.

2. D was well aware of the possibility that he himself might be the weak link in the current setup. The efforts he had already made to get Intelligence functioning efficiently again included everything he might have tried short of turning over the job to somebody else – bar one thing.

3. The Intelligence organization, being what it was, could neither commit suicide nor call in an outside troubleshooter. Therefore it had no choice but to go on bungling if it couldn't put its own house in order.

At the thought of bungling, Mark recalled the Navy Yard case and searched through the folder to see if there was anything about it. There was. He read the report carefully and then went back to the other room.

D looked up. 'Well?' he said stiffly.

Diplomatically Mark censored a lot he might have said. 'There's one thing you should have tried and haven't.'

'And what's that?'

'Cut out the Genius. Make all the decisions yourself.'

'But ... that's impossible. It's unthinkable. Anyway – there can't be anything wrong with the Genius. I test it every week myself. I run a whole pattern of logistic and mathematical problems –'

'Maybe the Genius can handle mathematics and logic but not Intelligence.'

'But it used to run Intelligence very well.'

'It's not running it well now.'

'If that's all you have to suggest –' D began coldly. Then he stopped himself, remembering how often Mark had been proved right by events.

'No,' Mark said, 'it's not all I have to suggest. But tell me one thing – now that I'm in on this, how much freedom do I have? What will you let me try?'

With a visible effort D forced himself to say: 'Anything you like.'

'Then I'm going to see S.'

'You can't do that. He's retired. He's not in Intelligence any more.'

Mark grinned. 'The old boy knows so many secrets that another wouldn't make any difference. And you have to admit that things ran pretty smoothly when he was boss here.'

'Yes –' said D unwillingly. Mark knew exactly what he was thinking. D had never had a high opinion of S's methods. He had thought when he took over that he was going to make Intelligence twice as efficient. Only now was he forced to admit that perhaps S had known what he was doing, after all.

'Well, do what you like,' said D crossly, looking down at the papers on his desk.

'One more thing. There's nothing wrong with the Genius, huh? Then what about the Navy Yard case?'

'What about it?'

'I've just learned that the distorter was found inside the casing of a machine which had just had a routine check. If I'd known that before –'

'If you think the technicians who did the job left it there, you're wrong,' said D, with a certain small triumph. 'There were three of them, working under the eye of a Yard security officer.'

'Exactly.'

'What do you mean, exactly?'

'The Navy Yard authorities knew the distorter wasn't there at the time of the routine check. So when they started looking, they didn't look there. Sure, they got round to it eventually. But that was about the last place they looked – naturally enough. Are you buying the coincidence? I'm not. *The distorter was put there by somebody who knew it was going to be the last place anyone would look.*

'And the Genius, with all these facts at its disposal, says one of seventeen visitors put it there. Visitors who couldn't possibly know that the machine had just been checked.'

'One of them could have been told to put it there.'

'Oh, sure. By the real saboteur – the one who works at the Navy Yard. But the Genius didn't see that.'

'And neither did I,' said D very quietly.

Mark rose to go. 'No,' he said. 'You didn't.'

Mark could have gone to see S that day, but he left it until the following morning, which was Saturday, because Paula might be at home then. The week-end wasn't a good time for Security investigations. People were relaxed then, off their guard, but they were also less willing to talk about their jobs and the trials and tribulations of the week. A man who on Wednesday would be eager to pour out his troubles to a willing listener would shrug everything off and change the subject on Saturday.

Mark's guess proved correct. In the swimming pool, a pool which hadn't been there thirteen years ago, he found Paula.

She climbed out, shaking herself and removing her bathing cap.

'You didn't wear a swimsuit last time I was here,' Mark reminded her.

'Look, let's drop the subject of my not wearing clothes, huh?' said Paula. 'What are you doing here?'

'Looking for your father.'

'Oh.' Her disappointment showed. For the second time Mark suspected that she wasn't a very good Security agent. She was too transparent. Still, perhaps she would learn. Heredity should count for something.

'And to see you, of course,' he added politely.

'My father's in the house.'

'I'm in no hurry.'

'You're out of a job?'

'I wouldn't say that.'

'So –' She stopped herself.

Mark laughed. 'Paula, your father and I were never the ultra-cautious type of Intelligence men like D is. I don't mind discussing things with you, and you needn't be too careful with me. I don't think for a moment that Mercaptan could buy you.

'Did anybody ever try to buy you?'

'Sure. Two men who tried have been shot.'

'The Mercaptan spy service never does its own spying. They bribe Terrans to do it. It's regrettably easy.'

She spread a towel and sat on it. 'Why, Mark? Why are so many people ready to turn traitors?'

'Because this is such a long-range, theoretical war. We'll never see spaceships battling it out over our heads – the only Mercaptan ships that ever venture into the Solar System are spy ships, coming and going like shadows. Maybe it isn't really a war at all. Hardly anybody ever gets killed, even near Mercaptan. It's a conflict more like a chess game than a war. And you can't expect people to be intensely patriotic over a chess game.'

'I see what you mean. It's not the kind of war people feel involved in. No personal danger, nobody gets killed. They don't see why they shouldn't make some easy money if the chance is offered.'

'That's it exactly.'

'And that's why Intelligence always has so much on its hands . . . Mark, what are you thinking?'

'That I didn't play my cards right that night I met you. If I'd only been harder to crack, we might have been practically married by now.'

'That's what you think,' she said coolly. 'I told you I wasn't . . . that I didn't –'

'I still think, the way you acted, I might have done better.'

'Well, maybe,' she admitted, rather to his surprise. 'But that's because it was you.'

'Huh?'

'As you said – my father isn't ultra-cautious. I've heard about you . . . and when I was a kid you were a hero of mine.'

'Now that you're old, of course, it's different?'

'My father says you could look at twenty people you'd never seen before and pick out the spy among them.'

He grinned. 'That's a slight exaggeration. But picking out spies is pretty easy – on account of what we were just saying.'

'What were we just saying?'

'In this war most spies are amateurs. Half-spies and half-saboteurs. Not like the dedicated professionals of hard, bitter, close-contact wars. They're not careful or patient enough. They spend their bribes too freely. They –'

He saw S approaching from the house, and got up reluctantly. 'Don't go,' he said. 'I'll be back.'

S was still lean and erect, although he was over seventy.

'Mark!' he exclaimed. 'What brings you here?'

'Trouble,' said Mark, grasping S's hand firmly. 'Although if I'd known about Paula it wouldn't have taken trouble to bring me here.'

Rapidly he sketched the present situation in Intelligence, and asked for S's opinion.

S was indignant, both because his beloved department was in such a bad way and because nobody had consulted him before.

'It's all young Drayton's fault,' he exclaimed. 'Well, call him D if you like. I knew you should have been appointed in my place. He's a nincompoop.'

'It may be partly D's fault,' Mark said more cautiously, 'but it's more than that. S, how could the Genius be tampered with?'

'It couldn't,' S declared flatly. But he frowned thoughtfully when Mark explained the details of the Navy Yard case.

'In my time the Genius would never have made a mistake like that,' he admitted. 'I guess this needs some consideration. Mark, do you know why I recommended you and not D?'

Mark shook his head.

'You were extremes, the two of you. He's cautious, careful, patient. You're casual, maybe sometimes reckless. He uses his head, you use your nose. And I knew the man who replaced me would have to work with the Genius. Well, D would rely on it absolutely, leaning heavily on it and trusting it implicitly. That's just what he's done. You'd use it more like a pocket calculating machine. In other words, D would rely on it too much and you wouldn't rely on it enough.'

'That's true enough,' Mark admitted.

'I picked you because you can adapt yourself. D can't. If you found that you got on better by cooperating more with the Genius, you'd do it. In any case, you wouldn't fail because you're not the type to fail. D is, if he doesn't have somebody keeping him right.'

'Anyway, D's the Security Chief, not me,' said Mark. 'Let's get back to the Genius. Assume it has been tampered with. How could that be done?'

'Not by technicians,' S said. 'No technician gets near the computer alone. And that only leaves department heads.'

'Sounds unlikely, I grant,' Mark mused. 'But somebody's done something to the Genius. I guess I could talk D into letting me check it myself –'

'It won't do the slightest good.'

'Huh?'

'Don't you know you can't get information out of the Genius?'

'Sure I know. I was a department head myself – S, nobody living understands the Genius better than you. Can't it be tricked? Can't you get information out of it in the form of a directive?'

'No,' said S positively. 'Frame such a case and the Genius won't play. It won't produce a solution.'

'Well, couldn't that be it? Couldn't something have been done ... I don't know what, but we'll come to that later ... to make the Genius think it's being asked to produce information?'

'I see what you mean, but the answer's no again. Because from what you say, the Genius has been producing directives all right, but *wrong* directives.'

'It comes to this, that once something's fed into the Genius's memory banks, it never comes out? So that if somebody fed fake information in, it's there for keeps, ineradicable, and we can never find out what it is, because the Genius will never tell us?'

'That's not quite right. The Genius constantly does its own erasing and modifying. And if anything doesn't check, it can always ask questions.'

'So the Genius couldn't be sabotaged by being fed false information?'

S pondered. 'You think you're on to something, Mark? I won't say that's impossible. Naturally with any computer you've always got to remember the thing hasn't got eyes and ears, and if you don't tell it something, it doesn't know. And every now and then, even if you're a cybernetics expert, you phrase information or questions ambiguously or plain badly, and the computer gets you wrong. So you get strange solutions at times, even when there's been no deliberate attempt to confuse the computer.'

'It could happen by mistake? Then suppose some very important item of information was recorded wrongly, perhaps months ago. Couldn't that –?'

S was shaking his head. 'Our computer, the Genius, is no ordinary electronic brain. It knows all about improbabilities and impossibilities, and it always automatically crosschecks. Try to get it to record – believe, if you like – something that just isn't so, and you'll get a flood of questions. And remember that while there's no record of what's fed into the Genius, there's an indestructible record of its questions and answers. I mean the answers it gives, not the ones it's given. So –'

'Yes, I see,' said Mark, disappointed. 'You couldn't keep feeding it false information, because even if it accepted any item without question, it would ask significant questions later, and the false item would soon be erased.'

'You might possibly get it to accept one vitally significant thing without question,' S said thoughtfully, 'and if you left it at that, it might be some time before it showed up. But what vitally significant thing would it record and act on and never correct?'

'I'll think about it,' Mark said.

S correctly took this to mean that Mark had no more questions at the moment. So he produced his own suggestion.

'Mark, there's an easy way to find out. Check all the department heads yourself. If one of them smells, you'll know. You wouldn't miss a thing like that. But I still say – Intelligence will never recover until young Drayton is kicked out on his ear.'

Mark thanked S and went back to the pool. Paula was gone, but she had left a note which read:

Sorry I have to go. How about tomorrow at two o'clock? Pick me up here. Unless, of course, you'd rather not.

Mark decided to be back at two the next day, and he was.

On Monday morning Mark went in at the usual time, although he wasn't quite certain what his position was. Presumably he was no longer Bergstein's deputy in CE. So he went straight to D.

D looked pale and tired. His desk was covered with agents' reports and yellow slips which Mark recognized as directives from the Genius.

'Did you see S?' D asked.

'Yes.'

'What did he say?'

Mark hesitated. Oddly enough, he no longer disliked D. One of the things he had most objected to had been D's bland self-assurance, and that had obviously been gone for months. And D's decision to call in a man he didn't like and place himself in his hands, belated though it was, showed bigness and humility which Mark had never suspected he was capable of.

'You needn't be polite,' D said, smiling faintly. 'He said Intelligence would never recover until I was kicked out on my ear.'

The exact quote made Mark jump. After he had done so, he remembered ruefully that he had concluded Paula wasn't a very good Security agent because she was so transparent.

'I thought so,' D remarked. 'And I guess he's right. I'm only beginning to realize now, Mark, that that's why I disliked you and S – you never seemed to put half the work into being right that I did. I thought you were just lucky, both of you.'

'Listen, D,' Mark said. 'There's something wrong with the Genius. I'm sure of it. If you'll authorize it, I'm going to check on the department heads, the only men who have access to the Genius. S says it can't be the technicians.'

D waved his hand. 'Sure. Do what you like. Then come back here.'

Mark didn't bother checking Bergstein. If there was a suspect department chief, it had to be one he hadn't had any dealings with. Otherwise he'd have smelled something sooner.

He had brief talks with the five other chiefs, all men he had never seen before, introducing himself as D's new assistant and hinting at a mysterious development which would shortly take place in the Intelligence organization.

This was merely a preliminary survey to give him some idea of the men he would have to investigate. Somehow he couldn't concentrate. He kept thinking of D.

D hadn't asked any questions. He hadn't asked what Mark was going to do or how long he'd be doing it. He had merely said, 'Sure. Do what you like. Then come back here.'

After the fifth brief interview, Mark found himself hurrying back to D's office. What he saw wasn't exactly a surprise, for it figured.

D was slumped across his desk, a hole in his head and the gun still in his hand.

Mark didn't instantly pick up the phone. The Intelligence Department had a small police section of its own – there wouldn't be hordes of outside cops swarming all over the building when the incident was reported.

Nevertheless, Mark wanted to reach his own conclusions before turning the matter over to anybody else.

One of the papers on the desk was the Navy Yard report, stapled to the relevant directives from the Genius. Another referred to an incident in Mercaptan which the Genius had had investigated at a cost of three Terran agents and with no worthwhile result. A third concerned the dismissal of an entire Washington Security wing, ordered by the Genius; it had transpired that a certain bodyguard was the real spy and the Security men were innocent.

There were other papers, all referring to incidents in which the Genius had made an order, D had executed it, and it later turned out that the Genius had been wrong. More than that – they were cases in which the Security Chief could and should have questioned the Genius's solution and tried to find another.

On the desk was D's record of personal failure. This was why he hadn't been encouraged when Mark spoke of his conviction that there was something amiss with the Genius. Of course there was – but that didn't let D out.

D had at last realized that there was more to the consistent success of S and Mark Swan than just being lucky.

Mark waited patiently while the three guards painstakingly established his identity and passed him through, locking the door behind him.

He was alone with the Genius for the first time in seven months. Since D put Bergstein over his head, he wasn't even a department chief, and thus no longer had access to the Genius.

Now he returned as Security Chief.

There had been a carefully confined storm over D's suicide. S had been consulted, and he said his piece bluntly. On retiring as Security Chief he had recommended Mark for the position and strongly opposed D as a replacement. This was on record. Also on record now was D's utter failure, finally recognized even by himself, and Mark's continued efficiency.

Not only was Mark's appointment as Security Chief rushed through; Washington itself shuddered, and the President himself very nearly bit the dust. A field marshal who had backed D's appointment, as the more reliable, more stable man, now found himself with plenty of time to devote to the affairs of his New England farm.

Mark was neither triumphant nor particularly elated. He had no power complex and would on the whole have been happier to go on working under S than to become Security Chief himself. Although it was pleasant to receive such overwhelming votes of confidence from all sides, he was well aware of the other side of the coin: if he wasn't brilliantly successful immediately, there would again be calls for a new Security Chief.

And looking at the gray-painted panels and teletype printers of the Genius, he wondered if he was looking at an enemy.

After D shot himself, everybody involved, whether red-faced or not, seemed to take it for granted that his suicide proved his incompetence and that there was nothing wrong with Intelligence but D's incompetence. Everybody but S.

S said: 'You've got quite a job on your hands, Mark. I guess you've no choice but to follow your own advice to D – cut out the Genius and run the whole show yourself.'

And this was exactly what Mark was doing.

He sat in front of one of the printers and tapped a brief item of information. There was a new Security Chief – directives should now be addressed to M.

The Genius accepted this item with placid indifference. Personalities were nothing to it. It asked no questions. It didn't care what had happened to D; it didn't care who M was.

Mark stared at the keyboard in front of him, remembering his talk with S. The Genius accepted this announcement without question. Could there have been another such announcement? No, because henceforth all Security directives would be addressed to M. Could the Genius have been told something and instructed not to reveal it even indirectly? No, because the Genius's inbuilt secrecy screen was unalterable. You couldn't make it reveal things it wasn't designed to reveal, or conceal anything it wasn't designed to conceal.

The Genius was a machine. Its one instinct, if you could call it that, was efficiency. It *wanted* to be efficient, because it was made that way. It *wanted* nothing else. It cared about nothing else.

RECORD (Mark tapped): Navy Yard concluded. Saboteur was naval technician. Replaced.

QUERY: Is any alteration in Navy Yard security arrangements recommended?

The reply came back, addressed to Security Chief M: No. The Genius, Mark knew, would never refer to the Navy Yard case again, except indirectly if new information fed to it failed to fit with the contents of its memory banks.

Mark typed again:

QUERY: Albert Kemp, former Personnel department chief killed eighteen months ago in car accident, suspected now as Mercaptan agent. Your verdict?

The Genius burst into activity. Four different machines started tapping at once.

It was unnecessary to repeat any information which the Genius had ever been fed. On receiving such a query, the computer would automatically scan all questions and information ever received under Kemp's name, all directives given, and the result of any action that was taken. It would assess Kemp – who was, to the Genius, nothing more than a working unit – and decide whether Kemp was an efficient working unit or not, much as another machine would test a radio tube and pass it or reject it. The Genius could never be concerned with appointments or dismissals. If a man –a working unit – made a mistake in typing, he was to the Genius inefficient and ought to be scrapped.

Mark didn't bother to read the material as it was typed. He could wait.

None of the department chiefs seemed to him to be possible saboteurs. But Kemp had been killed just after the Genius's directives began to be suspect. Suppose Kemp had been paid to do a job, had done it, and had then been liquidated by Mercaptan agents?

The Genius's four machines stopped clicking one after another. Mark moved to the first and read what was on it. It was a series of questions which added up to: What grounds are there for suspecting Kemp? Full information requested. There was a long list of items on which the Genius demanded specific information. Very little of it would now be obtainable, but the Genius knew that. Although it was always prepared to give an interim solution based on the material it already possessed, there was no harm in asking for more. Possibly certain information had not been supplied purely because nobody had appreciated its possible significance. The Genius trusted nobody to decide that. It wanted to know everything, significant or not.

The second machine listed another series of questions. These were framed on the basis that Kemp might have been a spy – a deliberately inefficient working unit.

Mark looked at this list very carefully, and decided to study it minutely later. This was an example of the way in which the Genius, which could not reveal secret information directly, might reveal it indirectly. For these were the items on which Kemp had supplied information. The Genius, on the theory that Kemp might be suspect, wanted to check the accuracy of its own information.

Mark's first survey indicated that the Genius was very hard to trick in this way. For the questions were framed so that it was quite impossible to establish what Kemp had actually said. They were questions like:

How many security agents does Intelligence employ?
Give details of monthly identification checks.
List unsuccessful attempts to bribe Intelligence personnel.
List discovery of traitors in Intelligence.
List dismissals from Intelligence.
Give details of retired but still living personnel.
List all changes in personnel during the last three years.

Such questions gave no hint of the answers Kemp had given. This was how the Genius got new information and checked the information it already had without revealing anything.

The third machine had listed cases – by their security code numbers – which might be affected if it were true that Kemp had been working for Mercaptan. This list was marked tentative. It was a fairly short list, referring to Personnel cases. The Genius was well aware that it might have to be extended.

The fourth machine simply said that Kemp was not a saboteur. This was an interim conclusion, meaning that crosschecking revealed no indication that Kemp was guilty – which was only to be expected, for if it had been otherwise, the Genius would have drawn the conclusion long ago, and checked through D anything which Kemp communicated to it.

Mark answered none of the Genius's questions. They could wait. He was staring at the blank panels in front of him, thinking deeply.

As far as he could make out, the Genius was functioning perfectly. The questions it had asked were exactly what it might be expected to ask.

Was the Genius trying to lull him into a sense of false security, building up his confidence before it sabotaged him the way it had sabotaged D?

Mark kept expecting trouble, but it never came. Gradually the Intelligence organization deloused itself, regaining confidence in itself week by week. Mark adopted a practice of reaching a decision first on all subjects and then reporting all the facts to the Genius and asking for a solution. Almost invariably the Genius gave the answer he had already reached –

except for the occasional cases where any computer, in the nature of things, would be liable to give an impractical answer.

Unfortunately, this method of working couldn't go on forever. Mark was forced to the conclusion, as S had said he would be, that the Genius wasn't a luxury, it was a necessity. Coordination of all Intelligence operations was too big a job for one human brain, or any number of human brains.

Temporarily, Mark could and did limit operations to what he could control himself. And the trouble cleared itself, much as a restless city would settle under strict military control. But strict military control couldn't be maintained forever – and Intelligence couldn't reach top efficiency without the Genius.

So it was a top-priority matter to find out what had been wrong with the Genius and make absolutely certain it wasn't wrong any more.

Mark pulled Paula in off field operation and made her his secretary. Under M, Intelligence was driven on an even slacker rein than under S. Mark's principle was to find the right man for a job and let him get on with it. On the other hand, he was easy to approach when help was needed.

He and Paula were married six weeks after he became Security Chief, and for the moment at least Paula went on working as his secretary. It was an unusual arrangement but not without precedent.

One day after he'd sat for an hour without moving, Paula exercised the privilege of a wife rather than a secretary and asked him what was on his mind.

'I'll have to fire Bergstein,' he said. 'I've been leaning over backwards trying not to do it, because it looks like getting even with him. But he's still a D man – inflexible, unimaginative, with a slide rule in one hand and a book of rules in the other.'

Paula, after her one lapse, spoke as a secretary. 'Why not warn him first? Show him how CE is lagging behind the other departments, and tell him if he doesn't pull up his socks, he's out?'

'I'll do that,' said Mark. 'Send for him, will you?'

He sent Paula out when Bergstein arrived. He would rather have had her present, but it wasn't fair to reprimand Bergstein in front of her.

'Bergstein,' Mark said, 'I don't want to get tough with you, because people might think it was because D made you my boss when I was in CE. But CE just isn't keeping up with the other departments.'

'I know it,' said Bergstein defensively.

'You know it?' said Mark, surprised.

'How can you expect anything else, when I'm not allowed to consult the Genius any more?'

So that was his out. 'Other department chiefs can't consult the Genius either, and they're doing all right.'

'Maybe they don't need the Genius as much as Counterespionage does.'

'You've got a point,' Mark admitted. 'Look, Bergstein, you know the Genius was supplying D with wrong solutions. We still don't know why. Until we do, we can't trust it. D trusted it, and it ruined him.'

'Can't we get another computer?'

Mark grinned. 'Since the one we've got cost twenty million and nobody can demonstrate that there's anything wrong with it, I doubt it. Look, Bergstein, send all the questions you want to put to the Genius to me, and I'll send you the Genius's answers. It's not that I don't trust you, but the Genius is still very much under a cloud and I don't want anybody to follow it blindly. If I suspect any of the Genius's directives, I'll come and see you.'

'That's fair.' Bergstein stood up. After some hesitation he said: 'M, you called me here to give me a warning. Let me give you one. You get results by your own particular brand of inspired guessing – I'm not denying that. But don't build an Intelligence empire on your personal crystal ball. Some of us are slow and deliberate and painstaking and don't believe anything we can't see. And those methods work, too. D would have been a good Security Chief if the Genius hadn't let him down.'

'Sit down again,' Mark said. 'You knew D well, didn't you? Why do *you* think he failed?'

'Well, maybe he trusted the Genius too far. I knew he had his doubts sometimes. But he always said the Genius must be right.'

'And I always approach every directive with the idea that the Genius is probably wrong,' Mark mused. 'Well, look, Bergstein. To be quite honest with you, I've never had the slightest indication since I took over that the Genius is anything but efficient. You want to use it. OK, you can – and I'm going by results. If the Genius helps CE back on its feet, fine. If it doesn't –'

'I know,' said Bergstein irritably. 'You don't have to spell it out for me.'

When he had left, Mark felt vaguely depressed and couldn't think why. Perhaps it was the same old thing – until he found out if anything had been done to the Genius, and what, he felt as if he were sitting on a bomb. Intelligence needed the Genius. Sooner or later Mark was going to be forced to use the Genius, whether he had found the secret of its psycho-neurosis or not, whether it was over or not.

Did that mean the Genius was going to do to him what it had done to D?

Paula came back, took one look at his face and sat down quietly at her desk.

Suddenly he woke up. 'Paula, suppose you're a saboteur. You want to sabotage the Genius. How would you do it?'

'Exactly as it was done, I guess. Exactly like the Navy Yard case. Not with a bomb. Not with anything that would show up. With a distorter that would do minor but significant damage for a long time, rather than with anything that would do concrete, obvious damage that could be fixed.'

Mark nodded. 'The usual Mercaptan plan. But what? How would you distort the Genius?'

'It's up to you to find out.'

'It can't reveal information,' Mark murmured. 'It's patient, it cares about nothing but efficiency. Long-term efficiency. It knows nothing about personalities ... personnel –'

He jumped up. 'Paula,' he said excitedly. 'I think I've got it. Why didn't I put myself in the place of a Mercaptan agent before?'

'You've got what?'

'The answer. And if I'm right, the Genius is perfectly OK now.'

'Then you can stop worrying,' said Paula practically.

'Yes, but am I right?'

'You're always right.'

He was in no mood for frivolity. 'Listen. Time is nothing to the Genius. It cares for nothing but the efficiency of Intelligence. It can't reveal information, it can only ask questions. If there was a saboteur, it was Kemp, Personnel department chief. And when I told the Genius there was reason to suspect Kemp, these are some of the questions it asked: How many security agents does Intelligence employ? Give details of monthly identification checks. List unsuccessful attempts to bribe Intelligence personnel. List discovery of traitors in Intelligence. List dismissals from Intelligence. Give details of retired but still living personnel. List all changes in personnel during the last three years.'

'I give up,' said Paula.

He grabbed her arm and dragged her from the office. Outside the Genius's control room, he had to sign three copies of a special authorization before he could take Paula in with him.

At one of the keyboards he tapped briefly and waited. The Genius was silent. It asked no questions.

Paula leaned over to see what he had written, but he held her back. The message was rolled into the gray casing.

'Now you'll never know what I wrote,' Mark said, 'unless I tell you. The Genius never will, because it's secret. Everything that anybody tells the Genius is secret.'

'Was it important?'

'Very important.'

'Was it true?'

'No.'

'Then why didn't the Genius question it?'

'Because I added: "No further information available at this time."'

'I get it. There's no point in asking questions if the informant doesn't know any more. Mark, did you put it in under your own name?'

'No. Under Bergstein's.'

'Well, don't keep me in suspense. What now?'

'I want you to put a query from me. We'll use the Navy Yard case again – same problem but different facts.'

'As a test?'

'Exactly. Put this under my name.'

He dictated a long, wholly imaginary case which was in essence identical to the Navy Yard affair, concerning a time bomb planted in a Washington conference room. He detailed similar times and security arrangements, and supplied a party of fifteen visitors who had been shown over the conference room.

When he paused at last, Paula said: 'I hope that's all.'

'Yes. End it there.'

Paula ended the message, and at once the Genius replied:

TO M, SECURITY CHIEF: CHECK FIFTEEN VISI-TORS. PROBABLE MOTIVE: SABOTAGE FOR GAIN.

'That's exactly what it said last time,' Paula said.

'Yes – and on the facts I presented, now as before, the saboteur must have been an inside man. Paula, as of now the Genius is working for Mercaptan.'

'How do we put it right?'

'I guess the easiest way is to take a new initial. From now on I'm S, Security Chief. Your father won't mind, and the Genius won't care. It won't even ask what happened to M.'

'Mark, just what did you tell the Genius?'

'That M was a saboteur. And, of course, that there was no further information available.'

Paula still looked puzzled. Mark said: 'A computer has to believe what it's told, so long as the information isn't intrinsically impossible. It isn't intrinsically impossible that anyone should turn saboteur. That doesn't necessarily mean there was anything wrong with his loyalty before.

'Kemp told the Genius nearly two years ago that D was a saboteur. He may have added a few other things to corroborate it, and then said that no further information was available. And every other scrap of information he ever supplied to the Genius was correct.

'What could the Genius do? There was no reason why it should disbelieve the information, for what Kemp said was perfectly possible. It couldn't fire D, because the Genius isn't the boss, the Security Chief is. It couldn't tell anybody else, partly because it can't give information, partly because it would be no use telling D he was a spy, and all directives go through the Security Chief. But it wanted to be efficient, and a spy is an inefficient working unit.'

'I get it,' Paula exclaimed. 'The only way it could get rid of D was to give wrong answers until he was fired!'

'That's it. It wasn't a good way, for the Genius's one desire is to be efficient. But the Genius knows that Intelligence can't possibly be efficient when the Security Chief is a saboteur. So the *only* way to be efficient again, whether it was a good way or not, was to get rid of D. And the only way the Genius knew to get rid of its own boss was to be temporarily so inefficient that D had to be removed.'

He sighed with satisfaction. 'I'll have to do some thinking about this, Paula. I'll talk to your father about it. But now that we've got the answer, we should be able to find a way to block such tactics in the future.'

'I married a smart guy,' said Paula complacently.

'You sure did. Poor D – I always did have an idea he was being framed somehow. OK, now you can tell the Genius that S is the new Security Chief.'

Two minutes later the Genius gave a new solution to the imaginary Washington case:

TO S, SECURITY CHIEF: INVESTIGATE INSIDE STAFF. ONLY THEY KNEW THAT BOMB WOULD NOT BE DISCOVERED IN HIDING PLACE SELECTED.

The Genius had changed sides again.

WHILE-U-WAIT

Edward Wellen

When the multinational conglomerate took over the firm Neil Purley had helped build into something worth taking over and told him, in effect, 'Sorry, Social Security No. 129-03-7652, but there's nothing you can do that a computer can't do better and more cheaply,' Purley burned with a cold flame. If man was no match for the computer's speed, the computer was no match for man's tricky mind.

He would show them. It went deeper than that. He would show himself as well. A man's insight, intelligence, intuition should not go for nothing, be of no worth, wither for want of use.

With his severance pay he rented space, leased equipment, ran an ad. And waited for his first client.

The conglomerate would be his unwitting ally. He would be using the conglomerate's identifying codewords to gain illegal access to the computer. He nicened it up by thinking of it as 'timesharing in an unauthorized manner'. Still, the upholders of law and order would not look kindly on that. So for safety's sake he had set up his office on the cheesebox principle.

Just as bookies interpose unmanned phones, Purley interposed closed-circuit television. The office the ad directed you to held only a cathode-ray-tube screen, a TV camera, and a client's chair. Purley himself sat at a time-division multiple-access data link in another part of town. The connection would break at the first sign of trouble. The law would never catch Purley red-handed – or touch-tone fingered.

And that was why his first client seemed slightly puzzled when an image on the screen welcomed him. Parenthetically, the image looked nothing like Purley.

'Please sit down.'

The man did not sit down. He held a clipping up to the camera eye. 'This mean what it says?'

It said: *WHILE-U-WAIT Computerized Detecting. One-hour maxi-*

mum per case. The lost found. Fee: (includes all expenses) $500 certified check.
Satisfactory job or your money refunded. And gave the address.

The image smiled. 'It means what it says. Let me add up front, though, that we're not a detective agency and don't have a license to operate as such. We don't send operatives gumshoeing around. We're purely and simply a data-processing service that specializes in retrieving information from data banks to help clients retrieve persons, places, and things. We *locate*, in other words; the physical retrieval is up to you.

'You've brought your certified check for five hundred dollars? Kindly place it in the escrow slot. That's it.' Purley scanned the signature, saw the man's name was Albert Uhl. 'Now, Mr Uhl, take note of the time. If we fail to locate your someone inside one hour, you get your check back. All right, Mr Uhl, who are you looking for?'

Uhl sat down before the visual display. He gave the image a slightly dubious smile, as though suspecting WHILE-U-WAIT relied more on theatrics than on technology. But his need appeared greater than his doubt. He wanted to believe WHILE-U-WAIT would help him. And if he had to pay extra for his need by submitting himself to showmanship, he was willing to do so. But he looked a man who would demand results. He leaned forward.

'I'm trying to locate a friend of mine. He's playing around with another man's wife.' He paused. 'This all just between us?'

'Of course. Privileged communication. Go on, Mr Uhl.'

'My friend went abroad to meet the woman. What he doesn't know is that the husband knows about them. This husband can be violent. He has a temper – and a gun to go with it. I'm anxious to get in touch with my friend and head him off before he runs into trouble. Only my trouble is I don't know just where he is or what name he's using.' He leaned back.

Purley kept the image smiling but in his own person he grimaced in dismay. 'We have to have *something* to go on, Mr Uhl. There can't be feedback without input.'

'Sure, I realize that.' Swiftly and smoothly Uhl produced a snapshot. 'That's why I brought this. It came from somewhere abroad about a week ago. All you have to do is figure out the exact spot it shows. I'll do the rest.'

The snapshot, amateurishly blurry, showed a man standing in front of a thatch-roofed cottage. Purley zoomed in on the snapshot. That gave him a bigger blur. He grimaced again, then tapped out instructions for the computer to enhance the snapshot electronically, sharpen it up to make the man's features and those of his surroundings as clear as possible.

While the computer worked on the snapshot, Purley picked up on his client.

'That's all you have to go on?'

'Yes.'

'Let's try it from the other angles of the triangle. I gather the husband is shadowing the wife to the rendezvous. We can trace them through plane or ship bookings and hotel reservations. You can take a fast jet there and be on the lookout for your friend to warn him. What's the husband's name?'

Uhl frowned. He shook his head. 'I don't know that. If I did I wouldn't need you.'

'I see.' Purley did not see anything but a total blur. If all his cases were going to be like this first one, maybe he had bitten off more than he could chew. 'All right, let's see if you can give me a description of your friend.'

Uhl's frown deepened. 'You have the snapshot.'

The image smiled patiently. 'It doesn't tell me his age, eye color, height, weight – a few little details like those.'

Purley presented a display on the screen in place of the image. The display consisted of a list of physical and social characteristics – sex, race, age, marital status, height, build, weight, complexion, eye color, hair color, scars, and so on. He asked Uhl to take up the light pen attached to the set and tick off his friend's profile.

Something in the tigerish way Uhl moved, the man's reflexes, plus his almost willful lack of helpful input, the failure to supply the husband's name, gave Purley to think again. He did not let the light pen work.

'Sorry, Mr Uhl. The light pen seems to be out of order. But the computer can sense it just as well if you use your finger.'

Uhl hesitated a fraction of a second, then touched his finger to the screen to indicate his friend's characteristics.

'Fine.' Purley winked out the display and presented his surrogate image again. 'While we work on what we have, you can relax and listen to music. Do you have any preferences?'

The man stared. 'No, no preferences.'

'All right.' Purley faded the image from the screen and let Uhl enjoy Mantovani and colored lights that pulsed to the soothing strains.

Purley himself felt far from relaxed. Uhl bothered him. While working on locating Uhl's friend, it would not hurt to get a make on Uhl.

Besides recording Uhl's state of tension in his finger tremors as he touched the screen, the computer had registered Uhl's fingerprint. Uhl seeemed the right age and the right physique to have served in Vietnam. Subsidiaries of the conglomerate that had found Purley redundant did national defense work. If you knew the codeword, you had access to Department of Defense files. Purley knew the codeword. He had the computer classify Uhl's fingerprint and look for the print's match among the whorls, loops, and arches of all those who had served in the armed forces.

It took two minutes. The fingerprint matched the right index finger of one Steve Kinzel.

Purley retrieved Kinzel's service record. Kinzel had received a less-than-honorable discharge from the Army – but not before winning every sharpshooting award the Army had to offer.

Using the conglomerate's plant-security contact with the FBI – another codeword – Purley patched into the National Criminal Identification Centre in Washington.

Steve Kinzel's FBI yellow sheet showed that the FBI's antisyndicate task force suspected Kinzel of being a hit man with a long string of contracts to his credit. Never caught in the act.

Purley eyed Uhl–Kinzel through the camera. The man sat seemingly relaxed, sound-bathing. A sunning snake looks relaxed. Purley felt a hollow tightness in his belly.

The hit-man angle would seem to rule out the possibility Purley had been considering – that this client was the husband in the story he had fed Purley.

But the purpose in hiring WHILE-U-WAIT remained the same. Even stronger. To locate and waste the 'friend'.

Purley turned to the enhanced snapshot on one of his screens. The computer had made a number of identifications and deductions.

The architecture put the cottage in the British Isles. The thatched roof was not of the kind you find in Suffolk, Essex, or Cambridgeshire; there the roof cocks up at the gable end. This cottage stood rather in a western or southwestern county, where the gables droop or have hipped hoods. That narrowed it down to Cornwall, Devon, or Somersetshire.

The gentle swells of land visible in the distance further narrowed it down to Somersetshire. Purley blew up white dots on the nearest slope into grazing sheep – Southdown breed, the computer said after a nanosecond's glance at its memory banks.

A speck in the snapshot's sky blew up into a seagull. The computer gazed at its gazetteer. The hills would be the Mendip Hills, the seagull's drink would be the mouth of the Severn.

In short, the cottage stood on property near a Southdown sheep pasturage some five miles southeast of Weston-super-Mare.

The front of the cottage had a freshly whitewashed look. The man posing in front of it had probably just recently taken possession. The foliage of the oak tree dominating the grounds told Purley the man had taken possession of it in early spring. The shape of the oak tree also showed the orientation – the northern branches reaching for light, the southern branches taking it easy. Therefore the road the cottage faced on ran east and west.

Shadows showed it to be midafternoon; they also helped Purley and the computer, using the man's height as a yardstick, to determine the dimensions of the cottage. Only the man's identity remained in shadow.

Purley turned to his 'blue box', an electronic device for placing overseas calls without paying for them. He put through a call to Taunton, the county town of Somersetshire.

There Purley found an obliging records clerk. The important sound of 'overseas call', plus Purley's tone of urgency, proved contagious. Inside of five minutes she identified the property from Purley's detailed description and came up with the name of the present owner of Oak Cottage.

Roger Nugent.

It was all over. Investigation successfully completed, fee earned. He had not bitten off more than he could chew. Purley now had all the information his client wanted. All that remained was to astonish the client by letting the image smile modestly and say, 'Your man is Roger Nugent, at Oak Cottage, between Weston-super-Mare and Axbridge, in Somerset, England.'

Purley stole another look at Uhl–Kinzel. He saw beneath the relaxed form the unsoothed beast. Purley glanced at the hour. He decided to stall the man another ten minutes.

Through the computer of a correspondent bank obligating and obligated to the conglomerate, Purley determined that Roger Nugent had paid for Oak Cottage with funds from a Taunton bank account. Purley backtracked the deposits, following a suspiciously complex trail.

He traced the laundered money in Nugent's account ultimately to a US Justice Department special fund. The pattern of payments told him Roger Nugent's name had been Larry Shedd.

Now Purley knew why his client had been shy about telling WHILE-

U-WAIT the missing man's name up front. Anyone who kept up with the news would have recognized the name Larry Shedd and have realized the phoniness of the love-triangle tale.

Larry Shedd, before disappearing and surfacing as Roger Nugent, had testified before a Senate committee looking into the activities of a leading crime-syndicate figure, Vincent Minturn. Minturn, according to 'reliable sources', had put an open $500,000 contract out on Larry Shedd.

Because of this contract, the Justice Department had paid for plastic surgery on Larry Shedd, spirited him out of the country, and set him up under a new identity. Away from hit men, away from front pages.

WHILE-U-WAIT's client was not a newspaperman. His reason for discovering Shedd's present identity and whereabouts was not to expand on Shedd's life story but to contract Shedd's life span.

WHILE-U-WAIT's client's client had to be Vincent Minturn.

Purley glanced again at the hour and quickly followed up the Minturn lead.

A search of the computerized morgue of the largest wire service – the conglomerate whose facilities Purley was borrowing owned newspapers and radio and TV stations – turned up that Minturn, like Shedd, was hiding out under another name somewhere overseas.

Minturn had slipped out from under FBI and Interpol surveillance to evade a grand jury investigation arising out of the Senate hearings. Minturn had often voiced his love for the American way of life and his scorn for all other ways, but he dared not risk returning as long as Shedd lived to testify against him. The $500,000 contract was a measure of that love.

Purley smiled an unlovely smile. It had hit him that Minturn and the conglomerate had a lot in common. Money was root, stem, and flower of the evil they did. He had no self-pity, but he thought *poor Shedd*.

While he was at it, he had the computer look up everything the wire-service morgue had on Shedd. The latest reference to the vanished Shedd appeared in an item about a minor burglary a week ago at a Chicago nursing home. The minor burglary had a major outcome. Larry Shedd's aging and ailing mother had died of shock shortly after the intrusion, though as far as anyone knew, nothing of any worth was missing.

Purley knew what was missing.

The snapshot.

Shedd–Nugent had mailed it to his failing and fearful mother to reassure her that he was alive and well and doing fine ... somewhere. He must have had sense enough to arrange for the envelope to bear a misleading postmark. Otherwise, Uhl would not have needed WHILE-U-WAIT's help.

A thought burned bright in Purley's mind. But for it to become deed required Minturn's present identity and whereabouts.

Purley had not even a blurred amateurish snapshot to help him locate Minturn. A glance at the hour told him time was running out.

According to news accounts, Minturn had haunted the hangouts of the show-biz crowd. He would be homesick for those haunts, eager for some reminder or taste of them.

Again Purley twitched the conglomerate's tentacles. He traced all overseas air shipments of Lindy's cheesecake, Nathan's hot dogs, and Stage Door Delicatessen pastrami in the past month. He narrowed the field to one Frank Fratto in Rome.

Fratto's Rome bank account led back to a Stateside account of Vincent Minturn's that Minturn had cleaned out just before disappearing. Fratto's handwriting on his bank signature card matched Minturn's on his – there were distinctive *t*s. The computer gave it as a 98.6666 percent probability that Frank Fratto was Vincent Minturn.

The man's checking account gave Purley the man's present address – a Rome hotel. The checks led Purley to invoices of places where Fratto shopped. Among the earliest purchases were a red-brown wig and prescription sunglasses. Best of all, the measurements on file at the leading Rome tailor's for Fratto's new suits reassured Purley that Fratto had roughly Nugent's build.

Purley switched off Montevani and the lights and threw his smiling surrogate image at his client.

Uhl leaned forward. 'The hour's up. Do you have a name and a place?'

Purley gave him a name and – 'He's not where you might think he'd be' – a place.

Uhl sat staring at the image. 'Are you sure you got the right man?'

The image drew itself up. 'We're 98.6666 percent sure.'

Uhl smiled. 'That's good enough for me.' He got up to go but stopped to shake his head. 'I wish I knew how you –' He shrugged. 'No time. I have to catch a plane. So long.'

'Good-by.'

Purley watched Uhl set out toward his doom. He sat bemused awhile, then stirred himself to forge and send an IPCQ alert – Interpol Paris to all national bureaus – warning the *carabinieri* in Italy to be on the lookout for the arrival of Steve Kinzel, a.k.a. Albert Uhl, suspected hit man. The Italian police would tail him and should catch him red-handed, trigger-fingered, gunning down Frank Fratto, a.k.a. Vincent Minturn.

WHILE-U-WAIT awaited its next client.

GETTING · ACROSS

Robert Silverberg

I

On the first day of summer my month-wife, Silena Ruiz, filched our district's master program from the Ganfield Hold computer center and disappeared with it. A guard at the Hold has confessed that she won admittance by seducing him, then gave him a drug. Some say she is in Conning Town now; others have heard rumors that she has been seen in the Morton Court; still others maintain her destination was The Mill. I suppose it does not matter where she has gone. What matters is that we are without our program. We have lived without it for eleven days and things are starting to break down. The heat is abominable, but we must switch every thermostat to manual override before we can use our cooling system; I think we will boil in our skins before the job is done. A malfunction of the scanners that control our refuse compactor has stilled the garbage collectors, which will not go forth unless they have a place to dump what they collect. Since no one knows the proper command to give the compactor, rubbish accumulates, forming pestilential hills on every street, and dense swarms of flies or worse hover over the sprawling mounds. Beginning on the fourth day our police also began to go immobile – who can say why? – and by now all of them stand halted in their tracks. Some are already starting to rust, since the maintenance schedules are out of phase. Word has gone out that we are without protection, and outlanders cross into the district with impunity, molesting our women, stealing our children, raiding our stocks of foodstuffs. In Ganfield Hold, platoons of weary, sweating technicians toil constantly to replace the missing program, but it might be months, even years, before they will be able to devise a new one.

In theory, duplicate programs are stored in several places within the community against just such a calamity. In fact, we have none. The one kept in the district captain's office turned out to be some twenty years obsolete; the one in the care of the soul father's house had been devoured by rats; the program held in the vaults of the tax collectors appeared to be intact, but when it was placed in the input slot it mysteriously failed to activate the computers. So we are helpless: an entire district, hundreds of thousands of human beings, cut loose to drift on the tides of chance. Silena, Silena, Silena! To disable all of Ganfield, to make our already burdensome lives more difficult, to expose me to the hatred of my neighbors ... Why, Silena? Why?

People glare at me on the streets. They hold me responsible, in a way, for all this. They point and mutter; in another few days they will be spitting and cursing; and if no relief comes soon, they may be throwing stones. Look, I want to shout, she was only my month-wife and she acted entirely on her own. I assure you I had no idea she would do such a thing. And yet they blame me. At the wealthy houses of Morton Court they will dine tonight on babies stolen in Ganfield this day, and I am held accountable.

What will I do? Where can I turn?

I may have to flee. The thought of crossing district lines chills me. Is it the peril of death I fear or only the loss of all that is familiar? Probably both: I have no hunger for dying and no wish to leave Ganfield. Yet I will go, no matter how difficult it will be to find sanctuary if I get safely across the line. If they continue to hold me tainted by Silena's crime, I will have no choice. I think I would rather die at the hands of strangers than perish at those of my own people.

II

This sweltering night I find myself atop Ganfield Tower, seeking cool breezes and the shelter of darkness. Half the district has had the idea of escaping the heat by coming up here tonight, it seems; to get away from the angry eyes and tightened lips, I have climbed to the fifth parapet, where only the bold and the foolish ordinarily go. I am neither, yet here I am.

As I move slowly around the tower's rim, warily clinging to the old and eroded guardrail, I have a view of our entire district. Ganfield is like a shallow basin in form, gently sloping upward from the central spike that is the tower to a rise on the district perimeter. They say that a broad lake once occupied the site where Ganfield now stands; it was drained and covered over, centuries ago, when the need for new living space became extreme. Yesterday I heard that great pumps are used to keep the ancient lake from breaking through into our cellars, and that before very long the pumps will fail or shut themselves down for maintenance, and we will be flooded. Perhaps so. Ganfield once devoured the lake; will the lake now have Ganfield? Will we tumble into the dark waters and be swallowed, with no one to mourn us?

I look out over Ganfield. These tall brick boxes are our dwellings, twenty stories high but dwarfed from my vantage point far above. This sliver of land, black in the smoky moonlight, is our pitiful scrap of community park. These low flat-topped buildings are our shops, a helter-skelter cluster. This is our industrial zone, such that it is. That squat shadow-cloaked bulk just north of the tower is Ganfield Hold, where our crippled computers slip one by one into idleness. I have spent nearly my whole life within this one narrow swing of the compass that is Ganfield. When I was a boy and affairs were not nearly so harsh between one district and its neighbor, my father took me on holiday to Morton Court, and another time to The Mill. When I was a young man I was sent on business across three districts to Parley Close. I remember those journeys as clearly and vividly as though I had dreamed them. But everything is quite different now and it is twenty years since I last left Ganfield. I am not one of your privileged commuters, gaily making transit from zone to zone. All the world is one great city, so it is said, with the deserts settled and the rivers bridged and all the open places filled, a universal city that has abolished the old boundaries, and yet it is twenty years since I passed from one district to the next. I wonder: Are we one city, then, or merely thousands of contentious, fragmented, tiny states?

Look here, along the perimeter. There are no more boundaries, but what is this? This is our boundary, Ganfield Crescent, that wide curving boulevard surrounding the district. Are you a man of some other zone? Then cross the Crescent at risk of life. Do you see our police machines, blunt-snouted, glossy, formidably powerful, strewn like boulders in the broad avenue? They will interrogate you, and if your answers are un-easy, they may destroy you. Of course they can do no one any harm tonight.

Look outward now, at our horde of brawling neighbors. I see beyond the Crescent to the east the gaunt spires of Conning Town, and on the west, descending stepwise into the jumbled valley, the shabby dark-walled buildings of The Mill, with happy Morton Court on the far side, and somewhere in the smoky distance other places, Folkstone and Budleigh and Hawk Nest and Parley Close and Kingston and Old Grove and all the rest, the districts, the myriad districts, part of the chain that stretches from sea to sea, from shore to shore, spanning our continent border to border, the districts, the chips of gaudy glass making up the global mosaic, the infinitely numerous communities that are the segments of the all-encompassing world-city. Tonight at the capital they are planning next month's rainfall patterns for districts that the planners have never seen. District food allocations – inadequate, always inadequate – are being devised by men to whom our appetites are purely abstract entities. Do they believe in our existence, at the capital? Do they really think there is such a place as Ganfield? What if we sent them a delegation of notable citizens to ask for help in replacing our lost program? Would they care? Would they even listen? For that matter, is there a capital at all? How can I, who have never seen nearby Old Grove, accept, on faith alone, the existence of a far-off governing center, aloof, inaccessible, shrouded in myth? Maybe it is only a construct of some cunning subterranean machine that is our real ruler. That would not surprise me. Nothing surprises me. There is no capital. There are no central planners. Beyond the horizon everything is mist.

III

In the office, at least, no one dares show hostility to me. There are no scowls, no glares, no snide references to the missing program. I am, after all, chief deputy to the District Commissioner of Nutrition, and since the commissioner is usually absent, I am, in effect, in charge of the department. If Silena's crime does not destroy my career, it might prove to have been unwise for my subordinates to treat me with disdain. In any case we are so busy that there is no time for such gambits. We are responsible for keeping the community properly fed; our tasks have been greatly complicated by the loss of the program, for there is no reliable way now of processing our allocation sheets, and we must requisition and distribute food by guesswork and memory. How many bales of plankton cubes do we consume each week? How many pounds of proteoid mix? How much bread for the shops of Lower Ganfield? What fads of diet are likely to sweep the district this month? If demand and supply fall into imbalance as a result of our miscalculations, there could be widespread acts of violence, forays into neighboring districts, even renewed outbreaks of cannibalism within Ganfield itself. So we must draw up our estimates with the greatest precision. What a terrible spiritual isolation we feel deciding such things with no computers to guide us!

IV

On the fourteenth day of the crisis the district captain summons me. His message comes in late afternoon, when we all are dizzy with fatigue, choked by humidity. For several hours I have been tangled in complex dealings with a high official of the Marine Nutrients Board; this is an arm of the central city government, and I must therefore show the greatest tact, lest Ganfield's plankton quotas be arbitrarily lowered by a bureaucrat's sudden pique. Telephone contact is uncertain – the Marine Nutrients Board has its headquarters in Melrose New Port, half a continent away on the southeastern coast – and the line sputters and blurs with distortions that our computers, if the master program were in operation, would normally erase. As we reach a crisis in the negotiation my subdeputy gives me a note: 'District captain wants to see you.' 'Not now,' I say in silent lip talk. The haggling proceeds. A few minutes later comes another note: 'It's urgent.' I shake my head, brush the note from my desk. The subdeputy retreats to the outer office, where I see him engaged in frantic discussion with a man in the gray-and-green uniform of the district captain's staff. The messenger points vehemently at me. Just then the phone line goes dead. I slam the instrument down and call to the messenger, 'What is it?'

'The captain, sir. To his office at once, please.'

'Impossible.'

He displays a warrant bearing the captain's seal. 'He requires your immediate presence.'

'Tell him I have delicate business to complete,' I reply. 'Another fifteen minutes, maybe.'

He shakes his head. 'I am not empowered to allow a delay.'

'Is this an arrest, then?'

'A summons.'

'But with the force of an arrest?'

'With the force of an arrest, yes,' he tells me.

I shrug and yield. All burdens drop from me. Let the subdeputy deal with the Marine Nutrients Board; let the clerk in the outer office do it, or no one at all; let the whole district starve. I no longer care. I am summoned. My responsibilities are discharged. I give over my desk to the subdeputy and summarize for him, in perhaps a hundred words, my intricate hours of negotiation. All that is someone else's problem now.

The messenger leads me from the building into the hot, dank street. The sky is dark and heavy with rain, and evidently it has been raining some while, for the sewers are backing up and angry swirls of muddy water run shin-deep through the gutters. The drainage system, too, is controlled from Ganfield Hold, and must now be failing. We hurry across the narrow plaza fronting my office, skirt a gush of sewage-laden outflow, push into a close-packed crowd of irritable workers heading for home. The messenger's uniform creates an invisible sphere of untouchability for us; the throngs part readily and close again behind us. Wordlessly I am conducted to the stone-faced building of the district captain, and quickly to his office. It is no unfamiliar place to me, but coming here as a prisoner is quite different from attending a meeting of the district council. My shoulders are slumped, my eyes look toward the threadbare carpeting.

The district captain appears. He is a man of sixty, silver-haired, upright, his eyes frank and direct, his features reflecting little of the strain his position must impose. He has governed our district ten years. He greets me by name, but without warmth, and says, 'You've heard nothing from your woman?'

'I would have reported it if I had.'

'Perhaps. Perhaps. Have you any idea where she is?'

'I know only the common rumors,' I say. 'Conning Town, Morton Court, The Mill.'

'She is in none of those places.'

'Are you sure?'

'I have consulted the captains of those districts,' he says. 'They deny any knowledge of her. Of course, one has no reason to trust their word, but on the other hand why would they bother to deceive me?' His eyes fasten on mine. 'What part did you play in the stealing of the program?'

'None, sir.'

'She never spoke to you of treasonable things?'

'Never.'

'There is a strong feeling in Ganfield that a conspiracy existed.'

'If so I knew nothing of it.'

He judges me with a piercing look. After a long pause he says heavily, 'She has destroyed us, you know. We can function at the present level of order for another six weeks, possibly, without the program – if there is no plague, if we are not flooded, if we are not overrun with bandits from outside. After that the accumulated effects of many minor breakdowns will paralyze us. We will fall into chaos. We will strangle on our own wastes, starve, suffocate, revert to savagery, live like beasts until the end – who knows? Without the master program we are lost. Why did she do this to us?'

'I have no theories,' I say. 'She kept her own counsel. Her independence of soul is what attracted me to her.'

'Very well. Let her independence of soul be what attracts you to her now. Find her and bring back the program.'

'Find her? Where?'

'That is for you to discover.'

'I know nothing of the world outside Ganfield!'

'You will learn,' the captain says coolly. 'There are those here who would indict you for treason. I see no value in this. How does it help us to punish you? But we can *use* you. You are a clever and resourceful man; you can make your way through the hostile districts, and you can gather information, and you could well succeed in tracking her. If anyone has influence over her, you do; if you find her, you perhaps can induce her to surrender the program. No one else could hope to accomplish that. Go. We offer you immunity from prosecution in return for your cooperation.'

The world spins wildly about me. My skin burns with shock. 'Will I have safe-conduct through the neighboring districts?' I ask.

'To whatever extent we can arrange. That will not be much, I fear.'

'You'll give me an escort, then? Two or three men?'

'We feel you will travel more effectively alone. A party of several men takes on the character of an invading force; you would be met with suspicion and worse.'

'Diplomatic credentials, at least?'

'A letter of identification, calling on all captains to honor your mission and treat you with courtesy.'

I know how much value such a letter will have in Hawk Nest or Folkstone.

'This frightens me,' I say.

He nods, not unkindly. 'I understand that. Yet someone must seek her, and who else is there but you? We grant you a day to make your preparations. You will depart on the morning after next, and God hasten your return.'

V

Preparations. How can I prepare myself? What maps should I collect, when my destination is unknown? Returning to the office is unthinkable; I go straight home, and for hours I wander from one room to the other as if I face execution at dawn. At last I gather myself and fix a small meal, but most of it remains on my plate. No friends call; I call no one. Since Silena's disappearance my friends have fallen away from me. I sleep poorly. During the night there are hoarse shouts and shrill alarms in the street; I learn from the morning newscast that five men of Conning Town, here to loot, had been seized by one of the new vigilante groups that have replaced the police machines and were summarily put to death. I find no cheer in that, thinking that I might be in Conning Town in a day or so.

What clues to Silena's route? I ask to speak with the guard from whom she wangled entry into Ganfield Hold. He has been a prisoner ever since; the captain is too busy to decide his fate, and he languishes meanwhile. He is a small, thick-bodied man with stubbly red hair and a sweaty forehead; his eyes are bright with anger and his nostrils quiver. 'What is there to say?' he demands. 'I was on duty at the Hold. She came in. I had never seen her before, though I knew she must be high caste. Her cloak was open. She seemed naked beneath it. She was in a state of excitement.'

'What did she tell you?'

'That she desired me. Those were her first words.' Yes. I could see Silena doing that, though I had difficulty in imagining her long, slender form enfolded in this squat little man's embrace. 'She said she knew of me and was eager for me to have her.'

'And then?'

'I sealed the gate. We went to an inner room where there is a cot. It was a quiet time of day; I thought no harm would come. She dropped her cloak. Her body –'

'Never mind her body,' I could see it all too well in the eye of my mind, the sleek thighs, the taut belly, the small high breasts, the cascade of chocolate hair falling to her shoulders. 'What did you talk about? Did she say anything of a political kind? Some slogan, some words against the government?'

'Nothing. We lay together naked a while, only fondling each other. Then she said she had a drug with her, one that would enhance the sensations of love tenfold. It was a dark powder. I drank it in water; she drank it also, or seemed to. Instantly I was asleep. When I awoke the Hold was in uproar and I was a prisoner.' He glowers at me. 'I should have suspected a trick from the start. Such women do not hunger for men like me. How did I ever injure you? Why did you choose me to be the victim of your scheme?'

'Her scheme,' I say. 'Not mine. I had no part in it. Her motive is a mystery to me. If I could discover where she has gone, I would seek her and wring answers from her. Any help you could give me might earn you a pardon and your freedom.'

'I know nothing,' he says sullenly. 'She came in, she snared me, she drugged me, she stole the program.'

'Think. Not a word? Possibly she mentioned the name of some other district.'

'Nothing.'

A pawn is all he is, innocent, useless. As I leave he cries out to me to intercede for him, but what can I do? 'Your woman ruined me!' he roars.

'She may have ruined us all,' I reply.

At my request a district prosecutor accompanies me to Silena's apartment, which has been under official seal since her disappearance. Its contents have been thoroughly examined, but maybe there is some clue I alone would notice. Entering, I feel a sharp pang of loss, for the sight of Silena's possessions reminds me of happier times. These things are painfully familiar to me: her neat array of books, her clothing, her furnishings, her bed. I knew her only eleven weeks, she was my month-wife for only two; I had not realized she had come to mean so much to me so quickly. We look around, the prosecutor and I. The books testify to the agility of her restless mind: little light fiction, mainly works of serious history, analyses of social problems, forecasts of conditions to come. Holman, *The Era of the World City*. Sawtelle, *Megalopolis Triumphant*. Doxiadis, *The New World of Urban Man*. Heggebend, *Fifty Billion Lives*. Marks, *Calcutta is Everywhere*. Chasin, *The New Community*. I take a few of the books down, fondling them as though they were Silena. Many times when I had spent an evening here she reached for one of those books, Sawtelle or Heggebend or Marks or Chasin, to read me a passage that amplified some point she was making. Idly I turn pages. Dozens of paragraphs are underscored with fine, precise lines, and lengthy marginal comments are abundant. 'We've analyzed all of that for possible significance,' the prosecutor remarks. 'The only thing we've concluded is that she thinks the world is too crowded for comfort.' A ratcheting laugh. 'As who doesn't?' He points to a stack of green-bound pamphlets at the end of the lower shelf. 'These, on the other hand, may be useful in your search. Do you know anything about them?'

The stack consists of nine copies of something called *Walden Three*: a Utopian fantasy, apparently, set in an idyllic land of streams and forests. The booklets are unfamiliar to me; Silena must have obtained them recently. Why nine copies? Was she acting as a distributor? They bear the imprint of a publishing house in Kingston. Ganfield and Kingston severed trade relations long ago; material published there is uncommon here. 'I've never seen them,' I say. 'Where do you think she got them?'

'There are three main routes for subversive literature originating in Kingston. One is –'

'Is this pamphlet subversive, then?'

'Oh, very much so. It argues for complete reversal of the social trends of the last hundred years. As I was saying, there are three main routes for subversive literature originating in Kingston. We have traced one chain of distribution running by way of Wisleigh and Cedar Mall, another through Old Grove, Hawk Nest, and Conning Town, and the third via Parley Close and The Mill. It is plausible that your woman is in Kingston now, having traveled along one of these underground distribution routes, sheltered by her fellow subversives all the way. But we have no way of confirming this.' He smiles emptily. 'She could be in any of the other communities along the three routes. Or in none of them.'

'I should think of Kingston, though, as my ultimate goal, until I learn anything to the contrary. Is that right?'

'What else can you do?'

What else, indeed? I must search at random through an unknown number of hostile districts, having no clue other than the vague one implicit in the place of origin of these nine booklets, while time ticks on and Ganfield slips deeper day by day into confusion.

The prosecutor's office supplies me with useful things: maps, letters of introduction, a commuter's passport that should enable me to cross at least some district lines unmolested, and an assortment of local currencies as well as bank notes issued by the central bank and therefore valid in most districts. Against my wishes I am given also a weapon – a small heat-pistol – and in addition a capsule that I can swallow in the event that a quick and easy death becomes desirable. As the final stage in my preparation I spend an hour conferring with a secret agent, now retired, whose career of espionage took him safely into hundreds of communities as far away as Threadmuir and Reed Meadow. What advice does he give someone about to try to get across? 'Maintain your poise,' he says. 'Be confident and self-assured, as though you belong in whatever place you find yourself. Never slink. Look all men in the eye. However, say no more than is necessary. Be watchful at all times. Don't relax your guard.' Such precepts I could have evolved without his aid. He has nothing in the nature of specific hints for survival. Each district, he says, presents unique problems, constantly changing; nothing can be anticipated, everything must be met as it arises. How comforting!

At nightfall I go to the soul father's house, in the shadow of Ganfield Tower. To leave without a blessing seems unwise. But there is something stagy and unspontaneous about my visit, and my faith flees as I enter. In the dim antechamber I light the nine candles, I pluck the five blades of grass from the ceremonial vase, I do the proper ritual things, but my spirit remains chilled and hollow, and I am unable to pray. The soul father himself, having been told of my mission, grants me audience – gaunt old man with impenetrable eyes set in deep ebony rims – and favors me with a gentle feather-light embrace. 'Go in safety,' he murmurs. 'God watches over you.' I wish I felt sure of that. Going home, I take the most roundabout possible route, as if trying to drink in as much of Ganfield as I can on my last night. The diminishing past flows through me like a river running dry. My birthplace, my school, the streets where I played, the dormitory where I spent my adolescence, the home of my first month-wife. Farewell. Farewell. Tomorrow I go across. I return to my apartment alone; once more my sleep is fitful. An hour after dawn I find myself, astonished by it, waiting in line among the commuters at the mouth of the transit tube, bound for Conning Town. And so my crossing begins.

VI

Aboard the tube-train no one speaks. Faces are tense; bodies are held rigid in the plastic seats. Occasionally someone on the other side of the aisle glances at me as though wondering who this newcomer to the commuter group may be, but his eyes quickly slide away as I take notice. I know none of these commuters, though they must have dwelt in Ganfield as long as I; their lives have never intersected mine before. Engineers, merchants, diplomats, whatever – their careers are tied to districts other than their own. It is one of the anomalies of our ever more fragmented and stratified society that some regular contact still survives between community and community; a certain number of people must journey each day to outlying districts, where they work encapsulated, isolated, among unfriendly strangers.

We plunge eastward at unimaginable speed. Surely we are past the boundaries of Ganfield by now and under alien territory. A glowing sign on the wall of the car announces our route: CONNING TOWN – HAWK NEST – OLD GROVE – KINGSTON – FOLK-STONE – PARLEY CLOSE – BUDLEIGH – CEDAR MALL – THE MILL – MORTON COURT – GANFIELD, a wide loop through our most immediate neighbors. I try to visualize the separate links in this chain of districts, each a community of three or four hundred thousand loyal and patriotic citizens, each with its own special tone, its flavor, its distinctive quality, its apparatus of government, its customs and rituals. But I can imagine them merely as a cluster of Ganfields, every place very much like the one I have just left. I know this is not so. The world-city is no homogeneous collection of uniformities, a global bundle of indistinguishable suburbs. No, there is incredible diversity, a host of unique urban cores bound by common need into a fragile unity. No master plan brought them into being; each evolved at a separate point in time to serve the necessities of a particular purpose. This community sprawls gracefully along a curving river, that one boldly mounts the slopes of stark hills; here the prevailing architecture reflects an easy, gentle climate, there it wars with unfriendly nature; form follows topography and local function, creating individuality. The world is a richness – why then do I see only ten thousand Ganfields?

Of course it is not so simple. We are caught in the tension between forces that encourage distinctiveness and forces that compel all communities toward identicality. Centrifugal forces broke down the huge ancient cities, the Londons and Tokyos and New Yorks, into neighborhood communities that seized quasi-autonomous powers. Those giant cities were too unwieldy to survive; density of population, making long-distance transport unfeasible and communication difficult, shattered the urban fabric, destroyed the authority of the central government, and left the closely knit small-scale subcity as the only viable unit. Two dynamic and contradictory processes now asserted themselves. Pride and the quest for local advantage led each community toward specialization: this one a center primarily of industrial production, this one devoted to advanced education, this to finance, this to the processing of raw materials, this to wholesale marketing of commodities, this to retail distribution, and so on, the shape and texture of each district defined by its chosen function. And yet the new decentralization required a high degree of redundancy, duplication of governmental structures, of utilities, of community services; for its own safety each district felt the need to transform itself into a microcosm of the former full city. Ideally we should have hovered in perfect balance between specialization and redundancy, all communities striving to fulfill the needs of all other communities with the least possible overlap and waste of resources; in fact our human frailty has brought into being these irreversible trends of rivalry and irrational fear, dividing district from district, so that against our own self-interest we sever year after year our bonds of interdependence and stubbornly seek self-sufficiency at the district level. Since this is impossible, our lives grow constantly more impoverished. In the end, all districts will be the same and we will have created a world of pathetic, limping Ganfields, devoid of grace, lacking in variety.

So. The tube-train halts. This is Conning Town. I am across the first district line. I make my exit in a file of solemn-faced commuters. Imitating them, I approach a colossal Cyclopean scanning machine and present my passport. It is unmarked by visas; theirs are gaudy with scores of them. I tremble, but the machine accepts me and slams down a stamp that fluoresces a brilliant shimmering crimson against the pale-lavender page:

- DISTRICT OF CONNING TOWN •
- ENTRY VISA •
- 24-HOUR VALIDITY •

Dated to the hour, minute, second. Welcome, stranger, but get out of town before sunrise!

Up the purring ramp, into the street. Bright morning sunlight pries apart the slim, sooty, close-ranked towers of Conning Town. The air is cool and sweet, strange to me after so many sweltering days in program-less, demechanized Ganfield. Does our foul air drift across the border and offend them? Sullen eyes study me; those about me know me for an outsider. Their clothing is alien in style, pinched in at the shoulders, flaring at the waist. I find myself adopting an inane smile in response to their dour glares.

For an hour I walk aimlessly through the downtown section until my first fears melt and a comic cockiness takes possession of me: I pretend to myself that I am a native, and enjoy the flimsy imposture. This place is not much unlike Ganfield, yet nothing is quite the same. The sidewalks are wider; the street lamps have slender arching necks instead of angular ones; the fire hydrants are green and gold, not blue and orange. The police machines have flatter domes than ours, ringed with ten or twelve spy-eyes where ours have six or eight. Different, different, all different.

Three times I am halted by police machines. I produce my passport, display my visa, am allowed to continue. So far getting across has been easier than I imagined. No one molests me here. I suppose I look harmless. Why did I think my foreignness alone would lead these people to attack me? Ganfield is not at war with its neighbors, after all.

Drifting eastward in search of a bookstore, I pass through a shabby residential neighborhood and through a zone of dismal factories before I reach an area of small shops. Then in late afternoon I discover three bookstores on the same block, but they are antiseptic places, not the sort that might carry subversive propaganda like *Walden Three*. The first two are wholly automated, blank-walled charge-plate-and-scanner operations. The third has a human clerk, a man of about thirty, with drooping yellow moustachios and alert blue eyes. He recognizes the style of my clothing and says, 'Ganfield, eh? Lot of trouble over there.'

'You've heard?'

'Just stories. Computer breakdown, isn't it?'

I nod. 'Something like that.'

'No police, no garbage removal, no weather control, hardly anything working – that's what they say.' He seems neither surprised nor disturbed to have an outlander in his shop. His manner is amiable and relaxed. Is he fishing for data about our vulnerability, though? I must be careful not to tell him anything that might be used against us. But evidently they already know everything here. He says, 'It's a little like dropping back into the Stone Age for you people, I guess. It must be a real traumatic thing.'

'We're coping,' I say, stiffly casual.

'How did it happen, anyway?'

I give him a wary shrug. 'I'm not sure about that.' Still revealing nothing. But then something in his tone of a moment before catches me belatedly and neutralizes some of the reflective automatic suspicion with which I have met his questions. I glance around. No one else in the shop. I let something conspiratorial creep into my voice and say, 'It might not even be so traumatic, actually, once we get used to it. I mean, there once was a time when we didn't rely so heavily on machines to do our thinking for us, and we survived, and even managed pretty well. I was reading a little book last week that seemed to be saying we might profit by trying to return to the old way of life. Book published in Kingston.'

'*Walden Three*.' Not a question but a statement.

'That's it.' My eyes query his. 'You've read it?'

'Seen it.'

'A lot of sense in that book, I think.'

He smiles warmly. 'I think so too. You get much Kingston stuff over in Ganfield?'

'Very little, actually.'

'Not much here, either.'

'But there's some.'

'Some, yes,' he says.

Have I stumbled upon a member of Silena's underground movement? I say eagerly, 'You know, maybe you could help me meet some people who –'

'No.'

'No?'

'No.' His eyes are still friendly but his face is tense. 'There's nothing like that around here,' he says, his voice suddenly flat and remote. 'You'd have to go over into Hawk Nest.'

'I'm told that that's a nasty place.'

'Nevertheless, Hawk Nest is where you want to go. Nate and Holly Borden's shop, just off Box Street.' Abruptly his manner shifts to one of exaggerated bland clerkishness. 'Anything else I can do for you, sir? If you're interested in supernovels we've got a couple of good new double-amplified cassettes, just in. Perhaps I can show you –'

'Thank you, no.' I smile, shake my head, leave the store. A police machine waits outside. Its dome rotates; eye after eye scans me intently; finally its resonant voice says, 'Your passport, please.' This routine is familiar by now. I produce the document. Through the bookshop window I see the clerk bleakly watching. The police machine says, 'What is your place of residence in Conning Town?'

'I have none. I'm here on a twenty-four-hour visa.'

'Where will you spend the night?'

'In a hotel, I suppose.'

'Please show your room confirmation.'

A long moment of silence; the machine is conferring with its central, no doubt, keying into the master program of Conning Town for instructions. At length it says, 'You are advised to obtain a legitimate reservation and display it to a monitor at the earliest opportunity within the next four hours. Failure to do so will result in cancellation of your visa and immediate expulsion from Conning Town.' Some ominous clicks come from the depths of the machine. 'You are now under formal surveillance,' it announces.

Brimming with questions, I return hastily to the bookshop. The clerk is displeased to see me. Anyone who attracts monitors to his shop – 'monitors' is what they call police machines here, it seems – is unwelcome. 'Can you tell me how to reach the nearest decent hotel?' I ask.

'You won't find one.'

'No decent hotels?'

'No hotels. None where you could get a room, anyway. We have only two or three transient houses and accommodations are allocated months in advance to regular commuters.'

'Does the monitor know that?'

'Of course.'

'Where are strangers supposed to stay, then?'

The clerk shrugs. 'There's no structural program here for strangers as such. The regular commuters have regular arrangements. Unauthorized intruders don't belong here at all. You fall somewhere in between, I imagine. There's no legal way for you to spend the night in Conning Town.'

'But my visa —'

'Even so.'

'I'd better go on into Hawk Nest, I suppose.'

'It's late. You've missed the last tube-train. You've got no choice but to stay, unless you want to try a border crossing on foot in the dark. I wouldn't recommend that.'

'Stay? But where?'

'Sleep in the street. If you're lucky the monitors will leave you alone.'

'Some quiet back alley, I suppose.'

'No,' he says. 'You sleep in an out-of-the-way place and you'll surely get sliced up by night bandits. Go to one of the designated sleeping streets. In the middle of a big crowd you might just go unnoticed, even though you're under surveillance.' As he speaks he moves about the shop, closing it down for the night. He looks restless and uncomfortable. I take out my map of Conning Town and he shows me where to go. The map is some years out of date, apparently; he corrects it with irritable swipes of his pencil. We leave the shop together. I invite him to come with me to some restaurant as my guest, but he looks at me as if I carry plague. 'Good-bye,' he says. 'Good luck.'

VII

Alone, apart from the handful of other diners, I take my evening meal at a squalid, dimly lit automated cafeteria at the edge of downtown. Silent machines offer me thin acrid soup, pale spongy bread, and a leaden stew containing lumpy ingredients of undeterminable origin, for which I pay with yellow plastic counters of Conning Town currency. Emerging undelighted, I observe a reddish glow in the western sky. It may be a lovely sunset or, for all I know, it may be a sign that Ganfield is burning. I look about for monitors. My four-hour grace period has nearly expired. I must disappear shortly into a throng. It seems too early for sleep, but I am only a few blocks from the place where the bookshop clerk suggested I should pass the night, and I go to it. Just as well; when I reach it – a wide place bordered by gray buildings of ornate façade – I find it already filling up with street-sleepers. There must be eight hundred of them, men, women, family groups, settling down in little squares of cobbled territory that are obviously claimed night after night under some system of squatter's rights. Others constantly arrive, flowing inward from the plaza's three entrances, finding their places, laying out foam cushions or mounds of clothing as their mattresses. It is a friendly crowd; these people are linked by bonds of neighborliness, a common poverty. They laugh, embrace, play games of chance, exchange whispered confidences, bicker, transact business, and join together in the rites of the local religion, performing a routine that involves six people clasping hands and chanting. Privacy seems obsolete here. They undress freely before one another and there are instances of open coupling. The gaiety of the scene – a medieval carnival is what it suggests to me, a Brueghelesque romp – is marred only by my awareness that this horde of revelers is homeless under the inhospitable skies, vulnerable to rain, sleet, damp fog, snow, and the other unkindnesses of winter and summer in these latitudes. In Ganfield we have just a scattering of street-sleepers, those who have lost their residential licenses and are temporarily forced into the open, but here it seems to be an established institution, as though Conning Town declared a moratorium some years ago on new residential construction without at the same time checking the increase of population.

Stepping over and around and between people, I reach the center of the plaza and select an unoccupied bit of pavement. But in a moment a little ruddy-faced woman arrives, excited and animated, and with a Conning Tower accent so thick I can barely understand her, she tells me she holds claim here. Her eyes are bright with menace; her hands are not far from becoming claws; several nearby squatters sit up and regard me threateningly. I apologize for my error and withdraw, stumbling over a child and narrowly missing overturning a bubbling cooking pot. Onward. Not here. Not here. A hand emerges from a pile of blankets and strokes my leg as I look around in perplexity. Not here. A man with a painted face rises out of a miniature green tent and speaks to me in a language I do not understand. Not here. I move on again and again, thinking that I will be jostled out of the plaza entirely, excluded, disqualified even to sleep in this district's streets, but finally I find a cramped corner where the occupants indicate I am welcome. 'Yes?' I say. They grin and gesture. Gratefully I seize the spot.

Darkness has come. The plaza continues to fill; at least a thousand people have arrived after me, cramming into every vacancy, and the flow does not abate. I hear booming laughter, idle chatter, earnest romantic persuasion, the brittle sound of domestic quarreling. Someone passes a jug of wine around, even to me; bitter stuff, fermented clam juice its probable base, but I appreciate the gesture. The night is warm, almost sticky. The scent of unfamiliar food drifts on the air – something sharp, spicy, a heavy, pungent smell. Curry? Is this then truly Calcutta? I close my eyes and huddle into myself. The hard cobblestones are cold beneath me. I have no mattress and I feel unable to remove my clothes before so many strangers. It will be hard for me to sleep in this madhouse, I think. But gradually the hubbub diminishes and – exhausted, drained – I slide into a deep, troubled sleep.

Ugly dreams. The asphyxiating pressure of a surging mob. Rivers leaping their channels. Towers toppling. Fountains of mud bursting from a thousand lofty windows. Bands of steel encircling my thighs; my legs, useless, withering away. A torrent of lice sweeping over me. A frosty hand touching me. Touching me. Touching me. Pulling me up from sleep.

Harsh white light drenches me. I blink, cringe, cover my eyes. Shortly I perceive that a monitor stands over me. About me the sleepers are awake, backing away, murmuring, pointing.

'Your street-sleeping permit, please.'

Caught. I mumble excuses, plead ignorance of the law, beg forgiveness.

But a police machine is neither malevolent nor merciful; it merely follows its program. It demands my passport and scans my visa. Then it reminds me I have been under surveillance. Having failed to obtain a hotel room as ordered, having neglected to report to a monitor within the prescribed interval, I am subject to expulsion.

'Very well,' I say. 'Conduct me to the border of Hawk Nest.'

'You will return at once to Ganfield.'

'I have business in Hawk Nest.'

'Illegal entrants are returned to their district of origin.'

'What does it matter to you where I go, so long as I get out of Conning Town?'

'Illegal entrants are returned to their district of origin,' the machine tells me inexorably.

I dare not go back with so little accomplished. Still arguing with the monitor, I am led from the plaza through dark cavernous streets toward the mouth of a transit tube. On the station level a second monitor is given charge of me. 'In three hours,' the monitor that apprehended me informs me, 'the Ganfield-bound train will arrive.'

The first monitor rolls away.

Too late I realize that the machine has neglected to return my passport.

VIII

Monitor number two shows little interest in me. Patrolling the tube station, it swings in a wide arc around me, keeping a scanner perfunctorily trained on me but making no attempt to interfere with what I do. If I try to flee, of course, it will destroy me. Fretfully I study my maps. Hawk Nest lies to the northeast of Conning Town; if this is the tube station that I think it is, the border is not far. Five minutes' walk, perhaps. Passportless, there is no place I can go except Ganfield; my commuter status is revoked. But legalities count for little in Hawk Nest.

How to escape?

I concoct a plan. Its simplicity seems absurd, yet absurdity is often useful when dealing with machines. The monitor is instructed to put me aboard the train for Ganfield, yes. But not necessarily to keep me there.

I wait out the weary hours to dawn. I hear the crash of compressed air far up the tunnel. Snub-nosed, silken-smooth, the train slides into the station. The monitor orders me aboard. I walk into the car, cross it quickly, and exit by the open door on the far side of the platform. Even if the monitor has observed this maneuver, it can hardly fire across a crowded train. As I leave the car I break into a trot, darting past startled travelers, and sprint upstairs into the misty morning. At street level, running is unwise. I drop back to a rapid walking pace and melt into the throngs of early workers. The street is Crystal Boulevard. Good. I have memorized a route: Crystal Boulevard to Flagstone Square, thence via Mechanic Street to the border.

Presumably all monitors, linked to whatever central nervous system the machines of the district of Conning Town utilize, have instantaneously been apprised of my disappearance. But that is not the same as knowing where to find me. I head northward on Crystal Boulevard – its name shows a dark sense of irony, or else the severe transformations time can work – and, borne by the flow of pedestrian traffic, enter Flagstone Square, a grimy, lopsided plaza out of which, on the left, snakes curving Mechanic Street. I go unintercepted on this thoroughfare of small shops. The place to anticipate trouble is at the border.

I am there in a few minutes. It is a wide, dusty street, silent and empty, lined on the Conning Town side by a row of blocky brick warehouses, on the Hawk Nest side by a string of low, ragged buildings, some in ruins, the best of them defiantly slatternly. There is no barrier. To fence a district border is unlawful except in time of war, and I have heard of no war between Conning Town and Hawk Nest.

Dare I cross? Police machines of two species patrol the street: flat-domed ones of Conning Town and black hexagon-headed ones of Hawk Nest. Surely one or the other will gun me down in the no-man's-land between districts. But I have no choice. I must keep going forward.

I run out into the street at a moment when two police machines, passing each other on opposite orbits have left an unpatrolled space perhaps a block long. Midway in my crossing the Conning Town monitor spies me and blares a command. The words are unintelligible to me and I keep running, zigzagging in the hope of avoiding the bolt that very likely will follow. But the machine does not shoot; I must already be on the Hawk Nest side of the line and Conning Town no longer cares what becomes of me.

The Hawk Nest machine has noticed me. It rolls toward me as I stumble, breathless and gasping, onto the curb. 'Halt!' it cries. 'Present your documents!' At that moment a red-bearded man, fierce-eyed, wide-shouldered, steps out of a decaying building close by me. A scheme assembles itself in my mind. Do the customs of sponsorship and sanctuary hold good in this harsh district?

'Brother!' I cry. 'What luck!' I embrace him, and before he can fling me off I murmur. 'I am from Ganfield. I seek sanctuary here. Help me!'

The machine has reached me. It goes into an interrogatory stance and I say, 'This is my brother who offers me the privilege of sanctuary. Ask him! Ask him!'

'Is this true?' the machine inquires.

Redbeard, unsmiling, spits and mutters, 'My brother, yes. A political refugee. I'll stand sponsor to him. I vouch for him. Let him be.'

The machine clicks, hums, assimilates. To me it says, 'You will register as a sponsored refugee within twelve hours or leave Hawk Nest.' Without another word it rolls away.

I offer my sudden savior warm thanks. He scowls, shakes his head, spits once again. 'We owe each other nothing,' he says brusquely, and goes striding down the street.

IX

In Hawk Nest nature has followed art. The name, I have heard, once had purely neutral connotations: some real-estate developer's highflown metaphor, nothing more. Yet it determined the district's character, for gradually Hawk Nest became the home of predators that it is today, where all men are strangers, where every man is his brother's enemy.

Other districts have their slums. Hawk Nest *is* a slum. I am told they live here by looting, cheating, extorting, and manipulating. An odd economic base for an entire community, but maybe it works for them. The atmosphere is menacing. The only police machines seem to be those that patrol the border. I sense emanations of violence just beyond the corner of my eye: rapes and garrotings in shadowy byways, flashing knives and muffled groans, covert cannibal feasts. Perhaps my imagination works too hard. Certainly I have gone unthreatened so far; those I meet on the streets pay no heed to me, indeed will not even return my glance. Still, I keep my heat-pistol close by my hand as I walk through these shabby, deteriorating outskirts. Sinister faces peer at me through cracked, dirt-veiled windows. If I am attacked, will I have to fire in order to defend myself? God spare me from having to answer that.

X

Why is there a bookshop in this town of murder and rubble and decay?
Here is Box Street, and here, in an oily pocket of spare-parts depots
and flyspecked quick-lunch counters, is Nate and Holly Borden's place.
Five times as deep as it is broad, dusty, dimly lit, shelves overflowing
with old books and pamphlets, an improbable outpost of the nineteenth
century, somehow displaced in time. There is no one in it but a large,
impassive woman seated at the counter, fleshy, puffy-faced, motionless.
Her eyes, oddly intense, glitter like glass disks set in a mound of dough.
She regards me without curiosity.

I say, 'I'm looking for Holly Borden.'

'You've found her,' she replies, deep in the baritone range.

'I've come across from Ganfield by way of Conning Town.'

No response from her to this.

I continue, 'I'm traveling without a passport. They confiscated it in
Conning Town and I ran the border.'

She nods. And waits. No show of interest.

'I wonder if you could sell me a copy of *Walden Three*,' I say.

Now she stirs a little. 'Why do you want one?'

'I'm curious about it. It's not available in Ganfield.'

'How do you know I have one?'

'Is anything illegal in Hawk Nest?'

She seems annoyed that I have answered a question with a question.
'How do you know *I* have a copy of that book?'

'A bookshop clerk in Conning Town said you might.'

A pause. 'All right. Suppose I do. Did you come all the way from Ganfield just to buy a book?' Suddenly she leans forward and smiles – a warm,
keen, penetrating smile that wholly transforms her face: now she is keyed-
up, alert, responsive, shrewd, commanding. 'What's your game?' she asks.

'My game?'

'What are you playing? What are you up to here?'

It is the moment for total honesty. 'I'm looking for a woman named
Silena Ruiz from Ganfield. Have you heard of her?'

'Yes. She's not in Hawk Nest.'

'I think she's in Kingston. I'd like to find her.'

'Why? To arrest her?'

'Just to talk to her. I have plenty to discuss with her. She was my
month-wife when she left Ganfield.'

'The month must be nearly up,' Holly Borden says.

'Even so,' I reply. 'Can you help me reach her?'

'Why should I trust you?'

'Why not?'

She ponders that briefly. She studies my face. I feel the heat of her scrutiny. At length she says, 'I expect to be making a journey to Kingston soon. I suppose I could take you with me.'

XI

She opens a trap door; I descend into a room beneath the bookshop. After a good many hours a thin, gray-haired man brings me a tray of food. 'Call me Nate,' he says. Overhead I hear indistinct conversations, laughter, the thumping of boots on the wooden floor. In Ganfield, famine may be setting in by now. Rats will be dancing around Ganfield Hold. How long will they keep me here? Am I a prisoner? Two days. Three. Nate will answer no questions. I have books, a cot, a sink, a drinking glass. On the third day the trap door opens. Holly Borden peers down. 'We're ready to leave,' she says.

The expedition consists of just the two of us. She is going to Kingston to buy books and travels on a commercial passport that allows for one helper. Nate drives us to the tube-mouth in midafternoon. It no longer seems unusual to me to be passing from district to district; they are not such alien and hostile places, merely different from the place I know. I see myself bound on an odyssey that carries me across hundreds of districts, even thousands, the whole patchwork frenzy of our world. Why return to Ganfield? Why not go on, ever eastward, to the great ocean and beyond, to the unimaginable strangenesses on the far side?

Here we are in Kingston. An old district, one of the oldest. We are the only ones who journey hither today from Hawk Nest. There is only a perfunctory inspection of passports. The police machines of Kingston are tall, long-armed, with fluted bodies, ornamented in stripes of red and green: quite a gay effect. I am becoming an expert in local variations of police-machine design. Kingston itself is a district of low pastel buildings arranged in spokelike boulevards radiating from the famed university that is its chief enterprise. No one from Ganfield has been admitted to the university in my memory.

Holly is expecting friends to meet her, but they have not come. We wait fifteen minutes. 'Never mind,' she says. 'We'll walk.' I carry the luggage. The air is soft and mild; the sun, sloping toward Folkstone and Budleigh, is still high. I feel oddly serene. It is as if I have perceived a divine purpose, an overriding plan, in the structure of our society, in our sprawling city of many cities, our network of steel and concrete clinging like an armor of scales to the skin of our planet. But what is that purpose? What is that plan? The essence of it eludes me; I am aware only that it must exist. A cheery delusion.

Fifty paces from the station we are abruptly surrounded by a dozen or more buoyant young men who emerge from an intersecting street. They are naked but for green loincloths; their hair and beards are untrimmed and unkempt; they have a fierce and barbaric look. Several carry long unsheathed knives strapped to their waists. They circle wildly around us, laughing, jabbing at us with their fingertips. 'This is a holy district!' they cry. 'We need no blasphemous strangers here! Why must you intrude on us?'

'What do they want?' I whisper. 'Are we in danger?'

'They are a band of priests,' Holly replies. 'Do as they say and we will come to no harm.'

They press close. Leaping, dancing, they shower us with sprays of perspiration. 'Where are you from?' they demand. 'Ganfield,' I say. 'Hawk Nest,' says Holly. They seem playful yet dangerous. Surging about me, they empty my pockets in a series of quick, jostling forays: I lose my heat-pistol, my maps, my useless letters of introduction, my various currencies, everything, even my suicide capsule. These things they pass among themselves, exclaiming over them; then the heat-pistol and some of the currency are returned to me. 'Ganfield,' they murmur. 'Hawk Nest!' There is distaste in their voices. 'Filthy places,' they say. 'Places scorned by God,' they say. They seize our hands and haul us about, making us spin. Heavy-bodied Holly is surprisingly graceful, breaking into a serene lumbering dance that makes them applaud in wonder.

One, the tallest of the group, catches our wrists and says, 'What is your business in Kingston?'

'I come to purchase books,' Holly declares.

'I come to find my month-wife, Silena,' say I.

'Silena! Silena! Silena!' Her name becomes a jubilant incantation on their lips. 'His month-wife! Silena! His month-wife! Silena! Silena! Silena!'

The tall one thrusts his face against mine and says, 'We offer you a choice. Come and make prayer with us or die on the spot.'

'We choose to pray,' I tell him.

They tug at our arms, urging us impatiently onward. Down street after street until at last we arrive at holy ground: a garden plot, insignificant in area, planted with unfamiliar bushes and flowers, tended with evident care. They push us inside.

'Kneel,' they say.

'Kiss the sacred earth.'

'Adore the things that grow in it, strangers.'

'Give thanks to God for the breath you have just drawn.'

'And for the breath you are about to draw.'

'Sing!'

'Weep!'

'Laugh!'

'Touch the soil!'

'Worship!'

XII

Silena's room is cool and quiet, in the upper story of a residence overlooking the university grounds. She wears a soft green robe of coarse texture, no jewelry, no face paint. Her demeanor is calm and self-assured. I had forgotten the delicacy of her features, the cool, malicious sparkle of her dark eyes.

'The master program?' she says, smiling. 'I destroyed it!'

The depth of my love for her unnerves me. Standing before her, I feel my knees turning to water. In my eyes she is bathed in a glittering aura of sensuality. I struggle to control myself. 'You destroyed nothing,' I say. 'Your voice betrays the lie.'

'You think I still have the program?'

'I know you do.'

'Well, yes,' she admits coolly. 'I do.'

My fingers tremble. My throat parches. An adolescent foolishness seeks to engulf me.

'Why did you steal it?' I ask.

'Out of love of mischief.'

'I see the lie in your smile. What was the true reason?'

'Does it matter?'

'The district is paralyzed, Silena. Thousands of people suffer. We are at the mercy of raiders from adjoining districts. Many have already died of the heat, the stink of garbage, the failure of the hospital equipment. Why did you take the program?'

'Perhaps I had political reasons.'

'Which were?'

'To demonstrate to the people of Ganfield how utterly dependent on these machines they have allowed themselves to become.'

'We knew that already,' I say. 'If you meant only to dramatize our weaknesses, you were pressing the obvious. What was the point of crippling us? What could you gain from it?'

'Amusement?'

'Something more than that. You're not that shallow, Silena.'

'Something more than that, then. By crippling Ganfield I help to change things. That's the purpose of any political act. To display the need for change, so that change may come about.'

'Simply displaying the need is not enough.'

'It's a place to begin.'

'Do you think stealing our program was a rational way to bring change, Silena?'

'Are you happy?' she retorts. 'Is this the kind of world you want?'

'It's the world we have to live in, whether we like it or not. And we need that program in order to go on coping. Without it we are plunged into chaos.'

'Fine. Let chaos come. Let everything fall apart so we can rebuild it.'

'Easy enough to say, Silena. What about the innocent victims of your revolutionary zeal, though?'

She shrugs. 'There are always innocent victims in any revolution.' In a sinuous movement she rises and approaches me. The closeness of her body is dazzling and maddening. With exaggerated voluptuousness she croons, 'Stay here. Forget Ganfield. Life is good here. These people are building something worth having.'

'Let me have the program,' I say.

'They must have replaced it by now.'

'Replacing it is impossible. The program is vital to Ganfield, Silena. Let me have it.'

She emits an icy laugh.

'I beg you, Silena.'

'How boring you are!'

'I love you.'

'You love nothing but the status quo. The shape of things as they are gives you great joy. You have the soul of a bureaucrat.'

'If you have always had such contempt for me, why did you become my month-wife?'

She laughs again. 'For sport, perhaps.'

Her words are like knives. Suddenly, to my own astonishment, I am brandishing the heat-pistol. 'Give me the program or I'll kill you!' I cry.

She is amused. 'Go. Shoot. Can you get the program from a dead Silena?'

'Give it to me.'

'How silly you look holding that gun!'

'I don't have to kill you,' I tell her. 'I can merely wound you. This pistol is capable of inflicting light burns that scar the skin. Shall I give you blemishes, Silena?'

'Whatever you wish. I'm at your mercy.'

I aim the pistol at her thigh. Silena's face remains expressionless. My arm stiffens and begins to quiver. I struggle with the rebellious muscles, but I succeed in steadying my aim only for a moment before the tremors return. An exultant gleam enters her eyes. A flush of excitement spreads over her face. 'Shoot,' she says defiantly. 'Why don't you shoot me?'

She knows me too well. We stand in a frozen tableau for an endless moment outside time – a minute, an hour, a second? – and then my arm sags to my side. I put the pistol away. It never would have been possible for me to fire it. A powerful feeling assails me of having passed through some subtle climax; it will all be downhill from here for me, and we both know it. Sweat drenches me. I feel defeated, broken.

Silena's features reveal intense scorn. She has attained some exalted level of consciousness in these past few moments where all acts become gratuitous, where love and hate and revolution and betrayal and loyalty are indistinguishable from one another. She smiles the smile of someone who has scored the winning point in a game the rules of which will never be explained to me.

'You little bureaucrat,' she says calmly. 'Here!'

From a closet she brings forth a small parcel which she tosses disdainfully to me. It contains a drum of computer film. 'The program?' I ask. 'This must be some joke. You wouldn't actually give it to me, Silena.'

'You hold the master program of Ganfield in your hand.'

'Really, now?'

'Really, really,' she says. 'The authentic item. Go on. Go. Get out. Save your stinking Ganfield.'

'Silena –'

'Go.'

XIII

The rest is tedious but simple. I locate Holly Borden, who has purchased a load of books. I help her with them, and we return via tube to Hawk Nest. There I take refuge beneath the bookshop once more while a call is routed through Old Grove, Parley Close, The Mill, and possibly some other districts to the district captain of Ganfield. It takes two days to complete the circuit, since district rivalries make a roundabout relay necessary. Ultimately I am connected and convey my happy news: I have the program, though I have lost my passport and am forbidden to cross Conning Town. Through diplomatic channels a new passport is conveyed to me a few days later, and I take the tube home the long way, via Budleigh, Cedar Mall, and Morton Court. Ganfield is hideous, all filth and disarray, close to the point of irreversible collapse; its citizens have lapsed into a deadly stasis and await their doom placidly. But I have returned with the program.

The captain praises my heroism. I will be rewarded, he says. I will have promotion to the highest ranks of the civil service, with hope of ascent to the district council.

But I take pale pleasure from his words. Silena's contempt still governs my thoughts. *Bureaucrat. Bureaucrat.*

XIV

Still, Ganfield is saved. The police machines have begun to move again.

ALL · THE · TROUBLES · OF
THE · WORLD

Isaac Asimov

The greatest industry on Earth centered around Multivac – Multivac, the giant computer that had grown in fifty years until its various ramifications had filled Washington, DC, to the suburbs and had reached out tendrils into every city and town on Earth.

An army of civil servants fed it data constantly and another army correlated and interpreted the answers it gave. A corps of engineers patrolled its interior while mines and factories consumed themselves in keeping its reserve stocks of replacement parts ever complete, ever accurate, ever satisfactory in every way.

Multivac directed Earth's economy and helped Earth's science. Most important of all, it was the central clearing house of all known facts about each individual Earthman.

And each day it was part of Multivac's duties to take the four billion sets of facts about individual human beings that filled its vitals and extrapolate them for an additional day of time. Every Corrections Department on Earth received the data appropriate to its own area of jurisdiction, and the over-all data was presented in one large piece to the Central Board of Corrections in Washington, DC.

Bernard Gulliman was in the fourth week of his year term as Chairman of the Central Board of Corrections and had grown casual enough to accept the morning report without being frightened by it. As usual, it was a sheaf of papers some six inches thick. He knew by now, he was not expected to read it. (No human could.) Still, it was amusing to glance through it.

There was the usual list of predictable crimes: frauds of all sorts, larcenies, riots, manslaughters, arsons.

He looked for one particular heading and felt a slight shock at finding it there at all, then another one at seeing two entries. Not one, but two. *Two* first-degree murders. He had not seen two in one day in all his term as Chairman so far.

He punched the knob of the two-way intercom and waited for the smooth face of his co-ordinator to appear on the screen.

'Ali,' said Gulliman. 'There are two first-degrees this day. Is there any unusual problem?'

'No, sir.' The dark-complexioned face with its sharp, black eyes seemed restless. 'Both cases are quite low probability.'

'I know that,' said Gulliman. 'I observed that neither probability is higher than 15 per cent. Just the same, Multivac has a reputation to maintain. It has virtually wiped out crime, and the public judges that by its record on first-degree murder which is, of course, the most spectacular crime.'

Ali Othman nodded. 'Yes, sir. I quite realize that.'

'You also realize, I hope,' Gulliman said, 'that I don't want a single consummated case of it during my term. If any other crime slips through, I may allow excuses. If a first-degree murder slips through, I'll have your hide. Understand?'

'Yes, sir. The complete analyses of the two potential murders are already at the district offices involved. The potential criminals and victims are under observation. I have rechecked the probabilities of consummation and they are already dropping.'

'Very good,' said Gulliman, and broke connection.

He went back to the list with an uneasy feeling that perhaps he had been overpompous. – But then, one had to be firm with these permanent civil-service personnel and make sure they didn't imagine they were running everything, including the Chairman. Particularly this Othman, who had been working with Multivac since both were considerably younger, and had a proprietary air that could be infuriating.

To Gulliman, this matter of crime was the political chance of a lifetime. So far, no Chairman had passed through his term without a murder taking place somewhere on Earth, some time. The previous Chairman had ended with a record of eight, three more (*more*, in fact) than his predecessor.

Now Gulliman intended to have *none*. He was going to be, he had decided, the first Chairman without any murder at all anywhere on Earth during his term. After that, and the favorable publicity that would result –

He barely skimmed the rest of the report. He estimated that there were at least two thousand cases of prospective wife-beatings listed. Undoubtedly, not all would be stopped in time. Perhaps thirty per cent would be consummated. But the incidence was dropping and consummations were dropping even more quickly.

Multivac had added wife-beating to its list of predictable crimes only some five years earlier and the average man was not yet accustomed to the thought that if he planned to wallop his wife, it would be known in advance. As the conviction percolated through society, women would first suffer fewer bruises and then, eventually, none.

Some husband-beatings were on the list, too, Gulliman noticed.

Ali Othman closed connections and stared at the screen from which Gulliman's jowled and balding head had departed. Then he looked across at his assistant, Rafe Leemy and said, 'What do we do?'

'Don't ask me. *He's* worried about just a lousy murder or two.'

'It's an awful chance trying to handle this thing on our own. Still if we tell him, he'll have a first-class fit. These elective politicians have their skins to think of, so he's bound to get in our way and make things worse.'

Leemy nodded his head and put a thick lower lip between his teeth. 'Trouble is, though, what if we miss out? It would just about be the end of the world, you know.'

'If we miss out, who cares what happens to us? We'll just be part of the general catastrophe.' Then he said in a more lively manner, 'But hell, the probability is only 12.3 per cent. On anything else, except maybe murder, we'd let the probabilities rise a bit before taking any action at all. There could still be spontaneous correction.'

'I wouldn't count on it,' said Leemy dryly.

'I don't intend to. I was just pointing the fact out. Still, at this probability, I suggest we confine ourselves to simple observation for the moment. No one could plan a crime like this alone; there must be accomplices.'

'Multivac didn't name any.'

'I know. Still –' His voice trailed off.

So they stared at the details of the one crime not included on the list handed out to Gulliman; the one crime much worse than first-degree murder; the one crime never before attempted in the history of Multivac; and wondered what to do.

Ben Manners considered himself the happiest sixteen-year-old in Baltimore. This was, perhaps, doubtful. But he was certainly one of the happiest, and one of the most excited.

At least, he was one of the handful admitted to the galleries of the stadium during the swearing in of the eighteen-year-olds. His older brother was going to be sworn in so his parents had applied for spectator's tickets and they had allowed Ben to do so, too. But when Multivac chose among all the applicants, it was Ben who got the ticket.

Two years later, Ben would be sworn in himself, but watching big brother Michael now was the next best thing.

His parents had dressed him (or supervised the dressing, at any rate) with all care, as representative of the family and sent him off with numerous messages for Michael, who had left days earlier for preliminary physical and neurological examinations.

The stadium was on the outskirts of town and Ben, just bursting with self-importance, was shown to his seat. Below him, now, were rows upon rows of hundreds upon hundreds of eighteen-year-olds (boys to the right, girls to the left), all from the second district of Baltimore. At various times in the years, similar meetings were going on all over the world, but this was Baltimore, this was the important one. Down there (somewhere) was Mike, Ben's own brother.

Ben scanned the tops of heads, thinking somehow he might recognize his brother. He didn't, of course, but then a man came out on the raised platform in front of all the crowd and Ben stopped looking to listen.

The man said, 'Good afternoon, swearers and guests. I am Randolph T. Hoch, in charge of the Baltimore ceremonies this year. The swearers have met me several times now during the progress of the physical and neurological portions of this examination. Most of the task is done, but the most important matter is left. The swearer himself, his personality, must go into Multivac's records.

'Each year, this requires some explanation to the young people reaching adulthood. Until now' (he turned to the young people before him and his eyes went no more to the gallery) 'you have not been adult; you have not been individuals in the eyes of Multivac, except where you were especially singled out as such by your parents or your government.

'Until now, when the time for the yearly up-dating of information came, it was your parents who filled in the necessary data on you. Now the time has come for you to take over that duty yourself. It is a great honor, a great responsibility. Your parents have told us what schooling you've had, what diseases, what habits; a great many things. But now you must tell us a great deal more; your innermost thoughts; your most secret deeds.

'This is hard to do the first time, embarrassing even, but it *must* be done. Once it is done, Multivac will have a complete analysis of all of you in its files. It will understand your actions and reactions. It will even be able to guess with fair accuracy at your future actions and reactions.

'In this way, Multivac will protect you. If you are in danger of accident, it will know. If someone plans harm to you, it will know. If *you* plan harm, it will know and you will be stopped in time so that it will not be necessary to punish you.

'With its knowledge of all of you, Multivac will be able to help Earth adjust its economy and its laws for the good of all. If you have a personal problem, you may come to Multivac with it and with its knowledge of all of you, Multivac will be able to help you.

'Now you will have many forms to fill out. Think carefully and answer all questions as accurately as you can. Do not hold back through shame or caution. No one will ever know your answers except Multivac unless it becomes necessary to learn the answers in order to protect you. And then only authorized officials of the government will know.

'It may occur to you to stretch the truth a bit here or there. Don't do this. We will find out if you do. All your answers put together form a pattern. If some answers are false, they will not fit the pattern and Multivac will discover them. If all your answers are false, there will be a distorted pattern of a type that Multivac will recognize. So you must tell the truth.'

Eventually, it was all over, however; the form-filling; the ceremonies and speeches that followed. In the evening, Ben, standing tiptoe, finally spotted Michael, who was still carrying the robes he had worn in the 'parade of the adults'. They greeted one another with jubilation.

They shared a light supper and took the expressway home, alive and alight with the greatness of the day.

They were not prepared, then, for the sudden transition of the home-coming. It was a numbing shock to both of them to be stopped by a cold-faced young man in uniform outside their own front door; to have their papers inspected before they could enter their own house; to find their own parents sitting forlornly in the living room, the mark of tragedy on their faces.

Joseph Manners, looking much older than he had that morning, looked out of his puzzled, deep-sunken eyes at his sons (one with the robes of new adulthood still over his arm) and said, 'I seem to be under house arrest.'

*

Bernard Gulliman could not and did not read the entire report. He read only the summary and that was most gratifying, indeed.

A whole generation, it seemed, had grown up accustomed to the fact that Multivac could predict the commission of major crimes. They learned that Corrections agents would be on the scene before the crime could be committed. They found out that consummation of the crime led to inevitable punishment. Gradually, they were convinced that there was no way anyone could outsmart Multivac.

The result was, naturally, that even the intention of crime fell off. And as such intentions fell off and as Multivac's capacity was enlarged, minor crimes could be added to the list it would predict each morning, and these crimes, too, were now shrinking in incidence.

So Gulliman had ordered an analysis made (by Multivac naturally) of Multivac's capacity to turn its attention to the problem of predicting probabilities of disease incidence. Doctors might soon be alerted to individual patients who might grow diabetic in the course of the next year, or suffer an attack of tuberculosis or grow a cancer.

An ounce of prevention –

And the report was a favorable one!

After that, the roster of the day's possible crimes arrived and there was not a first-degree murder on the list.

Gulliman put in an intercom call to Ali Othman in high good humor. 'Othman, how do the numbers of crimes in the daily lists of the past week average compared with those in my first week as Chairman?'

It had gone down, it turned out, by 8 per cent and Gulliman was happy indeed. No fault of his own, of course, but the electorate would not know that. He blessed his luck that he had come in at the right time, at the very climax of Multivac, when disease, too, could be placed under its all-embracing and protecting knowledge.

Gulliman would prosper by this.

Othman shrugged his shoulders. 'Well, he's happy.'

'When do we break the bubble?' said Leemy. 'Putting Manners under observation just raised the probabilities and house arrest gave it another boost.'

'Don't I know it?' said Othman peevishly. 'What I don't know is why.'

'Accomplices, maybe, like you said. With Manners in trouble, the rest have to strike at once or be lost.'

'Just the other way around. With our hand on one, the rest would scatter for safety and disappear. Besides, why aren't the accomplices named by Multivac?'

'Well, then do we tell Gulliman?'

'No, not yet. The probability is still only 17.3 per cent. Let's get a bit more drastic first.'

Elizabeth Manners said to her younger son, 'You go to your room, Ben.'

'But what's it all about, Mom?' asked Ben, voice breaking at this strange ending to what had been a glorious day.

'Please!'

He left reluctantly, passing through the door to the stairway, walking up it noisily and down again quietly.

And Mike Manners, the older son, the new-minted adult and the hope of the family, said in a voice and tone that mirrored his brother's, 'What's it all about?'

Joe Manners said, 'As heaven is my witness, son, I don't know. I haven't done anything.'

'Well, sure you haven't done anything.' Mike looked at his small-boned, mild-mannered father in wonder. 'They must be here because you're *thinking* of doing something.'

'I'm not.'

Mrs Manners broke in angrily, 'How can he be thinking of doing something worth all – all this.' She cast her arm about, in a gesture toward the enclosing shell of government men about the house. 'When I was a little girl, I remember the father of a friend of mine was working in a bank, and they once called him up and said to leave the money alone and he did. It was fifty thousand dollars. He hadn't really taken it. He was just thinking about taking it. They didn't keep those things as quiet in those days as they do now; the story got out. That's how I know about it.

'But I mean,' she went on, rubbing her plump hands slowly together, 'that was fifty thousand dollars; fifty – thousand – dollars. Yet all they did was call him; one phone call. What could your father be planning that would make it worth having a dozen men come down and close off the house?'

Joe Manners said, eyes filled with pain, 'I am planning no crime, not even the smallest. I swear it.'

Mike, filled with the conscious wisdom of a new adult, said, 'Maybe it's something subconscious, Pop. Some resentment against your supervisor.'

'So that I would want to kill him? No!'

'Won't they tell you what it is, Pop?'

His mother interrupted again, 'No, they won't. We've asked. I said they were ruining our standing in the community just being here. The least they could do is tell us what it's all about so we could fight it, so we could explain.'

'And they wouldn't?'

'They wouldn't.'

Mike stood with his legs spread apart and his hands deep in his pockets. He said, troubled, 'Gee, Mom, Multivac doesn't make mistakes.'

His father pounded his fist helplessly on the arm of the sofa. 'I tell you I'm not planning any crime.'

The door opened without a knock and a man in uniform walked in with sharp, self-possessed stride. His face had a glazed, official appearance. He said, 'Are you Joseph Manners?'

Joe Manners rose to his feet. 'Yes. Now what is it you want of me?'

'Joseph Manners, I place you under arrest by order of the government,' and curtly he showed his identification as a Corrections officer. 'I must ask you to come with me.'

'For what reason? What have I done?'

'I am not at liberty to discuss that.'

'But I can't be arrested just for planning a crime even if I were doing that. To be arrested I must actually have *done* something. You can't arrest me otherwise. It's against the law.'

The officer was impervious to the logic. 'You will have to come with me.'

Mrs Manners shrieked and fell on the couch, weeping hysterically. Joseph Manners could not bring himself to violate the code drilled into him all his life by actually resisting an officer, but he hung back at least, forcing the Corrections officer to use muscular power to drag him forward.

And Manners called out as he went. 'But tell me what it is. Just tell me. If I *knew* – Is it murder? Am I supposed to be planning murder?'

The door closed behind him and Mike Manners, white-faced and suddenly feeling not the least bit adult, stared first at the door, then at his weeping mother.

Ben Manners, behind the door and suddenly feeling quite adult, pressed his lips tightly together and thought he knew exactly what to do.

If Multivac took away, Multivac could also give. Ben had been at the ceremonies that very day. He had heard this man, Randolph Hoch, speak of Multivac and all that Multivac could do. It could direct the government and it could also unbend and help out some plain person who came to it for help.

Anyone could ask help of Multivac and anyone meant Ben. Neither his mother nor Mike were in any condition to stop him now, and he had some money left of the amount they had given him for his great outing that day. If afterward they found him gone and worried about it, that couldn't be helped. Right now, his first loyalty was to his father.

He ran out the back way and the officer at the door cast a glance at his papers and let him go.

Harold Quimby handled the complaints department of the Baltimore substation of Multivac. He considered himself to be a member of that branch of the civil service that was most important of all. In some ways, he may have been right, and those who heard him discuss the matter would have had to be made of iron not to feel impressed.

For one thing, Quimby would say, Multivac was essentially an invader of privacy. In the past fifty years, mankind had had to acknowledge that its thoughts and impulses were no longer secret, that it owned no inner recess where anything could be hidden. And mankind had to have something in return.

Of course, it got prosperity, peace, and safety, but that was abstract. Each man and woman needed something personal as his or her own reward for surrendering privacy, and each one got it. Within reach of every human being was a Multivac station with circuits into which he could freely enter his own problems and questions without control or hindrance, and from which, in a matter of minutes, he could receive answers.

At any given moment, five million individual circuits among the quadrillion or more within Multivac might be involved in this question-and-answer program. The answers might not always be certain, but they were the best available, and every questioner *knew* the answer to be the best available and had faith in it. That was what counted.

And now an anxious sixteen-year-old had moved slowly up the waiting line of men and women (each face in that line illuminated by a different mixture of hope with fear or anxiety or even anguish – always with hope predominating as the person stepped nearer and nearer to Multivac).

Without looking up, Quimby took the filled-out form being handed him and said, 'Booth 5-B.'

Ben said, 'How do I ask the question, sir?'

Quimby looked up then, with a bit of surprise. Pre-adults did not generally make use of the service. He said kindly, 'Have you ever done this before, son?'

'No, sir.'

Quimby pointed to the model on his desk. 'You use this. You see how it works? Just like a typewriter. Don't you try to write or print anything by hand. Just use the machine. Now you take booth 5-B, and if you need help, just press the red button and someone will come. Down that aisle, son, on the right.'

He watched the youngster go down the aisle and out of view and smiled. No one was ever turned away from Multivac. Of course, there was always a certain percentage of trivia: people who asked personal questions about their neighbors or obscene questions about prominent personalities; college youths trying to outguess their professors or thinking it clever to stump Multivac by asking it Russell's class-of-all-classes paradox and so on.

Multivac could take care of all that. It needed no help.

Besides, each question and answer was filed and formed but another item in the fact assembly for each individual. Even the most trivial question and the most impertinent, insofar as it reflected the personality of the questioner, helped humanity by helping Multivac know about humanity.

Quimby turned his attention to the next person in line, a middle-aged woman, gaunt and angular, with the look of trouble in her eye.

Ali Othman strode the length of his office, his heels thumping desperately on the carpet. 'The probability still goes up. It's 22.4 per cent now. Damnation! We have Joseph Manners under actual arrest and it still goes up.' He was perspiring freely.

Leemy turned away from the telephone. 'No confession yet. He's under Psychic Probing and there is no sign of crime. He may be telling the truth.'

Othman said, 'Is Multivac crazy then?'

Another phone sprang to life. Othman closed connections quickly, glad of the interruption. A Corrections officer's face came to life in the screen. The officer said, 'Sir, are there any new directions as to Manners' family? Are they to be allowed to come and go as they have been?'

'What do you mean, as they have been?'

'The original instructions were for the house arrest of Joseph Manners. Nothing was said of the rest of the family, sir.'

'Well, extend it to the rest of the family until you are informed otherwise.'

'Sir, that is the point. The mother and older son are demanding information about the younger son. The younger son is gone and they claim he is in custody and wish to go to headquarters to inquire about it.'

Othman frowned and said in almost a whisper, 'Younger son? How young?'

'Sixteen, sir,' said the officer.

'Sixteen and he's gone. Don't you know where?'

'He was allowed to leave, sir. There were no orders to hold him.'

'Hold the line. Don't move.' Othman put the line into suspension, then clutched at his coal-black hair with both hands and shrieked, 'Fool! Fool! Fool!'

Leemy was startled, 'What the hell?'

'The man has a sixteen-year-old son,' choked out Othman. 'A sixteen-year-old is not an adult and he is not filed independently in Multivac, but only as part of his father's file.' He glared at Leemy. 'Doesn't everyone know that until eighteen a youngster does not file his own reports with Multivac but that his father does it for him? Don't I know it? Don't you?'

'You mean Multivac didn't mean Joe Manners?' said Leemy.

'Multivac meant his minor son, and the youngster is gone, now. With officers three deep around the house, he calmly walks out and goes on you know what errand.'

He whirled to the telephone circuit to which the Corrections officer still clung, the minute break having given Othman just time enough to collect himself and to assume a cool and self-possessed mien. (It would never have done to throw a fit before the eyes of the officer, however much good it did in purging his spleen.)

He said, 'Officer, locate the younger son who has disappeared. Take every man you have, if necessary. Take every man available in the district, if necessary. I shall give the appropriate orders. You must find that boy at all costs.'

'Yes, sir.'

Connection was broken. Othman said, 'Have another rundown on the probabilities, Leemy.'

Five minutes later, Leemy said, 'It's down to 19.6 per cent. It's *down*.'
Othman drew a long breath. 'We're on the right track at last.'

Ben Manners sat in Booth 5-B and punched out slowly, 'My name is Benjamin Manners, number MB-71833412. My father, Joseph Manners, has been arrested but we don't know what crime he is planning. Is there any way we can help him?'

He sat and waited. He might be only sixteen but he was old enough to know that somewhere those words were being whirled into the most complex structure ever conceived by man; that a trillion facts would blend and co-ordinate into a whole, and that from that whole, Multivac would abstract the best help.

The machine clicked and a card emerged. It had an answer on it, a long answer. It began, 'Take the expressway to Washington, DC, at once. Get off at the Connecticut Avenue stop. You will find a special exit, labeled 'Multivac' with a guard. Inform the guard you are a special courier for Dr Trumbull and he will let you enter.

'You will be in a corridor. Proceed along it till you reach a small door labeled "Interior". Enter and say to the men inside, "Message for Doctor Trumbull!" You will be allowed to pass. Proceed on –'

It went on in this fashion. Ben could not see the application to his question, but he had complete faith in Multivac. He left at a run, heading for the expressway to Washington.

The Corrections officers traced Ben Manners to the Baltimore station an hour after he had left. A shocked Harold Quimby found himself flabbergasted at the number and importance of the men who had focused on him in the search for a sixteen-year-old.

'Yes, a boy,' he said, 'but I don't know where he went to after he was through here. I had no way of knowing that anyone was looking for him. We accept all comers here. Yes, I can get the record of the question and answer.'

They looked at the record and televised it to Central Headquarters at once.

Othman read it through, turned up his eyes, and collapsed. They brought him to almost at once. He said to Leemy weakly, 'Have them catch that boy. And have a copy of Multivac's answer made out for me. There's no way any more, no way out. I must see Gulliman now.'

*

Bernard Gulliman had never seen Ali Othman as much as perturbed before, and watching the co-ordinator's wild eyes now sent a trickle of ice water down his spine.

He stammered, 'What do you mean, Othman? What do you mean worse than murder?'

'Much worse than just murder.'

Gulliman was quite pale. 'Do you mean assassination of a high government official?' (It did cross his mind that he himself —)

Othman nodded. 'Not just *a* government official. *The* government official.'

'The *Secretary-General*?' said Gulliman in an appalled whisper.

'More than that, even. Much more. We deal with a plan to assassinate Multivac!'

'WHAT!'

'For the first time in the history of Multivac, the computer came up with the report that it itself was in danger.'

'Why was I not at once informed?'

Othman half-truthed out of it. 'The matter was so unprecedented, sir, that we explored the situation first before daring to put it on official record.'

'But Multivac has been saved, of course? It's been saved?'

'The probabilities of harm have declined to under 4 per cent. I am waiting for the report now.'

'Message for Dr Trumbull,' said Ben Manners to the man on the high stool, working carefully on what looked like the controls of a strato-jet cruiser, enormously magnified.

'Sure, Jim,' said the man. 'Go ahead.'

Ben looked at his instructions and hurried on. Eventually, he would find a tiny control lever which he was to shift to a DOWN position at a moment when a certain indicator spot would light up red.

He heard an agitated voice behind him, then another, and suddenly, two men had him by his elbows. His feet were lifted off the floor.

One man said, 'Come with us, boy.'

Ali Othman's face did not noticeably lighten at the news, even though Gulliman said with great relief, 'If we have the boy, then Multivac is safe.'

'For the moment.'

Gulliman put a trembling hand to his forehead. 'What a half hour

I've had. Can you imagine what the destruction of Multivac for even a short time would mean. The government would have collapsed; the economy broken down. It would have meant devastation worse –' His head snapped up, 'What do you mean *for the moment*?'

'The boy, this Ben Manners, had no intention of doing harm. He and his family must be released and compensation for false imprisonment given them. He was only following Multivac's instructions in order to help his father and it's done that. His father is free now.'

'Do you mean Multivac ordered the boy to pull a lever under circumstances that would burn out enough circuits to require a month's repair work? You mean Multivac would suggest its own destruction for the comfort of one man?'

'It's worse than that, sir. Multivac not only gave those instructions but selected the Manners family in the first place because Ben Manners looked exactly like one of Dr Trumbull's pages so that he could get into Multivac without being stopped.'

'What do you mean the family was selected?'

'Well, the boy would have never gone to ask the question if his father had not been arrested. His father would never have been arrested if Multivac had not blamed him for planning the destruction of Multivac. Multivac's own action started the chain of events that almost led to Multivac's destruction.'

'But there's no sense to that,' Gulliman said in a pleading voice. He felt small and helpless and he was virtually on his knees, begging this Othman, this man who had spent nearly a lifetime with Multivac, to reassure him.

Othman did not do so. He said, 'This is Multivac's first attempt along this line as far as I know. In some ways, it planned well. It chose the right family. It carefully did not distinguish between father and son to send us off the track. It was still an amateur at the game, though. It could not overcome its own instructions that led it to report the probability of its own destruction as increasing with every step we took down the wrong road. It could not avoid recording the answer it gave the youngster. With further practice, it will probably learn deceit. It will learn to hide certain facts, fail to record others. From now on, every instruction it gives may have the seeds in it of its own destruction. We will never know. And however careful we are, eventually Multivac will succeed. I think, Mr Gulliman, you will be the last Chairman of this organization.'

Gulliman pounded his desk in fury. 'But why, why, why? Damn you, why? What is wrong with it? Can't it be fixed?'

'I don't think so,' said Othman, in soft despair. 'I've never thought about this before. I've never had the occasion to until this happened, but now that I think of it, it seems to me we have reached the end of the road because Multivac is too good. Multivac has grown so complicated, its reactions are no longer those of a machine, but those of a living thing.'

'You're mad, but even so?'

'For fifty years and more we have been loading humanity's troubles on Multivac, on this living thing. We've asked it to care for us, all together and each individually. We've asked it to take all our secrets into itself; we've asked it to absorb our evil and guard us against it. Each of us brings his troubles to it, adding his bit to the burden. Now we are planning to load the burden of human disease on Multivac, too.'

Othman paused a moment, then burst out, 'Mr Gulliman, Multivac bears all the troubles of the world on its shoulders and it is tired.'

'Madness. Midsummer madness,' muttered Gulliman.

'Then let me show you something. Let me put it to the test. May I have permission to use the Multivac circuit line here in your office?'

'Why?'

'To ask it a question no one has ever asked Multivac before.'

'Will you do it harm?' asked Gulliman in quick alarm.

'No. But it will tell us what we want to know.'

The Chairman hesitated a trifle. Then he said, 'Go ahead.'

Othman used the instrument on Gulliman's desk. His fingers punched out the question with deft strokes: 'Multivac, what do you yourself want more than anything else?'

The moment between question and answer lengthened unbearably, but neither Othman nor Gulliman breathed.

And there was a clicking and a card popped out. It was a small card. On it, in precise letters, was the answer:

'I want to die.'

BIOGRAPHICAL NOTES

POUL ANDERSON (1926–) is among science fiction's most honored writers, having been awarded six Hugoes, two Nebula Awards, and the Tolkien Memorial Award to date. He writes both hard science fiction and heroic fantasy, a rare combination. A number of his novels are considered major works in the field: *Brain Wave* (1954), *The High Crusade* (1960), *Three Hearts and Three Lions* (1961), and *Tau Zero* (1970) are only a few. That he is also an accomplished short-story writer is apparent from the numerous published collections of his works. Mr Anderson was the Guest of Honor at the 1959 World Science Fiction Convention.

ISAAC ASIMOV (1920–) is closing in on 300 published books as this is written, books that cover every area of science, most periods in world history, and both the Old and New Testaments, all in addition to mystery novels and stories and some of the most famous science fiction ever written. His *Foundation* series and robot stories and novels are cornerstones of modern science fiction. His most recent novels, *Foundation's Edge* (1982) and *The Robots of Dawn* (1983) both made the best-seller lists, but he still cares about introducing young people to the joys of science.

Canadian born GORDON R. DICKSON (1923–) has been entertaining science-fiction readers since the early 1950s. Among his honors are three Hugo Awards and one Nebula Award from his peers, the Science Fiction Writers of America, an organization for which he served as President from 1969 to 1970. His more than forty-five novels and short-story collections include such outstanding works as *The Alien Way* (1965), *Soldier, Ask Not* (1967), *The Dragon and the George* (1976), *Time Storm* (1977), and *In Iron Years* (1980). He is a long-time resident of the Minneapolis area and has been guest of honor at many science-fiction conventions.

STAN DRYER, the author of an 'An End of Spinach', works in Boston as a marketing representative for a computer manufacturer. Over the past twenty years he has published a variety of short stories under his 'Stan

Dryer' pseudonym. These have appeared in such publications as *Playboy*, *Cosmopolitan*, and *The Magazine of Fantasy and Science Fiction*.

JOE GORES (1931–) is a distinguished veteran of several genres. He is best known in the mystery field, where he won the Mystery Writers of America's Edgar Allan Poe Award for best novel for *A Time of Predators* in 1969, and is the only writer in the world to have won Edgars in three categories: novel, short story, and television script. Other outstanding crime novels of his include *Dead Skip* (1972), *Hammett: a Novel* (1975), and *Gone, No Forwarding* (1978). Although he has not published a novel in the science-fiction field, he has written a number of excellent science-fiction stories, and we wish he would do more.

A life-long resident of Rochester, New York, EDWARD D. HOCH (1930–) is a treasure to all those who love a good mystery. Easily the most prolific short-story writer in the crime-fiction field, his work appears in every issue of *Ellery Queen's Magazine*. His tremendous productivity (some 650 short stories published to date) has tended to obscure his considerable skill and imagination. Too few collections of his work have appeared, but they are all worth reading – *The Judges of Hades and Other Simon Ark Stories* (1971), *City of Brass and Other Simon Ark Stories* (1971), *The Spy and the Thief* (1971), and *The Thefts of Nick Velvet* (1978). He edits the annual *The Year's Best Mystery and Suspense Stories*.

J. T. MCINTOSH is a British writer whose career began in 1950 with 'The Curfew Tolls' in the December issue of *Astounding Science Fiction*. Since that date he has published more than twenty-five novels, including about eight outside the science-fiction field. He was an important figure in the 1950s where his novels, like *Born Leader* (1954), *One in Three Hundred* (1954), and *The Fittest* (1955), were highly regarded. Since then, his reputation has declined; he never again achieved the level of his novels. However, he also wrote outstanding short stories, and it is unfortunate that the best of his many score works have not been collected.

ROBERT SILVERBERG (1935–) is one of science fiction's most distinguished writers. He has had at least three major careers; in the first, from roughly 1955 to 1966, he produced a huge amount of solid, commercial science fiction; in the second, from 1967 to 1976, he was transformed into a major literary figure, with such seminal science-fiction novels as *Nightwings* (1969), *To Live Again* (1969), *The Book of Skulls* (1972), *Dying Inside* (1972), and *The Stochastic Man* (1975); and the third has been going strong since 1980 when, after a retirement of almost four years he wrote *Lord Valantine's Castle* (1980) and then *Valantine Pontifex* (1983). He has won several Hugo Awards and four Nebulas.

EDWARD WELLEN (1919–) was born and still lives in New Rochelle, New York. After graduating from high school he worked for a fuel oil company as a mechanic's helper, stock clerk, and dispatcher. He saw extensive action during World War II, serving a total of forty-two months (thirty-two of them overseas) and winning seven battle stars. After his discharge he worked as a mail-order stamp dealer, ad copy writer, and most recently as a free-lance writer. Over the years he has built up a very impressive body of work in both the mystery and science-fiction fields, selling regularly to such publications as *Ellery Queen's Mystery Magazine*, *Mike Shayne's Mystery Magazine*, and *The Magazine of Fantasy and Science Fiction*.